SECOND CHANCES

LIGHT *in the* EMPIRE

SECOND CHANCES

CAROL ASHBY

CERRILLO PRESS

Cover and interior design by Roseanna White Designs

Cover images from Shutterstock.com

ISBN: 978-1-946139-08-5 (paperback)
          978-1-946139-09-2 (ebook)
          978-1-946139-16-0 (hardcover)

Cerrillo Press
Edgewood, NM

Weeping may endure for a night, but joy comes in the morning.
Psalms 30:5 (NKJV)

And we know that for those who love God all things work together for good, for those who are called according to his purpose. Romans 8:28 (NKJV)

For I know the plans I have for you," says the LORD. "They are plans for good and not for disaster, to give you a future and a hope. Jeremiah 29:11 (NLT)

*To my children, Paul and Lydia,
for their love, support, and encouragement.
To Regina, now in the arms of Jesus, who helped so much
as I was writing every novel from Blind Ambition to Second Chances.
And especially to my husband, Jim,
who proves every day what a blessing it is to be his wife.*

And most of all, to Jesus.

Soli Deo gloria.

The price of love is that one of you will grieve.

I was only in my late teens when an elderly friend first told me that. Even then, long before I lost someone I loved, the truth of it struck home. The loss might be through death. It might be from someone moving away so you lose the intimacy of close friendship. It might be from a person you loved and trusted betraying you far more than what seems possible to forgive.

We grieve for what we've had and lost, and we grieve for what we've dreamed of and never found.

But there's a deeper truth that we should always remember. Weeping may endure for a night, but joy comes in the morning.

When things go horribly wrong, when life seems to turn against us, it's too easy to keep our eyes so focused on the wounds that we miss the healing waiting beyond the pain.

That's why it's so important to remind ourselves that God is the God of new beginnings and second chances. He can bring good out of the worst circumstances. But it can be so hard in the midst of the storm to remember that God promised all things would work together for good for those who love Him.

Sometimes He puts another person in our path to help us recover that joy. I've often found that God gives me a chance to help someone else, even when I'm hurting, and when I turn my mind to helping another instead of feeling sorry for myself, my own healing begins.

Second Chances tells the story of a Christian man haunted by the loss of his family and a Roman woman betrayed for many years by a husband who was neither faithful nor a good father. When one final betrayal forces Cornelia to risk everything to save her daughter's life, it launches a chain of events where God makes helping her daughter the catalyst for healing, forgiveness, and a new understanding of what's important in life. He creates a second chance for happiness for them all.

I hope you enjoy this story of God making all things work together for good as much as I've enjoyed guiding Hector and Cornelia toward all God had planned for them. When we face our own difficult times, may we always trust in God's power and love as He leads us toward the good He has planned for us.

Carol Ashby

Characters

Hector of Perinthus Family
Hector: (40) widowed sea captain; best friend of Philip, freedman
of Aristarchus
Damara: (deceased) Hector's wife of 17 years, died in an accident
one year earlier
Charissa: (deceased) Hector's 10-year-old daughter who died in
the accident with her mother
Marcario: (17) Hector's son

Claudius Drusus Family, Servants, and Slaves Based in Rome
Lucius (Fidelis): (41) paterfamilias of the Claudius Drusus family,
Drusilla's father
Cornelia Scipia: (39) ex-wife of Lucius
Tertius: (18) Lucius Fidelis's and Cornelia's third son, living with
Lucius in Rome
Drusilla: (10) daughter of Lucius Fidelis and Cornelia Scipia
Publius: (deceased) father of Lucius Fidelis, Titus, and Claudia;
executed for his Christian faith
Malleolus: (69) freedman steward of the Claudius Drusus family
Anthusa: (44) Cornelia's maidservant (slave) and best friend for 25
years

Claudius Drusus Family and Servants Based in Perinthus
Titus: (32) brother of Lucius (Fidelis) now living in Perinthus in
Thracia,
Claudia: (24) Lucius's and Titus's sister, wife of Philip, the son of
Aristarchus
Miriam: (27) wife of Titus, formerly Claudia's handmaid and
Titus's cook
Vania: (8) Titus's daughter, Drusilla's cousin
Nestor: Titus's freedman steward

Aristarchus of Thessalonica Family and Friends
Aristarchus: (58) wealthy Greek with merchant fleets and many estates, good friend of Publius
Helena: (54) Aristarchus's wife of 40 years
Philip: (33) youngest son of Aristarchus, house church leader, controls Thracian fleet and estates
Claudia: (24) Lucius Fidelis's sister, wife of Philip

Valerius Corvinus Family
Marcus: (41) Lucius's best friend
Gaius: (18) Marcus's son and Tertius's best friend
Gnaeus: (14) Marcus's violent younger son whom Lucius plans to betroth with Drusilla

Other Important Characters
Marcus Antonius Brutus: equestrian owner of a gladiator school in Rome
Didia Galla: wife of Lucius's friend, Sextus Flaccus
Manlius Atticus: Roman senator who admires Cornelia
Quintus Aemelius Lepidus: Roman equestrian with estate bordering Hector's farm

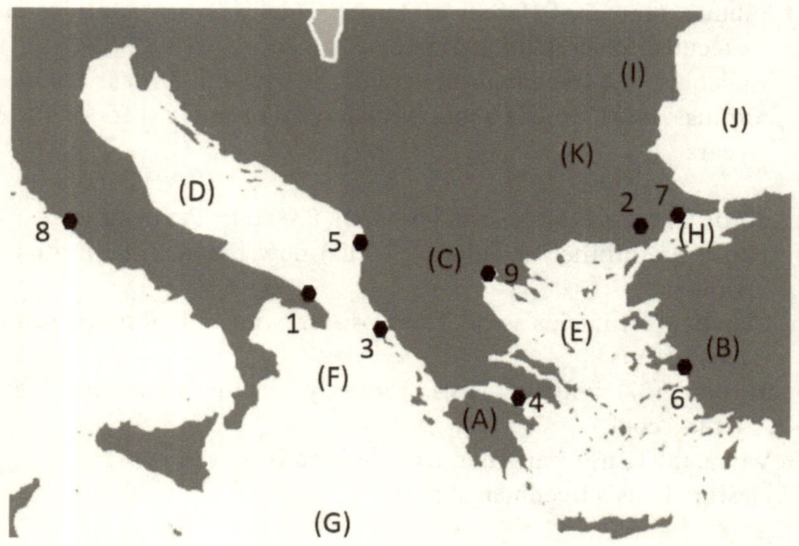

Cities and Towns

Achaia: (A) southern portion of present-day Greece

Asia: (B) Roman province, now Turkey

Brundisium: (1) port city on Adriatic coast of the bootheel of Italia, present-day Brindisi

Claudia Aprensis: (2) town in Thracia on Via Egnatia, near present-day Kermeyan, Turkey

Corcyra: (3) city on a Greek island in the Ionian Sea, present-day Corfu

Corinthus: (4) capital city of Achaia, present-day Corinth

Dyrrhachium: (5) port city on Albanian coast of Adriatic Sea, present-day Durrës

Ephesus: (6) capital city of Roman province of Asia

Macedonia: (C) Roman province, now northern portion of Greece, Albania, and Macedonia

Mare Adriaticum: (D) Adriatic Sea

Mare Aegeum: (E) Aegean Sea

Mare Ionium: (F) Ionian Sea

Mare Nostrum: (G) the Mediterranean Sea; "our sea," to the Romans

Mare Propontis: (H) Sea of Marmara, the inland sea connecting the Mediterranean and Black Sea

Moesia: (I) Roman province on the Pontus Euxinus (Black Sea), now Bulgaria and Romania

Perinthus: (7) capital of Thracia, present-day Marmara Ereğli

Pontus Euxinus: (J) Black Sea

Portus: (8) Port city at the mouth of the Tiber River serving as the port for Rome

Thessalonica: (9) capital of Macedonia, present-day Thessaloniki

Thracia: (K) Roman province north of the Mare Propontis; now Turkey, Greece, and Bulgaria

Via Appia: Roman road connecting Rome to Brundisium

Via Egnatia: Roman road that ran from Dyrrachium to Byzantium, passing through Perinthus

Chapter 1

Husbands and Fathers

Mare Nostrum, AD 122

Hector awoke, once more drenched in sweat. He rolled on his back and stared at the bottom of the bunk above him. As the ship rose and fell on the waves, he willed his breathing to match the rhythm of the swells.

The nightmares of his childhood were long past, the pain that caused them mostly forgotten. But now his dreams were red and raw, a stark reminder of reality, and they tore his heart each time he had one.

The dreams started well enough. It was the end of the final voyage of autumn. As his ship glided up against the pier and his crew prepared to secure it with ropes, his beloved Damara and their ten-year-old Charissa waved from the road above the wharves. Even after seventeen years of marriage, his heart beat faster as he thought about spending the cold winter nights in the warm embrace of the incredible woman God had given him to make him whole.

As the gangplank was lowered, his wife and daughter started down the ramp. He trotted down the plank and loped up the pier. As he dodged the crates and barrels waiting to be loaded, he lost sight of them. When he finally stepped clear of the stacks of cargo, Philip stood before him. He placed his hand on Hector's shoulder, tightened his lips, and shook his head.

Philip dissolved in a swirl of smoke, and Hector remained on the dock...alone.

The slower breaths lowered his heart rate, but the heartache remained. He'd known loneliness before God brought Damara into his life, or so he'd thought. But when two have become one, and suddenly one is gone... Those first four months when the sea was closed and he'd been home at his farm, where they'd planned on growing old together—the sweet memories of what he'd lost had engulfed him, tormenting his days and haunting his nights.

It hadn't been as bad when he was at sea, at least not during the daytime. He'd often been gone for weeks at a time, and he didn't expect to see Damara smiling at him when he turned around on deck or Charissa running to wrap her arms around him when he walked through the cabin doorway.

Hector rubbed his forehead with the back of his hand. If only Damara hadn't heard his ship might reach home port early and come to the wharf to see. If only he'd thought to tell her to stay well away from where the wagons unloaded, no matter how much Charissa begged to get closer to watch.

Experience told him sleep would not come again that night, so he rose and headed out to the ship's rail. There, alone in the moonlight, he watched his ship cutting through the waves and once more asked God why.

It had been almost a year since the accident, and the pain still cut deep. The shipping season was almost over. One more stop in Rome, then home to Perinthus...and another winter in a cold bed with empty arms.

Rome

Tertius didn't want to believe what his best friend Gaius had just told him. It shouldn't be true, but Tertius knew his father too well not to ask. He wasn't going to let anyone kill his sister if he could prevent it.

Lucius Drusus Fidelis was reading at his desk when Tertius walked into the library. Tertius's entrance drew a smile.

"I hadn't expected to see you today. I thought you were staying with Gaius at the Corvinus estate this week." His father set the scroll down and turned his attention to the youngest of his three sons.

"I hadn't expected to come, but Gaius just told me you were talking with his father about betrothing Drusilla to Gnaeus."

"That's true. Marcus is looking for the right girl for Gnaeus now that he's fourteen. Drusilla's ten, so she'll be the right age to marry him in five years."

"You can't do that, Father. Gaius says his brother is dangerous." He patted his closed fist twice with his palm. "Just last year, he and Gaius were riding out at their estate. His horse stumbled and threw him. He took a hoe from one of the slaves, and when he was through, Gaius had to slit the poor animal's throat to put it out of its misery. He's already beaten one of the house slaves to death and almost killed one of the slave girls after taking her."

Hands on the edge of the desk, he leaned toward his father. "Don't betroth Drusilla to him. He's vicious, and she's going to get hurt or killed."

His father had picked up a stylus and rolled it between his fingers while he listened; he paused, then shrugged. "Marcus is my closest friend, and he hasn't found anyone else who wants his daughter to be married to the boy. I have a daughter the right age, so I can solve Marcus's problem."

Tertius's jaw started to drop, but he stopped it while Father's eyes were still on the stylus. "You can't be serious about marrying Drusilla to a monster."

His father's brows dipped as a frown appeared. "What I choose to do with Drusilla is none of your business, Tertius. Marcus wants a wife for Gnaeus, and I can give him one. Gnaeus is no worse than many boys his age. Even if he did want to hurt her, Marcus wouldn't let him. She'll be safe enough."

Tertius masked the disgust swirling through him. It would be a huge mistake to let Father see it. "I hope you're right, Father. Drusilla's a sweet little thing. You'd really like her if you spent more time at the eastern estate. Mother and I would hate to see anything bad happen to her."

A sneer flitted across his father's lips. "What your mother thinks means less than nothing to me. Marcus will make sure nothing happens to Drusilla. Her safety is not your concern." He fixed irritated eyes on Tertius. "We won't discuss this again."

"As you wish, Father. I need to leave now, anyway. I'm meeting Gaius at the Circus Maximus for the afternoon races."

"I hope your faction wins. Enjoy yourself." His father turned his attention back to his scroll as Tertius walked out of the room.

When his father could no longer see him, Tertius let a frown furrow his brow as he tightened his lips. He should have known it would be pointless trying to convince Father not to put Drusilla in mortal danger. Time for a different approach to protect the little sister he loved.

Chapter 2

Time for a Change

The Drusus estate east of Rome

Father thought Tertius was going to the chariot races, but he headed to the eastern estate instead. He mostly stayed in Rome now that he was eighteen, but his mother and sister never came to the town house that had been his grandfather's before Father turned Grandfather in as a Christian so he'd die in the arena for his faith.

Father's sister, Aunt Claudia, had accused Father of murder. To punish her, Father had tried to marry her to a rich, sadistic old man from one of the noblest Roman families. Mother had tried to stop him, and she and Father had hardly spoken to each other in the eight years since.

Drusilla meant the world to Mother. It took no imagination to believe Father would let something terrible happen to her just to hurt Mother. But Father wouldn't hurt Drusilla if Tertius could stop it.

A slave scurried over to take his horse when Tertius trotted into the stable yard. He threw his leg over the horse's neck and slid to the ground. "Where's my mother?"

"In the garden, Master Tertius."

He tossed the reins to the slave and strode through the archway that separated the garden from the stable area. "Mother? Are you here?"

♦

Cornelia Scipia's eyes snapped up from her codex when she heard Tertius calling. She rose from the seat under the grape arbor and waved at him. When he reached her, she embraced her youngest son.

"What a pleasant surprise. I hadn't expected to see you until next week."

"There's something you need to know today."

The grim set of his mouth ramped up Cornelia's heart rate. "What's wrong? Are you well?"

"I'm fine, but Drusilla won't be if we don't do something to protect her."

A cold hand of foreboding gripped her heart. "What might happen to Drusilla?"

"Father is planning to betroth her to Gnaeus Corvinus."

"Marcus's youngest?" She'd heard too many rumors about the boy. "Are you sure?"

"After Gaius told me, I went to Father and asked him. I told him how dangerous Gnaeus is. He didn't care. He's planning to do it anyway just to help out his friend." Tertius sucked air between his teeth. "We can't let him do that, Mother. She'll end up hurt or dead."

Cornelia drew herself up to her full height, and her mouth set into a determined line. "Your father is a traitor to this family. He murdered your grandfather, he would have hurt Claudia if she hadn't escaped, and now he's planning to get Drusilla killed." She slapped her fist with her palm. "Well, I won't let him. I'll do whatever it takes to protect her."

"How can I help?" Eager intensity lit his eyes as he squared his shoulders.

Cornelia's brow furrowed as she pursed her lips. "First, don't tell your father you came here. He mustn't know I've been warned, or he'll take her away before I can do anything."

"I can't tell him. Father said we wouldn't discuss this again." His lips curved into a wry smile. "If I'm to be a good son, I must never say anything to him about it."

If Drusilla hadn't been in mortal danger, Cornelia would have laughed at her son's twisted interpretation of the duty to a *paterfamilias* that grown sons continue to obey their fathers in everything. Her mouth turned up a little anyway.

Cornelia clenched her hand and tapped the top of her fist against her pursed lips. "I've stayed married to your father only so he wouldn't take you all away from me, but you boys are grown. It's been eight years since he completely abandoned me for other women. It's time I divorce him and reclaim my dowry. Then I can take Drusilla where he can't hurt her."

"But children always belong to the father in a divorce. Where could you go that he couldn't get her?"

"Away from Rome. Maybe away from Italia. Far enough away that he might decide it's not worth the effort to find her and bring her back."

"I want to help. Tell me what to do."

Cornelia covered her mouth and stroked her cheek with her forefinger. "I think, for now, it's best that you not know what I'm going to do. If he thinks you're not part of this, we might get advance warning of what he's doing to get her back. Later, I'll let you know where we are so you can warn me of anything he's planning."

She wrapped her arms around Tertius's chest and stretched up to kiss his cheek. "I'm so proud of you and your brother Lucius. Two of my sons grew into fine men like your grandfather Publius. Marcus... well, he's too much like his father."

Tertius hugged her back. "If I can't help right now, I should go to the Circus Maximus. I told Father I was going there to meet Gaius, and I'd better know who won."

"Go. I already have an idea what to do, but I need to think about it more."

Tertius kissed his mother's cheek and left.

Cornelia began pacing. She would need her whole dowry back. As steward and overseer of all the Drusus estates and her despicable husband's under-the-table business ventures, Malleolus was the only person who could get it quickly and without Lucius knowing what she was planning. The moment he knew she was divorcing him, he'd come for Drusilla.

Secrecy was vital, but Malleolus would keep everything secret. Even though Lucius Fidelis was now head of the Claudius Drusus family, the old steward's loyalty still belonged to Publius, even eight years after his death. Saving Publius's granddaughter was something he'd be eager to do.

Rome

Breakfast was over, and Aristarchus and Helena walked Hector to the stable. It was a four-hour ride from their house near the eastern edge of Rome back to the ship in Portus. In a few days, Hector would sail back to Thracia, where he would spend the four months that the sea was closed due to winter storms at his farm near Perinthus.

Aristarchus expected his captain of the *Claudia* to dine with them and spend the night whenever he brought the ship to Rome. Hector was, without doubt, the most deserving man he had ever bought and freed. He had served in the family's merchant fleet for twenty-five years, first as a slave, then as a freedman whose maritime skills had elevated him to the rank of captain. He was loyal and honest to a fault, and he had been the best friend of Aristarchus's youngest son, Philip, since they worked together one summer fifteen years ago.

Each time Hector had visited this shipping season, Aristarchus saw the dark shadow enveloping him. He was worried about his captain, who was more son than employee. Hector's wife and daughter had died just before he reached home last fall. The deep grief had a grip on him that he could not shake. His smiles were sad, and his eyes seemed weary. He was barely forty, but sorrow made him seem much older this visit.

Helena, Aristarchus's wife of over forty years, wrapped her arm around Hector's as they walked him to the horse he had rented for the ride from the coast.

"I'm so glad you came up to see us. We love having you here." She stood on tiptoes and kissed his bearded cheek. "You're my sixth son. I'll be praying for you until I see you again."

Hector smiled in response, but there was no joy in his eyes. "God truly blessed me with both of you."

Aristarchus wrapped his arms around Hector in a crushing hug and slapped his arm when he let go. "May God be with you on your voyage and bring you happiness again."

"And may He continue to bless you both with a long life together."

The tightness at the corners of Hector's smile and the two hard blinks that stopped any tears betrayed his captain's longing for the years with Damara that would never be.

Hector mounted and waved before kicking the horse into a trot and heading down the street. Helena wrapped her arm around Aristarchus's and leaned her head against his shoulder as she watched Hector ride away.

"It breaks my heart to see him suffering so. I don't know if it's Damara or Charissa he's missing more. To lose them both at once..." She sighed. "He has so much love to give, and he needs someone to give it to. He needs to remarry and have more children."

Aristarchus shook his head as his mouth turned down. "That is not so easy for a man who has known the joy of having the perfect wife. I am not sure I could remarry if you died."

She slapped his arm before she hugged it. "Don't say that. I would want you to remarry and find happiness again, God willing. That will be my prayer for Hector. I'm going to ask God to bring a woman to heal his heart before we see him again next spring."

Aristarchus smiled down at the sweet, godly woman who had graced his life for so long. She might think a man can just remarry to replace a lost love, but some women were irreplaceable. He would know. He was married to one.

Chapter 3

THE PERFECT ALLY

The Drusus estate east of Rome

Early the next morning, Malleolus rode up to the stable at the eastern estate. It wasn't so easy to ride anymore. These days, his knees told him how far the ride from the town house was. It might not be long before he would need to take a sedan chair in the daytime or drive the two-wheeled *cisium* when the ban on wheeled vehicles on the streets of Rome ended two hours before dark. That would be a sad day. He was still a man of thirty from the inside looking out, but riding reminded him that the wrinkled old man in the mirror with the fringe of silver hair was him and not his father.

Although he came every week, he never found much needing his attention. Cornelia ran the estate herself better than the overseers at the other Drusus estates. The main reason he came was to visit Cornelia and Drusilla. Cornelia had become a dear friend in the eight years since Publius's murder, and Drusilla loved him like a grandfather. It felt good to spend a few hours with people who were like family. He had none of his own.

After he dismounted, he placed his hands on his knees and bent forward to limber up for walking. He flexed his rein fingers a few times. Too bad there wasn't axle grease for the joints of a man nearing seventy.

The stable slave bowed as he took the reins. "Mistress Cornelia said you were to come to her in the garden the moment you arrived."

Malleolus's face remained impassive when he heard the command, but those words triggered unease. He'd never been met with such a message before. He arched his back to loosen a few more muscles and walked as fast as was almost comfortable to find his mistress and friend.

When she saw him walk through the archway, Cornelia rose and held both hands out to him. "I'm glad you came early today. I have something important to ask of you, and it's vital that you start on it as soon as possible."

Malleolus's gaze swept the garden near them to see if any ears were listening.

Cornelia followed his gaze. "I've already given orders that no one is to come into this part of the garden until I say. I've been watching, and no one is here. Our conversation needs to be totally private. Drusilla's life depends on it."

Malleolus was a difficult man to upset, and he'd mastered the art of concealing his thoughts even when he was. Her words broke through his unflappable demeanor, and his eyebrows rose.

"Drusilla's life? What's going on?"

"That loathsome husband of mine is planning to betroth her to Gnaeus Corvinus. I'm sure you've heard all the rumors about the boy. I know at least some of the worst are true. We can't let that betrothal happen."

His brows dipped downward as he tightened his lips. "No, we can't."

She sat down and patted the bench so he would sit beside her.

"I've decided to divorce Lucius and take Drusilla away from Rome before he commits her to that marriage. I need my dowry money as soon as possible, and I need your help in getting it without him knowing I'm preparing to leave."

Malleolus rubbed the underside of his jaw. "Normally it would take some time to get you that much money, but as luck would have it, I can do it as soon as this afternoon. I was about to buy two estates ten miles up the Via Aurelia to make one large one. I've already arranged to have more than enough gold at my disposal to make the purchases. I only need to have most of it delivered here instead." One corner of his mouth rose in a wry smile. "Lucius is required by law to return your entire dowry immediately when you divorce him. I guess he'll have to wait to get his new estate northwest of Rome."

She leaned over and embraced him. "I knew you'd be able to help." The smile that had appeared at the news of the gold dimmed. "The next part might be harder, and I'm not sure how to do it." Her gaze swept the garden from the arched entrance to the farthest wall. "I plan to go to Thracia, where Titus and Claudia are living. I'm sure they'll be glad to let me stay with them for a short time while I find an estate of my own to buy where no one will recognize us."

Her brow furrowed. "I want to go by sea, but I'm not sure how to arrange everything. You've shipped things all over the Empire. Can you find a good ship for us without Lucius suspecting anything before we sail?"

He stroked the bottom of his chin. "If he's still living in Rome, I know the perfect man to ask to help with this." The corner of his mouth lifted. "The same man helped me sneak Claudia out from under Lucius's nose eight years ago. Actually, help isn't the right word. He did everything. Publius called him a good friend, and he couldn't have been a better one. I think he'll be willing to help save Publius's granddaughter as well."

He rose. "I'll go now to see if he can help. When I return, we can make final plans."

Chapter 4

To the Rescue...Again

Rome

Malleolus reentered Rome through the Porta Esquilinas and immediately turned south to look for Aristarchus's house near the Gardens of Maecenas. But what if the Greek merchant had moved in the last eight years? If he had, would whoever owned the house now know where he went?

He found it with no difficulty. Even the door color hadn't changed in the intervening years. He dismounted and led his horse to the door with the same small window he remembered.

When he knocked, the window opened to reveal the face of the doorkeeper.

"Is this still the house of Aristarchus of Thessalonica?"

"Yes. Your name and business with him?"

"Claudius Malleolus." His voice dropped to a near-whisper. "I have an urgent request for help for the family of Publius Drusus. He was a close friend of Aristarchus eight years ago." Even the whisper seemed to echo off the garden walls lining the street.

"Take your horse to the side gate and tell the gatekeeper Vitellus said you can enter. Someone will meet you to take you to the master."

The window in the door closed. Malleolus led his horse around to the gate and knocked. When its small window opened, he repeated the doorkeeper's instruction. The gate swung open just enough for him to lead his horse through.

A stableman took his horse as a curly-haired boy of about nine scurried toward him. "Please come with me. The master will see you now."

Malleolus followed the boy into the atrium. When Aristarchus emerged from one of the adjoining rooms, Malleolus fought his eyebrows rising. How little the Greek merchant had changed. There were more and deeper wrinkles, but his eyes still sparkled with the enthusiasm of youth. Eight years earlier, his hair and beard had been silver-streaked black. Even though they were silver now, he still looked fit enough for a hard day of work. As he approached, he made a sweeping gesture toward a bench by the pool.

"Malleolus, steward of my brother Publius. I did not expect to see you again. Vitellus tells me you have a problem. Tell me about it, and I will see if I can help."

As Malleolus lowered himself to the bench beside Aristarchus, tension drained from his body. Once again, he had the perfect ally for thwarting Lucius's plans.

He drew a deep breath before launching into his request. "Last time I asked you to help save my master's daughter. This time I'm asking for his granddaughter. Lucius Fidelis plans to betroth her to his friend's son."

Malleolus's disgust pulled the corners of his mouth down. "The boy is vicious, but her father doesn't care. His wife is going to divorce him and take Drusilla far from Rome to protect her. She wants to join Claudia and Titus in Thracia and then buy an estate where Fidelis can't find them. Cornelia will be very wealthy once she reclaims her dowry, so payment is not a problem."

He raised hopeful eyebrows. "Can you help arrange her passage so Lucius won't know she's leaving or where she's going? All must be done secretly, or he'll take Drusilla before Cornelia can get her away."

Aristarchus nodded slowly. "So, you are asking me to join in another kidnapping." His lips curved into a wry smile. "That seems to be my specialty when serving my brother Publius." He slapped his knees. "I will be glad to help. I even have the perfect ship anchored in the harbor at Portus right now. It is the same one that took Claudia."

A sigh of relief escaped Malleolus. "Excellent. I already have the gold to return Cornelia's dowry, and she'll pack a few trunks of personal items." He massaged his neck. "Now I only need to arrange for a freight wagon and *raeda* to get Cornelia, Drusilla, and Cornelia's maid to the port. I can't use the ones from the estate and keep anything secret. When and where should I plan on having them arrive in Portus?"

Aristarchus stroked his beard. "I think it will be much safer if I provide the carriage and wagon. My own men will drive and be armed guards. Fidelis can never trace them. Can you have everything ready in the morning four days from now?"

"Yes. I'll return to Cornelia's estate when I leave here to tell her our plan. She's a very capable woman. Three days will be more than enough for her to do everything needed."

"And what will you do after you arrange their escape?" The Greek's brow furrowed. "Fidelis never discovered the role you played when Claudia vanished, but he will suspect you when Drusilla also disappears. You will never convince him you knew nothing of Cornelia's plans since you are recovering her dowry gold."

Malleolus tightened his lips as he nodded. "He'll know I was her accomplice. I have legal authority to recover her dowry, but he will be furious that I didn't tell him of her plan to divorce him. What he will do to me...well, the most he can legally do is take stewardship of the Drusus affairs away from me. At least I think that's all."

He shrugged. "I can find another to hire me. I have a reputation for growing a fortune from a modest amount of money. I've been approached before by some who didn't know I only want to do it for Publius's grandchildren."

Aristarchus pursed his lips. "The way evil men react is not limited by Roman law. Your loyalty to the family of Publius deserves more than being cast out by his son. I will help Cornelia save her daughter, but you must go with them."

Malleolus's eyebrows shot up. "Me go, too?"

"Yes. It is too dangerous for you to stay this time. Too dangerous for me as well if you stay. We fooled Fidelis last time, but this time he will know who to blame."

The thought was tempting. Cornelia and Drusilla were the two people he cared for most in this world. Life would lose most of its pleasure once they were gone. He had some money from investing his modest salary as he invested the Drusus fortune. Perhaps it was enough.

"What would the passage cost?"

"Nothing. Claudia is now my daughter-in-law. My son Philip was the man who planned her escape, and they grew to love each other on the voyage to Thracia. She would want you to spend your final years with her. Your passage will be my gift to her."

"I would love to see her again, and Titus as well."

"Then you should go to them. Besides, someone who knows his

way in the world will be needed to care for Cornelia and her daughter. I think that should be you."

Malleolus's eyes crinkled as he tightened his lips to hold back the laugh. "You haven't met Cornelia. She could manage anything that might arise quite well without me, but I will gladly go with them."

Aristarchus and Malleolus spent half an hour planning the details of the escape. Then Aristarchus escorted him to his horse. After Malleolus mounted, Aristarchus stood with his hand resting on the horse's neck.

"When you get to Perinthus, be sure to tell Claudia you are my gift. It will be the best one I ever sent her."

Malleolus grinned down at him. "I will, and I thank you for everything."

As he rode through the gate and down the street, thoughts about the plan and especially his own role in it triggered repeated smiles. He'd never even dreamed of once more being with the young woman he'd always loved like his own daughter.

And nothing could give more satisfaction than spiriting Drusilla and her mother away to thwart the plans of Lucius Fidelis. Getting them safely to Thracia would be his final act of service to his dead master Publius, the man he would always consider the true head of the Claudius Drusus family.

Portus, port city of Rome

The last person Hector expected to see in Portus the next morning was Aristarchus. His ship was moored in the harbor, awaiting its turn to dock at a pier and load in three days. When one of his crewmen reported a boat approaching on the port side, he walked over to stand where the rope ladder would be lowered if he decided to let the visitor board.

When he saw Aristarchus, his knuckles whitened as he gripped the railing. The master of all the family enterprises had never come to his ship in the harbor before.

He flicked his hand to order the rope ladder lowered. As Aristarchus reached the top, Hector held out his hand to help him onto the deck.

"Welcome to the *Claudia*. Is anything wrong?" His jaw clenched.

"Not with me, but I have an urgent problem to solve for someone else, and you can help me do it."

Hector released the breath he'd been half holding. "What's the problem?"

"I must get four people to Perinthus as soon as possible."

"I have no passengers this trip, so I can take them. Who is it?"

"Claudia's sister-in-law Cornelia, her daughter, her maid, and Malleolus, the old steward of Publius Drusus who asked me to save Claudia from her brother Lucius."

"Come to the canopy and tell me all about it."

The two men walked to the stern and settled into the chairs kept there for passengers.

Aristarchus pulled a deep breath. "I miss the salty smell of the sea. I should come to Portus more often."

The corner of Hector's mouth rose. "And the faint aroma of dead fish?"

Aristarchus chuckled. "That smell I can do without. But my own pleasure is not why I came."

Hector leaned toward the man who meant more to him than any other. "Cornelia's party—is it urgent that they reach Perinthus...or that they leave Rome?"

"Leave Rome." Aristarchus stroked his beard. "Malleolus came yesterday to ask my help. Cornelia must get her daughter away from Lucius Fidelis. He wants to marry Drusilla to the son of his best friend. The boy is vicious."

His lips tightened. "How any father could do that... Cornelia has decided to divorce Fidelis so she can reclaim her dowry and take her daughter to Thracia to protect her. She cannot let Fidelis know where she is, or he will try to get the girl back. He is paterfamilias and has every right to keep Cornelia from even seeing Drusilla again. You could say Cornelia will be kidnapping her own daughter to save her."

Aristarchus ran his hand through his silver hair. "Cornelia has made a courageous choice. She is leaving her old life behind and can never return. Malleolus asked my help in secretly arranging passage for her, her daughter, and her maid. I told him I would help only if he went, too. He has grown old serving Publius's family. He deserves to end his days with people who love him. I know Claudia will want him with her."

"So, Lucius Drusus hasn't changed since I helped Claudia escape from him eight years ago." Hector shook his head; then a smile crept out. "God used his evil plan to bless Philip and Claudia with each other. It was a pleasure to help with that. I'll gladly help with this as well."

Aristarchus leaned over and slapped Hector's shoulder. "I can always count on you. Malleolus has started recovering her dowry. I will provide a wagon for her trunks and the carriage to transport the four of them. My raeda bears no markings, and it is closed in so they can travel without being seen and recognized.

He leaned back in the chair and crossed his arms. "I will also provide the drivers and guards to lay a false trail to the northeast and then bring them through the city at night when wagons are allowed. They will wait at the warehouse just south of the city gate until morning. That should get them here midmorning on the day you are loading."

"Is there anything I need to do to help them get here?"

"No. I will take care of the land portion of their escape. Cornelia has ample money and will pay full passage for three. I told Malleolus his passage is a gift from me to Claudia."

"I'm set to load and sail in three days. I can delay a couple of days if you need me to."

"That should not be needed, but I will send word if it is." Aristarchus rose. "Time for me to return home." He arched his back. "I am getting too old for riding most of the day when I do not do it very often, but saving Publius's granddaughter is worth the soreness."

Hector rose as well. "I'll take good care of them for you and deliver them safely to Philip and Claudia."

The two men walked back to the rope ladder. Aristarchus turned and rested his hand on Hector's shoulder.

"You truly are my sixth son, Hector. May God bless you and protect you on this voyage."

Those words and touch—they were balm for the ragged hole in Hector's heart. For more than twenty years, Aristarchus had filled the place of the father he never knew.

"And may He continue to bless you. Give my love to Helena."

◆

A gull screamed overhead as Aristarchus climbed down the ladder and settled into the rowboat that would return him to the pier. As the boat pulled away from the ship, his gaze locked on Hector's face.

Helena was right. He looked too sad. He needed someone to give his love to again. Philip had found the love of his life saving Claudia from her evil brother. Might God use another evil choice by Lucius Fidelis to heal Hector's broken heart?

Helena was praying, and she was a mighty woman of prayer. Had he just put in motion something that would help her prayers come true?

Chapter 5

Beginning the Great Adventure

The Drusus estate east of Rome

The morning of their departure arrived. Malleolus had personally supervised the delivery of five chests filled with gold coins two days earlier. Last night, he had arrived with his two small trunks. Cornelia had all the trunks for her, Drusilla, and her maid Anthusa packed and waiting. All that was needed was their transportation, and their escape could begin.

As the eastern clouds brightened from gray to pink, a black raeda and a freight wagon rolled into the stable yard. The armed guard on the raeda jumped down and asked for Malleolus. Then he stood by the carriage and waited.

Malleolus emerged from the house. After exchanging a few words with the guard, he returned to the house and ordered most of the trunks to be loaded into the wagon. The chests containing Cornelia's gold and jewelry and her box of perfumes were loaded into the raeda.

◆

While everything was being loaded, Cornelia and Anthusa walked through the garden for the last time. When Cornelia turned to look back at the façade of the villa as the rising sun chased shadows across it, her breath caught. Then a deep sigh drained her lungs.

"This has been my home since I married Lucius. I watched my boys grow into men here. I love this place." The marble columns blurred, but she shook her head slightly and squared her shoulders. A quick flick with her fingertips, and the tears that might raise suspicions were gone.

"But now it's time to leave. Drusilla is more important than any memories, and I can make a good life for us some other place."

She directed a steady smile toward Anthusa. "Ready for the great adventure?"

"Yes, mistress. I'm ready to go wherever you take us."

Cornelia took a deep breath and blew it out. "Then it's time for us to get into the raeda and head toward the northeastern estate."

The corner of Cornelia's mouth lifted into a wry smile as she pronounced their direction. The two women walked through the archway that led to the stable yard where the carriage waited.

Drusilla was standing beside the raeda, and she skipped over when they emerged from the garden. "Since we're going to the other estate for a couple of months, I packed all my scrolls and codices."

"That's good, dear. You'll have plenty of time to read where we're going."

"Why aren't we taking our raeda?"

"A friend thought it was a better idea to use his."

"The outside is plain, but I looked inside. It's even nicer than ours."

"Climb in. I need a word with the understeward, and then we'll be leaving."

As soon as she was in, Drusilla's head popped out the window.

Malleolus fell in beside Cornelia. "Everything is ready."

She nodded. The understeward saw her coming and strode over to meet them.

"Primus, you'll be in charge of everything while I'm gone. Malleolus is going to accompany me to take care of some special business. If anyone should need to find me, they should look for me at the northeastern estate. I may be gone for some time."

"Yes, mistress."

"There's a chest on the desk in the library. The next time Lucius Fidelis comes out here, he is to look at what's in it. No one except him is to open that chest. Understood?"

"Yes, mistress."

She strolled back to the raeda while Malleolus gave the understeward some final instructions.

"Time to leave, Anthusa." Cornelia rested her hand on her maid's arm. Then they both climbed into the carriage. Anthusa took the side-facing seat opposite Drusilla as Cornelia settled onto the thick upholstery of the bench seat at the rear.

Cornelia watched through the door as Malleolus slapped the arm of his understeward and headed toward the raeda himself.

He climbed in and leaned his head out the window. "Let's go."

As he settled onto the seat next to her, the reins slapped against the mules. The raeda lurched as they began their journey toward an unknown future. Cornelia's spine relaxed against the well-padded seat, and her satisfied smile blossomed into a grin. "We did it, Malleolus."

He grinned back. "We did, indeed."

The two wagons first headed toward the northeast on the Via Tiburtina. Cornelia knew that road well. It led to another Drusus estate, but it also led to several estates of the Cornelius Scipio family.

Cornelia's brother and several cousins had rural villas in that direction. Lucius would think she'd gone to one of those when he discovered she hadn't gone to theirs. Her jaw clenched as she fought the regret that she might never see any of them again.

They had driven three miles when the raeda turned off the main road paved with stone onto a narrow dirt road leading south.

Drusilla's brow furrowed. "Isn't the estate up that other road?"

"Yes, dear, but we're not going to the estate." She took a deep breath. It was time to tell her daughter what was going on. "We're leaving Italia and going to your uncle in Thracia."

"Why?"

"Your father was going to betroth you to Gnaeus Corvinus."

Drusilla's eyebrows shot up. "Gnaeus? Isn't he Gaius's crazy brother? The one who's so mean?"

"Yes, and I'm not going to let your father marry you to a boy like that. I've divorced him, and you and I are going to start over in Thracia where he can't find you."

"You mean we'll never, ever come back home?"

"No. At least not as long as your father is alive. By then, Thracia will feel like home, and we probably won't want to come back."

"Will our friends come visit sometimes?"

"No. We can't even let them know where we're going. Your father might find us."

◆

Drusilla saw sadness pass across her mother's face before she hid it behind a smile. But that smile wasn't a good enough mask when

Mother's eyes gave her away. Drusilla wrapped her fingers around her mother's.

Never see their friends again? Mother had two friends who were like sisters. They often visited, and when they did, Mother talked and laughed so much...no sadness, no worries, just like Drusilla was with her own friend, Flavia. Who would make Mother happy when they were in Thracia?

And what about Tertius?

We're only leaving because of me. Why is Father so horrible that Mother has to leave all her friends? It's not fair!

Drusilla blinked twice to keep the tears trapped inside. If Mother could pretend she wasn't sad to make leaving easier to bear, Drusilla could, too.

She faked her happiest smile. "That's all right. We can make new friends. Everyone will want to be your friend."

She wrapped both arms around her mother, and Mother returned the hug.

"Yes, we can. This will be a great adventure for us. We'll see and do so many new things." She pushed some stray hair behind Drusilla's ear. "We'll both love that."

Mother's stiff smile didn't fool Drusilla, but she could pretend it did. Anything to make this easier for Mother.

"I love seeing new things. I'm glad we're going. It should be fun."

She turned to look out the window. If Mother could give up everything to protect her from Father giving her to Gnaeus, she'd make sure Mother never saw her tears.

The raeda rocked and jostled them as it traveled the rutted dirt of the back road, but a little discomfort couldn't dim Cornelia's satisfaction over thwarting Lucius.

Drusilla's enthusiasm brought frequent smiles to Cornelia's lips as they made their way through the countryside. Her curious daughter pointed out different things and asked Malleolus about them. He had explanations for everything, and Drusilla had a seemingly endless supply of new questions.

Having Malleolus along made the unknown road ahead seem less worrisome...and less lonely.

He'd been part of her life since she married Lucius, and she'd quickly grown to love him as a friend. No matter what the problem was, he'd dive in and solve it for her. Not just because it was his job as steward, but because he cared.

He loved Claudia and Titus as if they were his own. He'd even loved Lucius before he betrayed Publius.

Drusilla loved him, too. She had no grandfather, but Malleolus was everything a child could want in one.

He'd grown old serving Publius's family. He could take a small fortune and turn it into a large one, and that was the only reason her rat of a husband kept him on after getting Publius killed. Lucius would have cast him off when he was no longer any use to him. She would have found a place for him with one of her brothers, had she stayed in Rome.

Drusilla pointed out the window, and Malleolus launched into another explanation that drew Cornelia's smile.

By taking him to Thracia, she would still have her dear friend, and he would always have a home.

The carriage and wagon stayed on the back road for several miles until they intercepted the Via Tuscana, where they doubled back toward the southwest.

When Drusilla finally ran out of questions, Malleolus flicked his fingers to invite her onto the bench beside him. As she snugged against his side, he draped his arm around her shoulder. No words were necessary as they both watched the orchards, vineyards, and pastures flow past the window.

After several hours of driving, they pulled off the road.

The raeda rocked as the driver jumped down. His head poked into the carriage. "We're a little more than a mile from the Porta Asinaria at the southeastern edge of Rome. It's a few hours until the gate opens. We'll wait here until then. We're heading across the river and south on the Via Portuensis. Wagon traffic is always heavy...and slow. It could take more than two hours to pass through the city and get to the warehouse, but we have torches if it gets dark before we reach it."

Malleolus stuck his own head out when the driver withdrew his. "A long day's travel, but worth it."

There were dozens of wagons and carriages waiting with them, and food venders wandered among them. Malleolus turned toward Anthusa.

"Come with me. We can get something for our escorts and ourselves to eat while we wait."

He and Anthusa wandered among the vendors until they found some rosemary-laced bread, dried dates, and wine. As they started back to their companions, four armed men drew Malleolus's gaze. They were winding through the parked carriages, tracing Malleolus's path and getting closer.

"Faster, Anthusa. Don't look, but we're being followed."

The men were gaining on them, and Malleolus quickened his steps as much as he could without actually jogging. A swift glance over his shoulder revealed the men less than sixty feet behind them, still gaining. At least they were almost back to Aristarchus's guards. He was puffing when they reached the raeda.

The driver stood and waved his arm at the four men. "Myron. Alexander. Over here."

Malleolus's tense shoulders relaxed, and he chuckled at himself. Aristarchus had said he would be providing extra guards for the trip through the city itself.

Being an accomplice in a kidnapping made a man much jumpier than usual.

For Cornelia, the hours spent waiting for the city gate to open to wheeled traffic felt like days. She longed to get out of the raeda and stretch her legs. But she weighed the risk of someone recognizing her against the cramps in her legs, and caution won over comfort.

The sun was low in the sky when they merged into the long line of wagons, carts, and carriages as it crept toward the stone arch that spanned the cobblestone road. Inside the city wall, they headed southwest from the Porta Asinaria to catch the Via Appia. With so much traffic, it was very slow going.

Cornelia's eyes drifted shut, but the occasional lurch as the wheels rolled over the cobblestones kept her from sleeping. She stayed away from the window as they got closer to central Rome, where the odds of encountering a senator who might recognize her rose.

Drusilla leaned her elbow on the window frame, transfixed by the monuments to the greatness of Rome.

As they drove past a building that stretched for at least a quarter mile, her daughter gasped. "Look at that huge building, Mother. What is it?"

"The Circus Maximus. That's where they race the chariots your brother likes to watch so much."

"I think it would be exciting to drive one. Maybe someone can teach me in Thracia."

Cornelia choked back a chuckle. Her daughter's daring nature matched her curiosity. "Maybe, but I won't let you compete in races. Those are too dangerous."

Drusilla turned to grin at her. "That's all right. Driving fast on a road should be fun enough."

Drusilla remained pasted to the window as they passed to the west of the area of the Forums. As they began to cross the Tiber on the Pons Aemilius, she turned again. "I've never been on such a big bridge. I didn't know the river was so wide. There's even an island in the middle of it." She craned her neck for a final view of the water as the carriage rolled off the bridge and headed for the city gate west of the river.

Cornelia flexed her shoulders and shifted on the bench. Even the best cushions couldn't make an all-day ride comfortable. "You'll love it when we reach the sea. When you stand on the shore, you can look across the water for miles."

The sky flamed gold and crimson as the carriage turned south onto the Via Portuensis. A steady stream of heavy wagons snaked into the city. A man driving a team of mules cursed at an ox driver for going so slowly. Start-and-stop traffic headed north, but the traffic heading south moved at a steady, if slow, pace.

They'd been traveling for almost twelve hours, and Cornelia was bone-weary. She leaned against the raeda wall, only to have her head smack into the wood as the carriage rocked its way along the cobblestone road.

Malleolus patted her hand. "We're almost there. It's only a mile and a quarter from the gate to the warehouse."

Dusk was turning into dark when the mules finally pulled the carriage through a large gate and stopped by a grain warehouse. The face of their driver appeared in the door's window.

He opened the door and held out his hand to assist Cornelia. "You'll be spending the rest of the night here. There are some beds waiting for you inside. It's about another three hours down to the harbor, and we want to get there midmorning. Someone will wake you for breakfast."

Cornelia stepped down from the raeda and stretched. The carriage was built to cushion the ride over rough roads and stone paving, but it still rattled and shook. One more day to the ship, four to five weeks to Thracia—soon she would buy an estate and start over. Almost everything would be different, but she would still have Drusilla, Anthusa, and Malleolus with her.

She tipped her head back and her gaze swept the sky. The stars sparkled against the blackness. She'd always loved looking at them. So much was changing, but the night sky would remain the same.

A cot in a warehouse should not have encouraged a good night's sleep, but Cornelia awoke well-rested and eager for what the day might bring. Her mirrors were packed in the wagon, but Anthusa could be trusted to replace her elaborate crown of curls and tidy her hair so it wouldn't look like she'd slept in it.

The breakfast of bread, cheese, and raisins satisfied better than her last banquet. The future awaited beyond the hills that lay between them and the wharves at Portus. As she climbed into the raeda for the final stretch of the escape from Rome, she shook off the dust of regret over what lay behind. Fifteen more miles, and Italia would become the stuff of memories, good ones to keep and sad ones to discard. She was ready to embrace the future.

Portus, port city of Rome

As they stopped above the wharves, Cornelia's view of the harbor was blocked by Drusilla hanging out the window of the raeda. Her daughter sprang out first, followed by Malleolus and Anthusa. The driver hopped down and held his hand out to Cornelia to steady her as she climbed out.

His other hand swept toward a ship tied to the pier below them. "That's the *Claudia.*"

Cornelia had never been to a harbor before, and her eyes widened as her gaze followed his hand.

The line of slaves carrying cargo up a plank and into a hole in the deck seemed more like children than men compared to the massive ship. The *corbita* that would carry them to Thracia was ninety feet long and twenty-five feet wide. Toward the rear was a cabin, about ten by twenty feet, with a canopy roughly half that size attached to it.

Just past the canopy, the bright white of a carved neck and head of a swan caught her eye. Two large, paddle-like rudders hugged the ship's sides just past the cabin. Poles for controlling them extended over the cabin roof where whoever was steering must stand.

A little forward of the center of the ship was a huge mast, about half as tall as the length of the ship. A second mast about a third as long as the tall one stuck out at an angle past the bow of the ship. The sails on each were tied up to the long spars that were mounted at right angles to the masts.

Drusilla's eyebrows shot up. "Is that our ship? It's huge. I never thought it would be so big."

"It takes a big ship to go safely on the sea."

The size of it did calm Cornelia's nerves. Sea voyages this late in the season could be especially dangerous. The fall weather was often unpredictable, and she'd heard sad tales of ships being lost in October gales that no one had expected. Still, the uncertain danger of a sea voyage was nothing compared to the certain suffering of her daughter if they stayed.

She drew a deep breath, raised her head, and stepped toward the ramp. The future belonged to those brave enough to take a risk.

Chapter 6

The Captain

Drusilla held Malleolus's hand as they started down the ramp to the pier. She looked back over her shoulder at Cornelia and grinned.

"I can hardly wait to see what it's like to be on a ship."

Her daughter's enthusiasm and endless curiosity drew Cornelia's smile. "I've never been on one, either. We'll stop in several ports before we get to Perinthus, where your uncle is. I'm sure we'll see many interesting things."

One interesting thing had already captured Cornelia's attention as they walked along the pier: the man standing on the deck of the ship ahead of her. Something in his bearing and the way the other crewmen acted toward him marked him as the captain.

The brawny man wore a white tunic that barely reached the knees of his sinewy legs. That seemed odd. The captain of a ship this size wouldn't be poor, and she'd expected something more befitting a well-to-do merchant. Only the color distinguished his attire from that of his crew. A broad leather belt held his tunic snug around his waist, accentuating the breadth of his shoulders and his athletic build.

His hair was short and curly, and he wore a short beard. That hair had once been totally black, but now it was gray at the temples and a sprinkling of gray could be seen in his beard. He was deeply tanned, as expected for a man who worked outdoors most of the year.

He stood with his legs spread, fists resting on his hips as he looked up at a crane-load of cargo as it was lowered toward a gaping hole in the deck. He reached up to steady the large crate that swung too much as it approached the opening, and his bulging biceps reminded her of the field slaves who did the heavy labor at her estate.

Perhaps he was not unusual for a ship's captain, but she'd expected someone who looked more like the cultured, spoiled men of aristocratic Rome, men like her ex-husband who relied on others to do any real work. Lucius Fidelis hadn't been that fit even during his mandatory service as a tribune in the army, but her ex-husband had only served near Rome, not in a fighting legion in a frontier province.

With his intensely masculine physique and his ruggedly handsome face, the captain would be the perfect model for a statue, but no statue could capture the animal magnetism she felt the moment she saw him. The maidenly flutter he provoked was unexpected. She was a grown woman long past any foolish mooning over handsome men.

As Malleolus and Drusilla paused at the foot of a broad wooden plank, a crewman spoke to the captain, and he turned to view his passengers. He signaled to the man who stood atop the cabin. When that man took his position by the opening, the captain strode to the edge of the deck where the plank rested.

"Come up, and welcome aboard. I'm Hector, captain of the *Claudia*."

His deep voice speaking accented Latin was accompanied by a welcoming smile. His warm brown eyes made his greeting feel like more than a formality. There was that flutter again.

◆

Hector watched the old man motion for the girl to step on the gangplank that moved up and down as his ship rode the gently lapping waves. She scampered up and smiled at Hector as she passed. He barely glanced at her. His eyes were fixed on her mother.

Cornelia Scipia and her maid remained standing on the pier beside Malleolus. Hector gazed down at the rich Roman noblewoman, proud descendent of a long line of consuls and senators, who was abandoning her privileged life in Rome to protect her daughter.

The first word that sprang into his mind was regal. She had a confidence in her bearing that he'd rarely seen in a woman. She seemed taller than she was as she stood gracefully erect with her head slightly tilted as she gazed up at him. The *palla* draped across her head and shoulders was as white as a billowy cloud with the sun shining on it. Her tunic and *stola* were fine linen, and silver cords wrapped all the right places to reveal her womanly curves. The deep blue fabric enhanced the color of her eyes.

Her nut-brown hair was piled high in the crown of curls that was the current fashion in Rome. Her nose was large and aquiline, more like a man's than a matron's. Her mouth was too wide as well, and her jaw too square.

Not ugly, but definitely plain. Still, she was a woman a man would notice. The confident intensity of her eyes and slight curve of her mouth as she surveyed him in return held his attention more than a pretty face could.

Those blue eyes shifted to follow her daughter as she hopped off the end of the gangplank and moved to lean against the railing where she could look down on the pier. They shone with the same love that had filled Damara's eyes when she watched Charissa playing in the garden.

He shoved that thought to the back of his mind. Now was not the time to let the grief tear into him again. He would hold it off until tonight, when he would be alone.

◆

The captain strode down the gangplank and joined Cornelia on the pier.

"Welcome, Claudius Malleolus, Cornelia Scipia, and...?" He turned his gaze on Cornelia's slave. Anthusa's eyes widened at the captain's greeting, and she froze without answering.

Malleolus broke the awkward silence. "Anthusa."

"Anthusa." Hector turned his attention back on Malleolus. "We need to get your chests from the wagons. My first mate, Clitus, will oversee that." He focused again on Cornelia. "Most will go into the hold where you can't get to them, so anything you want to use during the voyage should be moved into the two trunks that can be stowed in your room."

Malleolus turned to Cornelia. "I'll help with this to make sure everything is properly handled."

She nodded her approval. The security of the six small chests filled with her gold and jewelry was paramount. That dowry was essential to their future in Thracia. The weight of the chests would make anyone suspect what they might contain. Whoever carried them should be escorted.

Captain Hector stepped back onto the gangplank and offered his hand to Cornelia. "If you'll follow me, I'll show you where you'll be sleeping in the cabin. Then you can relax under the canopy while you wait. We'll be sailing on the evening tide."

She placed her petite hand in his large one and felt his work-roughened fingers wrap securely around hers. That simple act flexed the muscles in his forearm. Every part of this man exuded a controlled power she found exciting. She flipped the smile triggered by that silly response into a gracious acknowledgement of his help.

"Thank you, Captain."

The slight smile that he flashed in return brought another flutter. Foolishness! He was only a ship's captain.

"Watch your step at the end." His deep voice didn't help her control her reaction to him.

The captain led her up the plank and stepped off ahead of her. He continued to hold her hand until she had stepped down onto the deck.

He released it too soon. It had been a long time since a man treated her like someone delicate to be protected. She was a capable woman of thirty-nine, accustomed to taking care of herself for the many years since Lucius Fidelis ceased caring about her. She wasn't some silly girl who giggled over flattering words and fawning attention, but what seemed to be genuine concern in the way the captain helped her onto his ship—she liked it. It had, in fact, been a very long time since a man treated her that way. She had missed it.

Hector led them past the opening in the deck to the cabin at the rear. As she walked close behind him, his shoulders appeared even broader. He stepped through the door that opened on the side facing the pier, and they followed him into the room.

"This is the galley where my cook prepares meals. My ship isn't meant to carry many passengers, but I think you'll find the accommodations satisfactory."

Cornelia hadn't known exactly what to expect, but this most certainly was not it. A counter and cabinets lined the wall to the left. Four doors filled the opposite wall.

Each room couldn't be more than six feet deep and five feet wide. Satisfactory wasn't the first word that leaped into her mind. But there wasn't much space on a ship, and the main purpose of this one was the transport of cargo, not people. Lucius would never suspect she and Drusilla had left Rome on something like this. Besides, it would only be for a few weeks. Directly across from the door was a small window with its shutters wide open, so at least the room wasn't dark and stuffy.

The furnishings consisted of a set of bunks on the left side, a small table beside the bunks and beneath the window, and a chair that fit under the table. Above the table was an oil lamp that was shaped to fit securely in a metal rack, probably to prevent it starting a fire in rough seas. While the lower bunk had enough headroom for a tall man to sit comfortably, the upper bunk was close enough to the ceiling that it would only be useful for sleeping. Under the bunk was space for storing chests.

It was Spartan, but it would have to do.

◆

Hector hid the smile triggered by the shock in Cornelia's eyes before she veiled it. No surprise there. She was used to luxurious furnishings and the spaciousness of a large villa. These rooms were probably smaller than what she allowed the least of her house slaves.

His hand swept toward the two rooms farthest from the door. "Cornelia, I've planned for you to have the largest room here on the end. Anthusa will need to sleep either in the bunk above you or here in the room next to yours with your daughter."

Hector then stretched out his hand toward the room nearest the door. "Malleolus, this will be your room. Mine is between yours and the child's."

He turned back to Cornelia. "The cabin is small, but my passengers only spend time in these rooms at night and during storms. Behind the cabin, you'll find a canopy with some comfortable chairs and a couch." A slight smile accompanied his shrug. "I can't offer you the luxury you're accustomed to, but I think you'll find it pleasant there during the day. I mostly sail close enough to the coast that the view is entertaining."

◆

Cornelia stepped to the door of her room. As she looked in, she took a deep breath and blew it out. It was worth putting up with anything to get Drusilla safely away from her father.

"I'm sure this will be quite acceptable. There is one thing, though." She turned to face the captain. "I have a rather large amount of gold with me, so it will be essential to lock my room after it's brought in. I see no lock on the door, so how do you propose to do that?"

The door was hung to swing into the room. The latch was only a narrow piece of wood pierced near one end by a rod that stuck through the door. That piece could be lifted from its cradle inside the room by turning the rod. It could just as easily be opened by anyone from either side.

The captain didn't even glance at the door. "That won't be necessary. Your gold will be safe on my ship."

"I don't feel comfortable leaving it in an unlocked room where a thief can easily get to it."

The captain's friendly brown eyes cooled. "There are no thieves in my crew. I won't have any man work for me who isn't honest."

"I'm sure you think so, but slaves often fool their masters. Most are thieves and liars."

A crease appeared in his forehead as the corners of his mouth turned down. The chill in his eyes grew icy.

"You know nothing about how hard it can be for a slave to be honest. Would you starve before you'd steal when your master didn't care if you ate or not? Would you choose to die instead of lie when he might beat you to death if you told the truth?" His eyes snapped. "I don't think so."

Her eyes widened. That scowl on the face of someone so strong he could snap her like a twig was quite frightening. What kind of man was this captain? Was she placing her daughter and herself in the hands of a dangerous person during this voyage?

He took a deep breath and blew it out. The edge was off his voice when he spoke again. "Besides, my crewmen are not slaves. They're all freedmen who have worked for me for years, and I would trust any of them with anything, including my life."

She'd never seen a man switch from angry to calm that fast, as if nothing had happened. And surely a calm man could see the reasonableness of her request. It was too important to drop.

"Even if you do, that is no assurance to me that I can trust them."

"You can trust me. I give you my word that no one will take any of your treasure."

"I still don't feel it's safe to leave my 'treasure,' as you call it, unprotected in my unlocked room." She drew herself up to her full height and lifted her chin. She locked her eyes on his, determined to make her point and get him to do something about it.

His lips tightened as the fire reignited in his eyes. Why was he getting so upset? It wasn't as if she was questioning his own integrity. Having thieving servants didn't mean she doubted his honesty.

His muscled chest began to expand and contract faster. Another deep breath, and he slowed it down.

"Then leave your treasure in my room...unless you don't trust me."

The edge was back on his voice, and his eyes challenged her to impugn his honor as she had that of his crew.

Regret over her last words surged through her. He looked truly angry again, and angry men could be dangerous.

"I trust you completely, Captain. If you think the chests would be safer in your room, by all means, let's put them there."

"They would be just as safe in your room, your daughter's room, Malleolus's room...but they can go in mine if it will make you feel better."

He closed his eyes longer than she expected. It seemed like he momentarily left the cabin and the argument they were having. When he opened them again, the anger had faded, leaving a remote coolness. His whole body seemed more relaxed. Hers relaxed as well. Seeing a powerful man like him tensed for a fight was more than a little unnerving.

Still, she wasn't convinced of the honesty of his crew, even if he was. Her dowry was too important to let the matter drop, even at the risk of making him mad again.

"Maybe some in mine and some in yours would be wise. A thief might not look both places, and he should be afraid to take something from his captain's room."

He rolled his eyes at the suggestion. His lips started to tighten until she saw his broad chest expand as he took a deep breath.

His face relaxed again. "I understand that your treasure is important to you, Cornelia." His words sounded calm, even patient, but his eyes were still hot.

"As I said, my crew is trustworthy, but if it will make you feel safer when we're in port, I'll have one of my men keep watch to guard your treasure while the dockworkers load and unload the cargo. The honesty of those men I cannot guarantee."

She almost asked how she could be sure the guard could be trusted, but she stopped herself. That would have been throwing oil on a smoldering fire, and she didn't want to hit his flashpoint. Time to get away from the topic that had made this imposing man so angry. They would be in close quarters for several weeks, and she didn't want to start out as enemies.

"Thank you, Captain. That would help put my mind at ease."

He had calmed down enough to offer her a stiff smile, and his eyes had cooled as well. "Then that is what we'll do. Now, if you'll excuse me..."

He turned and walked away before she could respond.

She stared at his back as he exited the cabin. From so angry to calm with only a few deep breaths—she'd never seen anyone do that before. She couldn't even do that herself.

He made her feel off balance, an unusual sensation for her. She was an expert at reading the aristocratic men of her acquaintance. This Captain Hector was an enigma.

For some reason she couldn't quite explain, that was something she hoped to change before they reached Perinthus.

Chapter 7

Curiosity

Cornelia and Anthusa left the cabin and strolled back to the canopy. They settled into the cushioned chairs after Cornelia turned hers to face the roadway. Malleolus had joined Clitus to get the various trunks and chests from the raeda and freight wagon that Aristarchus had lent them. She planned to watch the progress in bringing aboard her "treasure," as the captain had insisted upon calling it.

Drusilla had not accompanied the others into the cabin. Instead, she'd worked her way along the rail, often leaning over to watch the activity on the pier below. She walked past Cornelia to the swan that rose at the rear of the boat.

She ran her hand along the smooth white wood of the swan's neck. Then she looked over her shoulder at her mother. "Why is there a swan's head here?"

Cornelia glanced at it before returning her eyes to the ramp where Malleolus was carrying her jewelry chest while Clitus carried one of the chests containing her gold.

"I don't know, dear. I've never been on a corbita before."

"Would Malleolus know?"

"Maybe. You can ask him later."

"I could ask the captain. I'm sure he would know."

Cornelia and Anthusa exchanged glances. The captain might not be a man who liked children, and she certainly didn't want to irritate him anymore today. "I wouldn't bother him with any questions right now. He's very busy loading everything onboard."

Drusilla moved back over to the rail and leaned against it. "Malleolus is almost back. Who is that with him?"

"Probably the first mate. The captain said he would be in charge of getting all our things onboard."

"I hope they bring my library box soon. I might want to read something later."

Cornelia focused on her daughter's cheerful eyes. "You are so much like your aunt Claudia. She always loved reading, too. You'll get to meet her when we get to Perinthus, and I'm sure you'll get along wonderfully."

"And I'll meet my cousins. It'll be fun to live with them for a while."

"Yes, it will. We might start out with Claudia or maybe with Titus until we get our own home. Your uncle Titus is a fine man. He probably picked a fine woman to marry. I'm sure we'll like them all."

Many times, she'd wished Lucius Fidelis was like his brother or his father. But there was no point in thinking about that now. Those sad years of marriage to Lucius were over, and she would make sure Drusilla never had to suffer like she had.

Drusilla alternated between leaning on the rail so she could report what was coming from the wagon and watching what was being stowed in the cabin. The cook had just delivered a selection of cheese, fruit, and rolls for their lunch. A pitcher and several brass goblets sat on a tray beside the bowls of food.

Malleolus came from the cabin, lowered himself into a chair, and blew out a slow breath. "There are days I wish I were still a younger man, but it's done. The two trunks you packed with things for the voyage are in your room with your perfume and jewelry boxes. The special chests are stowed two in your room, three in the captain's. They wouldn't all fit in yours. The captain has one of his men sitting in the galley, as you wanted. Anthusa's trunk had to go into Drusilla's room."

Drusilla stood with her hands resting on the back of his chair. "And my library box is where I can get to it easily."

He lifted a brass goblet from the tray and filled it. He raised it toward Cornelia. "To the future. May it be everything we hope."

Cornelia raised her own, then took a sip. "Everything we hope... and more."

A flash of white caught her eye, and she turned to see the captain slap his first mate's arm before walking down the gangplank.

A few hours, and they would set sail. What lay beyond the horizon in Thracia remained to be seen. But she was free of Lucius, and Drusilla would be safe. That would be enough, but would there be more?

Drusilla had checked the contents of her small library trunk and pushed it back under her bed where it was easy to pull out. Now she was back at the rail, watching the activity on the pier.

She started out near the chairs behind the cabin. The crane grabbed her full attention as it raised crates from the pier and swung them to where they were lowered out of sight behind the cabin. She moved forward along the rail until she could see where the captain stood with his back toward her. He sometimes stopped a crate swinging before it was lowered into the big hole.

She gradually worked her way up the rail to a point just to the rear of the opening. From there, she could almost see into the hole if she stood on tiptoe. Almost, but not quite. If she were full grown, that wouldn't be a problem, but she was still only ten-years' tall.

A stream of slaves carried sacks of something up the gangplank, across the deck, and down a set of stairs into the dim recesses of the ship. One stream in, another stream out. Where exactly were they putting the sacks? Were they near their trunks? Could she see her trunk if she peeked in?

She left the rail and stepped over to the edge of the opening. As she leaned over and stretched her neck to see, she wasn't watching the crane anymore.

◆

Hector listened to the creaking as the crane lifted the heavy crate behind him. When he heard it begin to swing the crate toward the ship, he turned to follow its motion. From the corner of his eye, he saw the girl leaning over the edge. He snapped his attention on her when she straightened. The crate was headed right for her head. He leaped toward her, grabbed her, and dropped to the deck with her wrapped in his arms as the crate swung over and past them.

He stood and pulled Drusilla to her feet. "What were you doing, child? You almost got yourself killed."

Her eyes were wide and her face pale as she stood, shaking, in front of him. "I'm sorry, Captain." She bit her lip. "Please don't tell Mother what almost happened. I don't want her to know I did something so stupid." She bowed her head, then raised it just enough to look at him. "It's just that...well...I've never been on a ship, and I wanted to see what they were doing down there. I won't do that again."

Her large brown eyes were pleading with him. Charissa had always been curious like that, and more than once she'd placed herself in danger because she was trying to see what was going on or how something was done. Those eyes reminded him of the times she'd begged him not to tell Damara. A hand squeezed his heart again. He tilted his head as he looked into those imploring eyes and sighed.

"We won't tell your mother...this time."

"Oh, thank you, Captain!" Her eyes sparkled, then dimmed. "Can I still stay by the rail and watch, or are you going to make me go back to the canopy?"

He furrowed his brow. "I should send you back, but...would you like to stand up there instead?" He pointed to the cabin top. "You can stay out of the way and still watch everything."

Her face lit up. "That would be wonderful."

"Up the ladder with you. If you want to come down, you ask me before you do."

"Yes, Captain. I'll do anything you say." She was beaming as she headed for the ladder.

He started to smile as he watched her climb. Then the smile faded, and a sigh escaped. Charissa would have loved to stand up there and watch, too.

Cornelia and Anthusa were both dozing in their chairs, so Malleolus decided to join Drusilla at the rail watching the activity on the pier. He walked to the port rail and looked along it. She was not where she had been. He crossed to the starboard side, assuming she must have moved over there to watch the ships being pulled into the other piers by the rowboats. She wasn't there, either. He walked into the cabin to see if she'd gone inside to read. She was nowhere to be found.

His brow furrowed as he hurried out to find the captain. If she had left the ship, surely he would know.

Hector stood watching another crate being lowered into the hold when Malleolus approached him.

"Captain. I can't find Drusilla. Did you see her get off the ship?"

The captain turned to face Malleolus, then pointed toward the cabin top.

"She was curious. She's safe watching from there."

Malleolus heaved a sigh of relief. "Thank you for letting her watch instead of sending her back to her mother. She wants to know how everything works. Sometimes her curiosity gets her in harm's way."

Hector glanced up at Drusilla, and she waved at him. He raised his hand. "Curiosity is a good thing. She can stay up there until supper."

Malleolus turned his eyes on Drusilla, and a huge grin lit her face as she waved down at him. He smiled as he waved back. He glanced once more at the captain before heading back to the canopy. After the argument with Cornelia, he thought Hector might be a short-tempered, difficult man. He'd just seen another side of the captain of the *Claudia*, and he liked what he saw.

Chapter 8

One She Can Trust

Hector crossed his arms as he watched his men drop the cover over the hatch and secure it with ropes. The corbita was fully loaded. It was still tied to the pier, but the rowboats would soon come to pull it into the open harbor. It was time to join his passengers for the light supper of cheese and bread his cook always served on the day of departure.

He chose a chair next to Malleolus, who sat alone on the couch. Hector was not a talkative man, and that should be the least likely place for too much conversation. At least he wouldn't have to talk too much with his rich female passenger. She and her people were welcome on his ship, but he didn't want a repeat of their earlier disagreeable encounter. The regal woman of enormous wealth and inherited privilege had questioned his integrity, and his one point of pride was that he was an honest man. She had an uncanny ability to make him angry, and that was never pleasing to God.

◆

Cornelia wasn't feeling talkative, and Anthusa always followed her lead. They were about to sail away from Rome and everything she had ever known, and Cornelia's confidence was wavering. She glanced at the captain, who sat in silence as he watched the other ships in the harbor.

She couldn't explain why, but something about him made her feel safer just because he was there. He looked about her age, so he'd probably made this voyage many times. Publius's close friend had personally arranged for her to sail with this man, and Malleolus had learned from the first mate that Hector had played a key role in rescuing Claudia from Lucius's cruel plans eight years ago. She could trust him just as he said.

After their energetic disagreement about the appropriate way to protect her dowry and the way he turned his back on her so abruptly when he left the cabin, she'd expected him to avoid speaking to her. Not so. He hadn't said much, but he had asked her whether she enjoyed the afternoon as if he genuinely hoped she had.

Genuine—that was a good word to describe him. There was something about his eyes that made her feel he was exactly what he seemed with no pretense. During her many years with Lucius Fidelis, she'd become expert at detecting those tell-tale signs around the mouth and the corner of the eyes that betrayed a lie in progress. She saw none of them with the captain.

◆

Hector's attention was drawn from the ships when the old steward spoke.

"I've been looking forward to this trip, Captain. For years, I've been arranging shipping to many parts of the Empire for some of the businesses of the Drusus family, but I've never actually been down to the wharves or on a corbita before. I have some questions."

He focused on Malleolus. He already found himself liking this man who'd proven himself the most loyal of servants to the family he loved. "What would you like to know?"

Malleolus began asking about the cargo capacity of the ship, how fast it sailed, the ports where they would be landing, how long it usually took to unload and load cargo in a port before moving on, and other assorted topics.

Drusilla had been sitting quietly by her mother, but when Malleolus noticed her listening to their conversation, he motioned for her to come over. With a big smile, she hopped off her chair and settled on the couch beside him. He wrapped his arm around her, and she snuggled against him.

Her bright eyes locked on Hector. She hung on every word he spoke as he answered Malleolus's questions. She was just like her aunt Claudia, as Malleolus claimed. Curious, smart—she would have gone far if she were a boy and had a chance to actually do something.

After several minutes discussing his ship, Hector rose. "I must leave you now. We'll be casting off soon."

Drusilla bit her lip as she looked up at him. "Captain?"

He looked down at hopeful eyes. "What, child?"

"Captain, is there somewhere I can watch everything as we leave? Someplace where I won't get in the way of anybody? I would love to see what happens when we leave the pier and the sails go up."

At first, he was going to tell her no, that she should just stay at the stern under the canopy with her mother. Then her eager eyes got to him. She looked so excited, as if getting to watch would be like a gift she'd been waiting for a long time.

"If you stay right beside me so you'll be out of the way of the crew, you can watch from the cabin top." He turned to Malleolus. "Will that be all right with her mother?"

He didn't want to ask Cornelia himself.

A smile accompanied Malleolus's nod. "If I say it's all right, Cornelia will agree."

Drusilla took Malleolus's hand in both of hers. "I promise I'll do exactly what the captain tells me if you'll just let me watch."

He rested his free hand on the side of her head. "You can go with the captain."

Drusilla gave him a quick hug and stood, looking up expectantly at Hector.

"Up the ladder with you, child. I'll be up in a moment."

She scampered away to climb to the cabin top. Malleolus watched her, a smile playing on his lips, before turning back to Hector. "Thank you for letting her join you. She's a special one. Too bad her father never bothered to find that out."

Hector nodded once before heading to the ladder himself. Charissa had been a special one, too.

The ship was well out to sea. The weather was clear, and the wind was light, so the rocking of the boat was rather soothing.

Cornelia's eyelids were heavy as she sat at the tiny table in front of the open window. The gentle sea breeze carried the faint scent of salt and freedom. She glanced at the bed beside her. Not a cloud-soft, thick mattress like she'd left behind, but she expected to sleep deeper than she had for many days.

Anthusa pulled out the sapphire-tipped pins holding the crown of curls on Cornelia's head and placed the wig in its box. Pulling the rest of the gold pins released all the braids wrapped at the back of her head.

"I won't be wearing that silly thing for a few weeks." She ran her fingers through the hair that fell freely across her shoulders after Anthusa unbraided it. "And maybe not even after that." Cornelia sighed. "It will be a relief to wear my hair more simply. I really don't know why we all decided we had to spend so much time copying whatever style the Emperor's wife likes."

"You'll look lovely, no matter how you wear your hair, mistress."

Anthusa began slowly brushing her thick, lustrous tresses. The silver mirror from Cornelia's dressing table at the estate stood on the table in front of her and reflected her smile to the loyal slave standing behind her.

"You and I both know that isn't so anymore. I never was a pretty woman, even when I was young, and now...let's just say I look old enough to have a twenty-four-year-old son."

Anthusa continued brushing. "You have beautiful hair. And no one can deny how lovely your eyes are. Those don't change as time passes."

Cornelia turned to smile directly at the slave who had become her confidante and closest friend since Lucius bought her shortly after they married. That was twenty-five years ago, and Anthusa knew her better than anyone. She was the one person Cornelia could trust with the deepest concerns of her heart.

"I can always count on you to make me feel better, even if what you tell me isn't exactly the truth. I could never leave you behind."

"I'm glad you didn't, mistress."

She turned back to the mirror so Anthusa could continue with the brushing.

"I hope going to Thracia turns out to be the best thing for Drusilla. I'm sure Titus and Claudia will be glad to see us and will help us start over. I couldn't let Lucius get Drusilla killed. That's what would have happened if we'd stayed, but it's still hard to leave everything and everyone behind. Except Malleolus and you, of course."

She twisted to face Anthusa directly. "I made sure Malleolus specifically listed you as part of my dowry repayment so Lucius could never try to take you away." She sighed deeply. "I just hope this all turns out well."

◆

The mistress's words were like an embrace to Anthusa. To be that important to Mistress Cornelia was almost like freedom. All the slaves belonged to Master Lucius, and she shuddered to think what he might have done to her after he discovered Mistress had taken Drusilla and she hadn't warned him.

She couldn't imagine a better mistress than Cornelia had been. Others might think her too reserved and too proud, but Anthusa knew how much Lucius Fidelis had made her suffer over the years. Her pride had carried her through what would have crushed the spirit of a weaker woman.

"I'm sure it will. As you've said before, Master Titus is a good man like his father, and he'll help make sure it does."

Mistress was silent for a few moments as the brushing continued. "What do you think of the captain?"

Anthusa raised her eyebrows. "What do you mean, mistress?"

"After we had that argument, I thought I'd made him angry enough that he'd stay angry with me at least for the rest of the day. He didn't. And he was so kind to Drusilla, the way he let her stay up on the cabin top with him while we sailed out of the harbor. She looked so happy up there. She kept telling me about it when I went in to kiss her good night."

"He is different. I don't know what to make of him."

Anthusa had been dumbstruck when he asked the name of a slave as if she were one of his passengers. But she didn't tell Mistress how good that made her feel. Her mistress always treated her like a person when no one else was watching, but the captain had done it where everyone would see.

Mistress leaned her elbows on the table and rested her chin in her palms. "I'm not sure why, but I feel better...safer...knowing he's the one taking us to Titus." Mistress moved from the chair to the bed. "There's something about his eyes...I just know I can trust him. I'm sorry I implied that I couldn't when I wanted some way to lock the door. I'm glad he didn't stay mad at me."

Anthusa pulled the covers over her mistress and tucked them around her. "Sleep well, mistress."

Mistress nodded as she closed her eyes.

Before blowing out the lamp and climbing into her own upper bunk, Anthusa smiled down at the mistress who was also her friend, the mistress who had sacrificed everything because she loved her daughter so dearly. If only she could find a new husband who would see her for the wonderful woman she was. But how was the mistress going to find a man like that in Thracia?

Chapter 9

Good for Each Other

It had been another night with the dream. Hector stood at the rail for half an hour before deciding to lie down and try to sleep again. As he crept through the galley, soft sounds came from the room next to his.

Someone was crying.

He tapped on the door before opening it enough to stick his head in. "Is something wrong, child? Should I get your mother?"

Drusilla sat up and flicked the tears from her cheeks. "No." Distress colored her whisper. "Please don't tell her I've been crying. I don't want her to think I'm not happy. She gave up everyone and everything to save me from Father." She stared at the floor before lifting her eyes to his again. "And where we're going...it's so far, and everything will be so different, and that's scary. Even Malleolus has never been there before."

"You're going to your aunt and uncle. You don't need to be afraid."

She clutched the sheet and pulled it up to her neck. "I know, and I'm trying to be brave, but...Captain, would you please stay with me until I go back to sleep? I promise it won't be long. Please?"

Even in the dim moonlight streaming through the window, he couldn't miss the quivering smile and desperate eyes pleading for him to stay.

"Lie down and close your eyes. I'll stay with you for a while."

He slipped into the room and turned the chair so he could sit beside her bed. She reached out, and his large hand enveloped her small one. She wrapped her other hand around his and pulled it over against her cheek as she rolled on her side to face him.

"Thank you, Captain." She smiled through the remains of her tears before closing her eyes.

In almost no time, her slow, steady breathing told him she was asleep. Her hands had relaxed, and he inched his hand out of hers so he wouldn't awaken her.

So many times, he'd told Charissa a bedtime story and then held her hand as his little treasure went to sleep. The memory tore at the hole in his heart. How he ached for that nighttime closeness that would never be again.

Drusilla stirred but didn't waken.

Poor child. At least his little girl had known the love of a father who adored her. The great wealth of the Drusus family was worth nothing without love. Drusilla was a fatherless child no less than one whose father was dead and buried. But the worst part was she'd never had the father she deserved.

Hector's lips tightened. Cornelia had abandoned everything to save her from her father marrying her to a sadistic monster. Lucius Drusus hadn't changed at all since he tried to do the same to his sister Claudia eight years earlier.

But even with her mother's great love, Drusilla felt loneliness and fear. He knew too well what it was like to be alone and frightened as a child.

At least for now, she needed his help. And as he gazed at her in the moonlight, a small voice inside whispered that maybe he needed hers as well.

Before they retired for the night, Hector had informed his passengers that a breakfast of fruit, cheese, and bread would be served shortly after dawn, but they could eat later if they didn't want to dine that early. In his experience, upper-class Roman women seldom appeared before the sun was well up in the sky. It took too long to put on their beauty potions and fix their hair.

Cornelia had worn one of those ridiculous hairstyles. He'd be able to eat and leave long before she appeared. The corner of his mouth turned up at that thought. It must take a long time to arrange herself to look so regal. No chance for her to irritate him if he was already on the cabin top when she finally came out.

Malleolus had risen early and was sitting under the canopy. Hector had enjoyed their conversation at supper, and the old steward shouldn't have to eat alone.

He climbed down the ladder at the front of the cabin and rounded the corner. As he approached the door, his gaze drifted to the clouds forming on the horizon.

Movement at the corner of his vision snapped his head forward. Cornelia was stepping out of the cabin, and he was one step from ploughing into her.

She startled and stepped back to avoid him, but her foot caught on the raised threshold. She lost her balance and, with a soft gasp, began to fall backward.

◆

Two strong hands gripped Cornelia's arms as the captain stopped her fall. Two dark brown eyes met hers, and her breath caught as she gazed into them. A woman could drown in their depths. As he pulled her back into a standing position, heat blazed on her cheeks. Why did those eyes being so close ramp up her sensitivity to his virile attraction? The captain shouldn't affect a mature noblewoman like her that way. The heat spread to her ears.

"I'm sorry, Cornelia. I should have been watching, but I didn't expect you up so early. Are you hurt?"

His hands were still on her arms. His grip had been tight, but now it was relaxed. Her eyes were level with his chest. It was so broad, and his biceps were disturbingly muscular. Just standing so close to him raised her heart rate. She slapped herself mentally. It was silly to be affected this way by a man she'd just met—and a ship's captain at that.

She raised her blue eyes to fix them on his brown ones. "No, Captain. I'm unscathed. Thank you for catching me. I'll watch out for that step in the future."

He let go of her arms, and she was sorry. A pleasant smile lifted the corners of his mouth. "Good. I'd hate to have one of my passengers get hurt the first day out. I was just going to join Malleolus for some breakfast. I hope you'll enjoy what my cook has prepared."

He motioned with his hand. "Please, go ahead of me. I'll try not to knock you over again."

She offered him a gracious smile over her shoulder. "Thank you, Captain."

As she turned away from him and took a step, the heat rose in her cheeks again. *This is childish. I'm no giggling maiden watching some handsome young man.* His upturned mouth and warm eyes had started her heart beating faster. Had her ears turned pink enough for him to notice from behind? He was only a ship's captain, so why was she fourteen again when he stood so close to her and smiled?

Her lips twitched as she silently laughed at herself. A ship's captain with the build of a gladiator and the eyes of a man who could be trusted. Perhaps the difference between a girl of fourteen and a matron of thirty-nine wasn't that great after all.

◆

As Cornelia walked ahead of him, Hector caught a whiff of the subtle, musky perfume in her hair. That hair surprised him. A single long, thick braid had been wrapped around itself and pinned at the back of her head. That would take only a few minutes. Nothing like the fancy styles he expected on a wealthy noblewoman.

Her hair was simple today, but regal still described her perfectly as she glided ahead of him. Regal, but not arrogant. Perhaps having her as a passenger for the next few weeks wouldn't be as trying as he'd feared.

They'd been at sea for two days, and the novelty of the passing shoreline had worn off for Drusilla. She hung over the rail, watching how the ship cut through the waves. She moved up the rail toward the bow to see if that changed depending on where she was on the ship. She was near the front when a dolphin broke through the water's surface below her.

She startled and stepped back from the rail. When a second dolphin joined the first, she grabbed the rail again and stood transfixed as she watched them.

◆

Hector walked up beside her. "They're dolphins."

She turned bright eyes up to his face. "I've read about them, but I never thought I'd see one. They look like they're playing together." A wistful look dimmed their brightness. "It must be nice for them to have someone to play with." She sighed. "My brother Tertius used to play board games with me...I wonder if I'll ever see him again." Another sigh escaped her. "I miss playing with my best friend, Flavia, too. I wonder if I'll ever have another best friend to play with."

Hector's lips tightened. She'd been forced to leave most of the people she loved behind. That first night in the dark, she'd said she didn't want her mother to know she wasn't happy. How much of the happy way she acted was only a show to protect her mother?

He knew too well how hard it was to hide the sadness over loved ones lost.

"I have some games in the cabin. I'll play with you for a while, if you want. I can teach you a game if you don't know any of the ones I have."

The sparkle in her eyes and her instant smile made him glad he'd offered. "Really, Captain? You will?"

He smiled down at her eager little face. "Yes. Let's go pick something out."

She followed him into his room. He lifted a small wooden chest and a game board down from the top bunk. The board was inscribed on one side with a checkered pattern and on the other side for *tabula*. He handed her the board while he tucked the small chest under his arm.

"We can play under the canopy."

"You should pick the game, Captain." She beamed up at him. "Thank you so much for doing this with me."

He simply smiled before he led her out the door and back to the canopy. Once there, he placed one of the small tables in front of an empty chair and pulled another over to face it. She set the board on the table with the checkered pattern up.

"So, what do you know how to play?" He set the box of game pieces on the table and opened it.

"I know how to play Pebbles. Tertius taught me, and I could beat him half the time. I like that one."

"Set it up."

She reached into the box to get out the white and blue disks made of sliced bone. While she was picking them out of the dice and knucklebones that were also in the box, she picked up two carved bone pyramids.

"What are these, Captain?"

"Those are the kings for Mercenaries. It's a strategy game popular with my adult passengers."

"I like strategy games. I'd love to learn a new one. Will you teach me?"

"If you wish. The rules are simple, but to play it well takes a lot of practice. It's not an easy game."

"We have lots of time before we get to Perinthus, and I like learning hard things."

Cornelia watched Hector as he explained the rules to Drusilla. Maybe a captain didn't have that much to keep him busy while the ship was at sea, but why was he back under the canopy playing a game with her daughter?

Not that she would complain. It gave her another chance to watch him up close. She was no moon-eyed maiden, but his unassuming masculinity made her feel like one. When she thought about it, she saw how absurd it was, but he attracted her. It was a pleasure to watch such a handsome man, but it wasn't just his appearance that drew her to him.

He'd been so kind to Drusilla on this voyage already. That had to be the main reason her daughter seemed so happy since they left Rome. She loved standing with him on the cabin top, watching everything the crew was doing.

Cornelia had never before met a man with such a kind heart toward a child that wasn't even his own. A man like him would probably have a wife and children in his home port. Maybe even grandchildren from his oldest.

She sighed. To be a child in his household must be wonderful when he wasn't out to sea.

◆

They had almost finished the first game. Hector shifted in the chair and arched his back to relax his tight muscles. Even though she was losing, Drusilla had played well enough that he found himself having to concentrate on the game.

As he took her last piece, she grinned at him. "I like this game. It's hard enough to be really fun."

"You played well for your first time. You remind me of your aunt Claudia. She played many games of Conquest with Philip when she was going to Thracia on this ship. She's very good at strategy games, too."

"My aunt Claudia was on this ship? How funny that it has her name."

"Your uncle Philip owns this ship. He and your aunt met and fell in love here eight years ago, and Philip renamed it in her honor."

"Will I get to meet them soon after we get to Perinthus?"

"Maybe even the day you arrive, and you'll get to meet their two boys, too."

"I can hardly wait to get to know my cousins. I hope we get to be friends."

"I expect you will. You'll meet the rest of your cousins, too. Your Uncle Titus and his wife Miriam also live in Perinthus with their two boys and their daughter. She's only a little younger than you."

"A girl cousin? Maybe we can become best friends. Do you have any children, Captain?"

"My son is almost seventeen. He lives at our farm and works for Philip. I had a daughter your age, but she died."

His throat began to tighten. He hadn't expected that question from her, so he hadn't braced for it. He fought to get the grief back behind the barrier that restrained it during the day.

Drusilla's smile faded at the sudden sadness he couldn't keep out of his eyes. She reached across the board to touch his hand. "I'm sorry, Captain."

That small act of sympathy broke the barrier, and the pain came flooding in. Hector furrowed his brow, swallowed hard, and clenched his jaw, fighting to keep the tears from forming. He looked away from the board, away from her, out over the waves.

She rose to move over beside him. She wrapped her arms around him and rested her cheek on the top of his head. He kept looking at the waves, but he raised one hand and rested it on her arm. She lifted her head to look down at him. When he finally took his eyes off the waves and looked up at her, she offered him a sympathetic smile.

The smile he returned was sad, but it was still a smile.

"Will you play another game with me now, Captain?"

He still couldn't speak for the lump in his throat, but he nodded. She started to set the game up again and began talking as if nothing had just happened.

"I like Mercenaries. We should keep playing this until I can beat you at least half the time. I don't want you to let me win just because I'm a child. I expect you to play to win."

He found his voice, and it sounded almost normal. "There are still many days left in the voyage, so there will be plenty of time for all the games you want."

She grinned at him. "You won, so I go first. I'll try to win so you get to go first next time."

◆

Cornelia had been chatting with Anthusa while she stole frequent glances at the captain. Watching Hector had become one of her favorite pastimes, especially when he wasn't aware of it. The last thing she expected to see was this strong man suddenly on the verge of tears. She focused her eyes on Anthusa during his silence so he wouldn't feel she was intruding on his unintended display of grief.

When his attention was once more fixed on her daughter and their new game, she returned to watching him. What could possibly have happened to the daughter of this self-controlled man that could affect him like that?

She had to know. Malleolus should be able to get her the details. He had frequent conversations with Calamus, the cook, and Clitus, the first mate. If either of them knew, Malleolus could ferret out the information she desired.

Chapter 10

A TRULY GOOD MAN

The next morning, Malleolus saw his opportunity. Hector was talking with Clitus near the bow of the ship, and the cook was alone in the galley. He stepped inside for the conversation that should satisfy Cornelia's curiosity.

"Calamus, I noticed something yesterday, and I hope you can explain it to me."

Calamus set down his knife. "What?"

"The captain. When he was talking with Drusilla, he said he had a daughter who died. Then he stopped talking. What happened to her?"

Calamus shook his head. "Sad story, that. Captain's wife and daughter used to meet us at the pier in Perinthus. He always lit up when he saw them. Charissa was the same age as Drusilla and so sweet and smart. The whole crew loved her. She and Damara, Captain's wife, died ten days before we reached port on our final voyage last season. Ropes on a log wagon came loose when they were walking by. The falling logs killed them. Captain thought he was coming home to four months with his family. Instead, Master Philip met him at the pier with the news."

The cook tightened his lips and shook his head again. "It's been hard for him. Captain and Damara were so happy together, and suddenly she's gone. Charissa, too. Captain loved that girl. He couldn't stand being at his farm at night without them, so Master Philip had him over almost every evening to eat with his family and spend the night. He took Captain along on his trips away from Perinthus until we began sailing again this spring."

He picked up the knife. "This is our last voyage until next spring, and I don't know how Captain's going to be when we get home. He used to be a joyful man, but his grief—it's a cloud over him. Daytime doesn't seem so bad, but some nights I see him standing at the rail in the moonlight, just staring at the waves. On this trip out from Perinthus, I saw that more often. I think he's dreading another winter at the farm with only his son."

He felt the knife's sharp edge. "Having a girl the age of Charissa on this voyage—I was afraid Captain would find it too hard. But she seems to have lifted his spirits, so I guess I was wrong. Only God knows what's best for each of us, and maybe He brought Drusilla to help Captain."

As Malleolus left the cabin to return to the canopy, he weighed what he should and should not tell Cornelia. The captain was a private man, pleasant but reserved. He would not want the depth of his pain revealed to her.

◆

Cornelia was watching the shore go by when she heard Malleolus returning. She turned to face him, a question in her eyes. He settled into the chair beside her.

"The captain's wife and daughter died in an accident just before his return from his final voyage last year. He's still grieving."

"I'm sorry to hear that. I can imagine how hard that must be for him."

She turned her eyes back on the shoreline, but her thoughts were on the intriguing man who captained the *Claudia*. Almost a year, and still torn up when he spoke of their death? For a man to love his wife so much that losing her was still that painful after so long—that was incredible. The contrast between their two marriages couldn't be starker. Lucius would probably have welcomed her death since that would make her dowry his to keep and use however he wanted.

As for loving his daughter, Lucius hadn't paid much attention to Drusilla even when he still lived at the eastern estate before he got Publius killed in the arena. Since he moved into the house in town, he hadn't seen his daughter more than a dozen times in the last eight years, and he treated her as if she weren't even in the room when he did see her. Drusilla didn't exist as far as he was concerned...until he could use her to help his friend. He didn't care whether she lived or died.

The mere thought of Lucius made Cornelia's jaw set as her eyebrows lowered. With his countless adulteries, he'd cheated her out of the affection a husband and wife should share. He was even willing to allow the murder of their daughter. Why couldn't he have been like the captain?

Cornelia stood and walked to the rail. When she looked toward the bow of the ship, Hector was walking back toward the cabin. He saw her watching him and raised his hand in greeting before he turned to climb the ladder to the cabin top.

Funny how even his wave could make her breath catch. She'd never met another man like him. From the first day, he'd impressed her with his kindness to her daughter and his considerate treatment of her, of everyone. Without him doing anything in particular, just being close to him awakened the same excitement that simmered when she was a girl awaiting her wedding night. Why couldn't she have had a husband like the captain instead of Lucius?

Cornelia rested her chin on her hands as she contemplated her image in the mirror. "It was a lovely day. I can see why a man would enjoy spending time at sea. The captain certainly does."

Anthusa pulled out the pins that kept her braid coiled at the back of her head. "The shore we passed was very pretty, mistress. And the sky—I've never seen it so blue."

Cornelia held her head still as Anthusa began the unbraiding. "Malleolus found out what happened to the captain's family. An accident last fall just before he got home. He must have really loved them."

Anthusa began brushing the loose tresses. "He did seem very sad when he spoke of it."

"Just think. A whole year and he's still mourning like that. I can't say I know another man who would do that. Lucius certainly wouldn't."

"No, mistress, but the master never was wise enough to see what a wonderful wife you were."

Cornelia turned in the chair to look at her faithful slave. "He's so good to Drusilla. Can you imagine how wonderful he must have been to his own daughter? I bet he'd never have put her at risk just to make a friend happy, like that disgusting man I married."

"I don't think the captain would put anyone at risk if he could help it."

Cornelia turned back to the mirror so Anthusa could resume brushing. "You're probably right. Malleolus told me he was the one who got Claudia at the bath and led her through the city when she escaped from Lucius. That was very dangerous for him. Lucius would have had him crucified as a kidnapper if they'd been caught. He didn't even know her. Why would he take such a risk for a stranger?"

"I don't know. Maybe he's just a truly good man."

Cornelia's lips twitched. "A truly good man. Yes, I think he might be, and that's a rare thing. The only men I would call truly good are Malleolus and Publius." She sighed. "I still miss Publius. I never understood how Lucius could betray his own father like that." She ran her hands into her hair and shook it before drawing her fingers through. "My life would have been so much happier if Lucius had been like his father...or like the captain."

"Yes, mistress." Anthusa finished brushing and laid the brush on the table. "There."

Cornelia rose and turned to the bed. One step and she sat on the edge. "Such a tiny room, but it's really not bad. I thought it ridiculous when the captain said I'd find the accommodations satisfactory, but I rather like this ship. Drusilla loves it. I have the captain to thank for that."

"He is wonderful to her."

Cornelia stretched out on the bunk, and Anthusa pulled the sheets up to her chin. "Good night, mistress."

Cornelia closed her eyes. "Good night, Anthusa."

Anthusa blew out the lamp and climbed into the upper bunk.

In the darkness, Cornelia was more aware of the gentle rocking of the ship. It was strangely soothing. It had been a good choice to take Drusilla away from Rome. Publius's friend had chosen well in picking Captain Hector to be the one to take them to safety. It had been a little frightening to leave everything she knew behind, but it seemed less frightening with the captain escorting them to Titus. The captain truly was a good man.

It was the crack of dawn on Sunday. Hector crept through the galley and headed to the crew quarters at the bow of the ship. He always began the week with a worship service with his men. It was best when his passengers were believers, too. Then they could enjoy the luxury of worshiping on deck and for as long as the Spirit moved them.

Today's worship would have to be quick and quiet since he had nonbelievers aboard. His passengers probably posed no real danger, but it was best to be careful until he knew for certain. He was more than willing to take Claudia's relatives to Thracia, but it would make his Sundays less enjoyable this trip. He didn't want to put his whole crew at risk of arrest and execution.

Chapter 11

Unwelcome Changes

Rome

Lucius had expected Malleolus in his office on *dies solis* with the weekly report of how much wealthier he'd become in the last seven days. When his steward failed to appear by noon and sent no explanation of his delay, that was surprising but not cause for alarm.

When the old man still hadn't appeared by evening the next day, Lucius asked the doorkeeper and the slave in charge of the stable if either of them knew where Malleolus had gone. The doorkeeper knew nothing, but Malleolus had told the stableman he had some business to attend to at the eastern and northeastern estates. He'd driven off in the two-wheeled *cisium* shortly before sundown, when the city streets opened to carriage traffic.

That had been a week ago.

The third morning found Lucius sitting at his desk, drumming on the edge of a wax tablet with his stylus. Malleolus still hadn't sent any message or returned.

Lucius had sent slaves to both estates to see if his steward was still at either of them. The eastern estate, where his wife and daughter usually stayed, was only a half-hour's walk from the city gate. The other estate was half a day by carriage northeast of Rome.

It had been a little over an hour when the slave from the eastern estate appeared at the library door.

Lucius closed the tablet. "Well?

"Steward Malleolus was not there, master, but he was a week ago.

Then he, Mistress Cornelia, your daughter, and her maid went to the northeastern estate."

"Did he tell anyone why?"

"No, master, but Understeward Primus wondered why they didn't take the estate raeda."

Lucius's head snapped back. "What did they take?"

"A raeda and freight wagon came for them the morning after Steward Malleolus came. Primus didn't know who owned them. The drivers and guards only spoke with Malleolus. Then they loaded a dozen trunks and chests into the wagon and some very heavy small chests into the raeda."

"Why so many trunks?"

"Primus didn't say, but he did say Mistress Cornelia left a box in your library with orders that only you were to open it."

"Anything else?"

"No, master."

Lucius flicked his hand to dismiss him and began to pace.

If Cornelia was taking Drusilla to the northeastern estate, why wouldn't she use the estate's raeda? And what about the freight wagon? Why take that many trunks when she wouldn't have needed more than two or three? And why not use his slaves as drivers and guards?

He strode through the atrium and peristyle to the stable.

The stableman's jaw started to drop when he saw Lucius, who always sent a slave to tell him which horse or chariot he wanted before coming himself. The stableman snapped it shut and bowed. "Master, what shall I prepare for you?"

"I need the gray immediately." Lucius spun and headed to his room to dress for the ride.

When he returned, his stallion stood saddled and ready. As he took the reins and mane in hand to mount, the slave he'd sent on horseback to the northeastern estate trotted through the gate.

Lucius swung around on him. "Was Malleolus there?"

"No, master. They haven't seen him since his regular visit three weeks ago."

"Was my wife there?"

"No, master."

Lucius uttered a string of curses and mounted. He kicked the horse into a trot as he headed out the gate. Whatever Cornelia had left for his eyes only, he wasn't going to like it.

The Drusus estate east of Rome

When Lucius arrived at the eastern estate, he went immediately to his library. A small chest sat on the desk. In case it held a venomous snake, he jumped back as he flipped the lid open with a stylus.

Nothing moved. When he peered in, he found several wax writing tablets.

His mouth twitched. It was stupid to think Cornelia would booby-trap the box. She might wish he were dead, but she wouldn't risk an innocent bystander's life.

He lifted the first tablet from the stack and opened it.

It was Cornelia's official certificate of divorce, signed and witnessed by five senators who disliked him. Below it was another tablet, signed by Malleolus and witnessed by the same men, describing what was returned to Cornelia as her dowry in a combination of gold and a few household items, including her favorite slave.

The curses he uttered would have done credit to a drunken sailor. The last thing he wanted was for those senators to know what Cornelia had done to him.

She would have heard the rumors about Marcus's violent son and how no one wanted him to marry their daughter. She must have heard from one of her many friends that he was planning to let Gnaeus marry Drusilla. She had every right to her entire dowry, but she had no right to their daughter. By Roman law, she was his to do with as he pleased.

Lucius clenched his jaw until his teeth hurt. Cornelia might think she'd outsmarted him, but she was sadly mistaken. Even if he might have reconsidered giving the girl to his friend's son, he would never do that now she'd taken her to prevent it. He would find their daughter, drag her back to his own house, betroth her to Gnaeus, and maybe even bring charges against Cornelia for kidnapping.

Lucius rubbed his chin. But first he had to find the pair of them.

Cornelia had a large extended family, including three brothers who despised him and numerous cousins. One of them might have been willing to take them in, especially if they didn't know about the divorce. She'd headed northeast, and her family had several estates in that direction. As the first step toward recovering Drusilla, he'd send pairs of slaves to see if they'd gone to any of them. Two slaves should be enough to drag the girl back to him immediately...if they found her.

If Cornelia hadn't gone to her family, the problem of finding her became more difficult. He'd paid her so little attention in the last eight years that he had no idea who her close friends might be. If one was willing to help her conceal Drusilla from him, it might be a long time before he found them.

His hand fisted, and he struck his palm.

The chest held more tablets, and he placed the stack on the desktop. The first listed all the estates of the Drusus family, their approximate worth, and the names of the men Malleolus had placed in charge of each.

The next tablet listed the many commercial activities Malleolus had established in his own name with Lucius's money. Some, while extraordinarily profitable, were illegal for a man of the senatorial order to own. It named the men in charge and officially transferred them all to Lucius as a "gift." The details of Malleolus's withdrawals of his own share from each were described without implicating Lucius as the real owner, but the same five senators had signed it.

Lucius opened the final tablet to find a personal letter from Malleolus.

Publius Claudius Malleolus to Lucius Claudius Drusus Fidelis, greetings. I am writing to inform you that I will no longer be serving as the steward and overseer of the Claudius Drusus estates and business ventures.

My duty of service was to my noble master and patron, Publius. My obligation to the man who freed me was fulfilled eight years ago when you betrayed him and he was killed in the arena. I have willingly continued to serve Publius by growing the fortune that would someday belong to his beloved grandchildren. I find myself no longer able to serve since you are willing to give his granddaughter to a brute who will hurt her.

As my final act of service, I have withdrawn exactly the sum of money required to return Cornelia Scipia's dowry, as required by Roman law and enumerated in the dowry document also in this chest, which was witnessed by five highly respected senators.

Lucius slammed his fist into the desktop as he swore. As soon as the divorce became public knowledge, those senators would revel in telling the gory details at the baths. If they reported his illegal businesses, he could be in real trouble.

He shook his hand. Hitting the unyielding wood had been stupid.

> The financial empire I have built for Publius and his grandchildren is in good order. The records of all legitimate business loans are in the strongbox at the town house, as are the deeds for the estates. The estates themselves are in the hands of highly skilled and honest men. I have carefully trained them to take excellent care of their respective parts. The Drusus fortune should continue to grow for Publius's grandchildren to someday enjoy.
>
> I have also provided an accurate accounting of the withdrawal of my own savings that had been invested in the family businesses, again witnessed by the same five senators. I have grown old serving this family, and I do not expect to live many years more. But as Publius's son, I still have a duty to give you a number of hours of service each year until you or I die. Since I do not expect that to be more than ten years, I have deducted the value of ten years of *operae* from my own money to pay that obligation.
>
> For the sake of the grandchildren, I have not revealed to those honest men that you have been breaking Roman law by engaging in trade other than selling the produce of your estates and lending money at interest. Since I don't know any man who is both honest enough to run those businesses and give you their profits and dishonest enough to pretend you don't own them, I suggest you convert the businesses to gold as soon as possible and invest that in more land for your sons to inherit.
>
> I do not expect to ever see you again. May the gods give you what you deserve.

Lucius took a deep breath and released it slowly. The old steward had at least kept his lawbreaking from the senators. He probably should have expected that. Malleolus's loyalty to his father would keep him from willingly damaging the Drusus reputation.

He didn't like the old man, but he'd always acknowledged how fortunate he was to have such a gifted steward multiplying his wealth for so long. It would be impossible to replace him. He was genuinely sorry to have Malleolus leave.

He wasn't sorry that Cornelia had left...he was furious. The only thing he would actually miss about her was having the use of her dowry to increase his own wealth, but he would never be content for her to think she got the better of him by taking Drusilla. He would find them and bring the girl back to marry Gnaeus. His motivation had switched from helping his friend Marcus to hurting Cornelia. Drusilla was only a pawn in that game now.

Chapter 12

TIME WITH THE CAPTAIN

Off the coast of Italia

During lunch, Cornelia found herself once more watching the captain eat with Malleolus. Hector was usually quiet until Malleolus selected something for them to discuss, but then he seemed to enjoy their conversation.

What would make him choose to sit next to her instead? She didn't know exactly what they would talk about, but she would find something. She never had any problem conversing with men, even the shy ones.

How pleasant it would be to have those brown eyes looking into her own, his head cocked as he listened to her. She would pick a topic that would cause the corners of his mouth to lift into a smile as he nodded, like he did when he talked with Malleollus. That smile might even broaden enough to crinkle the corners of his eyes, like when Drusilla was excited about something he was showing her.

Cornelia suppressed a sigh. Drusilla was on the couch next to the captain, happy just to sit with the two men. She would have rather been sitting there herself.

The moon, framed by Hector's window, slipped behind a veil of thin clouds, but he could still see the bunk above him. He'd expected the dream. He seldom made it five nights without it, and the last one had come after he almost broke down the first time he played Mercenaries with Drusilla.

He'd prayed for the eight months at sea to be enough to get him past the worst of the pain. It had been. Searing grief had been replaced by cold heartache. He could face living at the farm again with only his son. He wasn't looking forward to it, but he could bear it. He was doing better, but the dream still came.

He rose and headed out to the rail. A few minutes at the rail were sometimes enough to let him return to his bed and sleep. Sometimes it took many more than a few. Tonight felt like one of those.

◆

Drusilla's eyes popped open. A smile tugged at the corners of her mouth as she stared at the bunk above her.

In her dream, she'd been strolling through flowers in a meadow. Mother was on one side, Captain on the other. She smiled up at Captain, and he scooped her up to place her on his shoulders. Then Mother moved over next to Captain and wrapped her arm around his. He turned toward her and leaned over to kiss her tenderly on the lips. Then they kept walking together until she woke up.

The soothsayers claimed dreams could foretell the future. What if they really did?

Every day, she liked the captain more. Malleolus liked him, too, and she'd heard Mother say good things about him to Anthusa. Maybe Captain and Mother could fall in love. Captain would be wonderful to have as a father.

As she lay smiling at the thought of the three of them becoming a family, the hinge on Captain's door creaked. She slipped out of bed and tiptoed over to open her own door a crack. His form blocked the moonlight in the cabin doorway before he shut the door behind him.

◆

Hector was standing at the rail, staring across the waves, when he heard a soft rustle behind him. He twisted around to see Drusilla standing in the moonlight.

"Captain? Is anything wrong?"

"No. You should be in bed, child."

She stepped up to the rail to stand beside him. "I heard you go out. I thought maybe you needed some company."

His hands rested on the rail again. She placed one of her own on the rail and the second on his hand. "Can I stay here with you for a while? I like the moonlight dancing on the waves. I've never seen that before."

He gazed down at the hopeful smile she directed at him and sighed. "You can stay. I won't be out here long."

She stood in silence beside him for several minutes. Then she shivered in the cool night breeze. He wrapped his arm around her and drew her against his side to warm her. "It's getting cold for you. Time to go back in."

She turned a little and wrapped both arms around him as well. "So soon? That cloud is about to hide the moon. Can we stay here until it does? The waves are so pretty, and I want to watch them a little longer."

"But then we go in."

"Yes, Captain." She grinned up at him and snuggled closer.

As he stood in the moonlight with his arm around her, he found himself focusing on the beauty of the moon reflecting from the waves, as seen by the eyes of a little girl. For that moment at least, he forgot about the hole in his heart.

The next day, when Hector came from the cabin top to join his passengers for the midday meal, he picked up a codex from the chair next to Malleolus and moved it to the couch before he settled in.

Malleolus's usual smile greeted him. "It's a beautiful day, Captain. It seems we're making good time."

"We are. In four days, we'll have crossed the Mare Ionium to dock in Corcyra. Then along the coast of Macedonia and Achaia to Corinth, some open-water sailing to Ephesus, then up the coast of Asia to the Mare Propontis and Perinthus. Less than four weeks and you'll reach your new home."

"And you'll have earned four months rest at home while the sea is closed."

Home...without Damara and Charissa. His smile faded. "Rest is not always a blessing. I'd rather be at sea."

Drusilla wandered over and picked up the codex. Malleolus opened his arm, and she snuggled against him.

Hector stood. "Please excuse me, Malleolus."

The old man's brow furrowed, then relaxed. A sympathetic smile accompanied his nod, as if he knew what it was to bury himself in work as a balm for pain.

Hector jerked when Drusilla's fingertips touched his arm.

"Captain? Can I ask you something?"

"What, child?"

She held out the codex. "Would you read to me? I can read myself, but this story is so much better when someone reads it to me."

He hadn't read to a child since Charissa died. He didn't want to now. He could tell Drusilla he needed to get back to the cabin top, but those eyes were looking at him with such hope in them.

"I can read for a while if the writing is Greek. My Latin is good enough to get by in Roman ports, but I don't read it well."

"I brought all my scrolls and codices, and many of them are Greek. When we finish those, I can read the Latin ones to you."

Malleolus stood and waved his hand toward the couch as he moved to the chair.

Hector settled onto the couch, leaving plenty of room for her to sit beside him. Instead, she crawled into his lap and snuggled in...just like Charissa used to do.

The sharp claw of regret dug into his heart. Could he bear holding another little girl in his lap? He was about to tell her he remembered something else he needed to do. Then she turned her face up toward his, and the happy glow in her eyes as she smiled stopped him.

"I already read part of it, but we should start over at the beginning so you don't miss any of the story."

His little girl was gone, but he could make another little girl happy, a girl who truly needed someone willing to do that. "Open it wherever you want me to start."

As he began reading from the beginning, he wrapped his arms around her and held the codex in front of them both. After the first few words, Drusilla relaxed against him and sighed.

◆

Cornelia sat watching Hector, as she usually did whenever he joined them under the canopy, and she couldn't stop her smile. It was sheer delight to see this brawny man with her daughter in his arms, to hear his deep voice pronouncing the Greek, to see the glow in Drusilla's eyes as she turned each page when he finished it. Her friends in Rome would laugh at her if she told them how extraordinarily masculine and appealing he seemed as he sat reading a child's story.

She would be sorry when they reached Perinthus. The captain must have been a wonderful father. Drusilla lit up whenever he did something with her. At first, she'd been glad to see that, but it was becoming a little worrisome. For the first time in her life, her daughter was receiving the attention from a man that a good father would have given her. She craved spending time with him, no matter what they were doing.

Drusilla would miss the captain terribly when he was gone. How could she prevent her daughter's grief over losing him when the voyage was over? Perhaps there was some way she could get them together after they left the ship.

If anyone were to ask, she would have told them she wanted to continue contact with Hector for Drusilla's sake. Truth be told, she found herself more strongly attracted to the man with every passing day.

She only knew four things about him: he was a widowed ship's captain with a farm near Perinthus, he had a heart that could love someone so deeply he still struggled a year after losing them, he was so very kind to her daughter, and he made her feel both safe and off balance at the same time. She wanted to know more...much more. She'd be at least as sorry as Drusilla if he were to disappear completely from their lives after the voyage ended.

Chapter 13

JUST LIKE GRANDFATHER

The predawn sky was still gray when Hector headed toward the crew cabin at the bow of the ship. It was Sunday again, time for the weekly worship with his men. Even Malleolus didn't get up this early, so none of his passengers would be looking for him. His scripture reading and their prayers should remain unnoticed.

◆

Drusilla had been awake for several minutes. She turned around on her bunk so she could lie under her blanket as she watched the dark gray lighten. Why did the sky look so different out here at sea than it had back at the villa?

The soft creak of Captain's door hinge interrupted her thoughts. She slid off the bed and opened her own door a crack to peek out. She got there just in time to see the cabin door close behind him.

She stepped back to her bed to get the blanket. If the captain had gone out to watch the waves, like he did at night, she planned to join him. Maybe he knew why the sky looked so different. Even if he didn't, maybe he would let her stand with him and hold her snug against him to keep her warm. That part was almost as much fun as watching the waves dancing in the moonlight. Time with Captain was the best part of each day.

She wrapped her blanket around her shoulders and tiptoed toward the cabin door. So close to morning, any noise might awaken her mother or Anthusa. She was about to open the door when she froze. Captain might not think she was cold if she had her blanket. She crept back to her room to toss it on the bed before following him out the door.

She pushed against the door with one hand as she pulled back on it with the other so it wouldn't make any noise as it latched. When she finally stepped past the front of the cabin where she could see where he usually stood at the rail, the captain was nowhere to be seen. She moved far enough forward of the cabin to see if he was on the cabin top, but only the crewman who was on night duty at the rudders was up there. She slipped back along the cabin to check for him under the canopy. No captain. As she walked back toward the center deck again, she caught sight of a light flickering under the door of the crew quarters.

The captain had told her the crew quarters were off limits. He told her to stay out of them, and she obeyed him. Still, what could the men be doing so early in the morning that needed a light? She worked her way along the rail to find out. If she didn't actually go in, she wouldn't be disobeying him.

When she reached the cabin wall, quiet voices leaked through the closed door. The captain's deep voice silenced them.

"We thank you, Father, for the gift of your son, Jesus, to save us from our sins, and for this gospel that You have given us that we may know Him. May your Spirit fill me and give me Your words this day. In the name of Jesus, I pray."

Silence, then Captain's voice again. "One day Jesus said to his disciples, 'Let's go over to the other side of the lake.' So they got into a boat and set out. As they sailed, he fell asleep. A squall came down on the lake, so that the boat was being swamped, and they were in great danger. The disciples went and woke him, saying, 'Master, Master, we're going to drown!' He got up and rebuked the wind and the raging waters; the storm subsided, and all was calm. 'Where is your faith?' he asked his disciples. In fear and amazement they asked one another, 'Who is this? He commands even the winds and the water, and they obey him.'"

Silence. She placed her ear against the door.

"Many times, we've faced storms. A few times, they've been far beyond what we thought the ship could stand. But each time, we've asked our Lord Jesus to protect us from loss at sea. He's always answered us, and we've come safe into port. But even if this ship should go down, we know there's nothing to fear. Jesus promised to always be with us. He promised us eternal life with him as our Lord and Savior. No matter what happens to us in this life, we can be certain of what will happen in the next, when we will be with Jesus forever. Always remember how much He loves us and that we never have to be afraid.

"Until we gather next week in worship, may the Lord bless and keep us. May he make his face shine upon us and give us peace."

She jumped at the sound of footsteps and hands slapping backs.

"The Lord's peace be with you, Clitus."

Captain was just on the other side of the wooden slats. What if he came out and found her there? Was standing right against the wall part of what he considered off limits?

Drusilla scurried back along the rail and re-entered the main cabin. She crept into her room and closed the door. After sliding back under the covers, she lay there, her mind racing.

Who was the Jesus that Captain was talking about? She couldn't ask the captain, or he would know she was listening where she shouldn't have been.

She wiggled a little under the covers. As soon as she heard Malleolus moving, she'd get up and ask him. Malleolus knew about almost everything. He would know who Jesus was.

When Malleolus emerged from his room, Drusilla popped out of hers and took his right hand. He rested his left hand on the side of her head as he smiled down at her.

"Well, this is a nice surprise. I didn't expect you up this early."

"I've been awake a while. I've been waiting for you. I have a question."

"Well, come with me to the canopy, and we can talk about it over breakfast."

After they'd both collected their fruit, bread, and cheese from the serving trays, Malleolus sat on the couch and patted the spot beside him. "Now, what is your question?"

"Who is Jesus?"

Malleolus's eyebrows shot up. "Before I answer, tell me why you want to know."

She glanced around to make sure no one was listening. "I heard Captain talking about him this morning."

"You did? Where?"

"I was listening by the crew quarters. He told his men a story about something Jesus did." She dropped her gaze. "I'd ask Captain, but he told me not to go into the crew quarters. I didn't really disobey him because I didn't go in, but he might not like me being that close."

"Before I tell you, I want you to promise me you won't mention this to anyone else. It might be dangerous for the captain."

Her eyes grew large as she nodded. "Dangerous for the captain? Why?"

"Because the captain must be a Christian. Your grandfather was killed in the arena because he became a Christian. For three years, he worshiped the Jewish god as the one true god. He refused to worship the Roman gods anymore because the Jewish god commands his people to worship only him. Roman law allows that because the religion of the Jews has demanded that since ancient times.

"Then he decided to follow Jesus. Your grandfather believed Jesus was the son of the Jewish god, that he came to be the sacrifice for everyone's sins if they only believed in him. Jesus doesn't allow his worshipers to worship any other gods, so your grandfather refused to sacrifice to Caesar as a god and deny Jesus as his lord. The Christians don't get the special treatment the Jews do. That's why he was killed."

"So if I say anything to the wrong person, Captain might get killed?"

"Yes."

She tightened her lips. "Then I won't say anything to anybody, not even to Mother and Anthusa. I don't want anything bad to ever happen to Captain."

"Neither do I, so this will be our secret."

Approaching footsteps warned of someone walking along the cabin. Malleolus held his finger to his lips and winked at Drusilla. She mimicked his motion just before Hector came around the corner.

"Good morning!" His voice bounced with energy, and his eyes sparkled, exactly as Malleolus had seen with Publius when he returned from Christian worship.

As the captain gathered his fruit, cheese, and bread before sitting down with them, Malleolus pursed his lips. The captain being a follower of Jesus explained many things. The Christians were notorious for treating everyone the same, with aristocrats, freedmen, and slaves all worshiping together and treating each other with kindness and affection like they were family. The captain certainly did that. He treated Anthusa with the same consideration he showed Cornelia. He was so kind to Drusilla and so patient and forgiving with Cornelia when other men might stay angry.

Publius had been killed before Malleolus had a chance to decide whether his closest friend's belief in Jesus was something he might want to embrace himself. Now that he knew another Christian, perhaps he'd have a chance to ask the questions that could help him decide.

Chapter 14

A Handsome Man

The corbita arrived at the harbor in Corcyra late enough in the afternoon that they would stay the night. That presented an opportunity, and Cornelia was ready to seize it.

The greatest hardship of being on the ship was the lack of a proper bath. Cleansing with scented oils and rinsing with a small basin of water was a poor substitute for soaking in warm water up to her neck. Her villa had its own room for bathing, and she'd always enjoyed a private soak there when she didn't join a friend at the exclusive private bath nearby. After so long, almost any bath would be acceptable. Surely a port town must have a decent public bath, and there should be time to go there before they had to leave.

Hector was leaning on the rail, watching the activity on the pier. She strolled over to stand beside him. He glanced at her, smiled a distracted smile, and returned his eyes to the cargo being moved onto the ship across from them.

"Captain, I have a request."

He straightened and focused his attention on her. "What would that be, Cornelia?"

His muscular physique was unnerving as he stood looking down at her. His aura of mental and physical strength stirred her like no man before him. Being so close felt good. It felt even better when he fixed those eyes on hers like he really cared what she was about to say...like now.

"The last time I enjoyed a leisurely bath was before I left my villa.

That's much too long. Since we'll be here until tomorrow, is it possible to go to the baths?"

His eyebrow rose; then he shook his head. "This is a very rough town, especially at night."

"But it's only afternoon. Surely it would be safe enough this time of day."

"A woman like you would be a tempting target for robbers even now. It's best if you stay onboard."

"A woman like me? What exactly makes me a target?"

"Your hair, your clothes, the way you move...everything about you says wealthy."

"What if I were to borrow a tunic from Anthusa and leave all my jewelry here?"

He crossed his arms. "The public bath here is not a safe place for you and Drusilla."

"Well, is there a private bath that might be?"

◆

Hector gazed into the blue eyes that showed no sign of giving up. "Is it that important to you?"

"Yes, Captain. It is."

He opened his mouth, then shrugged instead of speaking. She always assumed he could do anything she asked, no matter how difficult. He felt the compliment, even when it might not be wise to do what she wanted. This time, the request was not unreasonable. He would like a bath himself.

"Go change. I'll see what I can do."

As she headed into the cabin, he followed her. Corcyra was a town where it was wise to carry a dagger in plain sight. He threaded his belt through the two leather loops on the sheath before striding down the gangplank and up the pier. The harbor master would know if there was a place he could safely take her.

When Hector returned, Cornelia stood by the rail. Her hair was down, and she wore one of Anthusa's plain beige tunics. She had Drusilla and Anthusa in tow.

"We're ready, Captain."

"I need my gladius; then we'll go. The harbor master said there's a nice private bath about a quarter mile off the forum. We have time to go there if we hurry."

He ducked into the cabin and returned with the sword in its scabbard hanging from the strap draped across his chest.

"Stay right beside me."

Cornelila rested her hand on Drusilla's shoulder. "Of course, Captain. Lead the way."

◆

The captain led Cornelia and her party down the gangplank and up the pier. As they moved away from the water, it became obvious why he'd said it was a dangerous town. She tried to project a confident air as they walked past the rough-looking men who eyed them like jackals as they moved through the narrow streets just above the wharves. To appear afraid might provoke an attack. She squared her shoulders and raised her chin, but she did move closer to Hector and placed Drusilla between them.

"Perhaps this wasn't the best idea, Captain. Should we go back?"

He kept his hand on his sword and his eyes on the men around them as he answered. "We're almost to the forum. It's safer to keep going. It should be fine past there."

The dark, narrow street suddenly opened up into a spacious forum. As they moved into the bright sunshine, the captain took his hand off his sword. He led them across the square and down the broad street on the other side. When they'd walked about a quarter mile, he turned left onto a narrow street. About half a block down, he turned through a gate with a small sign saying "bath" above it. He paid the fee for all of them to the attendant just inside.

Hector scanned the courtyard before directing them toward the doorway on the left. "Women's bath is that way. You can take about an hour. I'll be waiting for you when you're done."

"Will that be enough time for you to bathe?" The men Cornelia knew were usually gone for at least two hours when they went to the baths.

As he struggled to contain the laugh her question had provoked, she regretted her words, but her thoughts were safe from him. He had no skill at all in hiding his emotions, but she'd practiced blocking an ill-timed blush for years.

"I'm no Roman aristocrat, Cornelia. I'm only here to bathe, not plan the affairs of the Empire. I'll be ready to take you back as soon as you're ready."

She offered him her most gracious smile. "Thank you for bringing us, even if it was against your better judgment. We'll try to hurry so we can return while it's still somewhat safe."

He nodded to acknowledge her appreciation, but the corners of his eyes crinkled as one corner of his mouth turned up. He was still laughing at her, but it was worth it to see that smile. Too bad this bath separated men and women.

She turned and walked toward the entrance into the women's side of the bathhouse. Exactly what he found so funny wasn't obvious, but the twinkle in his eyes charmed her no matter what caused it. She glanced back at him before following Anthusa and Drusilla through the door. He was such a handsome man when he was almost laughing. Truth be told, he was a handsome man no matter what he was doing.

Hector watched Cornelia until she disappeared. Then he headed into the men's bath. Even dressed in the clothing of her slave, she moved like a queen. Regal wasn't just a matter of jewels and fine linen after all.

Anthusa had just finished brushing the mistress's hair for the night. Mistress rested her elbows on the table and her chin in her hands as she gazed at her reflection in the mirror.

"I wonder what the captain's wife looked like. He's such a handsome man. I think she must have been very pretty." She sighed. "I never believed it when the young men told me I was pretty. Lucius never said it. At least he was honest in that. I think I always knew he was mostly attracted by my being a Claudius Scipio and the size of my dowry. Well, maybe not the dowry so much. His father was even richer than my father was. He got tired of me so fast. I'm not sure he waited even a year before he was with other women."

"He was a fool, mistress. None of the others were worth anything compared to you."

Mistress sighed. "It shouldn't have been that way. I actually loved him when we first married. I thought he cared for me, too. Until he got Publius killed, I kept hoping we could get that love back." She looked up at Anthusa. "If he'd loved me even half as much as the captain loved his wife, we wouldn't be on this ship."

Anthusa didn't know what to say, so she just nodded.

"It must have been wonderful to have the captain as a husband. He must have been a wonderful father, too. He's so good to Drusilla."

"The captain is very kind. I've never seen another man like him."

Mistress Cornelia leaned forward to inspect her face closely in the mirror. "I never was pretty, and now, well..." She turned to offer a wry smile to Anthusa. "I'm sure my dowry will make me look attractive to the men in Perinthus." Her lips tightened. "But I don't want that kind of man."

"The captain's not that kind of man, mistress."

"No, he isn't. Quite the opposite. If he ever acted as if he liked me, I'm sure he really would."

"And I don't think he's the kind of man who would choose a woman only because she was pretty."

"No, probably not." Mistress stood and moved over to her bed. "He's not like any man I've known. I would like to know him better. I'm going to work on that."

Anthusa nodded again. If the captain were a Roman aristocrat, he'd be the perfect second husband for her dear mistress. But if he were a Roman aristocrat, he probably wouldn't be the kind of man he was.

Chapter 15

RISK OR REWARD?

The next day, when Hector rounded the corner of the cabin to join Malleolus for lunch, Cornelia rose and stepped into his path.

"Captain, please sit with me for a while. I have many questions about Perinthus, and I hope you can answer them." She offered her most gracious smile.

His brow furrowed. A long conversation with Cornelia wasn't as appealing as talking with Malleolus, but it made sense that she'd want to know something about her future homeland. Leaving Rome with only four days' notice—she'd had no time to find out much before the voyage.

"Of course. I'll try to answer what I can."

Regal was the perfect word for her as she turned and walked ahead of him. When she moved, it was almost like a dance. Sometimes that made her seem like nothing and no one could touch her, but he knew that wasn't true. She looked at her daughter with the kind of love he had for Charissa. She did it often, and she was actually quite attractive then in spite of her large nose and wide mouth. The deep blue of her eyes was like the Mare Aegeum under a cloudless sky, and her lips curved into a warm smile. She seemed like a flesh-and-blood woman then, not an untouchable queen.

When Damara had looked at Charissa that way, it made him want to scoop her into his arms and kiss her. That memory usually triggered a fresh shot of pain. Surprise coursed through him when it didn't happen...and relief. God was finally answering his months of prayer for the pain to end.

As she turned to seat herself, she invited him to sit in the chair beside her with a wave of her upturned hand. The elegant gesture and the way she seemed to float as she settled into her own chair made it look like a dance. The word regal popped into his mind again. The polish and poise of a patrician woman was evident in her every move. That might have seemed fake and pompous for many women. But after so long together on the ship, anything else would seem unnatural for her.

He settled into the chair beside her. "What would you like to know first?"

"When we first arrive, we will probably be living for a while with Titus or Claudia while I arrange something more permanent. Titus was a fine young man when he left for Thracia twelve years ago. I expect he remained one, just like his father. I'm sure he will welcome us and be glad to help me decide the best way to start over there. The last time I saw Claudia, she was a very sweet girl, but she was only sixteen and more of a child than a woman. I heard you tell Drusilla that she married the man who owns this ship. I'm sure Claudia would welcome us and want to help, but will her husband?"

"I know both men. Titus is as good a man as you expect, but Philip is even better. Anyone would call him an honest, generous man. I expect he'll be as much and maybe more help than Titus. He has estates and other business in both Thracia and Moesia. I'm sure he'll help with anything you need."

"I'm glad to hear you speak so glowingly of him. Claudia was always unusually intelligent in scholarly matters but rather helpless about practical things. She probably needs someone like that to care for her."

The corner of Hector's mouth twitched up. "You'll find her very different from the girl you remember. Philip and Claudia are well matched. Theirs is a very happy marriage."

"So, how do you know my relatives so well?"

"Philip worked the summer he was eighteen on the ship where I was first mate. When he bought this ship thirteen years ago, he made me captain. He's my friend."

The best friend a man could have, one who'd sheltered him during his crushing grief last winter.

Cornelia's unperturbed smile revealed a heart that had never known that kind of grief. She'd left all her friends to save Drusilla, but she didn't know what it was like to be married to someone whose death could make you feel as if half of you had died as well.

◆

The captain was a friend of her in-laws. Cornelia couldn't have asked for a better opening to learn more about him. But how best to exploit it? She'd always been able to draw out even the shyest men by revealing something personal first. The captain should be no different.

"I'm glad to hear that Claudia doesn't have the kind of marriage I have...had. We were married less than four years when my husband started spending most of his nights with...others. Lucius and I have had nothing even remotely resembling a marriage since I opposed what he tried to do to Claudia after he got their father killed. I was delighted when she escaped from him.

"I only stayed married to him because I didn't want him to take my boys and Drusilla. He would never have let me see them if I'd divorced him. Once he decided to do something that would hurt Drusilla, that was the end of it. There was no reason to stay and every reason to leave. I have my dowry to start over well in Perinthus. Titus will know how to help me. It sounds like Philip is wealthy enough that he'll know how as well."

Hector had been leaning toward her, but he leaned back at her comment on two rich men helping her reinvest her dowry. She kicked herself for those words. She should have expected that response. He was totally uninterested in her money. He must have a good idea of how rich she was from the weight of the gold chests in his room and hers. He'd spoken of her "treasure" during their first argument like a man who didn't particularly worry about wealth.

That lack of interest made him even more intriguing. She already knew there would be men in Perinthus who would eagerly pursue her hand in marriage because of it. She'd seen that happen several times with friends who divorced and retrieved their ample dowries, and hers was even greater than most of theirs. Those second marriages turned out as bad as the first ones. She would stay single before going down that path again.

"My only regret in leaving Lucius is that I will see less of my boys."

He leaned forward again. "So you have sons as well as Drusilla?"

Satisfaction surged as she smiled at the first personal question he'd asked her. Perhaps the first sign of some interest in her.

"I have two sons, Lucius and Marcus, who are tribunes serving in Judaea, so I don't get to see them often. My third son, Tertius, is eighteen. He lives with his father in Rome, but he came often to the villa to see Drusilla and me. He warned me of my husband's plans."

His eyes were fixed on hers. She had his full attention, and that unleashed the flirtatious girl in her. It had been years since she fished for a compliment, but somehow, she couldn't resist.

"When you have three grown sons, it's hard to fulfill the Roman ideal of beauty anymore." She combined a wistful smile with a slight shrug.

"Motherhood hasn't made you look any older than you are."

He meant that to be a compliment, but it was the clumsiest one she'd ever received. The laugh she fought to suppress escaped anyway. What should she expect but an unusual compliment from the most unusual man she'd ever had the good fortune to meet?

◆

Hector straightened at Anthusa's soft gasp. Cornelia had laughed at his unintended insult, but maybe she laughed only to hide the hurt. He often smiled to mask his pain.

"That came out wrong. I'm sorry if what I said offended you. I meant no offense. I don't move in circles where words are twisted to make people think well of you so you can get what you want."

She laughed again at his summary of her world. "No offense taken, Captain. It's refreshing to talk with a man who doesn't play games with words."

"Word games are sometimes just lies in pretty language. God made me an honest man."

He liked the amused smile that lifted the corner of her lips and put a sparkle in her eyes. It made her seem more like a woman and less like a queen.

"I wish more men valued honesty as much as you do. That's rare among my acquaintances in Rome."

He returned her smile. He liked a woman who didn't take offense when no offense was meant. He sometimes put things too bluntly when talking with women and hurt their feelings. She wasn't some fluttery young woman he had to be careful around. There was something about her that made it comfortable to speak his mind, even when they disagreed—which was not infrequent.

He wasn't sure what to say to her next, so he stood. He scooped up a handful of dates and selected a piece of bread.

"If you'll excuse me, Cornelia, it's time for me to return to work. We can talk more about Perinthus another time."

◆

"Of course, Captain."

Their conversation had ended too quickly. Cornelia hadn't learned anything important about him at all.

She watched him walk away. He was a remarkable man—honest, handsome, strong, reliable, kind. Especially kind. That was so rare among the men she'd known.

The more she saw of the captain, the more she admired him. If she could find a man like him, she would seriously consider remarrying.

In fact, if he were to show the interest in her that she felt in him, she would give serious consideration to marrying the captain himself.

He was not a wealthy man by her standards, but he didn't need to be. She had more than enough herself. He'd been a captain for many years, and he probably made good money from his share of the profits on the cargo of a ship this size. He already had a farm, so he knew about being a landowner. He should be comfortable as her partner in running an estate.

He wasn't Roman, but after twenty-five years with Lucius, she'd had her fill of aristocratic Roman men. None in her broad acquaintance ever stirred her like this Greek sea captain.

And there was one thing she knew for certain. Drusilla would be thrilled if he became her husband. Hector would make the finest father a girl could ever have.

Leaving Rome and taking Drusilla to Perinthus was risky, but the greatest rewards often came from the greatest risks.

Cornelia stroked her cheek as she stared at the corner of the cabin where Hector had disappeared. Would life with the captain be more of a risk or a reward?

Chapter 16

Better Than Money

Circus Maximus in Rome

The murmurs of a quarter million spectators waiting for the races to start filled the Circus Maximus with an ocean of sound. Lucius wove through the crowd on his way to join Marcus Corvinus in the senatorial seating.

His progress was blocked by a well-fed equestrian and his even-better-fed wife arguing over whether he should sit by a willowy young woman or move up a row.

A hand rested against his upper arm, and he turned to find Didia Galla, her other hand fondling a necklace of spun gold and rubies.

"Lucius, how delightful to find you here." She looked past his shoulder. "And alone. My husband has gone to Corinth for business and... pleasure. I'm missing the company of a man."

Her mouth curved into a seductive smile. "One particular man's company would be most welcome this evening."

If Didia had been a tigress, her tail would have been swishing as she eyed him.

"I knew Flaccus was out of town. We dined together at Marcus Corvinus's just before he left. Since you're feeling lonely, you must be glad he'll be home in less than a week."

"Yes, well..." She fingered the ruby earring that matched the necklace. "We are no longer each other's favorite evening companion. Neither of us minds if the other enjoys...conversation with another. We agree that we may part soon."

Another seductive smile and she moved closer to him. "Rather like

"

you and Cornelia. I hear she's left you...no great loss and not that you'd care. A handsome man like you shouldn't waste his time with a plain, proud woman who's a fool not to want you and would run off with your daughter."

Lucius straightened. "What do you mean?"

"Didn't she divorce you and just disappear, taking your daughter with her?"

Lucius flipped to full alert. This was one cat it paid to be nice to. She moved in all the gossip circles, and whatever tale he could get her to believe about Cornelia's actions would soon make the rounds of Rome.

"We did agree to divorce, but she didn't just disappear. She's traveling with our daughter, expanding her knowledge of the Empire before I betroth her."

Her smile broadened. "What a fine idea. I should have done the same with my girls before they married."

"You must excuse me, Didia. I'm already late meeting someone, and we have some business to discuss before the races start." He patted her hand before lifting it from his arm.

"Of course, Lucius. But do remember what I said."

He graced her with an appreciative smile. "I will. Not this week, but perhaps another trip will offer an opportunity."

As he continued down the steps to join Marcus, his smile broadened. Didia Galla would spread the tale he wanted abroad. No matter which faction won, he'd come out ahead with something better than money on this race day.

Chapter 17

Fit to be Tied

Midmorning the next day, Cornelia heard Drusilla's laughter as she came around the corner of the cabin. She watched for the captain to step into view as well, and her heart quickened when he did. He looked directly at her and smiled as if he was glad to see her looking at him. But why was he carrying two lengths of rope?

Drusilla bounced over and took hold of both her hands.

"Come sit with us, Mother. Captain is going to teach me how to tie knots like a sailor. You should learn, too."

Hector settled himself on the couch after moving one of the small tables in front of it. "Your mother may not care to learn."

He was right that she didn't care whether she learned to tie knots, but the opportunity to sit close beside him as he taught her was irresistible. "Actually, Captain, I do. You never know when I might need to tie something up."

His eyebrows rose at the enthusiasm in her voice. "Very well." He patted the couch on each side of him. "Join me, and we'll begin."

Drusilla sat to his right, and Cornelia settled in to his left. She sat close enough that she sensed the warmth of his body beside her. Funny how just sitting next to him made her heart rate rise. She cast a sideways glance at his classic profile. He was focused on the ropes in his hands, oblivious of her watching him. He probably had no idea that he could tie her in knots as easily as he could tie the rope.

He handed one of the ropes to Drusilla and kept the other himself. "We'll start with something easy." He turned toward Drusilla. "You've

88

seen the loop in the rope that goes from the bow to the post on the pier." She nodded. "That's a bowline knot. Let's do that one first. Take the rope like so...now watch how I thread the rope around itself."

He tied the knot slowly so they could watch what he was doing. Drusilla watched his fingers attentively while Cornelia watched the captain's profile. Then he untied it.

"Now, copy me as I do it again."

Drusilla copied his motions exactly as he made the first small loop away from the end of the rope, then the larger loop that would go around a post. Then he threaded the end of the rope back through the first small loop, wrapped it around the rope behind the small loop, and finally threaded it back through the small loop before tightening. Her first attempt produced a knotted loop that looked almost like his.

He smiled broadly at her success. "Nice. You have the makings of a good sailor."

"If I were a boy, I'd love to work on your ship, Captain."

"And I'd be glad to have you on my crew. Now, you practice the bowline while I teach your mother."

Simply sitting next to Hector while she watched him teaching Drusilla was enough to distract Cornelia. She hadn't paid close attention to what he'd done, so she wasn't prepared when he handed her the rope and waited.

She made the first small loop and then the large one. She remembered that he'd threaded the end through the small loop, but she'd been watching his face and not his fingers after that.

"I'm afraid I didn't watch carefully enough, Captain."

"Let me help you." He leaned closer and wrapped his hand around hers to guide it.

His touch was unexpected, and her heart jumped at the contact. The sensation of his calloused palm on the back of her hand and his fingers lying against hers was delightful.

◆

As the subtle scent of roses filled Hector's nostrils, he was acutely aware of Cornelia being so close. She had several different perfumes, and he'd started to notice which one she wore each morning. This one was his favorite.

Her skin was silken, and the warmth of her small hand brushing against his palm increased his awareness of her perfume. He finished helping her wrap the rope around itself and thread it back through the small loop.

He leaned back and rested both hands on his knees. "You've got it. Now tighten it."

She pulled it taut to make a reasonable bowline.

"Not as good as Drusilla's. You'll have to practice more if you want to be part of my crew."

A playful smile drew his attention to her lips, and the twinkle in her blue eyes pulled his completely away from the rope. "You may have to show me a few more times. I'm not as quick a learner as my daughter is."

"I can do that. I need to teach you a reef knot, too. If I have to send you aloft to help, you'll need to know that one."

She laughed as she rested the elegant fingers of her petite hand on the back of his large, work-roughened one. "If you need to send me aloft, we are in serious trouble." As she pulled her fingers across and away, a tingle shot up his arm.

He grinned back. Her laughter was musical, and it made her seem less like a queen. "You never know what you can do until you have to do it. I'm sure you could do anything if your daughter needed you to."

"I'm honored by your confidence in me, Captain, but I probably don't deserve it."

The warmth of her smile and the sparkle in her eyes made her face almost pretty. If she had fished for a compliment today, he could have given her one that would make Anthusa smile instead of gasp. He could honestly say her love for her daughter softened her face in a way a man like him could admire.

Looking too long at Cornelia's laughing blue eyes was stirring up feelings he hadn't expected—an attraction both physical and mental. Sitting so close to her was unsettling, but that wasn't a bad thing.

It was good she wanted to tie knots.

He lifted the rope from her fingers. "Time for the next knot. Let's try the clove hitch. We use that to secure a line to a post or a rail." He pulled the table closer so each of them could reach a leg. "You start it this way..."

◆

A knowing smile tugged at Malleolus's lips as he watched the lesson. He had grown old living among the aristocrats of Rome, and he'd watched many Roman ladies play their seductive games with Lucius. Cornelia was not a game player. Lucius had abandoned their marriage bed eight years ago, and she'd still lived chaste and faithful to her marriage vows.

He'd have to be blind not to see she was attracted to Hector. She was even beginning to flirt with him. Could it be that her heart, so wounded by Lucius's cruelty and neglect, was ready to risk loving another man?

Since Cornelia's marriage into the Drusus family twenty-five years ago, he'd watched over her. He'd seen her grow from an innocent maiden to a wise woman made strong by years of caring for herself and raising her children virtually alone. He couldn't love her more if she were his own daughter. Like any good father, he longed to see her happy.

Her bell-like laughter and the captain's responding grins—perhaps two wounded hearts were opening up before him. She deserved a good husband, and the captain was as fine a man as he'd ever met. What did it really matter that they came from two different worlds? Cornelia had already rebelled against the rules of patrician society when she took Drusilla. She was wise enough to see the worth of a man wasn't set by the value of his property or the noble blood in his veins.

Perhaps by the end of this voyage they would discover they had much more to share than affection for Drusilla. He would do all he could to help them along.

Anthusa pulled the brush through Mistress Cornelia's hair as she leaned her chin on her hand and gazed into the mirror.

"It was a lovely day. I never would have imagined it could be so enjoyable to just tie knots."

Anthusa continued brushing. "I think the captain liked teaching you, mistress. Drusilla looked so happy when he praised her and teased her about joining his crew. The captain is so kind to her, the way he does things with her so she doesn't feel too lonely."

Mistress turned in the chair. "He is kind...and patient...and I like his eyes. When I talk with him, he looks at me like what I'm saying really matters. I find him one of the most attractive men I've ever known, and it isn't just because he's so handsome. Lucius is handsome, and he repels me. I'd find the captain attractive even if he were ugly. Does that seem odd to you?"

"No, mistress. Any woman would think the captain is attractive."

"When he was guiding my fingers so I made the knots right—he probably didn't mean anything by it, but it felt like he wanted to touch me. I know it sounds silly, but just sitting next to him and watching his fingers make the knots so quickly was so...well, I don't know how to describe it. The last time I felt like that was when I was a girl talking with Lucius in private before our wedding."

"The captain is a much better man than your husband ever was."

"He would make such a wonderful father for Drusilla. You know, I wasn't planning on ever marrying again. I didn't want to risk getting another man like Lucius. Men often aren't what they seem before you marry. They act one way, but then the ugliness comes out after the wedding. That would never happen with the captain. There's no ugliness inside him. I would actually consider marrying him. For Drusilla, of course."

Anthusa listened, nodding her head in agreement with everything her mistress was saying. Except for the final thing. The captain would be at least as good for the mistress as he would be for Drusilla. She should do whatever it took to get the captain to become her second husband. Mistress deserved to be happy, and being married to the captain would make her a happy woman, indeed.

Chapter 18

The Secret Revealed

Corinth

It had been a little over two weeks since they left Portus. The *Claudia* was tied to the pier in Corinth while some of its old cargo was being unloaded to make room for the new. As first mate, Clitus had been left in charge of that. Hector had gone to the shipping office to meet with Leander, the second-oldest son of Aristarchus, who ran the family operations in Achaia and Epirus.

Cornelia stood at the rail, watching the general bustle on the pier below. She soon tired of that and began watching for the return of the captain. It was not long before she spotted him on the road, heading toward the ramp that led down to the pier. As a Greek man in a Grecian port, one might expect him to blend into the crowd, but he stood out to her eyes. She moved along the rail to stand near the gangplank. The moment he boarded, she'd make her request.

◆

As Hector made his way past the line of slaves carrying cargo from his ship, he looked up and saw Cornelia waiting for him. As soon as she caught his eye, she raised her hand and waved. He started up the gangplank and saw that expectant look. She was about to ask him to do something. Would it be quick and easy? Knowing Cornelia, it might not be.

"Captain, I'm glad you returned so soon. There should still be plenty of time."

Hector stopped beside her. Plenty of time—that didn't sound good. "Time for what?"

"Time for a bath and a good dinner. Surely a city like Corinth is a place where both should be readily available."

"It is, but what Corinth considers normal could make even Rome blush. It would not be good to take Drusilla or even to go yourself to the public baths here."

"That might be, but perhaps you can find an alternative. You did in Corcyra."

She stood with her head tipped, looking at him with those eyes that assumed he could fulfill her request. In Corinth, he probably could. He'd worshiped many times with Leander's house church, and a brother had a restaurant not far from the harbor. Leander could recommend a good private bath and give him exact directions to the restaurant.

"I probably can. I need to go back to the shipping office for some directions. Then I'll escort you to bathe and eat."

"Thank you, Captain. We'll be ready when you return." She turned and headed for the canopy, where Malleolus and Anthusa were waiting.

He watched her. Gracious. Graceful. Every move like a dancer. His mouth curved up in appreciation. Cornelia was one persistent woman who didn't give up until she got what she wanted. Sometimes that was quite annoying. Still, the walk of a patrician woman would attract any man's eyes.

When Hector returned, Malleolus stood waiting by the gangplank. "Cornelia invited me to join you for a good dinner. She should be out in a moment."

Hector smiled at the old steward. "Good. I'd rather have another man along."

The thought of having only Cornelia to talk with during dinner was a little uncomfortable. He sometimes had trouble knowing how she'd respond to his words. Her eyes were usually so calm, but then they'd twinkle because he'd said something she found terribly amusing. He wasn't always sure what was so funny. Still, her eyes were pretty when they were laughing, so he didn't mind that she found him unintentionally entertaining.

"I'm ready, Captain."

He turned, and his head bounced back. He'd assumed she'd have the fancy crown of curls and her best clothes. Her hair was down, and she wore one of Anthusa's plain tunics.

His eyebrows rose as he stared at her.

She rested her hand on her chest and tipped her head. "Is something wrong?"

"You look very plain. You can dress fancy here in Corinth, like you did in Rome. Do you want to change?"

"No. I don't want to risk putting you in danger defending us from robbers. I don't mind being seen dressed like this."

There was that twinkle that lit her eyes when she teased him. What had he said?

"I've been a plain woman all my life. I can't change that, even if I want to, so you shouldn't expect it to bother me here."

"That's not what I meant, Cornelia. Just because you're not pretty doesn't mean you're so plain I thought it would bother you."

He glanced at Anthusa; her wide eyes confirmed that he had just insulted Cornelia...again.

The corners of Cornelia's mouth twitched, and the laughter danced in her eyes. "Thank you for clarifying that. Now shall we go?"

He didn't need to look at Anthusa again. His ears heated. He'd just dug himself deeper in the hole. He would have tried to fix it, but he wasn't sure he wouldn't just say something else that sounded like an insult. She really wasn't a pretty woman, so what could he say? He wasn't going to lie to her.

"I'll get my sword in case we return after dark." He stepped quickly into the cabin, glad of an excuse to get out of the conversation.

◆

Malleolus's eyes were laughing, even though he didn't make a sound.

Cornelia grinned at him. "I probably shouldn't have done that to him, but I couldn't resist."

"The captain is a strong man. I'm sure he can take it." The full grin broke out. He closed his eyes and took a deep breath as he tried to regain his composure before the captain saw him. Hector's natural honesty was no match for Cornelia's playfulness. He shouldn't laugh at him, but it was hard not to.

◆

When Hector returned, he led them down the gangplank and up the pier without speaking. If he didn't say anything, he couldn't accidentally insult her.

At the top of the ramp, he turned to Cornelia. "It is only a quarter mile to the bath that Leander recommends. Stay close to me."

"With pleasure, Captain."

He wasn't quite sure how to interpret her smile, but there was that teasing sparkle in her eyes. She might be plain over all, but no man could ever think her eyes were.

The bath was delightfully refreshing, but Cornelia had noticed one thing that all the baths he took them to had in common. Men and women were always separated. She was sorry for two reasons. Drusilla would have had a wonderful time playing with the captain in a communal swimming pool, and she would have enjoyed watching them. She always loved watching Drusilla enjoy herself, and, well, he really was a handsome man.

It was a short walk from the bath to the small restaurant Hector had selected. As they entered the courtyard, tantalizing aromas enveloped them: rosemary-laced bread fresh from an oven and a lamb and lentil stew, simmering with onion and garlic, seasoned with cumin and coriander. A half dozen tables were scattered under a canopy, and all but one were already occupied.

Hector motioned for them to take the empty one before he headed for the kitchen. He'd almost reached it when the proprietor burst through the door.

"Hector! It is so good to see you, my brother." The two men embraced with hearty slaps on each other's backs.

"It's even better to see you, Menelaites." Hector turned slightly and waved his hand toward Cornelia and the others. "I've brought some passengers from Rome who are eager for a good meal after so many days of Calamus's cooking."

"That I can understand. You are an excellent captain, and I would trust my life to you even in the worst of storms, but you are not known for feeding people well." He slapped Hector's back again. "You can trust that I will give them a meal to remember, brother."

Hector grinned. "I'm sure of that."

With one more slap of Hector's arm, Menelaites turned and vanished into his kitchen.

Hector stepped over to first one and then another of the other tables and exchanged very quiet words with the people there. From the smiles on all their faces, it was obvious he knew them well.

Cornelia's curiosity was aroused. The two men seemed to be good friends. The proprietor had called the captain "brother," but that wasn't possible. Hector was so obviously Greek, and his friend looked decid-edly Egyptian. She leaned over to whisper to Malleolus.

"The captain seems to know almost everyone here. Why do you suppose that Egyptian is calling him 'brother'?"

"I'll tell you later, when no ears are listening."

Cornelia cupped her chin and stroked her cheek with her forefin-ger. That was a conversation she'd be looking forward to.

The dinner had been truly delicious, and their small party had re-turned to the ship without Hector needing his sword. Clitus was wait-ing to discuss something about the cargo with the captain, and the two of them descended into the hold. Cornelia motioned with her head to invite Malleolus into the cabin while Drusilla and Anthusa continued on to the deck chairs to enjoy the sunset.

As soon as they were alone inside, Cornelia turned to Malleolus.

"There are no ears now. What were you going to tell me? Why did that Egyptian keep calling the captain 'brother'?"

"The captain is a Christian, like Publius. It is what Christian men call each other."

Cornelia's eyes widened before her brow furrowed. "Are you sure? How do you know?"

"Drusilla heard him leading their worship. I told her not to say anything to anyone because it could put the captain in danger."

"I appreciate the wisdom of that, considering what happened to Publius. I certainly don't intend to say anything to anyone, either. I would hate to have something happen to the captain."

Malleolus nodded his agreement, and the two of them headed back to the canopy.

As orange faded to red in the sunset sky, Cornelia pondered what she'd just learned. She didn't know much about the Christian religion, but the wisest man she'd ever known had decided his loyalty to Jesus was more important than his life. When Publius chose to die, she never understood it, but there had to be something extraordinary about fol-lowing Jesus for him to willingly leave Claudia when she still needed him.

And the most extraordinary man of her acquaintance was a Chris-tian, too. But she didn't care what his religion was. He would still be the perfect father for Drusilla and an excellent husband.

His secret was safe with her.

Anthusa unbraided Mistress's hair and ran her fingers through it. Hearing the thoughts of the mistress's heart as she brushed her hair was always the best part of the day.

Mistress Cornelia smiled contentedly at Anthusa's reflection in the mirror. "It's been nice spending most of the day in port. That dinner with the captain was truly delicious. It was good of him to take time away from his work to escort us himself. He gets embarrassed, but I think he likes it when I tease him. He's so handsome when he gets a little flustered and then his smile shows up. I like it when his eyes crinkle. He seems to smile more now than when we first sailed. I know I do. He makes me smile without even trying."

"I've noticed that, mistress. It's the same with Drusilla. I think the captain could make anyone smile."

Cornelia turned to face her. "Drusilla loves listening to him talk about the ship. When I was saying good night, she told me she wished she had something to read about ships and sea voyages. She pointed out a shop selling scrolls as we were coming back from dinner. It's only a short distance from the harbor. If there's time tomorrow, we should go there to see if I can find her one."

"I'm sure she'd love that."

Cornelia turned back to the table and rested her chin on her hand. "I'm sure she'll love having the captain read it to her. I'll enjoy that, too. He has such a wonderful voice for reading aloud."

"He does."

"The captain does almost everything well." Cornelia grinned at Anthusa in the mirror. "At least that's the way it seems to me."

Anthusa nodded and continued brushing. She liked the dreamy look on Mistress's face as she thought about the captain. She was well on her way to being in love with him. Each day, he seemed to like the mistress more as well.

A smile tugged at Anthusa's lips as she pulled the brush through Cornelia's nut-brown tresses one last time. It would be so good if the captain decided he wanted to marry Mistress. If only the voyage would take long enough for that to happen. The mistress deserved happiness, and no one could make her happier than a good man like the captain.

Chapter 19

Beginning to Care

Breakfast was over, and Cornelia was leaning against the rail by the canopy. When she glanced toward the bow, she saw Drusilla with Malleolus, watching the rowboats pull ships away from the nearby piers.

Anthusa joined her. "She always finds something worth watching, even when she's seen it before."

Cornelia turned her smile on her maid. "Yes, and things I've seen many times sometimes seem new when she tells me about them."

She strolled back to the fruit tray and ate the last slice of dried apple before settling once more into her chair.

When Calamus came to clear away the remains of breakfast, she drained her brass goblet and handed it to him. "How much longer will it be before we leave Corinth?"

He glanced at her as he continued stacking plates and bowls on a tray. "Should be at least an hour. Did you need anything before we sail?"

"Drusilla wanted something about ships to read. I saw a scroll vender just up the road from the harbor. An hour should be plenty of time to go there and back." She rose. "Come, Anthusa."

Calamus's brow furrowed. "Best check with Captain before you leave the ship."

"He's busy in the hold. No need to bother him. We'll hurry so we won't cause any delay."

He opened his mouth as if to speak but shrugged instead. Then he swept the bread crumbs from the small table before carrying the tray of dishes back into the galley.

Cornelia slipped into her room to get some money, and she and Anthusa headed down the gangplank.

All was properly secured in the hold, and Hector and his first mate returned to the deck. It was time to leave.

"Leander arranged good cargo for us, Clitus. This should be a very profitable trip. Prepare to cast off."

The crewman guarding the gangplank sucked air between his teeth. "Captain."

Hector turned to face him with eyebrows raised.

"We can't cast off yet, Captain. Cornelia Scipia and her maid aren't back onboard."

Hector tightened his lips. She was an exasperating woman sometimes. He'd hoped to make good distance today, and she'd chosen to wander off somewhere without telling him.

"Where did she go?"

"She said she was going to buy a scroll and would be right back."

Hector's nostrils flared. He exhaled sharply as his lips squeezed so tight they almost disappeared. Drusilla had pointed out the scroll vendor as they walked up to the bath. She was still talking about it at breakfast. It was just like Cornelia to go there to get something for her daughter. It was even more like her to do it without asking him first.

He turned to Clitus. "I know where she went. I'm going to fetch her. Be ready to cast off as soon as we return."

Clitus gave one quick nod. "Yes, Captain."

Hector trotted down the gangplank and up the pier.

Cornelia had made her purchase, and Anthusa carried the scroll as they started back.

Fingers of unease wrapped around Cornelia's spine as they worked their way down the crowded street. Perhaps this hadn't been the best idea. Passing this way with the captain had felt perfectly safe, but now predatory eyes appraised her. She'd made a mistake not changing out of her fine linen and gold hair picks that held her braid at the back of her head. She looked worth robbing, and with only Anthusa beside her, she looked like an easy target.

"Mistress."

Cornelia glanced at her maid. Anthusa jerked her head slightly toward the rear. "We're being followed."

Cornelia looked back over her shoulder in time to see the scraggly youth start his grab for the small purse that held 60 denarii after the scroll purchase. She spun around to face him as she swung her arm sideways and up to get the purse out of his reach. He anticipated her move and grabbed the sack of coins. She gripped it with both hands and braced against his efforts to pull it away from her.

"Let go! Now! You are not going to rob me!" She looked at the men standing nearby. "Help me."

But the bystanders did just that—stood by and watched. Not one moved to help.

◆

Hector had just caught sight of Cornelia when the thief struck. He broke into a dead run when she started yelling. His heart pounded faster than his feet when he saw the sheathed dagger on the thief's belt.

Hector's hand shot past her to grab and twist the thief's arm sideways and down as he seized her purse, too. She was pulled against him until she let go and stumbled back. The youth yelped in pain, let go of the purse, and sprinted away.

Hector spun around on her and stepped close. His body blocked the sun as he towered over her. His nostrils flared as his fist gripped the recovered purse tight enough to make his knuckles white and his forearm bulge.

"You are never to do this again. You do not leave my ship without asking me first. You do not go anywhere without an escort. You were a fool to fight with that thief. He had a dagger. You could be dead right now and over what? A pittance. If he stabbed you, what would happen to Drusilla?"

She blanched as his scowl drilled into her. "If anything happens to me, take care of her. Get her safely to Claudia."

Her enormous blue eyes blinked rapidly as they moistened. She was trembling. But why? She fought for her purse fearlessly, so why was she so scared now it was over?

Then it hit him. It wasn't the thief who frightened her. It was him.

He took a deep breath to calm himself. The anger faded, and deep concern replaced it. He handed her the purse before placing his hands on her upper arms. She tensed when he first touched her, but his grip was so gentle that she relaxed immediately.

An urge to pull her close surged through him. An urge to wrap her in his arms to protect and comfort her. Where had that come from? The fear had drained from her eyes, but clasping her to himself would probably replace it with anger. It was not his place to embrace her for any reason.

"I will, but you won't have to worry about that as long as you do what I tell you instead of something stupid like this. I don't want to see you hurt, Cornelia. I will get you safely to Perinthus if you just do what I say and let me take care of you."

She offered a rueful smile as she nodded. "I promise I'll consult you before I do anything stupid again." Her regret was clear in both voice and eyes.

He took a breath and blew it out. She was staring at the ground, so she didn't see the corners of his mouth tip up as he released her. "Good. Now let's go. It's past time we should have left the harbor."

He glanced down at her as she walked back at his side. He'd never seen her so subdued. She was looking at anything but him. So completely unlike what he'd come to expect from his regal passenger, and he didn't like it. Strange as it might seem, it was much better when she was so sure of herself with those joking eyes and playful words that he didn't always know how to answer. She shouldn't still be afraid of him. It was time to break the silence.

"Did you get what Drusilla wanted?"

She looked up at his face, then relaxed. "Yes. I found just the thing. I'm sure she'll want to read it with you." She took a deep breath as her eyes locked on his. "I don't want her to know I almost got hurt getting it. Please don't tell her."

He smiled down at her. She and her daughter were so much alike; each wanted to protect the other. "As you wish, but only if you don't try to do this again."

A slow breath escaped her, and she offered him an appreciative smile in return. "I won't, Captain. I seldom make the same mistake twice."

He kept glancing at her as he escorted her down the pier and up the gangplank. It had been an eye-opening morning. His stomach had knotted too much when he saw her in the fight. He hadn't meant to get so angry and frighten her, but seeing her in danger had really shaken him.

Who would have thought this woman who had a way of constantly disturbing his balance would no longer be just a passenger to him? Her daughter had become much more than a little girl in need of comfort. He would be sorry when they left his ship...and his life...when they reached Perinthus.

Anthusa pulled the brush slowly through Cornelia's luxurious hair as her mistress sat smiling at the mirror. It was one of those dreamy smiles that Anthusa particularly enjoyed.

Mistress's eyes glowed as she fingered the gold hair pick. "This morning was more exciting than I would have chosen, but it's been a lovely day anyway. I know I made the captain angry, but I'm still glad we got that scroll for Drusilla. She loved it, and I loved watching the captain read it to her."

She leaned close to the mirror and stroked the shallow crow's feet by her right eye. "I do wish that thief hadn't tried to rob me. I don't want him to think I'm a fool, and hanging onto the purse...well, I can't believe I did that." She sighed.

She turned to face Anthusa directly. "He was so mad at me for fighting the thief. It really was stupid of me. But you know, I think he got so angry because it scared him that I could have been hurt."

"I think so, too, mistress."

"Do you think that was only because he wanted to protect Drusilla from losing me? I guess the only thing he really did say was about how it would affect Drusilla. I can tell how much he cares about her. I might only be imagining anything more."

"I don't think so. I can see the captain loves your daughter, but I don't think that's all. I watched him as we walked back. When you weren't looking at him, I think he was looking at you like he cared about you, too."

Mistress's eyebrows lifted. "Really? You're not just saying that to make me feel good?"

"No, mistress. I also saw how he talked with you for a while at dinner before he moved over to sit with Malleolus. He hasn't been doing that before unless you asked him to. He did it himself tonight."

A thoughtful smile lit up Mistress's eyes. "You're right. He did, didn't he? Of course, we only talked about what it's like around Perinthus, but I did always have to ask him to join me before."

She turned back to the mirror. "Malleolus told me that Corinth was about the half-way point on the way to Perinthus. Two weeks isn't much time for a man to decide whether he wants a woman or not. I would really like the captain to want to marry me."

Her eyes turned sad. "The only men who ever wanted me only wanted me because of my money or my family connections. I would so love to have a man want me just for me." She leaned on her elbows to gaze at the plain face reflecting in the mirror. "I would so love to have the captain want me."

Anthusa nodded her agreement. Any man would be lucky to have the mistress as his wife. She had such a generous heart. Even as a girl of fourteen, Mistress Cornelia had appreciated her faithful service. She was only five years older than the mistress, and they had shared so much in the past twenty-five years. It was a pleasure to serve a mistress who always treated her like a friend.

If only there were something she could do to help the captain realize he wanted Mistress as much as she wanted him.

Chapter 20

In the Open

The next evening, supper had been cleared away, and a rising evening breeze made the canopy flutter. Cornelia's thoughts were aflutter, too. She'd spent most of supper listening to the conversation between Hector and Malleolus and wishing she'd been the recipient of the captain's focused attention for as long.

When he first came down from the cabin top, he'd chosen to sit next to her and ask how she'd enjoyed her day. He'd listened as if she were telling him something important as she described one exceptionally pretty part of the coast. Then she made the mistake of telling him she was especially enjoying herself at that moment, that telling him about what she'd seen was even better than seeing it. He'd turned silent, as if he hadn't known what to say. Then he'd excused himself and moved on to Malleolus.

As she watched him rest his forearms on his thighs and lean into the conversation she had no part of, she felt strangely hollow. She was hungry for his company, and she'd only had the appetizer instead of the full meal.

◆

Hector hadn't expected Cornelia to tell him so frankly that his attention pleased her. Since Corinth, he found himself wanting to spend more time talking with her. She was an interesting woman who could describe the most ordinary scene with words that painted its beauty vividly in his mind. She was good with words. Sometimes too good. That gave her an unfair advantage talking with a blunt-speaking man like him. She had a habit of taking something he said and turning its meaning into something funny or embarrassing that left him trying to explain what he really meant.

But even when it might seem she was laughing at him, the look in her eyes told him she wasn't. She just had a playful nature that couldn't resist teasing him sometimes, but somehow that felt good even when it made him uncomfortable. He found himself smiling when she did that. It had been a long time since he'd found it so easy to smile.

Something about her had begun attracting him as a man, and that could become a problem. That attraction surged when she said she especially enjoyed his company that evening. He'd like it to be true, but she was probably only playing with words again. An aristocrat like her was out of his class, and he'd be foolish to let himself become too fond of her.

As he rose to leave them to enjoy the evening by themselves, he yielded to the temptation to walk close to Cornelia. She smelled of roses today—his favorite. Even if she was beyond his reach, he could at least enjoy her perfume.

"Captain."

He was heading for the cabin top, but he stopped to hear what she had to say. "Yes, Cornelia?"

"I think there's something you should know that might increase your enjoyment this trip."

"What would that be?"

"My father-in-law, Publius, was a Christian. Since we went to the restaurant in Corinth, we all know you are, too."

He tensed. It probably wasn't dangerous for her to know, but he thought he'd been careful enough that she wouldn't.

◆

Cornelia saw him freeze at her words. She hadn't meant to worry him. She only wanted to say something that he might especially enjoy hearing. Since the next day was Sunday, she knew exactly what that might be.

"I believe tomorrow is the day Christians usually worship, and I don't want you to feel you need to hide your worship tomorrow morning, like you have the last two weeks. It is perfectly safe for you to do it in front of us."

His whole body relaxed. Then a warm smile spread across his face until he was beaming. His obvious delight that he and his crew would be able to enjoy their worship without time constraints and secrecy was even greater than she expected.

"I'm very glad to hear that. Thank you for telling me."

She smiled a gracious smile in return. She wasn't quite sure what else to say.

The captain tipped his head. "Now if you'll excuse me..."

She watched him walk quickly along the cabin until he turned the corner. The hollow feeling was gone. They hadn't talked much, but it warmed her own heart to have told him something that made him so happy, even if she didn't understand why.

Cornelia's braid tumbled down her back as Anthusa pulled out the last of the gold picks that held it in place. As Anthusa began untwisting the strands in preparation for brushing, Cornelia leaned on her elbows and gazed at her maid in the mirror.

"I did so enjoy talking with the captain at dinner tonight. The only problem was he didn't stay with me long enough. I'm not entirely sure what I said that made him want to leave. Could you tell?"

"Not really, mistress. I thought he was truly enjoying himself. He wasn't looking at anything but you. It seemed to me there was admiration in his eyes."

Cornelia turned to look directly at Anthusa. "Admiration? I wish it were so, but that's not likely."

She turned back to the mirror and gazed at her plain features. The brush slipped through her thick hair. "I certainly admire him. There isn't a single thing about the captain that isn't admirable."

"Any man who was smart could say the same of you, mistress."

"That's not true. We both know I'm not pretty...never have been."

"No one has prettier eyes. Besides, I said a smart man. A smart man would admire you for much more than whether you were pretty."

Cornelia smiled at her devoted slave. "Then let's hope the captain is a very smart man."

Anthusa had almost finished brushing when Cornelia spoke again. "I'm glad I told him we knew about him being a Christian. I've never seen him look happier. It was as if I'd given him a very expensive gift. Why should getting to worship on deck delight him that much?"

"I don't know, mistress, but I can't remember seeing a bigger smile on a man."

"I never understood why Publius wouldn't offer a sacrifice to Caesar and save himself. It seemed like such a small thing to ask. It's not like the sacrifices to the Roman gods actually mean anything. Publius himself convinced me they aren't real when he first became a God-fearer and tried to tell Lucius about it when he dined with us. I don't understand why Christians won't make the sacrifice when it would save their lives."

Anthusa nodded her head but didn't reply as she continued brushing.

"I hope he talks to his men close enough to the canopy that we can hear. I'm curious about what he's going to do that it made him so happy."

"You can stand at the rail where you can hear. I don't think the captain would mind that."

"No, I don't think he would, either."

Anthusa made the final brush strokes and set the brush down on the table.

"There. All loose and lovely. Any man would admire your hair, not just the smart ones." She pulled her fingers through the free-flowing tresses one last time.

Cornelia's eyes shone as she looked at Anthusa in the mirror. "If I were a vain woman, you'd be invaluable. You always point out my best and ignore my worst. It would be nice if that was what the captain saw, too."

"Perhaps he does, mistress. I do think I saw admiration."

Cornelia moved from the chair to her bed. "I hope you're right."

Chapter 21

FIRST STEPS

Sunday morning dawned bright and clear. Except for the sailor manning the rudders, Hector's whole crew had gathered on deck and was waiting for the worship to begin.

As Hector emerged from the cabin with his copy of the gospel written by Luke, Malleolus was waiting for him.

"Captain, if you don't mind, I would like to join you and listen. Publius wanted to tell me about his faith in Jesus, but he was killed before I let him."

Hector placed his hand on Malleolus's shoulder and beamed at him. "You are very welcome."

As the crewmen sat down on the hatch covering the hold and on the deck in front of Hector, Malleolus took his place at the rear of the group. Drusilla came over and sat down beside him. He smiled down at her as he wrapped his arm around her shoulders.

◆

Cornelia was reluctant to sit as close as Malleolus and Drusilla. She didn't want to be where Hector could see plainly what she was thinking. From his delighted response the night before, it was obvious this was extremely important to him. She didn't want him to see any negative reaction she might have, so she stayed back at the railing where she could listen relatively unobserved.

Hector closed his eyes and raised his hand. "We come this morning to worship You, Father, with our prayers and praise. Fill us with Your Spirit so our worship may be worthy for You to receive."

109

Calamus began strumming a lyre, and the voices of the crew blended in song. Cornelia drew a breath and held it. How could this collection of rugged men produce such beautiful music? The smiles on their faces and their glowing eyes revealed a delight like she'd never seen before. No wonder Hector was so glad when she told him they could worship in the open. They could never have sung like this hiding in the crew quarters.

Too soon, the singing ended. Hector held the codex to his chest and closed his eyes. An aura of tranquility surrounded him as he stood breathing slowly and smiling. Then he raised the codex over his head.

"We thank You, Father, for the gift of Your son, Jesus, to save us from our sins, and for this gospel that You have given us that we may know Him. May Your Spirit fill me and give me Your words this day. In the name of Jesus, I pray."

He opened his eyes and lowered the codex. Before he opened it, he looked directly at Cornelia. As his eyes met hers, a smile of sheer delight overspread his face. Cornelia's breath caught. She'd never seen a man look so happy. Was that because she'd come to hear him?

Her heart rate rose as her cheeks and ears warmed. She couldn't pull her eyes away from his. What was he thinking? His smile, his eyes—they looked like those of a man deeply in love, but that couldn't be. At least not yet.

He finally broke the connection. She was both relieved and sorry when he focused his eyes on the codex again. He turned to the page he wanted and began to read.

"Once when Jesus was praying in private and his disciples were with him, he asked them, 'Who do the crowds say I am?' They replied, 'Some say John the Baptist, others say Elijah, and still others, that one of the prophets of long ago has come back to life.' 'But what about you?' He asked. 'Who do you say I am?' Peter answered, 'The Christ of God.' Jesus strictly warned them not to tell this to anyone. And he said, 'The Son of Man must suffer many things and be rejected by the elders, chief priests, and teachers of the law, and he must be killed, and on the third day be raised to life.' Then he said to them all: 'If anyone would come after me, he must deny himself and take up his cross daily and follow me. For whoever wants to save his life will lose it, but whoever loses his life for me will save it. What good is it for a man to gain the whole world, and yet lose or forfeit his very self? If anyone is ashamed of me and my words, the Son of Man will be ashamed of him when he comes in his glory and in the glory of the Father and of the holy angels.

I tell you the truth, some who are standing here will not taste death before they see the kingdom of God.'"

Cornelia stared at Hector. Here was the explanation for the question that had plagued her for eight years. So many times, her anger at Lucius had burned white hot as she thought about the horrible way Publius had been killed. The question of why Publius let himself be killed in the arena had been unanswerable. One meaningless sacrifice to Caesar, and he would have been freed. Here, carried by the deep, rich voice of the man she wanted, was the answer.

But it was a confusing answer. How can a man save his life by losing it? That made no sense at all. But maybe there was meaning to the words that was hidden, that only the Christians could understand. Maybe it was some kind of secret code, but Publius had lived and died like it was literally true. The sacrifice would have been a public denial of his faith. It would have gained his freedom, preserved his wealth, and spared Claudia from heart-rending grief, but would he have lost himself? Would it have destroyed the man he was even while he still lived?

She pulled her thoughts back to what Hector was saying.

"So the things of this world mean nothing in themselves. Wealth, power, position—they only mean something if we use them to serve God. Let each of us be willing to give up anything except our love for Jesus, no matter what it might cost us."

Hector raised his right hand. "May the Lord bless and keep us. May He make His face shine upon us and give us peace."

He nodded at Calamus, and the singing began again. The music wrapped around Cornelia like a warm blanket on a rainy night. Hector's eyes closed, and his face tipped heavenward as he sang. The love she'd seen in his eyes before—it was for his god.

There was something here. Something she'd never felt before. Something that pulled her toward it, frightening yet welcoming at the same time. She wanted the singing to end, but she wanted it to go on forever.

When the last strum of the lyre sounded, the men rose and began embracing each other with hearty slaps and beaming smiles. It was good to be here. It was good to watch this. She could hardly wait for next Sunday, even though she couldn't have told anyone why.

Finally, Hector walked over to her at the rail, his eyes still glowing and a broad smile stretching his lips. "I'm very glad you joined us, Cornelia."

"I am, too, Captain. You explained something I've wondered about for the past eight years."

"What was that?"

"Why Publius chose to die. It never made sense to me before. He loved Claudia so much, and he knew what his death would do to her." She cupped her chin and stroked her cheek. "But if he truly loved Jesus, nothing else, not even Claudia, mattered as much as his commitment to his lord."

Hector nodded. "It doesn't."

She looked deep into his eyes. "Would you make that same choice?"

He nodded again. "I would."

She believed him.

◆

The silence that followed his words couldn't have pleased Hector more. She was thinking deeply about what she'd heard. That was the first step toward hearing God's call and coming. His heart warmed at the thought. Each day he cared about her more, and he knew the joy that awaited her if she decided to follow Jesus. Today was a good first step on the path that would change her forever.

He waved toward the canopy. "I've had the food for my soul. Time now for food for the body. Calamus is putting out the breakfast. Please go ahead."

Cornelia's eyes sparkled. "And I have food for thought. Thank you, Captain."

As she glided down the deck ahead of him, Hector smiled.

Chapter 22

A Contest of Wills

The Drusus town house, Rome

Dinner had been delicious, but it was getting late. Lucius swung his legs off the dining couch and sat up. His best friend, Marcus Corvinus, did the same.

"It's frustrating, Marcus. Three weeks since Cornelia disappeared, and still no sign of her. At least I was able to stop the rumors about her kidnapping Drusilla after I got Didia Galla to spread my version of why she and Drusilla aren't in Rome."

He swirled the wine in his goblet before draining it. "Your idea of having my searchers claim they had a letter for Cornelia worked well. I've sent them to more than a dozen women whom I thought might hide the two of them, and not one of them seemed to suspect I'm hunting for Drusilla. Or if they did, at least they didn't gossip about it."

He set the empty goblet on the table. "But I expect to find Cornelia's hiding place sometime. Then we can proceed with the betrothal. Drusilla will make a good wife for Gnaeus when she's fifteen."

Marcus traced the rim of his goblet with his finger. "Getting the right wife is the least of my worries about him right now."

"Why is that?"

"He crippled a favorite slave of my neighbor's wife. I had to pay three times what she was worth before he agreed not to file a civil suit against me."

Marcus ran his fingers through his hair. "Gnaeus is so unpredictable...most of the time he's fine, then something sets him off. I don't know what to do.

"When he turns fifteen, I should start him training with Brutus. That's when Gaius and Tertius started, but will learning how to use a sword well only make him want to use it? Almost anything can trigger the violence."

He massaged the back of his neck. "And what will happen when he starts the *cursus honorum* in six years? When he's a tribune and wearing a sword all the time, who knows what he might do or how a fellow officer might react to it. Even a centurion might try to stop him if Gnaeus is doing something outrageous enough. A legion commander would back his centurion against a tribune whose proven more trouble than he's worth, no matter who his family is."

His lips tightened. "I'm sorry Cornelia took Drusilla and ran, but maybe she was right. The more I think about it, the less I want to risk your daughter's life with my crazy son."

Lucius shrugged. "She's only ten. I have plenty of time to betroth her, so we don't have to commit them to each other right away. I still want Drusilla back, even if she isn't going to be the means of officially uniting our families."

He slapped Marcus's arm. "Don't despair about this. Gnaeus will get better about controlling his temper as he gets older. Most boys do as they mature. We don't have to make any final decisions on the betrothal for a few years."

Marcus's frown relaxed into a slight smile as he nodded. "True. A lot can change in five years." He slipped his feet into his sandals, and a slave came over to lace them around his calves. "It's been a pleasure, as always, but it's time to return home."

Lucius crossed his arms. "My pleasure as well. I'll probably see you tomorrow at the baths. *Vale*, Marcus."

They entered the atrium together, and Marcus headed toward the exit while Lucius turned toward the peristyle garden.

Through the opening in the roof, he looked up at the stars sprinkled across the night sky. Somewhere, Cornelia and Drusilla might be looking at the same constellations. As soon as he found them, Drusilla would be in his possession again and that was where she would remain. He might not marry her to Gnaeus, but she would always be his to control, not Cornelia's.

Cornelia was ahead at the moment in their contest of wills, but she would most certainly lose before he was through.

Chapter 23

One Step Closer

The week had passed much too quickly, but Cornelia was still glad it was Sunday again. This time she and Anthusa sat with Drusilla and Malleolus.

Hector held the codex in his hands as he closed his eyes. He raised it as he began to speak. "We come again to worship You, Father, with our prayers and praise. Fill us with Your Spirit so our worship may be worthy for You to receive."

Calamus struck the lyre, and again the emotion of the music engulfed Cornelia. It spiraled up and up until it suddenly stopped.

Hector's gaze settled on Cornelia, and his warmest smile lit his face before he dropped his eyes to the codex and began to read.

"'So I say to you: Ask and it will be given to you; seek and you will find; knock and the door will be opened to you. For everyone who asks receives; he who seeks finds; and to him who knocks, the door will be opened. Which of you fathers, if your son asks for a fish, will give him a snake instead? Or if he asks for an egg, will give him a scorpion? If you then, though you are evil, know how to give good gifts to your children, how much more will your Father in heaven give the Holy Spirit to those who ask him!'"

Hector closed the codex and held it to his chest. "Here Jesus is teaching His followers how the Father wants to answer the prayers of those who have become His children by believing in Jesus as their Savior, the perfect sacrifice Who paid for their sins."

Hector's gaze, which had been on Malleolus, locked onto Cornelia.

His eyes...so intense when they first caught her own, then warming like Publius's eyes once had when he spoke of his god.

"He's also teaching how He wants those who are not yet His followers to seek Him, and He promises they will find Him. To knock and He will open the way to Himself. To ask and they will receive salvation and the greatest possible gift, the Holy Spirit, God Himself dwelling inside them because of their faith in Jesus."

The slosh of the waves breaking against the ship and the flutter of the sails faded to silence. It was as if she and Hector and someone she felt but couldn't see were the only ones onboard.

"So whether you already have the peace and joy of knowing Jesus as your Savior or you are wondering about what He has done out of His great love for you, even before you believe in Him, you can be sure He wants to give you only what is best for you. And the best gift of all is Himself."

Hector closed his eyes and raised his right hand. "May the Lord bless and keep us. May He make His face shine upon us and give us peace."

The men began to sing, but this time Cornelia wasn't listening to the music. The echoes of Hector's words drowned out all other sounds.

Could it really be so simple? Just ask and God would live inside her? All she had to do was believe Jesus saved her and she'd be saved? What would that even be like? The thought was both tempting and scary.

Publius had talked about everyone being sinners because even good people made choices that separated them from the one real god, the God of Israel, Who was actually the god of the whole world. He'd talked about the holiness of that god, how He couldn't abide sin in His presence, so He'd told His people how to make sacrifices at the temple in Jerusalem to cover their sins, year by year. Publius had worried about how the sins could be covered after Emperor Titus destroyed the Jewish temple.

But then Publius decided to believe Jesus was the final perfect sacrifice who made any more animal sacrifices unnecessary, and her wisest friend died before he could explain his choice to her. But how could one man's death pay for all the sins of all people? And how could a god actually dwell inside everyone who believed in him?

She couldn't get her mind around it. But maybe that was what he meant by seeking. Maybe she just needed to learn more about it all, and then it would make sense. She didn't even have the questions clear enough in her own mind to ask Hector yet. Ask, seek...she would work on both.

She once more became aware of the rich male voices surrounding her. Then it was over, and the men were embracing and conversing happily.

Hector came to her side. "I hope you enjoyed the worship."

"More than you know, Captain."

She almost asked him her questions, but she stopped herself. She needed to plan out what she would ask. This was so important to him that she wanted to get the questions right, and she had to sort some things in her mind before she was ready.

"You've given me more food for thought. And I know food for our bodies awaits us under the canopy. I'm ready for that now."

Hector motioned for her to go ahead of him. "After you."

In the afternoon, Hector stood atop the cabin. His eyes scanned the clouds on the horizon, but he wasn't really seeing them. More important things occupied his mind. Today's worship had given him exceptional pleasure. Watching his passengers listen so intently to the gospel reading and then to his own words had made his heart sing. Nothing could make him happier than for Cornelia's whole party to decide to follow Jesus.

Especially her.

It was funny how each day he liked her more. Who would have thought when they argued that first day in Portus that it would take less than four weeks for his regal passenger to become a genuine friend? A friend...and a sister if she would only decide to follow Jesus. Maybe even a woman he could marry after she shared his faith.

His eyebrows shot up. Where had that thought come from? A laugh almost escaped his lips over that one. Cornelia Scipia would never consider marrying a ship's captain who had risen from being a farm slave to owning a farm himself. No one could be more truly an aristocrat than she was, and there was no way she would consider anyone but an aristocrat for her next husband. Yes, she liked him as a friend. There was no doubt about that, but to rise above friendship to marriage... that was beyond what was possible. Captains and queens only wed in children's stories, and this was real life.

Chapter 24

Two Fine Men

Ephesus

Drusilla stood by Hector atop the cabin as the ship was pulled into the Ephesus pier by the rowboats. As the crew began casting the ropes to the dockworkers to secure the ship, Hector smiled down at his little first mate.

"Go tell your mother I want to speak with her as soon as the gangplank is lowered."

"Yes, Captain." She walked briskly to the ladder and climbed down to go find Cornelia.

When Hector descended the ladder himself, he found Cornelia watching him from the rail. As he walked toward her, that playful upturn appeared at the corner of her lips, and the twinkling look in her eyes warned him something was coming. He was in for some teasing, but that was perfectly fine with him.

She was struggling to keep a straight face as she squared her shoulders and stood erect at his approach. He half expected her to salute him. "You summoned me, Captain?"

Her barely suppressed grin brought a smile to his face as well. "I did. I thought you might enjoy a trip to the bath and a good dinner tonight. Ephesus can safely provide both. It will be the last good opportunity before we reach Perinthus in about a week."

"What a lovely idea. Would you prefer I be plain or fancy for this excursion?"

He wasn't going to touch that one. Whatever he answered, she'd find some way to turn the words to tease him.

"Suit yourself, Cornelia. However you want to dress is fine here. Surprise me."

He was sure he'd chosen his words carefully enough to avoid the tease. Why then did her eyes suddenly sparkle as she gave him that smile that usually showed her delight in flipping his words around?

She turned without a word and headed into the cabin. He found himself looking forward to the surprise.

Cornelia emerged from the cabin in her Roman finery. Even with her hair in her usual simple style, she looked as regal as she had standing on the pier in Portus. But now Hector knew there was a loving mother and playful woman under that queenly demeanor. A woman whose company made him feel both comfortable and off balance. First a trip to the private bath he always visited when he docked in Ephesus, then a good dinner at a restaurant nearby where he'd never seen Romans wearing purple stripes. It should be an enjoyable evening for them both.

For greater privacy and quiet conversation, Hector had chosen a table near the back wall. Cornelia, Drusilla, and Anthusa had their backs angled toward the door, while he and Malleolus faced it.

A Roman dressed in his toga and tunic with the wide purple stripes marking him as a senator entered the restaurant. He condescendingly scanned the people seated at the tables. When his eyes locked on Cornelia, Hector's spine stiffened.

The senator's eyebrows shot up, and a broad smile appeared as he began his walk toward her.

Malleolus spotted him and spoke in a near-whisper. "Cornelia. We have company. Someone who knows you."

Hector focused on Cornelia. Her eyes widened like a deer facing a dog pack, and he kicked himself mentally. He'd picked this restaurant because he'd never seen a senator here before. Why did there have to be one today?

She took a deep breath and locked her gaze on her hands as they rested in her lap. Even before she completely released that breath, those eyes looked calm, collected. He'd never seen anyone so quickly mask great agitation. His eyes remained fixed on her face as she waited for the senator to approach her and speak.

"Cornelia Scipia?"

Her most gracious smile appeared as she turned in her chair to face the Roman.

"Manlius Atticus. What a pleasant surprise. It's been quite some time since we last met."

She held out her hand to him, and he wrapped his fingers around her own. The senator's eyes looked genuinely delighted to see her and not just as an acquaintance. The corners of Hector's mouth started to turn down. It took a conscious effort to keep that from happening.

"It has, indeed, Cornelia. Much too long. What brings you to Ephesus?"

"I grew tired of staying alone at the estate outside Rome. I felt like doing something different. I've heard for so many years about the wonders of Ephesus, so I thought a sea voyage to see them would be entertaining."

"And what do you think of the beauties of the city?"

"We've only just arrived, so I have no opinion yet. Have you been here long?"

"Not quite a week. I'm on my way home from Antioch. I'll be catching a ship to Thessalonica tomorrow. From there I'm going home on the Via Egnatia. It's too late in the season to go all the way by ship before the sea closes."

"Yes, I suppose that's true. I guess that means it would be a good idea for me to spend the winter here. That sounds appealing, actually. It might be quite pleasant to stay someplace other than Rome for a few months and return in the spring."

"But what about Drusus? Surely he'll miss you." Atticus's voice dripped sarcasm as one corner of his mouth pulled upward.

Hector switched his gaze from her aristocratic friend to Cornelia herself. She sat like a queen on a throne, bestowing her gracious smile on Atticus, but the flicker of distress in her eyes before she masked it triggered the start of another frown. He once more focused on blocking it.

She laughed, and it sounded genuine to him. How could she do that?

"I'm certain he'll miss me terribly if he ever bothers to go out to the estate to look for me, but I'm also certain his regular women will comfort him in my absence. He's found them sufficient for years. He won't lack for entertainment, so we don't have to worry about Lucius suffering while I'm gone from Rome."

With the sarcasm in her voice, she even seemed to be sharing in the senator's ironic humor. No trace there of the bitterness he would have expected after such treatment.

Atticus laughed again, and Hector's mouth tilted down until he forced it back up. What did that laugh mean?

The look in the Roman's eyes, that was too easy to interpret. He admired her as a woman…and he wanted her. "I always thought Drusus was a fool to trade you for the pretty, mindless things he's wasted his time with for so long. It's amazed me for years how such an intelligent man could make such a stupid choice."

Cornelia's gracious smile and nod were all the response she gave.

Atticus still held her hand. As he began to caress the back of it with his thumb, Hector found himself fighting the frown again.

"It amazes me even more that you've stayed married to him. If you ever do decide to divorce Drusus, I'm not the only man in Rome who would be glad to hear it. However, I might be the most eager to do something about it." His mouth turned up in the kind of smile that punctuated his meaning. Hector's mouth became an inverted reflection of the senator's until he forced it back into a straight line. "My wife has been dead for two years. Perhaps it's time I remarried. I would be much more appreciative than he's been."

Cornelia's laugh carried the chimes of tiny bells within it. "That's very kind of you to say, Atticus, and it's probably quite true. My dowry remains intact, thanks to the exceptional talent of Publius's steward for making money. I'm sure many would find marrying me appealing. Golden hair isn't the only gold that makes a woman irresistibly attractive to the men of our acquaintance."

Atticus laughed at her response. It sounded genuine to Hector, but these Roman aristocrats were so good at hiding their true thoughts that it was hard to know for sure. The senator was not trying to hide his romantic intentions. Hector's breath came faster as he watched the obvious interest flame in the senator's eyes.

"You have much more than your gold to recommend you, and you well know it."

Two men entered the restaurant and waved at Atticus.

"My dinner companions have arrived, so I'll leave you now. Perhaps I'll see you again in the spring when we're both back in Rome. We can spend some time together and see where that leads." There was that smile that got Hector breathing faster again.

"Perhaps so. I wish you a safe journey home."

With a final suggestive smile at Cornelia and a quick flick of his gaze toward Hector, Atticus left them to join his friends.

Cornelia turned back toward their table, blocking Atticus's view of her face. A barely perceptible furrow flitted across her brow. Her face relaxed, but there was still something off balance in her eyes. If he hadn't become so familiar with her every expression, he would have missed it.

Malleolus reached over and covered her hand where it rested on the table. "That was most unfortunate. I didn't expect to see someone who would recognize you here."

His voice was much quieter than normal, but his expression was relaxed and even happy as he spoke. Hector's gaze bounced between the two of them. They were both masters at deception.

"Neither did I. Atticus is not one of Lucius's good friends, but he's not his enemy, either. I don't know how often they meet or what they might talk about."

"Is he going to tell Father where we are?" Drusilla blinked twice as she whispered her question.

Cornelia directed a smile at her daughter that masked any worry. "I have no reason to think he will. He and your father are not close friends. By the time Atticus gets back to Rome, our meeting will probably be long forgotten. There's nothing for you to be afraid of, dear."

She turned her smile on Hector and lowered her voice even more "Perhaps I should explain, Captain. Lucius still may not know I've divorced him. I left the legal certificate in a box for him in the estate office, but he won't find it until he bothers to go to the estate. It would not surprise me if he hasn't been there since we left. He'll notice Malleolus is gone long before he'll miss me. I brought Drusilla with me without his consent. He was going to marry her to his best friend's son. The boy's a monster. I'll do anything I can to prevent that, no matter what it takes."

"I know some about why you're here, Cornelia. You don't need to explain."

"I want to explain. I want you to know everything."

He would have reached over and covered her hand with his if Malleolus hadn't beaten him to it. He didn't like seeing the tightness at the corners of her eyes and the strained smile that didn't quite hide her distress. Her acting might fool the Roman, but it wasn't perfect enough to fool him.

"I appreciate you taking me into your confidence."

"You're a man who inspires confidence in every way."

The total sincerity in her elegant eyes was unmistakable. It was nothing like the play-acting with her aristocratic friend. He felt the full force of the compliment, and his frown flipped into a smile.

Malleolus lifted his hand from hers. "We are being observed by the good senator. It would be wise to look like we're enjoying ourselves."

Cornelia nodded and immediately her demeanor changed. If Hector hadn't known how concerned she was that she'd been recognized, he would never have suspected. She and Malleolus were conversing as if they hadn't a care in the world. The Roman should suspect nothing. He shifted his gaze past her to Atticus and caught the Roman watching him as well.

Atticus and his friends ate quickly. As the other two headed toward the door, he approached their table again.

Cornelia put on her mask and turned to smile up at him.

He spoke softly so his companions wouldn't hear. "You needn't worry that Lucius will hear from me that you're in Ephesus. My father always spoke well of Publius Drusus, and I think your husband is a disgrace to the family name."

Atticus glanced at Drusilla, who sat staring up at him with wide eyes. "I know Corvinus can't find a wife for his crazy son. I rejected his request for my daughter. I'm glad to see you've protected yours. I hope you enjoy your stay in Ephesus. I fear you may need to remain for some time to keep her safe. Too bad. If you do return to Rome and divorce him, remember my interest. You know full well it's never been only your dowry that I consider worth pursuing."

"Thank you for telling me, Atticus." Gratitude brightened her voice.

The senator picked up her hand and held it between both of his. As his fingers caressed the back of it, the corners of Hector's mouth turned down and stayed there.

"If you want to know what's going on in Rome, write me. Your location will remain our secret." The genuine warmth in his eyes as he held her gaze kindled equal warmth in hers. "I'll leave you now to enjoy the company of your friends."

His eyes cooled as they lingered on Hector. "I can see you don't have to worry about finding someone to take care of you here." He flipped his gaze back on her face, and his eyes warmed again. "Don't forget there is someone in Rome with much more to offer."

He favored her with another meaningful smile before releasing her hand. Then he fixed cold eyes on Hector and nodded once before turning to follow his companions out the door.

Cornelia turned her gaze back on Hector. He was looking at her with his honest eyes and a slight smile on his lips. Atticus clearly did not like him being with her. What did Atticus see that she didn't? She'd love to think the captain wanted to be the man who'd take care of her, but she couldn't tell if that were the case.

Atticus had always been gifted at flattery. Perhaps what he said was only that, but the way he looked at the captain suggested otherwise. He was right that many men would be interested in her when her divorce became known, but there was only one man whose interest she desired. She had one more week with him on the ship. But would that be enough?

Anthusa had released the braid from its pins and was working her fingers through the plaits to free Mistress's hair for brushing. Mistress rested her elbows on the table and her chin in her hands. A sigh escaped as she gazed at her face in the mirror.

"That was a close call tonight. I'm so glad it was Atticus and not one of the men who are Lucius's friends. I'm sure I can trust him not to say anything."

"That's good, mistress. It would be best if the master had no idea which way you've taken Drusilla."

"Even if someone did see us here in Ephesus, it might not be a total disaster. Perinthus is so far off the normal routes. Still, if he knew we came so far east, Lucius would probably guess I was going to Claudia or Titus. He never believed them when they wrote that they forgave him for killing Publius and for trying to drag Claudia back to Rome to marry Sabinus. He'd suspect they would help me to get even with him. It's the sort of thing he would do. I don't know if Lucius has had any contact with Titus since he decided to stay in Perinthus when he finished his military service. Malleolus took care of everything at Titus's estate north of Rome. I'm not sure who will do that now."

Anthusa just nodded as she continued brushing. Mistress looked at her in the mirror.

"I'm glad Malleolus decided to come with us. I enjoy his company so much. So does the captain. I think they've become good friends."

Anthusa tightened her lips to keep her smile from becoming a grin. She enjoyed watching Mistress think about the captain. It always brightened her mistress's spirits, and sometimes it put a dreamy look in her eyes that made her look positively young again. She hated to see Mistress sad. She'd seen that too much in the last eight years.

"Did you see the way Atticus looked at the captain when he came to our table after he ate?"

"Yes, mistress. I don't think he liked the captain being there with you. I think he was jealous."

"Even when we were young, I often got the feeling that Atticus might have wanted to marry me if Lucius hadn't done it first. He always sought me out to talk awhile whenever he saw me somewhere. He's always said flattering things to me. I never thought he meant any of them, but given what he said tonight, maybe he did. It's certain he doesn't need my money. He's very rich himself."

"I'm not surprised that a smart man like him would admire you. The master was stupid not to appreciate you more."

Mistress turned in the chair to face Anthusa. "I really was surprised when Atticus said that about the captain taking care of me. I know he takes care of us by keeping us safe when we go ashore, but Atticus seemed to imply much more than that. Just being our escort wouldn't be something that would make him jealous."

"I think the captain likes you a great deal. I think he admires you as a woman, and the senator saw that."

"If he does, then why doesn't he say something or do something to let me know for certain? What did Atticus see that I'm missing?"

She turned back to face the mirror. "Maybe there's nothing there, but sometimes it really feels like there might be. We'll be talking, and I know I have his full attention. It seems like he's enjoying our conversation. Then suddenly he just excuses himself and leaves. Why does he do that if he's interested in me?"

She rested her chin on her hands again as Anthusa pulled the brush through her hair. "I don't know what to make of him. He's so unlike the men in Rome. I can predict how most of them will act. The captain still mystifies me."

She turned again to look at Anthusa. "There's only about a week left. What if he doesn't say anything before we land? I don't know if there will be any chance to see him again after we leave his ship. I already know he's the man I want. Why can't he see that and do something about it?" She sighed. "But maybe I've just been fooling myself.

Maybe he really has no interest in me, and he's just being kind. He is so very kind."

"I don't think that's what it is, mistress. I've seen how he looks at you sometimes when you're not looking at him. I'm sure there's admiration in that look."

"Then why doesn't he say something?" Cornelia sighed.

"I also think the captain didn't like the way the senator was interested in you. Maybe that's why the senator said that. Maybe it takes a man to know what another man is thinking."

Cornelia choked on a chuckle. "Two fine men jealous for my attention? That would be an amazing thing. Lucius would find it laughable if anyone tried to tell him that was possible."

"Like the senator said, the master has been a fool for years not to appreciate you. The captain is no fool. I think he'll decide you're exactly the woman he wants, just like you want him."

Cornelia turned to face Anthusa again "I am so glad I brought you with me. You always know exactly what to say to cheer me up. You're right. The captain is no fool, and there's still a week before we reach Perinthus. He lives there, too, so I really have until the sea opens again in the spring. I'm sure he'll want to see Drusilla, so he'll come visit if I ask him."

"I think he'll want to visit you as much as Drusilla."

"I hope so, Anthusa. I truly hope so."

Chapter 25

ONLY DREAMS

Hector awoke shortly after midnight. Many days had passed since he last dreamed about Philip meeting him in Perinthus. A new dream drove him out to the rail.

In the dream, he was at his farm. As he rode up to the house, he called out to let Damara and Charissa know he was home. He swung his leg over the horse's neck and slid to the ground. As he walked the horse to the stable, a pair of small arms wrapped around his waist from behind. When he turned in that embrace, it was Drusilla beaming up at him. He bent over and kissed her forehead.

When he straightened up, Cornelia stood before him, her playful eyes sparkling as she smiled. Drusilla stepped out of the way so her mother could wrap her own arms around him. She slowly rubbed his back as she rested her cheek against his chest. Then she tipped her head so she could look up at his face.

His heart beat faster as the love radiating from those deep blue eyes engulfed and embraced him. He wrapped his arms around her and drew her closer. As she placed her hand on the back of his neck and began pulling his lips down to hers, he awoke.

He stepped quietly from the cabin and walked to the rail. His fingers gripped its well-oiled surface as he stood alone in the moonlight. The ship was still tied to the pier, so he couldn't watch her cutting through the waves, as had become his custom after waking from a dream. He had to settle for watching for the flickering torch of the occasional person walking on the road above the wharves.

He slid his hand back and forth on the smooth wood and sighed.

If only that dream could become reality. He already loved Drusilla like a daughter. The more time he spent close to Cornelia, the more he wanted to be with her. There couldn't possibly be a more devoted mother. She was a gracious lady with a playful sense of humor that delighted even while it disturbed his balance. He'd been mired so long in sadness, but she'd made him laugh again. Those elegant blue eyes—a man could drown in them when she was serious, and no one could resist smiling when they were teasing.

She seemed to enjoy his company at least as much as he did hers. In time, who knew where that might lead? She hadn't decided to follow Jesus yet, but she was definitely interested. Surely faith would come. She was a woman a man could gladly spend a lifetime with.

There was only one problem, but it was a huge one.

She was Cornelia Scipia, daughter of one of the noblest Roman families, born and raised to move in circles of wealth and power. The gold in her chests was enough to buy even Philip's estates near Perinthus. The senator clearly wanted her as his wife. He'd practically proposed right there in the restaurant. There must be a dozen aristocrats who would find her as attractive as he did. Any man with half a mind would.

How could he possibly expect a woman like her to be willing to marry a man like him? He was only a ship's captain. He straightened up and kicked the deck. A deep sigh escaped before he turned and trudged back to the cabin.

Dreams were just that...only dreams. It was best not to expect they would ever come true.

Mare Propontis

When Sunday came around again, they were only two days out from Perinthus. As Hector came from the cabin with the codex in his hand, his gaze fell on Cornelia. She sat with Drusilla between her and Malleolus. A satisfied smile lifted the corners of his mouth. The three of them had all become much more than passengers. Malleolus was a good friend, and he loved both Drusilla and her mother. To see them so interested in learning about Jesus—it filled his heart with joy. Cornelia would never become his wife, but she still might become his sister.

As he stood in front of his assembled crew, it was Cornelia who drew his gaze. She was watching him with an eagerness that fired his own heart.

Hector closed his eyes and raised his hand. "We come this morning to worship you, Father, with our prayers and praise. Fill us with your Spirit so our worship may be worthy for You to receive."

Calamus strummed the lyre, and the men raised their voices in praise. After several songs, Hector raised his hand and began the reading.

"'A farmer went out to sow his seed. As he was scattering the seed, some fell along the path; it was trampled on, and the birds of the air ate it up. Some fell on rock, and when it came up, the plants withered because they had no moisture. Other seed fell among thorns, which grew up with it and choked the plants. Still other seed fell on good soil. It came up and yielded a crop, a hundred times more than was sown.' When he said this, he called out, 'He who has ears to hear let him hear.'

"His disciples asked him what this parable meant. He said, 'The knowledge of the secrets of the kingdom of God has been given to you, but to others I speak in parables, so that, 'though seeing, they may not see; though hearing, they may not understand.'

"This is the meaning of the parable: The seed is the word of God. Those along the path are the ones who hear, and then the devil comes and takes away the word from their hearts, so that they may not believe and be saved. Those on the rock are the ones who receive the word with joy when they hear it, but they have no root. They believe for a while, but in the time of testing they fall away.

"The seed that fell among thorns stands for those who hear, but as they go on their way they are choked by life's worries, riches, and pleasures, and they do not mature. But the seed on good soil stands for those with a noble and good heart, who hear the word, retain it, and by persevering produce a crop.'"

He closed the codex. "There is nothing God wants more than for each of us to listen to His word, hear His call, and come to Him through our faith in Jesus as our savior. There is nothing the devil wants more than to keep each of us from doing that. It's easy to hear the word and get excited about it right away. Many have done that. But then the hard part comes. There will be trials and testing that make it hard and even dangerous to stay firm in our faith, loyal to Jesus. There is the very real danger that we might die in an arena or be killed with a sword for refusing to deny Jesus as our Lord."

He glanced at Cornelia and saw her nodding slowly. Again, his heart thrilled that he'd had the chance to plant the seed in her mind and heart. It would be fed and watered whether she lived with Titus or Philip. He'd be praying that God brought it to full blossom.

"But there are other dangers, more subtle than the hostility of the Emperor and his governors. The choice between Jesus and betrayal is clear and swift then. There can be the slow drifting away from holding Jesus as important above all else. We can be like the seed among thorns, where we don't lose our faith or our life, but we let other things become too important so we never grow and bear the fruit God intends.

"We're about to spend four months on land, where the temptations are much greater. As we spend time apart, let each of us continue to pray for the others, that we may remain strong in the faith until we sail together again in the spring."

Hector raised his right hand. "May the Lord bless and keep us. May he make his face shine upon us and give us peace."

The men's voices blended in praise, lifting his own spirit higher. His eyes were drawn to Cornelia. She sat by Drusilla, her eyes closed, swaying to the music.

His heart swelled with love for her.

Thank you, Father, for bringing her to me. Thank you for using her and Drusilla to break the chain of the grief that had stolen my joy. Even though she'll never become my wife, I thank you for blessing me with her friendship. I thank you even more that you let me see the start of her walk toward You.

Even if nothing else came from her voyage with him, she would decide to follow Jesus, just as Titus and Claudia had.

Lucius Fidelis might be an unwitting servant of the devil himself, but God had used his evil intentions to produce the salvation of Titus and Claudia. Hector would be praying that God would do the same for his three passengers who had become treasured friends.

It was their last morning at sea. Breakfast was the same bread, fruit, and cheese that Calamus usually served, but it was all Cornelia could do to eat any of it. She watched Hector talking with Malleolus. His forearms rested on his knees, and he was smiling and nodding as he focused on Malleolus's words.

She'd hoped he would eat with her. She longed to have those honest eyes locked on her own, to make his mouth twitch as she teased him, to watch his eyes crinkle when she made him almost laugh.

She suppressed a sigh. Hector seemed to enjoy her company, but he'd given her no clear sign that he was planning to do anything to make their time together continue past when they docked in Perinthus.

And now, on the last morning she'd get to spend with him on his ship, he'd chosen to talk with Malleolus instead of her.

Then his eyes turned on her, and her pulse raced. Was that the same longing in his eyes that she knew must be in her own? Their eyes caught and held. Then he pulled his away as Malleolus asked a question.

How much she'd hoped five weeks would be sufficient for him to decide he wanted to marry her. Five weeks together every day...but it wasn't quite enough. Somehow, she had to find a way to spend more time with him before he sailed in the spring.

◆

Hector tried to stay focused on what Malleolus was telling him, but it was hard. Cornelia was close enough that he occasionally caught the scent of her rose perfume. After this voyage, he'd never be able to pass a rose bush without seeing her teasing blue eyes and laughing lips.

Why did she have to be Cornelia Scipia, noble daughter of Imperial Rome? Why couldn't she have just been Cornelia, a woman that a captain could hope to marry?

As much as he'd wanted to spend one last breakfast talking with her, he'd chosen Malleolus instead. There was no point in making her departure more painful by adding one more playful conversation to his memories. She was wealthy beyond the wildest dreams of most men, and her ancestors had ruled Rome for centuries. If she ever decided she wanted to remarry, she'd choose an aristocrat like the senator Atticus who'd approached her in Ephesus.

He glanced at her and their eyes locked. No matter how much he wanted it, she'd never be only Cornelia. Then Malleolus asked a question, and he focused on their conversation once more. He was glad to have the distraction.

Captains and queens moved in two different worlds, and only a fool let himself forget that.

Chapter 26

Coming Home

Perinthus, Thracia

As the ship slipped up to the dock, Hector looked down at Drusil-la standing beside him on the cabin top. She wasn't watching his crew. Her jaw was clamped as she stared at her feet.

"As soon as we finish docking, I'll go up to the shipping office and send word to your uncle's house. You and your mother will be home before dinner."

She slid her hand into his and held on tight. He gave it a gentle squeeze. She turned her face up to him. The tears weren't flowing yet, but they were close.

"I don't want to leave you, Captain."

He didn't want her to leave, but she wasn't his little girl, no matter how much he wanted her to be.

"I live near Perinthus, too. After you get settled in, maybe I can come visit you."

She brightened at the prospect. "Promise? I know Mother and Mal-leolus would like that, too."

"I promise."

"And you always keep your promises. Mother says you're the most honest man she ever met."

A lopsided smile twisted his mouth. He and Cornelia had come a long way since their argument about honesty and trust the day she boarded in Portus.

Conversations with Cornelia had become the high points of his day, even though they sometimes provoked him into saying things that came out wrong. Those laughing eyes captivated him when she twisted one of his simple, honest statements into something he didn't mean and then teased him about her twisted version.

He shook his head almost imperceptibly to end that foolish reverie and focused back on Drusilla.

"You can watch everything from here where it's safe. Stay on the cabin top unless Malleolus or your mother comes to get you. I'll be back shortly."

"Yes, Captain." She didn't look happy, but he'd stopped any tears when he promised to visit.

He climbed down and strode to the gangplank. Before stepping off the deck, he turned to look at her. Her eyes were locked on him, and her hand shot up and swung back and forth. His own hand swept the air twice before he headed down to the pier. When he reached the top of the ramp that led up to the road, he looked back. He saw her reaching as high as she could to wave again. He raised his hand before heading up the road to Philip's shipping office.

Hector's son, Marcario, looked up from his desk when the door opened. "Father! Welcome home!"

His father's broad smile and outspread arms as he approached spoke volumes. "It's good to be home." He embraced Marcario and slapped him on the shoulder as he stepped back.

The change in his father since he left for Rome raised Marcario's eyebrows. Father had departed ensnared by inconsolable grief. He'd returned with a smile in his eyes again.

"I need to send a message to Titus and Claudia. I have their sister-in-law Cornelia and her daughter on my ship. She's moving here and needs to stay with one of them for a while."

"I can take care of everything, Father. I'll send a messenger to get a raeda from Titus or Philip, and I have a wagon here. When the raeda comes, I'll send them both down to the pier."

"Good. She'll need a couple of armed men to escort her as well."

Marcario nodded. "Of course." He already knew theirs was a very wealthy family.

He took a deep breath before asking the question that would tell him how his father was really doing. "Will you be at the farm tonight?"

Father rested his hand on Marcario's shoulder. "Yes. I'll be at the farm most of the time until we sail again in the spring. God has given me peace with the past. It's time to look to the future instead."

Marcario's broad smile stretched his whole face. "I'm glad, Father. This past year was almost like I lost you as well when we lost Mother and Charissa. It's good to have you back."

The trunks that had travelled in the hold had all been loaded into the wagon. The trunks from their rooms sat on the ground, ready to load. Hector told the wagon driver to take everything to Philip's house as soon as they finished loading. Then he headed down the ramp and back to his ship. All that remained were her perfume box, her chest of jewels, and the five chests containing her dowry gold. He would oversee the loading of her treasure himself.

◆

Cornelia sat on her bunk and gazed out the window. That first day, she'd thought this room so small and Spartan. Now she wished she didn't have to leave it.

She partly wanted that because Hector made Drusilla so happy. He'd treated her like his own daughter, and Drusilla loved him dearly. She definitely wanted to keep him in their lives for Drusilla's sake. But that wasn't the main reason.

She wanted him in their lives for herself. He was so kind and honest and fun to tease and...the list of what made him wonderful was almost endless. If he would just ask her, nothing could keep her from saying yes in an instant. If he were a noble Roman like Atticus, she'd ask him herself. Her cousin had proposed to her second husband, and he'd been glad to marry into the rich Scipio family. But that wouldn't work with this Greek sea captain. He cared nothing for her wealth and noble birth. A man like him made up his own mind about things. He wouldn't like being told what she wanted him to do before he decided to do it himself.

She closed her eyes and wished he would step into her room, take her hand, and tell her right then and there that he wanted her as his wife. She opened them when she heard his footsteps in the galley. When his frame filled her doorway, the distance in his eyes told her that wish would not come true...at least not yet.

◆

Hector found Cornelia sitting on her bunk, her hand resting on the jewelry box on the bed beside her. Those jewels, the gold in the boxes under her bunk and his own...they anchored her in a noble world that could never include him. It had been too easy to forget that at sea, to think of her as simply Cornelia, not a woman richer than many kings. But it was time for her to return to her world and leave him behind in his.

"Cornelia, I know your future lies in these treasure boxes, so I thought I'd load them in the raeda myself."

She tipped her head and graced him with a smile. "Thank you, Captain. Of course, I would trust any of your crewmen to help me with the chests, but I especially appreciate your offer."

He pressed his lips together to keep the laugh from escaping as he remembered their discussion of what to do with her treasure chests when she boarded in Portus. He picked up her chest of jewels.

The flush of pink that swept across her cheeks betrayed her remembrance of that first conversation as well. He struggled to suppress the grin, but it broke free anyway.

It had often been his ears turning red over something he'd said that came out wrong. She blushed so seldom. That was too bad. She looked almost pretty when she did.

"The raeda is waiting." He indicated the door with a nod of his head. "After you, Cornelia."

"Thank you, Captain." She tilted her head and smiled at him as she rose. His eyes followed her as she preceded him through the door. Every step seemed effortless and elegant, like a dance. He was going to miss watching her.

Anthusa followed her mistress with the box of perfumes, and Hector fell in behind. As he emerged from the cabin, Drusilla stepped up beside him.

"You promised to come visit soon. When will you come, Captain?"

"In a few days. You'll want to get settled in first."

Malleolus fell in beside him. "I want to thank you, Captain. I'm sure I speak for Cornelia as well when I say it's been a pleasure sailing with you."

Hector's eyes remained fixed on Cornelia as she walked several paces ahead of him. "It's been a pleasure for me, too. I've enjoyed our many talks."

◆

Malleolus saw where Hector's eyes were focused. He hadn't lived almost seventy years without knowing the look of a man who wanted a woman but didn't know what to do about it. Perhaps there was one more service he could perform for Cornelia, even here in Thracia.

"I hope you'll come visit so we can have many more. I know Cornelia agrees with me that we couldn't have had a better man to bring us from Rome than you."

They had reached the raeda, where Cornelia stood waiting for them. Malleolus had seen enough of the patrician women of Rome to know what the look on her face meant. Her natural poise concealed the depth of her feelings, and the captain probably didn't even suspect the strength of her desire for him under that calm exterior. If Hector ever found the courage to ask for her hand, he'd find her just as eager.

Hector turned his eyes on Malleolus. "Nothing would please me more. It's been good to have you all with me." His eyes turned back on Cornelia. "I'm going to miss my little first mate."

Malleolus's lips twitched as he fought the grin that almost escaped. Miss his little first mate. Yes, that was probably true, but the captain's eyes spoke more clearly than his words. The mate he really wanted was a helpmate to fill his life with the love of a woman again. The captain might need some help getting what he wanted, but Malleolus was the right man to help them both get the desire of their hearts.

◆

Cornelia stepped aside so Malleolus could open the door, and Hector slid the jewel chest under the seat. Three of his crew were bringing the first installment of her gold chests up the ramp behind him. He slid those into place as his men returned for the final two.

She stepped closer to Hector. "I can't thank you enough, Captain, for making our voyage such a pleasure. I especially want to thank you for your kindness to Drusilla. I believe it's been the finest time she's ever had."

Drusilla stood beside her, her head bouncing in agreement.

Hector placed his hand on the side of Drusilla's head as he smiled down at her. The love in his eyes as he gazed at her daughter was as great as any father's could be.

"I enjoyed having your daughter on my ship as much as she did."

Drusilla beamed at him.

Cornelia's heart beat faster when he turned his eyes back on her.

"It was a pleasure having you all with me. I'm glad it worked out for you to come here on my ship." Those honest brown eyes—who could ever doubt his words?

She kept her gaze locked on his eyes, willing him to do the same.

How could she tell him she didn't want to leave him so he'd ask her to stay?

She was still struggling with that question when his crewmen arrived with the last two chests. His eyes broke free as he turned away to receive them. As he loaded them into the raeda, she held back a sigh. Why couldn't his men have taken longer?

When he withdrew from the carriage, he looked at Drusilla instead of her.

"In you go, child. You have cousins waiting for you."

Drusilla clambered in and turned to smile at him. "Maybe two days? No more than five."

"We'll see." He turned to offer his hand to Cornelia. "Allow me to assist."

"Thank you, Captain." She placed her hand in his. Even the simple sensation of his hand wrapped around hers made her heart feel like it was skipping beats.

◆

There was that gracious smile Hector had seen so often. Regal as a queen, but what a loving mother. She was the mother Drusilla deserved. Growing to love that precious girl had healed his own heart. God had truly blessed him the day He brought them to his ship.

Too bad the voyage was over.

He helped Cornelia up into the carriage. Anthusa climbed in, and Malleolus was right behind her.

Hector stood with his hand on the open door, in no hurry for them to leave. His eyes were riveted on Cornelia until Malleolus spoke.

He leaned forward in his seat and turned toward Hector. "I hope you'll visit soon, Captain."

Cornelia took up the refrain. "Yes, Captain. As Drusilla said, please make it no more than five days. We all look forward to seeing you again."

His eyes locked on hers again, and the satisfaction of her specific invitation triggered a broad smile. "As you and Drusilla wish, Cornelia. Not more than five days."

He broke eye contact and stepped back from the carriage. Then he slapped the side to tell the driver to leave, and the mules put the raeda into motion.

◆

The carriage started with a lurch. Cornelia's stomach lurched as well. It hurt to leave the man who'd be the perfect father for Drusilla...

and the perfect husband for her. But perhaps he wouldn't wait the full five days.

Drusilla hung out the window, waving goodbye to the only father she'd ever known. When she pulled herself back inside, she tried to smile. "He promised he'd come visit. I hope he really does."

Cornelia leaned forward and rested her hand on her daughter's cheek. "I'm sure he will. The captain would never break his word."

Drusilla's smile brightened as she nodded her agreement.

Cornelia gazed out the window, but she wasn't seeing the passing view. Her mind's eye was filled with curly black hair that was graying at the temples, a short silver-frosted beard, lips parted in a smile as he appreciated one of her teasing remarks, and eyes so honest she could never doubt a single word he spoke. There must be some way to win his heart as he had already won hers.

◆

Hector watched the raeda until it turned the corner. He hadn't expected it to hurt so much when he sent it to Philip's house instead of his own. He couldn't love Drusilla more if she were his own daughter. He could visit, but that was a pitiful substitute for seeing her every day.

And Cornelia—if she were an ordinary woman, he'd pursue her to see if her friendship could grow into love...and marriage.

But she wasn't an ordinary woman. She was the proud daughter of one of the most important political families of Rome. He didn't even know who his father was, and his mother had been sold before he was old enough to remember her. The gold in Cornelia's chests was enough to buy even the largest estates between Perinthus and Byzantium. He was a ship's captain with a farm.

He stared at the ground and kicked at the dirt. He took a deep breath, held it, and released it slowly as the corners of his mouth turned down. He drew two overlapping circles in the dirt with his toe, then erased them with the sole of his sandal. One more deep sigh and a slow shake of his head. Finally, he squared his shoulders before turning to head back down the ramp.

He still had cargo to unload and a ship to prepare for mooring until spring. He wasn't a man who allowed himself to waste time dreaming of gaining the unattainable. She was a gracious woman who'd enjoyed his company during the voyage, but no man with his history could expect to win the heart of a queen.

Chapter 27

GIFTS AND SURPRISES

The raeda carried them west from the harbor about two miles before it turned onto a side road. Cornelia leaned over to examine the large houses of the upper-class neighborhood on the hillside where Claudia lived.

About three quarters of a mile uphill, the mules slowed in front of a tall wall that flanked the road. The driver reined in and turned the mules through an open carriage gate.

Drusilla leaned out the window as the raeda passed through a small orchard.

"I see a house, but it's not very big." She pulled back in. "Our villa must be at least twice its size."

Cornelia leaned forward to look out the window beside her daughter. "No, it's not as large, but I'm sure it's very nice inside."

Drusilla was right. It wasn't nearly as large as she expected for the house of man with several estates in Thracia and Moesia. It wasn't much larger than the Drusus house in Rome where Claudia had grown up. They were only four people, so there should be room. But what if Philip didn't want to add so many to his small household?

The raeda passed along the side of the house and halted in front of a stable at the rear. A stableman hurried over to open the door and offer his hand to assist them.

Malleolus climbed out first, then Drusilla. She spun and stuck her head back inside.

"Mother, is that Aunt Claudia?"

Cornelia stepped out to see a stunningly beautiful woman with reddish-gold hair hurrying toward them with outstretched arms. "Yes, dear, it is."

"She's so beautiful."

"Yes, she is, and she's very nice as well."

Cornelia strode forward to greet her sister-in-law.

Claudia clasped both Cornelia's hands. "I could scarcely believe it when Hector sent word that you were on his ship. Philip will be home shortly before dinner. I can hardly wait for you to meet him. He'll be so pleased that you've come. Hector said you might only need to stay for a short while, but you're welcome to live right here with us as long as you want."

Claudia's warm smile and sparkling eyes erased the last trace of concern about their welcome.

"It's wonderful to see you again, Claudia. Thank you for taking us in. From the moment Tertius told me what his father was planning, I was certain you'd want to help me protect Drusilla from Lucius. He hasn't changed at all from the horrible man he was when you escaped."

Claudia shook her head. "Poor Lucius. Strange as it may seem, I owe him a debt of thanks. I would never have met Philip if he hadn't tried to marry me off to punish me. Maybe I owe him another for making you decide to join me here. I've missed you."

Cornelia's brow furrowed. Poor Lucius? Owe him anything, least of all thanks? Why on earth was Claudia talking like that?

Claudia looked past Cornelia to Malleolus standing behind her. "And I've missed you most of all, Malleolus." She stepped forward and wrapped her arms around the old man. "To be with you again is something I never even dreamed possible. Having you here is almost like having Father with me."

Malleolus embraced her and wiped beside his eye as he stepped back. "Aristarchus insisted I come. He said to tell you I was his gift to you."

Claudia rested her hand on his cheek. "Other than his asking Philip to rescue me, this is the best gift he's ever given me."

"We agreed it was too dangerous for him as well if I were to stay." Malleolus grinned. "Lucius has no idea how happy he's made me by forcing Cornelia to divorce him."

Claudia stepped back and knelt before Drusilla. "You were only two when I saw you last. Titus's little girl, Vania, is going to be so glad to have a girl cousin living close. She's been the only girl around four lively boys. Philip grew up with four brothers, and his sisters found it very trying sometimes."

Cornelia's smile broadened as she watched Drusilla grin when she heard about the cousins. Maybe she wouldn't miss the captain as much with cousins to play with.

The captain. She suppressed a sigh. It was impossible not to think about him. Those honest brown eyes. Those lips that twitched before curving into a smile as she teased him. A virile man who made her feel feminine and young again. Drusilla might find the cousins could fill the void left by his absence, but nothing she could imagine could replace his company.

Not more than five days. That's what he'd promised. Five days too many for her.

Cornelia and Malleolus were relaxing with Claudia in the garden when the hoof beats of Philip's stallion drew Cornelia's attention. Hector's glowing praise had piqued her interest in this man who'd earned Claudia's love and Hector's friendship.

Claudia rose and hurried over to greet him even before he dismounted. He swung his right leg over the stallion's neck and slid off. His feet had scarcely hit the ground before she caressed his cheek, smiling as if the clouds had just parted to reveal the sun.

"Welcome home. Hector brought us a wonderful surprise from Rome."

Claudia wrapped her arm around his and led him toward the circle of chairs where Cornelia and Malleolus waited. She waved her arm toward them. "My sister-in-law Cornelia and Drusilla have come to stay with us. Malleolus is here, too. Aristarchus sent him as a gift for me."

Philip's gaze shifted from his wife's face to the group. His loving smile transformed into a warm welcome for them all.

"The *Claudia* often brings us the best things from my father. Welcome."

Cornelia tried not to stare at him, but that was almost impossible. She'd expected Claudia to marry a handsome man. Before her stood the ugliest man she'd ever seen with horrible scars on the right side of his face and an eyepatch. But Claudia gazed at him as if he were an Adonis.

She glanced down when a small hand slid into her own. Drusilla stood at her side. Her eyes were enormous, and she alternated between staring at Philip and looking away. Cornelia squeezed her hand to re-mind her to say nothing.

Malleolus stood on her other side, smiling at the approaching cou-ple as if nothing were amiss.

Claudia reached over and took Cornelia's free hand. "Philip, this is Cornelia Scipia." She moved her hand to Drusilla's shoulder. "And this is my niece, Claudia Drusilla. We call her Drusilla. They've come to live with us because Lucius planned to betroth Drusilla to his friend's vicious son."

Cornelia offered her hand to her brother-in-law. "I'm very pleased to meet you, Philip. I apologize for coming without asking or at least letting you know we were coming. It was imperative that I get Drusilla away from my husband as quickly as possible. We left only four days after I learned about his plans for her. I'm very grateful for the wel-come we've received."

Cornelia focused on his good eye and found it much easier to look at him. The warmth of the welcome she found there mostly overcame the distraction of his scars.

"Your timing was perfect, or you would have missed our last ship coming from Rome this season. I'm glad you decided to come to us. Claudia and I will do all we can to make the move to Thracia easy for you."

A wry smile lifted the corner of his mouth as he shook his head. "So Lucius hasn't changed much in the last eight years. I'm glad Hec-tor had the *Claudia* in Portus. He specializes in rescuing women from Lucius Fidelis for me. I hope you had a good voyage."

"It was exceptionally enjoyable. Captain Hector took excellent care of us." She glanced down at Drusilla. "He was especially kind to Drusil-la. She learned about knots and sails and tides and all manner of things related to ships and the sea. She'll miss being onboard with him, I fear."

And I shall miss him at least as much. Hector's trustworthy eyes and friendly smile flashed in her mind. It had only been a few hours since she left his ship, and she already longed to be near him.

She pulled her mind back to the conversation.

Claudia's eyes warmed when she shifted her gaze. "And this is Malleolus. He was Father's steward since before I was born, but he was really more like my second father. Aristarchus sent him with Cornelia as a gift to me. Your father knows better than any man how to arrange the perfect gift." She caressed his scars again. "First you, now Malleo-lus."

Philip rested his hand on Malleolus's shoulder and beamed. "I owe you more than I can ever repay. If you hadn't gone to Father to ask his help, Claudia and I would never have met. You are most welcome."

"Aristarchus has given me a greater gift. These two women are like daughters to me, and to live where I'll be near them both is more than I ever hoped."

Philip went down on one knee to get eye-level with Drusilla. "I'm glad you're here, Drusilla. My boys will be better off having another girl cousin to teach them how to act around girls, and Titus's Vania will have an ally against them. What was the best part of your trip here?"

Drusilla still held Cornelia's hand and was staring at the ground to avoid looking at her uncle's scars. Her eyes rose to his at the question.

"The best part? Captain. He taught me Mercenaries and how to tie knots and how to read the clouds and...well, too many things to tell you."

"Hector taught me some of those things as well when I was eighteen. He's a very good teacher."

Drusilla beamed at him. "Captain is good at everything."

A grin escaped as he rose. "Yes, Hector is good at almost everything."

Claudia wrapped her arm around his once more. "Miriam was with me when the news of Cornelia's arrival came. She insisted we all celebrate with a special dinner at her house tonight. She's gone to prepare it for us. She'd like to have Cornelia and her maid and Drusilla stay with them so the girls can enjoy each other's company."

She turned to Cornelia. "Titus's house is only a quarter mile down the street. Our families spend a great deal of time together. Do you mind staying there for the girls?"

Drusilla squeezed her mother's hand.

When Cornelia glanced down, her daughter was nodding vigorously. "I think that's an excellent idea."

Claudia scooped up Malleolus's hand. "I want to keep you here with me. I've missed you so much."

Two boys of about six and four and a servant were walking up the drive toward them. The boys broke into a run when they saw Philip. When they reached him, they tackled his legs. He scooped up the larger one and placed him on his shoulders.

Claudia laughed at their exuberance. "These are our boys, Publius and Philetus. Boys, this is Malleolus. He'll be living with us from now on. He was like a father to me when I lived in Rome."

The four-year-old, Philetus, sidled over to Malleolus. His head was down, but he kept tipping it up to sneak a peek at him. When he was right in front of Malleolus, he tipped his head back. "Do I call you Grandfather?"

Malleolus's eyebrows shot up, and Claudia laughed. "Yes, dear. I think that's a wonderful name to call Malleolus." She placed her hand on his arm. "That is, if you don't mind."

He nodded his head and knelt to get eye-level with her son. "I'd be honored if you would call me Grandfather."

Philetus threw his arms around Malleolus's neck, and the old man wrapped his arms around the little boy. Tears brimmed in his eyes when Malleolus looked up at Claudia.

Claudia bent over and kissed his forehead. "Welcome home, dear Malleolus. Welcome home."

Chapter 28

Different and Better

Cornelia walked beside Claudia as they headed down the street to Titus's house.

"Miriam is a wonderful woman. I met her two days after I arrived in Perinthus. She ended my nightmares and pulled me out of my despair over Father's death less than two weeks after we met. She's truly a sister to me. Finding Miriam was the best thing that could ever have happened to Titus as well."

Cornelia smiled at Claudia's enthusiasm for her other sister-in-law. Since Hector spoke well of Titus's wife, too, Miriam must be quite a woman.

Their party entered Titus's house through the door that faced the road. Titus was standing near the opposite end of the inner courtyard by the kitchen door.

He leaned into the room. "They're here."

As he strode toward Cornelia, a warm welcome radiated from his eyes and smile. "Malleolus. Cornelia. Welcome to Perinthus. It's good to see you both again. I'm sorry you had to leave Rome under such circumstances, but we're very glad you've come."

Cornelia's smile concealed her surprise. Titus was not wearing a tunic with the narrow purple stripes worn by men of the equestrian order. He was a Claudius Drusus, and his estate north of Rome was worth at least three times the 100,000 denarii required to be a member of that order. So why was he dressed in a plain white tunic?

A small, pretty woman with thick brown hair cascading down her back limped out of the kitchen. She wore an apron dusted with flour. Cornelia's gaze was drawn to her deformed ankle as she approached them. Titus must have remained a kind man, like his father. A crippled slave was never cast off, just retrained at the Drusus estates.

Titus turned and held out his hand to the kitchen slave. When he wrapped his arm around her shoulders and drew her close to his side, Cornelia's eyes widened.

He smiled down at the woman. "This is my Miriam." His lips brushed her forehead. Her fingertips stroked his jaw before she turned to Cornelia.

"We couldn't be happier that you've come to stay with us while you plan what you want to do. Vania is so excited about sharing her room with Drusilla." Miriam grinned. "She said there have been too many boys and not enough girls for too long in this family."

Cornelia smiled her gracious social smile. "Thank you for such a warm welcome when we've come so unexpectedly. Drusilla has been looking forward to meeting her cousins since I first told her we were coming here."

She was expert in concealing her true thoughts, and today had certainly tested that skill. Miriam had clearly been working in the kitchen when they arrived, like a servant or slave. Why would Titus allow his wife to do that?

Just as she'd hidden her surprise, Cornelia concealed her flash of insight. Eight years ago, Lucius had been furious when Titus sent 400 denarii back with the men he'd sent to fetch Claudia, telling him it was Claudia's bride price and the same amount he'd given for his own wife.

She'd thought that a paltry amount, but that was the price for an inexpensive houseslave. Titus married the slave he bought to serve Claudia two days after her arrival.

Miriam rested her hand on Titus's arm. "It will be a little while before everything is ready. Why don't you take everyone into the garden to sit and relax until it's done?"

Titus nodded, and Miriam limped back into the kitchen.

A surge of envy shot through Cornelia when she saw the look in Titus's eyes as he watched his wife. Lucius had never looked at her like that. Not once in twenty-five years.

Claudia slipped her arm around Cornelia's. "The wait will be worth it. I've never tasted better cooking than Miriam's, not even from the chefs Father kept in Rome. It's a wonder she hasn't made Titus fat."

Cornelia glanced around the house, all of which could be seen from the courtyard. It appeared to follow a Greek floorplan. The central courtyard was cobblestone with a well near the door they'd entered. To her left was the bath chamber, and next to it a large sitting room where Titus would receive clients and visitors. To her right was the dining room, which would connect to the kitchen by a separate door through a pantry. Opposite the entryway were two small rooms. One was probably the private office, the other a sleeping room for the household slaves.

The stairs to the balcony level rose directly opposite the door to the center leg of a U-shaped balcony. There appeared to be a single bedroom just to the right of the stairs. Next to it was the women's room, which occupied almost two thirds of that side. Four doors opened onto the left-side balcony and a fifth door at the head of the stairs.

Cornelia masked her surprise at the smallness of the house. Would there be room for the three of them? The silliness of that thought triggered a smile. She'd happily spent almost five weeks in a five-by-six-foot room shared with Anthusa, and it had been enough. By comparison, this was palatial.

Claudia pointed to the bedchamber on the right. "That was mine when I first came. Now it's where Miriam and Titus sleep." She pointed back to the room at the far end of the left leg. "Titus used that room, but it's for guests now. It has two windows with lovely views. I think Miriam plans on that being your room."

Cornelia gauged the size and number of rooms. Two nephews, one niece—that would fill all the other rooms on that leg. Two small rooms left over for their nurse, chef and helpers, slaves to clean the house... definitely not much room for three extra people. Was there any room for an extra slave in the house itself? She wanted Anthusa nearby.

"Anthusa shared my room on the ship. Perhaps she can do that here."

Claudia nodded. "Miriam was my lady's maid when I lived here, and she slept in my room before I married Philip. I always liked that arrangement."

"Then I'll suggest it to Miriam." Suspicion confirmed. Miriam had been Titus's slave. His chef, Claudia's maid—she'd never had a slave with skills for both those jobs.

Titus led the group through the kitchen to reach the door into the garden. As they passed through, Miriam stood by the fire, stirring the simmering sauce with a long-handled spoon. Titus stepped close behind her, slid his hand down her arm, and tried to take the spoon from her. She slapped his hand before dipping the spoon in the pot and offering it for him to taste.

Titus blew on the steaming liquid until it cooled enough, then let Miriam tip a tiny taste into his mouth.

"Still the best cook in the city." A crooked grin accompanied his laughing eyes.

Miriam beamed at his words. "And still the best husband."

Once more, Cornelia needed to conceal her surprise. Miriam didn't just oversee the kitchen. She actually worked in it as if she were the chef instead of the mistress.

Titus's lips brushed Miriam's forehead before he turned to lead them out the door into the garden.

Cornelia settled into a chair under a spreading tree to await Miriam's summons to dinner. Claudia and Titus chatted with Malleolus. Philip listened with his fingers laced behind his head and his legs stretched out, the perfect image of relaxation as he gazed at his beautiful wife. Drusilla had followed Vania to the flock of chickens, where she was being introduced to each.

How different her in-laws were from the way she remembered them. Different, but also better. None of the pretention of aristocratic Rome remained. They were natural, open, real.

Like Hector. Her pulse jumped as images of him flooded her mind. Where was he now? Did he think of her as often as she thought of him? Did he think of her at all?

No more than five days. That's what he'd said. It wasn't even one day yet, but that was already several hours too many.

The exquisite combination of aromas coming from the kitchen made Cornelia's mouth water. If the taste matched the savory smells, the meal should be a culinary masterpiece.

Dinner was to be served to the six adults at one table with the four boys, Vania, and Drusilla at a second. Drusilla was all smiles and giggles as she talked with her cousins. Watching her obvious delight erased Cornelia's final doubts about the wisdom of coming to Perinthus. Bringing Drusilla here would have been a good choice even if Lucius hadn't been such a horrible father.

Miriam had exchanged her servant's apron for a linen tunic befitting her station as Titus's wife. She seated Cornelia at one end of the table between Claudia and herself, with Malleolus directly opposite between Philip and Titus.

Titus wove his fingers into Miriam's where her hand rested on the table. "You are in for a treat tonight. Father always kept a good chef, and I assume Lucius was wise enough to keep his kitchen staff. I remember some excellent meals when I was still in Rome, but they were nothing, I tell you, absolutely nothing compared to what Miriam can prepare. Her sauces and pastries put to shame the best I ever had in Rome."

His enthusiasm drew Cornelia's smile. "If the aromas are signs of what is to come, I expect the flavors will be extraordinary."

A pink flush swept across Miriam's cheeks. "Titus praises me more than I deserve, but making sure he has the best possible dinner is one of my greatest pleasures." She gave his hand a quick squeeze as her gaze caressed his face. "It's my gift of love to the finest husband."

Titus lifted her hand and kissed it. "I may not be the finest husband, but I'm certainly the most blessed."

All eyes turned to the pantry door as a servant carried in the carrots sautéed in Miriam's peppered wine sauce. After the dish was placed on the table, Titus offered his hands to Miriam and Malleolus. Cornelia and Malleolus joined as the circle of hands formed around the table.

Titus tilted his head back, eyes closed. "We give thanks, Lord, for the blessings of this day and for this food that will nourish our bodies. We give special thanks that Cornelia, Malleolus, and Drusilla have arrived safely and can share it with us. In Jesus's name, we give thanks."

"Amen" came from all, including Cornelia.

Malleolus turned to Philip. "Hector and I had many opportunities to talk during the voyage. Before we landed, he began to tell me about Jesus and what he did. I would like to learn more about the faith that Publius thought worth dying for. Hector told me you could help me with that."

Philip grinned. "Nothing would give me greater pleasure." He paused. "You talked a lot with Hector?"

"Yes. We became good friends. I'll miss our daily conversations. He's a fine man."

Philip's grin turned serious. "I've been worried about him since his wife and daughter died last fall. His grief has been too deep for too long. I haven't had a chance to speak with him since he returned from Rome. Is their loss still consuming him?"

"He's a quiet man, and he didn't speak of his grief to me. He did smile and laugh much more by the end of our voyage. He and Drusilla became good friends. Each seemed to make the other happier the longer they were together. I am certain they'll miss each other a great deal. I hope there will be some way for them to get together soon."

Philip's eye brightened as a broad smile appeared. "That is excellent news. I've prayed long and hard for him to get past the crushing grief." His head tilted as his eyebrow rose. "So he and Drusilla have become friends? Then I'll make sure the two of them have many opportunities to enjoy each other's company until Hector sails again in the spring."

◆

Cornelia stopped listening to the conversation between Miriam and Claudia that flowed around her. Her full attention focused on Philip and Malleolus the moment she heard Hector's name.

What was Philip planning to do? Would she have many opportunities to enjoy Hector's company as well?

It was all she could do not to sigh. If only he were sitting next to her at the table. If only he would entwine his fingers with hers, as Titus did with Miriam. If only he would gaze at her as if she were the light in the room, as Philip did with Claudia. Whatever Philip did to get Hector to come for Drusilla, somehow she must convince him to come for her as well.

After Claudia's family went home, Miriam led Cornelia along the balcony to the room that would be hers. She paused at the door to wave Cornelia in ahead of her. "I had Philip's servants bring down the two trunks you had in your cabin and your boxes of jewelry and perfumes. The rest are still at Claudia's until you sort them into what you want to use now and what you want to store until you have your own estate. She thought it would be safer for your dowry gold to remain at Philip's house. He has the locking caskets and guards to keep it safe."

Cornelia paused in the doorway and tipped her head. "Thank you. That sounds wise for my gold. The two trunks should be sufficient. I discovered on the voyage how little I actually need. If you have no objection, I'd like to have Anthusa sleep in my bedchamber rather than be quartered too far from me."

Miriam's smile broadened. "Of course. Claudia always wanted me to sleep with her even though there were spare rooms. She mentioned your wish, and I've had a cot for Anthusa placed in your chamber already. I thought Vania and Drusilla would enjoy sharing as well."

"I expect Drusilla will be very happy with that arrangement."

Titus reached the top of the stairs and walked along the balcony to join them.

Miriam's gaze remained fixed on her. "I'm so glad we'll get a chance to know each other before you move to your own estate. I hope it will be close enough for frequent visits. We won't wa—"

Titus had scooped Miriam up into his arms. After one gasp, she started to laugh.

"Put me down, Titus. What will Cornelia think?" She squirmed, but he held her tight.

"You can ask her tomorrow. That's enough women's talk for tonight." His lips moved close to her ear and he lowered his voice. "It's time for our nighttime entertainment."

Blood flooded Miriam's cheeks and ears.

Titus's grin grew bigger. "You're pretty when you turn pink, but red is even better." One tender kiss, then he turned his eyes on Cornelia.

"I'm glad you've come. We'll do all we can to help you start over here."

"Thank you, Titus. With you and Philip helping, I'm sure all will turn out well. Good night." She turned and stepped into her room.

When she heard his footsteps moving away, she turned back to watch. Titus still cradled Miriam in his arms. She snuggled into him and rested her head on his shoulder. When she caressed his face, he kissed her again. He carried her into their room and shut the door with his foot, unwilling to put her down.

The love that flowed between Titus and Miriam drew Cornelia's shuddering sigh. What would it be like to have a man love her like that? Even after eight years of marriage, it was as if it were their wedding night. It must have been like that for Hector. Why else would he grieve so deeply for almost a year?

Why couldn't I have married a man like Hector instead of a worm like Lucius? I was a fool. I've spent my whole life with no man who wants my love, no man who loves me in return.

She'd been a Cornelius Scipio marrying a Claudius Drusus, the perfect merger of bloodline and fortune, and everyone had congratulated her on arranging such a wonderful marriage. Instead, it had been miserable. Titus had married someone who didn't even have a last name, and it had turned out so perfectly for him.

Anthusa's voice came from within the room. "Are you ready to retire, mistress?"

One last, longing look at their closed door. "Yes. I'm coming."

Chapter 29

New Understandings

When Malleolus entered the dining room the next morning, Philip and Claudia were already enjoying a breakfast of dates, cheese, and rosemary-laced bread.

Claudia rose and embraced him. "It's so good to have you here."

Malleolus sighed, a contented smile brightening his face as he hugged her. "To be here with you...I never expected to see you again. I couldn't have chosen a better end for my life."

Malleolus seated himself next to Philip and across from Claudia. "Philip, I can never repay Aristarchus for what he's done for me. Cornelia and Drusilla are family to me, just as Claudia is like my own daughter. I thought I'd end my days alone after I sent them all to Thracia. When your father insisted I come with Cornelia, he gave me the chance to be with the three people I love most in the world. To live my final days with them all...I could ask for nothing more."

Claudia reached across the table and took his hand. "May that be many years from now, dear Malleolus. You'll never be alone now. No one ever should be."

Philip nodded. "I've seen too closely how losing a child can tear up a man."

Malleolus flipped his gaze from Claudia to Philip. "Hector?"

"Yes. He left for Rome sadder than any man should be."

"When we first boarded, I believe he still was. But I had the pleasure of watching that change. To cheer Drusilla, he played games, taught her sailor skills, let her follow him around. They've come to love each other like father and daughter. I am sorry their time together has ended."

Claudia turned with a wide smile. "But their time together doesn't have to end. I'll invite him to dine here tomorrow." She glanced at Philip. "He and Philip are closer than brothers. He often dines with our family."

"That should bring great pleasure to more than Drusilla."

Claudia cocked her head, a question in her eyes. "Cornelia?"

A grin split Malleolus's face. "Not just Cornelia. By voyage end, I'm sure I saw great interest in each other, but neither was any good at letting the other know."

A mischievous grin brightened Claudia's eyes as well. "We'll see what we can do to help them understand each other better."

Malleolus was content as he turned his attention back to the breakfast before him. It was a good first step in his final act of service to Cornelia.

Cornelia was seated for breakfast with Miriam when she heard Drusilla's happy chatter as she crossed the courtyard with Vania. What a pleasant way to start the first day of their new life in Thracia.

Drusilla bounced over to give her a hug when she entered the dining room.

Cornelia basked in her daughter's beaming smile. "Did you sleep well, dear?"

"Oh, yes, and breakfast was delicious, too. I'm so glad Aunt Miriam wanted us to stay with her."

Her words brought a smile to Miriam's lips. "I'm glad you feel that way. Do you have everything you need in your room?"

Drusilla bit her lip as she looked at her aunt. "In the room, yes, but I was hoping I might have some rope."

Miriam's eyes widened. "Rope?"

"Yes. I promised Captain I would practice my knots every day."

"Knots?" Miriam's eyebrows rose.

Cornelia couldn't suppress the huge smile triggered by Miriam's surprise. "Hector taught Drusilla how to tie many of the knots the sailors use."

Drusilla stood with her arm draped across Cornelia's shoulders. "Captain taught Mother how to tie knots, too, but he said I learned quicker. He said he'd be glad to have me on his crew, if I were a boy."

A laugh bubbled out of Miriam. "I'll have to remember you're both trained to tie knots if I need something tied. Of course you can have some rope." She caught Cornelia's amused gaze with her own. "In fact, get enough rope for both of you. Just in case Hector wants to check to see if your mother remembers his lessons as well. Go find Nestor and ask him for some."

"Thank you, Aunt Miriam." Drusilla skipped back into the courtyard with Vania behind her.

Miriam's eyes danced as she turned back to the table. "So Hector was training you both to be seamen?"

Cornelia's eyes drifted as she remembered the captain's hands touching hers as he helped her. Hands so strong yet gentle. How would his calloused palm have felt resting against her cheek?

She snapped her attention back to Miriam. "The captain was so kind to Drusilla the entire trip. He saw how lonely she was, and he tried to help. He played board games and read to her. He taught her all sorts of things about the ship and sailing besides the knots. He let her stand on the cabin top with him as much as she wanted."

Her lips tightened as she shook her head. "Lucius never wanted to have anything to do with her. It was as if she were a fatherless child in Rome. The captain was the first man to encourage her." She paused. "Drusilla loves him. I do hope we get to see him sometimes. I don't want him to disappear from our lives, not after he's become so important to us...to Drusilla. He promised he would visit. I hope he keeps that promise."

Miriam's eyes brimmed with questions. Perhaps she'd revealed more than she intended of her own desire for the captain.

A gleam entered Miriam's eyes as a smile overspread her lips. "I don't think you need to worry about that. Hector is one of the most honest men I know. If he said he would come, then he will."

Cornelia felt her cheeks heat under Miriam's gaze. She never used to blush, but there was something about the captain that made her lose control. "I'm glad to hear that. It's important he come...for Drusilla's sake."

Miriam fought to keep the smile from turning into a grin. "Of course. For Drusilla's sake." Miriam stood. "As soon as you'd like, I'll give you a tour of the house and grounds. I can get a second loom set up for you in the women's room this morning, if you wish. I know it can get boring quickly with nothing to do."

Cornelia stood as well, glad to have the discussion of the captain finished. "I would like that very much. For years, I've had an estate to run to fill my days. I'll miss that until I buy one here, but I've always found weaving a relaxing way to spend my free time. Perhaps we can set up another one for Anthusa. I'd like to take her on the tour as well. I'm sure you understand our relationship is much more than mistress and slave."

Miriam smiled broadly. "I understand perfectly. Claudia and I were the same before my marriage. Let me discuss dinner with my chef, and then we can take that tour."

They walked into the courtyard. Miriam turned into the kitchen as Cornelia climbed the stairs to fetch Anthusa from her chamber.

She glanced down at the kitchen as she walked along the balcony. Yes, Miriam understood about Anthusa, and she suspected about Hector. Miriam was more of a kindred spirit than she'd expected, in spite of her once being Titus's slave.

Cornelia had grown tired of weaving, so she wandered down to the kitchen to see what Miriam was doing. The savory aroma of pork roasting on a spit filled the room while a mysterious sauce simmered beside it. She sat at the table and leaned back in the chair, watching Miriam dip a spoon in the sauce, roll some on her tongue with her eyes closed, then add a pinch of some spice that she couldn't identify.

She couldn't blame Titus for having his wife continue to direct the kitchen after their marriage. If the dinner last night was typical of her culinary art, and the luscious aroma filling the kitchen suggested it was, it would have been virtually impossible to find a chef to match her skill.

Titus strode through the kitchen door. "Good evening, Cornelia. I hope you enjoyed your day."

"It's been most enjoyable."

"Good." Titus stepped close behind Miriam, scooped her into his arms, and spun around.

Laughter bubbled from Miriam. "Titus! Put me down if you want a good dinner tonight."

He set her down, but he didn't release her. He pulled her close against him and nuzzled her neck. "You smell better than the sauce."

Miriam caressed his cheek and he placed his hands on both sides of her face. He turned it up to draw her eyes to his before lowering his lips to hers. After the kiss, his lips brushed her ear as his voice dropped to a near whisper. "Best chef in Perinthus, but it's not your delectable dinners I enjoy most."

Miriam glanced at Cornelia, and her cheeks flushed.

"That's what I like about you, wife. Such a pretty little thing when you turn pink."

Cornelia averted her eyes for Miriam's sake.

Vania came running in from the courtyard with Drusilla right behind. Titus knelt so she could kiss his cheek before he scooped her up into the air and planted a kiss on her forehead. Close behind came the two boys, who tackled his legs. Titus tousled their hair before they disappeared out the kitchen door.

The love Titus had for all his family was hard for Cornelia to watch. Lucius had never done that with her or her boys and most definitely never with her daughter. Just watching Titus drove home the hollowness of her married life, even in the beginning when it had seemed good to her. It hurt to think about it. She'd tried so hard to be a good wife. Everything Lucius had done or failed to do felt so unfair.

The way Titus loved Vania—Hector had treated Drusilla like that by the end of their voyage. He must have been as good a father as Titus. Where was he now? What was he doing? Would he come soon to see Drusilla?

When he came to see Drusilla, would he be coming because he wanted to see her, too? She stifled a deep sigh. She longed for him to want her, but did he? There had been hints, but he'd never made it clear he did. Was all she thought she saw only wishful thinking on her part? If only he would come, maybe she could tell. If she only had more time with him, maybe she could get him to tell her he wanted her, too.

The silver mirror from her dressing table in Rome sat before Mistress Cornelia as Anthusa brushed her hair at bedtime.

Mistress leaned closer to her reflection. "Titus and Miriam have made us very welcome, but I wish we were still on the ship."

Anthusa nodded. "The captain, mistress?"

Mistress sighed. "The captain. I miss him."

Anthusa drew the brush through her hair again. "He did promise to come visit. It isn't five days yet."

"I know." Mistress turned to face her. "But even when he comes, it will probably only be because he misses Drusilla. He loves her. If only the voyage had been longer..."

"I think he must be missing you as well. I saw how he looked at you when we were leaving him at the pier. I think he cares about you, too."

Anthusa watched the spark appear in her mistress's eyes, then dim.

"Maybe. I hope so. I hope he comes soon and often. I need time with him before he starts sailing again."

Anthusa nodded again. "I expect he will, mistress, and I expect him to decide you belong together."

Mistress turned back to the mirror. "I shouldn't keep thinking he won't. There's almost four months before he leaves."

"That should be enough. The captain is a very smart man, and he'd have to be a fool not to want to marry you."

Mistress took a deep breath and released it. "Yes. The captain is a very smart man."

Anthusa smiled as the worry lines around her mistress's eyes relaxed. A man would have to be a fool not to want her mistress, and the captain was no fool.

Chapter 30

A Pleasing Invitation

Cornelia was savoring her second wedge of Miriam's breakfast bread when word came that Claudia wanted everyone to come to dinner early at her house. Titus accepted the invitation and sent the boy who delivered it back to Claudia.

Miriam touched his hand on the table. "How thoughtful of Claudia. This will give Drusilla a chance to get to know her boys better."

"True, but I won't eat as well as I do here." He rose. "I'm going to the estate, but I'll be back in plenty of time." He kissed Miriam on the forehead and left the room.

The prospect of dining at Claudia's triggered Cornelia's smile. "It will be good to spend some time with Malleolus. He's very dear to me. I miss him, and I'm sure Drusilla does as well."

Miriam offered her a plate of sliced cheese. "It's a very short walk. Anytime you want, one of the servants can escort you there."

Cornelia moved a slice to her plate. "It must be nice living so close to Claudia. Almost like living together."

"Philip owned this house and rented it to Titus when he brought her here. After he married Claudia, he sold it to Titus so we would still live close. He knew how much that meant to both of us."

"Philip seems like a fine man. I can see why Claudia fell in love with him, even with all those scars."

"Claudia says the burns that scarred him were a blessing in disguise for both of them. He would have been married long before he met her if it weren't for the scars. He thought a woman would only want him because he was rich, and he didn't want that kind of woman. He discovered that wasn't true during their voyage here from Rome."

"I understand his concern. I know men will want to marry me because of my large dowry, but I don't want that kind of man myself. If I marry again, it would only be to a man who didn't care about my wealth."

Miriam took another slice of cheese. "There are many good men who wouldn't care. Perhaps God will bless you with one of them."

"Perhaps." Cornelia already knew one such man. There didn't need to be any others. If only that man would ask her to marry him. But first he had to visit so she could help him decide he should ask.

When they entered the courtyard at Philip's house that evening, Cornelia felt the flutter.

Hector stood before her, talking with Malleolus. He wore a short white tunic with a broad leather belt, just as he had the first moment she saw him on the ship. A shiver ran up her spine as she drank in his handsome profile and athletic physique.

Malleolus spoke to him, and he turned to face her. A huge smile appeared as his eyes caught hers. Butterflies again.

Drusilla ran past her with her arms spread. Hector knelt to catch her. She planted a big kiss on his cheek, just as she'd seen Vania do when Titus came home. His face was all smiles as he scooped her up and swung her around like he had on the ship.

Hector set her feet back on the ground. "How's my little first mate?"

"I missed you. I've been practicing my knots, Captain, just like you told me."

"That's good to hear."

Drusilla fixed hopeful eyes on him. "I wish you'd come visit us tomorrow so we can play Mercenaries."

Cornelia reached his side. "Yes, Captain. Do come visit tomorrow. I'm very glad it wasn't five days before we got to see you. We'd welcome the chance to see you as often as you wish to come."

His eyes crinkled at her invitation. "I'd like that."

Nothing could have delighted her more than those three words.

"Do you think it will be morning or afternoon when you come? We'll be glad to receive you whenever suits you better." Cornelia's gracious smile concealed her fluttering heart. *Please say morning so you can stay longer.*

"Probably midmorning." His lips formed a smile to match his eyes. "Since we're not on the ship anymore, please call me Hector."

"Of course. At least I'll try. It may take me some time to make that change. Captain fits a man like you so well."

◆

Hector couldn't miss the welcome in her eyes, but that was what he expected of a regal, gracious hostess. Of course, she'd be glad to receive him...for Drusilla's sake. It wasn't likely she missed him as much as he missed her the past two days. To her, he was still the ship's captain, a friend of her daughter and herself. Only a fool would expect anything more.

Drusilla took his hand to draw his attention. "Will you come every day so we can play Mercenaries?"

"Not every day, but often."

"How often, Captain? At least every other day?"

Her request drew a broad smile. "Your mother might not appreciate me coming so often."

Drusilla shook her head vigorously. "That's not true, Captain. Mother likes to have you with us at least as much as I do."

Hector didn't reply. He wished that were so, but he knew better than to expect an aristocrat like Cornelia to want him visiting her so often.

Cornelia stepped closer and rested her hand on Drusilla's shoulder. Close enough that the scent of roses teased his nostrils. He'd missed her perfumes, especially that one.

"Quite the contrary, Captain. I mean Hector. I'd be very happy if you'd come every day. Drusilla and I would both be pleased to have your company as often as you can join us."

Hector's eyebrows started to rise, but he stopped them. Cornelia pleased with his company? He liked the sound of that. Of course, she might have said it because it was the gracious thing to say. She might say it only so he'd come for Drusilla. But could she also want him to come for herself? She'd said "both."

"Very well, Cornelia. As often as I can."

Her sparkling eyes and quick smile assured him she liked his answer. Liked it very much. She was an aristocrat forever beyond his reach, but at least she wanted his company. Even if they had no future as husband and wife, they could still be friends.

Hector couldn't have been more pleased with the seating arrangement at dinner if Claudia had asked him to choose who sat beside him. Philip sat on the end next to him, and to his left sat Malleolus. Of course Claudia sat by Philip, with Cornelia between her and Miriam, and Titus at the other end.

A slight turn of his head, and he could glance up from his plate and watch Cornelia. More often than not, when he looked at her, she was looking at him. And she was really looking at him, not just glancing his way. She smiled every time she caught his eye. A man might almost think she took special pleasure in having him so close to her.

There were too many people for him to feel comfortable talking with her. Their conversation almost always turned into her teasing him in a way he really liked, but he didn't want others listening. He wasn't certain what to say that wouldn't lead to a tease, so he said very little except when Malleolus pulled him into conversation. He'd missed Malleolus, but nothing like he'd missed Cornelia.

He watched her turn to Philip.

"Philip, I am so grateful for all your father did to help us escape from Lucius. What with providing the wagons and guards and getting us safely to the harbor without Lucius ever suspecting a thing, he made it all so easy."

"I'm certain he enjoyed doing it. Publius was his friend and brother, and saving his granddaughter from Lucius would give Father as much pleasure as saving Claudia did eight years ago."

She flashed a warm smile at Hector before turning back to Philip. "I'm especially grateful that he chose Hector to bring us here. He couldn't have chosen a finer escort." She flipped her gaze on him again. "I think Drusilla had the finest time in her entire life. He was so kind to her. He made the trip very pleasant for all of us."

Philip rested his hand on Hector's shoulder and grinned at him. "Hector specializes in bringing women running from Lucius Drusus to Thracia."

Hector fixed his gaze on Cornelia's deep blue eyes. "I enjoyed doing it."

Those eyes brightened. "I hope as much as I enjoyed having you do it. No man could have been kinder or more attentive to us all. It was a pleasure to spend so many days in your company."

Hector's brows rose, then settled. Was that just her speaking her gratitude for him treating Drusilla well? Or was she hinting that she enjoyed his company herself beyond that of any other man?

"I'm glad to hear it, Cornelia."

"I'm pleased to tell you, Captain." Those blue eyes sparkled. She wasn't a pretty woman, but even Claudia didn't have eyes as beautiful as Cornelia's when they lit up like they were at that moment.

Hector picked up his goblet and took a sip. Drusilla wanted him to visit every day, and Cornelia had repeated the request. He'd be sure to take her up on that invitation. Even if she only wanted him as her daughter's friend, he could still enjoy those beautiful eyes.

Claudia stood with one arm wrapped around Philip's and waved farewell as Hector turned his horse toward their gate.

"That was an interesting dinner, don't you think?" She hugged his arm before releasing it.

"It's always interesting to talk with Titus, and Malleolus is certainly wise in the ways of the Empire."

Her fingertip traced a swirl of scar tissue by his blind right eye. "That's not what I'm talking about. I mean Cornelia and Hector."

His eyebrow dipped. "What about them? They didn't talk to each other much. In fact, Hector hardly talked at all except when Malleolus asked him something."

"Didn't you see how they looked at each other? Malleolus was right. They are definitely interested in each other."

He pushed a strand of hair behind her ear. "Why do you say that? They were pleasant to each other, but I saw no sign of special affection."

"Oh, Philip. You just weren't watching. Cornelia's eyes said everything when she looked at him, and he spent a lot of time watching her even though he didn't say anything."

Philip chuckled. "I didn't see it, but then I wasn't too quick at recognizing your interest in me when we were on Hector's ship eight years ago. You had to tell me outright that you wanted me. If she wants him, Cornelia might have to do the same with Hector."

"Oh, she wants him. She's always been calm and self-controlled on the outside, but she has a very warm heart. I think Hector may have won it already. You heard her encouraging him to visit every day."

"I heard, but wasn't that just to play with Drusilla?"

"Of course not. The words weren't the full message. Her eyes, her smile...they were saying much more than the words."

"Well, I don't think Hector is any better at reading a woman's eyes and smiles than I am. Probably worse, so I doubt he got her message."

She stood on tiptoe and kissed his unscarred cheek. "If you're right, then I'll just have to find some way to help them along."

He pulled her close. After a lingering kiss, he caressed her cheek with the back of his fingers. "I know you will. My mighty general enjoys strategic maneuvering too much to pass up an opportunity like this. Just be careful you don't encourage one to think the other is in love with them when they might not be. Cornelia seems strong enough to take disappointment, but I don't want to see Hector's heart broken again."

"Don't worry. I never do anything without prayer, and God will keep me from doing harm instead of good. It would be wonderful if they're God's gift to each other."

Philip stepped back and took her hand. "If she wants Hector's love, she needs to accept God's love first. He won't marry a nonbeliever. I hope he doesn't lose his heart to a woman he can't marry."

"Neither would you, but God took care of that and led me to believe. I think that's going to happen with Cornelia, too." She took a step toward the house, leading him by the hand. "That's going to be my first prayer. Then we'll see what happens."

Anthusa liked Mistress Cornelia's dreamy smile as she brushed the mistress's hair before bedtime.

"I wish you could have seen him, Anthusa. He was dressed exactly like he was that day on the pier in Portus. Just the sight of him gave me a fluttery feeling. He is so handsome, so masculine, and totally unaware of the effect he has on a woman. I find that endearing. I've never met another man who pays so little attention to appearances."

The brush slid smoothly through the lustrous brown hair. "I'm sure your appearance there got his attention."

Mistress's eyes glowed. "Oh, yes. I'm sure it did. When Malleolus told him I'd arrived, he turned right away and gave me the biggest smile. It was as if he'd been waiting for me to come."

"I'm sure he was, mistress."

"You know how Vania greets Titus at night? That's exactly what Drusilla did to him, and I've never seen him happier. I'm sure he'd love having her as his daughter."

"And you as his wife."

"Perhaps. He certainly seemed glad to see me. Claudia had us sit across from each other at dinner. Almost every time I looked at him, he was watching me, too."

Cornelia leaned on her elbow as she gazed at her reflection. "I know I'm not pretty, but he kept watching me as if I were."

"Did he say he missed you? I'm sure he has."

"Actually, he barely said anything to me. He hardly talked at all except a little with Malleolus, and that was only because Malleolus got him started by asking a question." She turned to face Anthusa. "He did say he enjoyed bringing us here and he was glad I'd enjoyed his company aboard his ship."

"That sounds promising."

Mistress grinned. "I know. Even better, Drusilla asked him to come visit her every day. At first, he said he didn't think I'd want him to come that often. After I said I'd love to have him come as often as he could, he seemed so happy. He said he'd come very often."

"Will he come tomorrow?"

"Yes. Midmorning to play Mercenaries with Drusilla."

"And to see more of you. I'm sure that's part of why he's coming."

Mistress turned back to face the mirror. "When we left the pier, I wasn't sure if he cared much about whether he saw me again. After tonight, I'm sure he does."

Anthusa finished the last stroke of the brush. "Time to rest so you'll look your best when the captain comes."

Mistress lay down, and Anthusa pulled her covers up. "I expect the sweetest dreams tonight. Good night, Anthusa."

"Good night, mistress."

Anthusa's smile broadened as she blew out the lamp. The captain was eager to spend time with Mistress Cornelia. Surely it couldn't be long before he realized she loved him and he chose to love her back.

Chapter 31

Games with the Captain

Even though the day was cool, Cornelia had donned a cloak and sat with Anthusa under the spreading tree where she could see the captain's approach. Drusilla was pacing in front of the stable, watching the gate for the first sign of him. Outwardly, Cornelia was serene, but inwardly she was pacing as well.

When Hector finally guided his horse through the gate, Drusilla trotted toward him. Cornelia rose and strolled behind her daughter.

"We've been waiting for you, Captain." Drusilla hugged herself and rubbed her arms.

He swung his leg across his mare's neck and slid off. "It's cold enough today you should have waited inside."

Drusilla slid her hand into his and swung their arms as they walked toward Cornelia. "It didn't feel too cold."

A smile played on his lips as Cornelia approached, and his eyes crinkled as she reached him.

"Welcome, Captain. We're glad you've come. It should be a lovely morning for some games."

Palm up, she waved toward the kitchen door. "I've set up a table for you in the sitting room and had a brazier lit to make it warm and comfortable there."

Drusilla kept her grip on his hand as they walked along the side of the house. A stable boy appeared, and Hector tossed him the reins.

Hector's gaze focused on Cornelia. "Is it warmer in Rome this time of year?"

"A little, but I'd rather be cool in Thracia with you than warm in Rome alone."

Her words had the effect she wanted. His eyes crinkled even more and his smile broadened. She expected him to say something, but he didn't.

"What's the weather like where you come from?"

"About the same as Perinthus in the winter, hotter like Rome in the summer."

"Where was that?"

"Near Thessalonica."

"Like Philip and Aristarchus. Do you still have family there?"

"None I know of. Perinthus has been my home for many years."

They entered the kitchen, and the warmth from the oven wrapped around them. Miriam was speaking with her chef, but she stepped over to greet him.

"Welcome, Hector. It's good to see you again so soon." The question in her eyes flipped to amused knowing. "I hope you'll come often. I'll send some fruit and cheese over in case you get hungry playing games." The corners of her smile twitched.

Cornelia glanced at Hector's face. No sign of embarrassment—he clearly didn't realize why Miriam was amused. "Thank you, Miriam. That will be very welcome."

She led Hector across the courtyard, away from the smiling Miriam. Once inside the sitting room, she removed her cloak and handed it to Anthusa. She'd dressed for Hector in the blue tunic that intensified the color of her eyes.

Drusilla still held his hand as she led him over to the table. "Aunt Miriam didn't have the kings for Mercenaries, but Mother said we could just use dice for them."

Hector's eyes returned to Cornelia, and her heart skipped at the warmth in them. "Your mother is right. A good game depends only on the people playing, not on what you use for game pieces."

Cornelia picked up the dice and contemplated them. "So true, Ca... Hector. Even the game doesn't matter much when it's the right two people." She flipped her gaze from the dice to his eyes. The corner of her lips lifted slowly into a teasing smile. "Sometimes it doesn't matter at all."

◆

Hector breathed in the scent of her perfume. Roses. Was she wearing that one deliberately because she knew he liked it best? His lips twitched as he silently laughed at that thought. He'd never told her it was his favorite. There was no reason she should know. Even if she suspected, would that make a difference in what she wore?

Her eyes seemed bluer than normal. They shone with the delighted look he knew so well from when she flipped his words to tease him. And she had remembered to call him Hector.

"I agree. The person you play with matters most."

Their eyes remained locked. Her perfume filled his senses. Was she trying to tell him something about more than the games he'd come to play with Drusilla?

Drusilla sat down and began placing the blue and beige disks on the board. She held her hand out to her mother for the dice that were to be the Mercenaries kings. Cornelia dropped them into her palm.

"I've got it all set up, Captain. Ready to play?"

He broke the connection that was simmering between him and Cornelia and lowered himself into the chair. "Ready."

As Drusilla made her first move, Cornelia moved toward the nearby chair. She settled into it like a queen seating herself on a throne. Hector shook himself internally. Regal, wealthy—beyond his reach. So why did he keep thinking about her becoming more than a friend? She'd laugh if she knew his thoughts. He glanced over at her. Her eyes were fixed on his face, and a sudden smile made them sparkle. She was only talking about board games. Or was she?

Cornelia watched the ebb and flow of the board-game battle. Equally matched, her daughter and Hector. He was definitely intelligent even if he wasn't highly educated. And most definitely kind. How could any thinking woman not fall in love with this man?

He was attracted to her; no doubt about that. It should only be a matter of spending enough time together to get him to ask for her hand in marriage. Her lips curved in a satisfied smile.

The game ended with a close victory for Hector. Drusilla started to set up the pieces for the next one.

"That was the last for today. I need to return to the farm." He stood.

Cornelia rose and stepped close again. "Some special task awaits you?"

"I'm breaking a pair of young mules to harness. I'm taking them out to get them used to pulling different kinds of wagons."

Drusilla slid her hand into his, which pulled his gaze to her eager eyes. "My brother taught me how to ride, but I don't know how to drive. Would you teach me?"

Hector turned his eyes from Drusilla to Cornelia. "That depends on whether your mother wants me to."

"I think that's an excellent idea. I would trust you to teach Drusilla anything you think she might need to learn."

Drusilla tugged on his hand, and a mischievous smile twitched on her lips. "Mother doesn't know how to drive. She needs to learn, too."

Hector glanced at Drusilla before his gaze locked back on Cornelia. "Your mother has done very well without knowing."

Cornelia tipped her head and looked at him sideways. "But that was in Rome. This is Thracia. I believe Claudia and Miriam both know how to drive, so surely I should as well. Drusilla is right that you should teach me."

Yes, teach me to drive. Touch my hand as you help me hold the reins. Brush against my shoulder as we sit close on the driver's bench. The more time I spend close to you, the sooner you'll realize we belong together as husband and wife.

◆

Hector's arm jiggled up and down as Drusilla bounced with anticipation. "We went by the Circus Maximus in Rome. That's where the chariots race. Can you teach me to drive one?"

A laugh rumbled in Hector's chest. "I don't have a chariot, but I have a two-wheel *cisium* where you sit above the wheels. You'll have to settle for that."

"That sounds good, too, as long as you teach me to drive fast."

Hector's eyebrows rose. "I'll teach you both to drive, but not too fast."

He glanced at Cornelia. Her smiling lips were pressed tight to contain the laughter trying to break free. She was almost pretty when such delight lit her face.

Hector felt his own smile broaden. Why hadn't he thought to suggest driving lessons? They guaranteed more time close to her.

He tightened his lips, but most of the smile remained. Whatever the future held, there was still pleasure in her company.

Chapter 32

DISPATCHING THE HUNTERS

Rome

Lucius had almost finished his breakfast when Tertius joined him in the dining room.

"You came in late, son. Where were you?"

Tertius lowered himself onto the couch. He squeezed his eyes shut and ran his fingers through his hair. "Gaius and I were celebrating Sextus Flaccus's betrothal. There was too much food and wine. I should have left earlier."

Lucius scowled. "We should have been celebrating Drusilla's betrothal to Gnaeus Corvinus by now. Your mother has hidden her away too well. Still no trace of them. It's as if they vanished into thin air."

Tertius nodded. "Mother has a lot of friends. I don't know how you'll ever find her."

"And I have a few enemies who'd help her to spite me."

Lucius swung his legs off the couch and shot to his feet. "By the gods, I know what she's done!"

Tertius tipped his head as his eyebrows scrunched. "What, Father?"

"When Claudia ran away from her betrothal to Flavius Sabinus, she went to Titus in Thracia. I'd bet my best stallion Cornelia has done the same."

He balled his napkin and flung it to the floor. "She thinks she's bested me, but there's no way I'll let her win on this. Marcus hasn't found a wife for Gnaeus yet, but even if he had, I'd still take Drusilla away from Cornelia."

He turned to the slave waiting by the door. "Fetch Paullus."

Tertius placed a selection of fruit and cheese on his plate. He took a bite, then picked at the food.

Paullus, Lucius's new steward since Malleolus left, scurried into the room.

"You summoned me, master?"

"I need some reliable men willing to do whatever it takes to get my daughter back. Cornelia has almost certainly taken her to hide out with Titus or Claudia in Perinthus. I want Drusilla back here before the New Year."

Paullus's mouth twitched. "So soon? The sea is closing for the winter. An overland trip will take more than five weeks one way by horseback and more than eight by carriage."

"Nonsense. Malleolus sent horse-courier messages four times that fast."

"Yes, master, but the courier service changes horses and riders often, and they ride all night. Even if they change horses two or three times a day, your agents could travel half, maybe two thirds that fast since they will have to rest at night."

"So, they can get there in, what, three weeks or so?"

"Maybe a little less, master. But can your daughter ride?"

"If she can't, she'll learn." Lucius rubbed his chin. "Once they have her, they can bring her back at a slower pace."

Paullus bit his lip. "If she were nearby, I would go to one of the gladiatorial schools to hire some muscle and lead them myself. But to be gone so long...I think we need someone other than me to lead the search. To find someone we can trust to find and bring her here...that might take some time, master."

"Antonius Brutus can provide them. I've known Brutus since my boys started training for battle at his *ludus* after Marcus cut Lucius's face when they were sparring. Brutus can provide a pair of gladiators and find the right person to lead them to Thracia. His is the first name that's mentioned whenever my friends have a problem that requires a threat of violence for speedy resolution."

The corner of Lucius's mouth rose. "Who better to pick the men to bring her back than an equestrian of unquestioned integrity who can still spot a scoundrel before he's uttered a hundred words?"

Lucius rubbed his palms together. "He'll provide trustworthy men who'll do what they're supposed to and return with Drusilla. If the ones he owns aren't smart enough to go by themselves, he'll know someone honest to hire to lead the party."

"I will start on this today, master."

"I want them on their way within three days." Lucius's brow furrowed. Paullus was no Malleolus when it came to making special arrangements. "I'll talk with Brutus myself." He dismissed his steward with a flick of his hand.

Paullus bowed. "Yes, master."

Lucius turned back to Tertius to find him flat on his back on the couch with his arm draped across his eyes.

"What's wrong, son?"

"My head feels like a blacksmith's trying to hammer his way out, and my stomach…well it's not very steady. I should never have eaten that fourth serving of gazelle. Or maybe it was that eighth, maybe ninth cup of wine. I lost count."

Tertius sat up. "Gaius told me of an apothecary at the Baths of Trajan with just the thing to fix this. I'm going there, then I'm going to soak a while. If I run into Gaius or Sextus, I may not be home for dinner." He scrunched his eyes and rubbed the back of his neck as he stood up. "That's the last time I do that at a party…at least until the next time."

Lucius chuckled. "I made the same mistake when I was your age. You'll learn to pace yourself at banquets. Then you won't need that apothecary."

Tertius headed for the atrium, but he paused in the doorway. "If I don't see you tonight, I'll see you tomorrow, Father." Then he stepped out of view.

The corners of Lucius's mouth turned up. Tertius was a good son. His oldest son was too concerned about doing the right thing all the time, and Lucius felt his disapproval even though his son would never speak it aloud. His second son acted the part of the dutiful son, but there was something about Marcus that stirred up doubts of whether he could be trusted. Tertius was, indeed, the best of the lot.

Lucius paused at the head of the stairs that led down from the wealthy Fagutal district on the Oppian Hill to the Flavian Amphitheater. He'd walked that route many times to watch the games or on the way to the Forum, but it had been many months since he diverted up the Via Patricias to the Vicus Sandaliarius, where Brutus's training school occupied a full block.

Marcus Brutus was a wealthy equestrian with his finger in many financial ventures, but he seemed to particularly enjoy his reputation as the owner of a prominent *ludus* who was as skilled in combat as his junior gladiators.

While not a close friend, Lucius counted him among his friendly acquaintances, and Malleolus had often hired Brutus's gladiators as guards when he needed to transport a large sum of money.

Lucius's gaze locked on the ludus below. Had Malleolus contracted with Brutus for services during Cornelia's escape? His lips tightened. He should have thought to check earlier. Brutus might have provided men as escorts. Her whereabouts might be one question away. But would she be foolish enough to stay where they'd left her?

He rubbed his lower lip. Cornelia was too shrewd to make it that easy for him, but it would provide a starting point. There was a time when her intelligence had attracted him, even though she was plain, but that was long ago. A man was much better off with a stupid, pretty wife.

The savage roar of men enjoying the morning animal fights reverberated in the Amphitheater, and Lucius started down the steps.

If Brutus had men fighting in the one-on-one events that afternoon, he'd be difficult to find among the mass of equestrians who watched from the second-tier seats. He might even be in the service area that was closed to any except the combatants and their owners during the contests. And even if Lucius did find him, there would be too many ears to keep his problems with Cornelia from becoming gossip fodder.

He picked up the pace as he went down the stairs. The sooner he got Brutus's men on the hunt, the sooner Cornelia would pay for what she'd done.

Lucius barely glanced at the intricate stone carvings of men in combat that flanked the door of the Ludus Bruti. The door slave straightened as Lucius strode toward him.

"Where can I find Brutus?"

"In the practice arena, Master Drusus."

Lucius climbed the stairs to the balcony that overlooked the arena. Young women often watched the gladiators training below, but today none stood giggling and pointing at their current favorite. Lucius smiled at their absence. His request might spawn gossip if any overheard.

He gripped the railing as he scanned the sand below. Brutus was sparring with one of his men. Lucius headed down the second stairway that led to the arena to join him.

"*Salve*, Brutus."

Brutus parried another strike by his gladiator and stepped back.

"Salve, Drusus. I hope all has been well with you. It's been, what, eight months since you last came to check Tertius's progress? He told me Marcus volunteered to join Lucius serving in Judaea. Not an easy posting."

Brutus's smiling frown shifted toward a smile. "I'm proud to have trained two loyal sons of Roma."

Lucius masked his surprise. All well with him? Brutus usually had his ear tuned to the latest gossip.

"I think not as well as with you. I hear you're expecting a child. My warmest congratulations."

Brutus rested the blade in his palm. His brow furrowed as he fingered the edge. "I hope they'll be needed. My wife has lost three babies. The last time, the physician said the next pregnancy might kill her...but she's determined to give me a son. She kept begging to try again..." He shrugged.

Brutus's signature smiling frown returned. "Fortuna has smiled on you, Drusus, giving you three fine sons and a daughter. This will be Camilla's last baby. If she births a daughter, I might want to adopt Tertius. My estates and business ventures are worth more than the share he'll inherit from you. I'll need a fine young man to be paterfamilias after me."

Lucius faked a smile. "That would be a tempting offer for many, but even a fourth of my fortune is many times what a man needs to remain senatorial. Besides, Tertius is the best of my sons. If I did decide to help a childless friend, it would be Marcus or Lucius I'd give to him."

Brutus's chuckle was more of a snort. "I'd be proud to claim Lucius as my own, even if I'm not old enough to have fathered him. I've seen only one man who's his equal. He tracked his kidnapped friend from Germania to Roma after I bought the German in Octodurus. Crassus was barely taller than my chin, but he fought me for the chance to rescue his giant friend from the arena." The smiling frown returned. "But Tertius should grow into as good a man as his oldest brother."

Brutus flexed his wrist, tracing a Greek sigma with the gladius's tip. "I have men fighting this afternoon. Is there something you need this morning?"

"I have a new steward, so I need some information about Malleolus's last dealings with you."

Speaking the old man's name fanned his irritation, but Lucius forced his voice to sound calm. "He retired from my service and left Rome. Did he hire your men as escorts for his move?"

"No. The last time I saw him was a month or so ago. He hired four gladiators to accompany a cart to your eastern estate, but that was only for a few hours." The corner of his mouth turned up. "My condolences on his retirement. His reputation for making money earned you the envy of many."

Lucius kept his jaw from clenching. "I've already noticed his absence." He forced a smile. "In time, Paullus will be an adequate replacement, but for now, I must attend to some things myself. I need to hire two gladiators for a trip to Thracia and back. I might need a third man if your fighters aren't smart enough to handle a challenging situation."

Brutus placed one arm across his stomach and propped his elbow on it before resting the flat side of the sword on his shoulder. "That should be possible. Which men I would provide for that will depend on what you need them for."

"My former wife has kidnapped my daughter. I suspect Cornelia has taken her to Thracia. My brother and sister live there and would help her find a place where she can hide Drusilla from me. I'll need reliable men who are smart enough to see through any tricks Cornelia might pull."

Brutus's head tipped. "Why did she take Drusilla?"

Lucius stiffened. "We had a disagreement over her betrothal. Cornelia is one of those who thinks she's as smart as any man and should have her say in things that aren't her business."

"Not her business? Most mothers think that is their business. Who were you going to betroth her to?"

"Marcus Corvinus's son."

"Gaius? I've been training him as long as I've been training Tertius. No mother would object to him." Brutus's cocked eyebrow demanded more.

"His younger brother. Drusilla's only ten."

"Gnaeus? You can't be serious. Gaius has told me too many stories. That boy is crazy."

Lucius couldn't stop the frown. "She's my daughter, and I have the right to betroth her to whomever I see fit."

Brutus's eyes narrowed. "You do. But as paterfamilias, you should be guardian of your family and protector of your daughter. How could any father even consider giving her to a boy like that? If I had a daughter, I'd sooner let her play with a tiger than give her to someone like Gnaeus."

Brutus's jaw clenched, and he swung his blade toward the young gladiator. His man barely caught the slashing gladius before it cut into his side. "Stay alert."

His gaze locked on Lucius. "I'll have no part in the betrayal of all a father should be."

He struck at his man again, and his gladiator caught the sword sooner. "Better."

Brutus wrapped his hand around the blade. He stared at it as he slid his thumb along the dulled edge. "Children are a gift from the gods. No friendship is worth letting yours be killed."

He focused on Lucius, and his eyes chilled. "You have every right to recover your daughter." A smiling frown curved his lips. "But I hope you fail in the attempt. I won't be party to dragging a girl back from safety with her mother to certain harm, maybe even death."

Lucius crossed his arms. "Men say you'll rent gladiators to anyone for any purpose, no questions asked. It's not your place to deny my rights as paterfamilias. This will do your reputation no good."

A laugh rumbled in Brutus's chest. "You think you can threaten me? My estates and other businesses increase my wealth daily, and my gladiators are in great demand. You might be richer, and you have some friends of importance. But I have the friendship and respect of men greater than you."

Brutus placed the point of his sword against Lucius's breastbone and pressed. Lucius's heart galloped as he took a step back.

"Nothing you say will make me betray my own code of honor." Brutus lowered the sword and handed it to his gladiator. "It's time to drop this before one of us says or does something he'll regret." The smiling frown returned, but Brutus's eyes remained cool. "Come soon and watch Tertius spar. You'll be impressed by his improvement. I have men in the bouts this afternoon. I need to clean up before I go, so you must excuse me. *Vale*, Drusus."

He turned and walked down the narrow passage that opened by the armor room.

Lucius touched his chest where the blade had rested. He blew out a breath through pursed lips. Would any men who mattered more than Brutus share his opinion?

His jaw clenched. So what if they did? Roman law gave him the right, and Cornelia had earned whatever might happen.

Brutus wasn't the only man with gladiators for hire, and the others wouldn't question his choice as paterfamilias. Brutus's word could be trusted that he hadn't helped Malleolus spirit Drusilla away, but had another ludus provided guards? Paullus could ask at the others and then pick the right one to provide the men who would hunt for the pair of them.

Drusilla was his, and Cornelia would lose the contest over their daughter's fate.

Chapter 33

WORSHIP WITH THE CAPTAIN

Anthusa was brushing her hair when Cornelia heard the quiet knocking.

"Come in."

Miriam pushed the door open and stepped halfway into the room. "Tomorrow is Sunday, and we'll be going to Philip's early for worship. Our whole household goes, but I'll have something left in the kitchen for your breakfast and lunch. Of course, if you want, you're very welcome to come with us."

Cornelia stroked her jaw. "We listened to Hector three times on his ship, and I found what he said very intriguing. I would like to learn more." She pressed her lips together. "I do have a concern, though. Are there any Romans? More to the point, are they equestrians or senators?"

Miriam nodded. "There are some, and a few do wear the purple-striped tunics."

Cornelia shook her head. "I'm reluctant to go where someone might recognize me and let Lucius know I'm in Thracia. Until I know Marcus Corvinus has betrothed his son to some other poor girl, I don't want to risk any word about me getting back to Lucius."

"I'm sure they'd keep your secret if they knew they should."

"Perhaps, but if I don't know them myself, I can't be sure. We won't go."

"I'll say good night then. We may be gone before you get up, but we'll be back some time after lunch. All the worshippers share a meal before we go home."

"Good night, Miriam. I hope you enjoy your worship as much as Hector did onboard."

Miriam flashed a smile at her. "I always do." She turned and limped down the balcony toward her bedchamber.

Cornelia walked to the door and watched until she entered her room. She heard Titus's voice as he welcomed the woman he loved for their night together.

A deep sigh escaped. It would have been so nice to go with them, but Drusilla's safety was more important than anything she might enjoy. It was better to stay home.

Drusilla woke in the gray dawn when she heard Vania rising.

"Vania?" Her whisper sounded like a shout in the quiet room.

"Yes?" Vania's whisper was softer.

"What are you doing?"

"Getting ready to go to Uncle Philip's for worship."

"Oh. I didn't think about it being Sunday." Drusilla paused. "Is Captain Hector going to be there?"

"I think so. When his ship is here, he's always there." Vania tiptoed to the door and opened it slowly. Her finger touched her lips before she whispered. "Mother told me not to make any noise to wake you or Aunt Cornelia."

Drusilla's own finger touched her lips. "I won't tell her."

Vania flashed a smile before she slipped out the door and pulled it closed.

Drusilla pulled the sheets up around her chin. Captain would be at their worship. She'd loved listening to him read and teach on the ship. He'd looked so pleased when he saw how much she liked it. She knew the way to Aunt Claudia's house. She could get there herself to be with Captain and hear everything. Aunt Miriam had told Vania not to wake her, but she was already awake, so there was no reason not to go.

Drusilla slid off her bed and picked out a clean tunic from her trunk. After running a comb through her hair a few times, she was ready.

She pulled the door open a crack and peeked out. No sign of anyone moving on the balcony. She tiptoed along the balcony and down the stairs. When she peaked into the kitchen, a tray of bread, cheese, and fruit sat on the table, covered with a cloth. Everyone seemed to have left already, but they couldn't be too far ahead.

She hurried to the courtyard door that fronted the street, but it was barred and locked. Then she trotted back to the kitchen and passed into the garden. When she reached the carriage gate, it was locked, too. But straw was piled by the wall, and the stack was tall enough that she could stand on it and reach the top. She pulled herself up, swung her legs over, and dropped to the ground outside.

Far up the street, Aunt Miriam limped beside Uncle Titus, holding Vania's hand. Drusilla couldn't catch up before they reached Uncle Philip's house, but she wouldn't be far behind.

She lifted her tunic so it wouldn't shorten her stride and ran up the street.

Hector was talking with Philip when something small and warm slipped into his hand as it hung at his side. His head snapped back when he glanced down.

"Drusilla. What are you doing here?" He scanned the gathering. "Is your mother here, too?"

"No, Captain. I came so I could hear more about Jesus. Can I sit with you?"

"Of course." He wrapped his arm around her shoulder and returned to his conversation with Philip.

◆

The young men talking with Marcario split up to join their families for the worship. His eyebrows popped up when he saw his father's arm wrapped around the shoulder of a brown-haired girl he'd never seen before. Who was this, and why did his father's whole face soften when he glanced down at her?

A smile spread across his face. The daughter of Cornelia Scipia. God had answered all his prayers for his father's broken heart with a little girl.

He strolled over to Philip and his father. Philip acknowledged his arrival with a smile and a nod.

"Time for me to ask God's guidance before we begin. Hector. Marcario." He turned and walked to the stand where a gospel codex waited.

Marcario grinned at his father. "I see we have company today."

Hector placed his hands on Drusilla's shoulders. "We do. This is Drusilla. I just brought her from Rome."

Marcario bent over to rest his hands on his knees, putting his eyes level with Drusilla's. "Welcome, Drusilla. I'm Marcario. Hector is my father. I hope you'll sit with us while we worship. Do you already belong to Jesus?"

Drusilla's brow furrowed. "Belong to Jesus? I'm not sure what you mean, but Captain talked about Jesus on the ship. I liked everything he said."

Hector rested his hand on her hair, and she turned her face up to his. "Philip will tell you much more, and it will be even better than what you heard from me. Let's sit down. Worship is about to start."

The three of them settled on a bench. Marcario glanced at the little girl resting her head against his father's shoulder. Less than five weeks together on a ship, and she loved his father already. His glance shifted to his father's face. That love flowed both ways.

As Calamus strummed the lyre and the first song began, Marcario lifted his heart in thanksgiving. The dark cloud smothering his father was gone. God could heal anyone's heart with love.

◆

Hector reveled in the softness of the small hand holding his and the warmth of her head resting against his shoulder as Philip taught. Drusilla sitting next to him was almost like having Charissa beside him again. He tightened his jaw to keep his eyes dry, but it wasn't only sadness trying to moisten them. Charissa was gone forever from this world, but she was with Jesus. Someday he would join her and Damara, but for now, his heart warmed with the pleasure of loving the precious child beside him.

Thank you, Father, for brining Drusilla for me to love. Thank you for Cornelia, that she welcomes me so I can spend time with her daughter... and with her.

It was good that Cornelia wanted him to visit Drusilla. It would be even better if she wanted those visits for her own pleasure as well.

Chapter 34

FREED AGAIN

Malleolus sat beside Claudia, his heart pounding. During his long life, he'd faced many turning points. As a youth, he'd been bought to serve as Publius's manservant. The trust that grew during their time with the legion made him steward when Publius became paterfamilias. Trust became friendship and led to freedom. The day the praetor tapped him with the rod and pronounced him Publius Claudius Malleolus, freedman, had seemed the pinnacle of his life.

Then the heartbreak of the death of his best friend was followed by years of serving the worthless son who'd betrayed his father for power and wealth. Malleolus had borne that with patience for the sake of Publius's grandchildren. And thanks to Lucius's failure as a father, he'd come to Claudia to end his days with those he loved.

But everything paled in comparison to the new life he was prepared to embrace with every fiber of his being. The bondage of the past lay behind him, and he was ready to be freed a second time.

Philip picked up a codex and held it close to his chest. Then he closed his eye and lifted it above his head.

"Dear Father, may my words be inspired by the Holy Spirit and bring honor to You and to my Lord Jesus."

Malleolus tried to focus on what Philip was reading and the explanation that followed, but his mind kept racing forward to what lay ahead.

At last, Philip turned toward Malleolus, and pure delight flooded Philip's face. "And now, brothers and sisters, I want to share what our

Lord Jesus said to His disciples as they gathered with Him privately, what He still says to us.

"'If anyone would come after me, he must deny himself and take up his cross daily and follow me. For whoever wants to save his life will lose it, but whoever loses his life for me will save it. What good is it for a man to gain the whole world, and yet lose or forfeit his very self? If anyone is ashamed of me and my words, the Son of Man will be ashamed of him when he comes in his glory and in the glory of the Father and of the holy angels. I tell you the truth, some who are standing here will not taste death before they see the kingdom of God.'"

Philip closed the codex and returned it to the stand. "Jesus told us that no one can come to Him except when the Father calls Him. There is one among us who has heard that call, and today, in this gathering, he wants to proclaim his answer."

He offered his hands, and Malleolus took them before lowering himself to his knees.

Then Philip's hands moved to his shoulders. "In the presence of all gathered here, tell our Lord your decision to love and serve Him, and receive the Holy Spirit as He promised."

A wistful smile curved Malleolus's mouth. "Eight years ago, my best friend decided Jesus was the Son of God and his savior. He wanted to tell me why he made that decision, but I didn't want to listen."

He drew a deep breath and released it slowly. "I saw he was disappointed, but he said that was fine, that we could talk about it later. But in less than a month, he was dead, betrayed by his oldest son and killed in the Flavian Amphitheater because he refused to deny his Lord and offer incense to Caesar. Since that day, I've often wished I'd listened when I had the chance."

Malleolus looked at Hector with Drusilla snuggled against his side, and his smile grew. "When I found myself on a ship bound for Perinthus with Publius's granddaughter and daughter-in-law, the chance I thought I'd lost forever came. Hector became the second Christian I knew well enough to ask, and he began to answer my questions on that voyage."

His gaze swept the smiling faces before him. "I have decided Publius was right in his beliefs. He convinced me years ago that the God of Israel was real, not just the hero of stories created by men. And being real, God alone decides what it takes to earn His favor. Publius kept telling me anything less than perfection was not enough. But no man could ever be perfect. It seemed hopeless. Then, when he told me Jesus had chosen to be the sacrifice that let God look on him as being perfect when he wasn't and never could be, it seemed too good to be true.

"But the joy that belief gave him…I started to wonder. I was almost ready to ask when he died. When Publius was gone, I thought I would never know another person who could tell me if Publius spoke the truth.

"But God wasn't through with me. First Hector, then Claudia and Philip…they knew the same joy, and they answered all the questions I would have asked my friend. And today, before you all, I declare that I know Jesus did everything Publius said. He is the Son of God, His death paid for all my sins, His resurrection proved it, and I want to love and serve Him for the rest of my life."

The air around him pulsated with light and love, and his heart soared heavenward as he spoke words he'd never heard before. And when he finished, Calamus strummed the lyre. The voices of men, women, and children blended into a harmony ringing with joy and peace.

◆

Hector looked down at Drusilla when she poked his arm and whispered.

"I believe in Jesus, and I pray to Him, just like Vania."

He beamed at her. "You can't know how happy that makes me. It means that no matter what happens, we'll be together in heaven with Jesus. You'll meet my Charissa there, and I know you'll love each other like sisters."

Drusilla wrapped her arm around his and snuggled in. He breathed a contented sigh. It would be pure joy to have her with him through eternity.

If only Cornelia would make that same decision.

Chapter 35

TOO GREAT A RISK?

The silence of the house wrapped around Cornelia as she walked from her room to Drusilla's closed door. She tapped three times before pushing it open.

"Time to get up, dear. Breakfast is waiting for us."

The sunlight streaming through the window lit the room, revealing two empty beds with the covers piled up at the foot of each. Drusilla must have already gone down to eat.

At the foot of the stairs, Cornelia veered into the kitchen. A plate of cheese, fruit, and bread sat on the table. But no sign of Drusilla.

She stepped back into the courtyard. "Drusilla! Where are you?" No answer.

She turned to Anthusa, who'd come down behind her. "Check all the rooms. I'll check outside. She must be here somewhere."

Anthusa nodded and hurried back upstairs.

Cornelia searched the garden and the stables, calling Drusilla's name repeatedly.

Anthusa ran out the kitchen door. "She isn't in the house, mistress, and her trunk is open. She got a clean tunic out."

Cornelia's eyebrows dipped as she bit her lip. "Maybe she went to Philip's. But I told Miriam I didn't want us to go in case one of the Romans might tell Lucius. Why would she go against what I'd told her? It's not her place to decide to take Drusilla without my permission." Her lips pressed tight as her anger grew.

"I don't think Miriam would, mistress. Maybe Drusilla followed without her knowing."

Cornelia drew a sharp breath. "She just might do that. We must go up there right now to be sure." She gripped Anthusa's hand. "But what if someone came from Lucius and took her?" Her breath came faster at that thought. "Come. There's no time to waste."

The key for the small door by the carriage gate hung in the storeroom, and Anthusa dashed back into the house to fetch it.

Cornelia started up the road at a brisk pace while her maid locked the door behind them. She fought against the panic surging within. What if Drusilla wasn't at Philip's? Where else could she possibly be?

It was only a quarter mile, but it seemed like ten. When they reached Philip's pedestrian gate, it was locked. No one answered her pounding. She hurried on to the carriage gate. When she knocked, a small window opened to reveal the gatekeeper's face. It closed instantly, and the gate swung open to admit them.

The gatekeeper bowed. "Welcome, Mistress Cornelia."

She gripped his arm. "Have you seen Drusilla?"

"Yes, mistress. She ran up right after I admitted Titus and his family. She's at worship in the garden now. Do you want me to take you there?"

Cornelia closed her eyes, and her shoulders slumped as relief flooded through her.

"No. Now that I know she's here and safe, I'll take care of the problem later."

"Did you want to join them yourself?"

"No, I don't want to disturb the worship. When it's over, tell Miriam what Drusilla has done so she'll bring her home with her family."

"Of course, mistress. I won't let your daughter leave alone."

"I'm going back to Titus's now. How long will it be before they return?"

"Probably two or three hours, mistress."

The gatekeeper reopened the gate, and the two women returned to the street.

As they trudged back to the house, Cornelia's mouth drifted from frown to scowl. "I can't believe she did that. How could she be so foolish to run off alone? Anything might have happened to her."

"Perhaps she thought the captain would be there."

Cornelia's face relaxed as she took a deep breath. "You're probably right. Of course he would be. But that's still no excuse for her going without asking me."

"No, mistress. I'm sure she'll never do that again after you talk with her."

"She most definitely will not."

They walked on in silence.

With tightened lips, Cornelia shook her head. To be with the captain, Drusilla would take any risk without thinking. Her lips relaxed. It was hard to stay mad about that. She would almost be willing to do such a thing herself.

No real harm had come this time, and maybe it was a good thing she had gone. It would be a chance to impress on her daring daughter that she shouldn't do such things in the future. By now, Lucius was surely looking for them. Finding them was the one thing that must never happen.

When Cornelia finally heard voices in the courtyard, she left her loom in the women's room and leaned over the balcony railing. Drusilla stood below with Miriam holding her hand.

"Drusilla. You get up here right now." The edge on her voice matched the frown on her lips.

Drusilla looked up at her and swallowed hard. "Coming, Mother."

Miriam tipped her head back. "I'm very sorry, Cornelia. We didn't realize she was coming until we saw her with Hector. I would never have taken her without asking you."

"I know. The gatekeeper told me she ran up after you were already there."

Drusilla now stood before her mother, head lowered. Cornelia gripped her shoulder and pushed her into the women's room ahead of her.

"I have something to tell you, Claudia Drusilla." Cornelia lowered her voice. "And I don't want your cousins to hear me." Cornelia gripped both her shoulders and turned Drusilla to face her.

"You left this house without telling anyone and without my permission. You are never, ever to do such a thing again. Do you have any idea why?"

Drusilla shook her head.

"Someone might recognize you and let your father know where

you are. What if he sends someone to drag you back and they find you when I can't protect you?"

Drusilla's eyes widened as they filled with tears. Her lip quivered. "I'm sorry, Mother. I only wanted to learn more about Jesus. I wanted to sit with Captain so I could ask him questions. Families sit together there, and Captain let me sit with him like I was his daughter. I met his son, Marcario, but he won't tell anyone. I don't think anyone who would tell Father learned our secret."

Teardrops began to escape. Cornelia rested her palm on Drusilla's cheek and swept some away with her thumb. "There was probably no harm done today, but you should have asked first instead of just going. Never, ever do that again. You frightened me half to death when Anthusa and I couldn't find you. I was afraid someone your father had sent might have come and taken you."

She pulled Drusilla close and wrapped her tightly in her arms. "I love you, dear, and I want to keep you safe. In the future, ask my permission. If I think it's safe, I'll let you go."

Drusilla hugged her back. "I will, Mother. I promise, and I'll always keep my word, just like Captain." She tipped her head back to smile into her mother's eyes. "I think it was safe today. Captain would never let anything happen to me."

Cornelia pushed some loose hair behind Drusilla's ear. "I know the captain would protect you if he could, but we still don't want to take any chances."

"I promise I won't take chances."

Cornelia released her. "Good. Now you can go find Vania."

Drusilla wrapped her arms around her mother in one quick hug before darting out of the room.

Cornelia sighed as she turned to Anthusa. "I don't think she'll do something like that again. I can't blame her for wanting to be with Hector, and I know he would do anything he could to protect her."

"He would, mistress. He loves her like a daughter."

Cornelia massaged the back of her neck. "But sometimes love isn't enough to keep danger away. Sometimes it can even get you into more danger than you can handle. Sometimes it can get you killed."

A shiver of foreboding ran through Cornelia's body. What if Lucius figured out where they were? Drusilla would be in mortal danger again, and all the love in the world might not be enough to save her.

◆

Later that afternoon, Drusilla stood beside her mother in the women's room, watching her weave the shuttle back and forth through the warp threads. She leaned her head against her mother's shoulder. "I'm sorry I went without asking. I'll never do that again."

Mother turned to smile at her. "I know, dear." She parked the shuttle on the loom and tucked a strand of Drusilla's hair behind her ear. "So, was it like when the captain led worship on the ship?"

Drusilla shrugged. "Mostly. Uncle Philip talks longer than Captain, and they sang more songs. Everybody looked really happy, just like Captain's crew. Malleolus talked, too. He said he'd decided to follow Jesus, but I didn't understand everything he said. He started using words that weren't Latin or Greek."

With her head tipped, she raised questioning eyebrows. "May I go again? I'd like to."

"I would, too. Perhaps we can, if I can be certain no one there will let your father know we're here."

"I liked sitting with Captain and meeting Marcario. That's his son. He's nice."

"I would expect a son of the captain to be a nice young man."

Drusilla slid her hand into her mother's and swung them.

"Mother...do you like Captain?"

"Very much. He's a fine man."

Drusilla kept swinging their hands. "What I mean is...do you want to marry Captain?"

Cornelia met Drusilla's gaze with a smile. "If the captain were to ask me, I would say yes." Her smile broadened. "You'd like that, wouldn't you?"

Drusilla beamed "Oh, yes. I'd love to have Captain as my father." Her brows lowered as her smile dimmed. "When we were eating, I heard something. Marcario and his friend were talking about marrying. His friend said he would only marry someone who believed in Jesus."

Cornelia's head tipped as those words sunk in. "That's interesting. I guess I'm not surprised. Christian men love their god enough to do anything for him. Your grandfather died rather than offer a simple sacrifice to Caesar. He thought that would be denying Jesus as his lord. I can see where a Christian man would only want a wife who worshiped the same god."

Drusilla's lips straightened. "Do you think Captain feels that way?"

"I don't know, dear."

"Do you think you could follow Jesus?"

"Maybe. I found everything Hector read and taught us on his ship very appealing. I would like to learn more. Perhaps Philip can teach us sometime when it's just family."

Vania stuck her head in the door. "Want to feed the chickens?"

Drusilla looked at her cousin over her shoulder. "I'll be right there."

As Drusilla followed Vania down the stairs, she made a decision.

She would ask Captain to ask Mother to come to worship with them. Mother said she was interested in learning more about Jesus since listening to Captain teach about him. Everyone in their family in Thracia was a Christian, just like her grandfather. Mother always said Grandfather Publius was the smartest man she knew.

If the smartest man followed Jesus, surely Uncle Philip and Captain could convince Mother she should, too. Then Captain could marry her.

Drusilla smiled at that thought. Mother would be happy, and she could have the best father in the world.

Chapter 36

Horse Play

On Monday morning, Quintus Aemilius Lepidus rode through Titus's carriage gate. He needed a new stallion, and Titus Drusus was known as one of the best horse breeders west of Byzantium.

Titus was talking with his steward as Quintus rode up.

"Greetings, Drusus."

Titus spun at his voice. "Lepidus. What brings you here today?"

"I was speaking with Brutus at the palace yesterday, and he told me you have a pair of two-year-old colts in your stable now. He said you planned to sell them, and I'm in the market for a young stallion."

Titus waved his hand toward the stable. "Brutus spoke the truth. I do have the colts here, and I am thinking about selling them. Come and see."

Quintus swung his leg across his horse's neck and slid to the ground. When the steward took his reins, Quintus fell in step beside Titus. The well-formed head of a handsome bay looked over the half-door of the first stall.

Titus rested his hand on the door frame. "This is Tonitrui. When he runs, it's like the sound of thunder." He stepped to the next stall and whistled. A black colt with a long white blaze sauntered over to get his nose rubbed. "And this is Fulgur, the lightning that travels even faster than the thunder."

Quintus reached out to stroke Tonitrui's nose. The colt flipped his head, snorted, and stepped back. "A pretty animal, Drusus, but jumpy. Let me see Fulgur closer."

Titus opened the stall door and led the colt out. Quintus stroked his neck, and the colt turned his head to contemplate the strange man who touched him. Quintus ran his hands over the colt's back, across his flank, and down his shoulder. He felt the legs, nodding as he did so. The animal was sound and confident. He would be good for riding and breeding.

"A decent animal. What are you asking for Fulgur?"

Titus stopped stroking the blaze, and Fulgar bumped him with his head, demanding more attention. "He's already faster than several of my fast four-year-olds. With his size and conformation, he's likely to be a superb stallion. I'm in no great hurry to sell him."

Quintus nodded. "But if you were to sell him, what would you want?"

Titus rubbed his chin as he considered the question. "I would consider three thousand denarii a reasonable price."

Quintus stopped his brows from rising. That was a lot of money. More than he was comfortable spending. His net worth had been drifting down lately. He was in no immediate danger of falling below the 100,000 denarii required to remain in the equestrian class, but he didn't have the surplus that would make a 3000-denarii horse seem inexpensive.

"That seems too much to me. I could see 500, maybe even 750, but not 3000."

Titus kept stroking Fulgur's nose. "That's not enough for this colt, but I have some others at the estate that would be in that price range. Perhaps you'd like to ride out some time and see the others."

Quintus nodded. "I'm not in a great hurry, so perhaps I will."

He heard the sound of women's voices behind him and turned to see who it was. One was the pretty little Jewish slave Titus had married, but the other was a Roman woman in her late 30s. "I see you have female company. Who is she?"

Titus appeared to tense, then relax. "She's just a distant relative who's visiting for a while."

The square jaw, the wide mouth, the prominent nose—Quintus knew that face, and it belonged to Cornelia Scipia, wife of Lucius Claudius Drusus, one of the wealthiest men in Rome.

"Is she married now?"

Titus shook his head. "No."

Quintus kept a straight face. Cornelia Scipia, now divorced and surely in possession of an enormous dowry. A plain woman, but it was well known how attractive a large dowry can make even an ugly one. It might be worth his while to seek out her company and flatter her into marrying him. A dowry like hers would remove all concern about the future.

"I'm already expected somewhere else this morning, but I would like to go with you to your estate sometime soon. Or even better, perhaps you could bring what you think suitable here for me to see."

Titus resumed stroking Fulgur's nose. "I have two that might particularly interest you. I'll send word when I have them here."

Quintus gestured for the steward to bring his horse. He jumped and swung his leg over the horse's rump. As he settled into the saddle, he looked down at Titus. "I look forward to receiving your message."

As he swung his horse toward the gate, his gaze lingered on the plain woman with Titus's pretty wife. Divorced, plain enough to be swayed by flattery, exceedingly wealthy. The perfect woman to become his second wife. He'd married once and found deep love. No man could expect that twice. A good companion with a good dowry would be enough the second time. He would, indeed, look forward to his next visit to the Drusus house, but a rich, plain woman was much more interesting than any horse.

Drusilla was bouncing with excitement the next morning, and Cornelia was scarcely less excited herself. Hector was coming to teach them to drive.

It was a cool day, so they watched for Hector's arrival from the window in the women's room.

"I see him. He's got a cisium, just like Malleolus used to drive to the estate sometimes." Drusilla snatched up her new cloak from the couch. "I thought he would bring horses. It's a pair of mules."

Cornelia threw her cloak around her shoulders. "Perhaps mules are better for learning. I'm sure the captain knows what's best for teaching us."

Drusilla trotted down the balcony and skipped down the stairs ahead of her. Cornelia followed, walking slower but just as eager to reach the captain's side. Sitting close to him on the seat of a cisium—she could think of no better way to spend the morning. Horses, mules—either was fine with her as long as Hector held the reins.

◆

Hector turned from his conversation with Nestor when Drusilla took his hand.

"I thought you'd bring horses, Captain. Can't they run faster?"

"They can, but I'm not going to let you run them." He smiled at the bright eyes staring up at him. "Your mother wouldn't want me to risk it."

He knew Cornelia was close when the faint scent of flowers teased him. It wasn't roses, but he wasn't sure what it was. He turned to face those deep blue eyes and found them dancing with pleasure.

"Good morning, Captain...Hector. It's a beautiful day for our driving lesson."

"It should be a good day, except for being cool. I brought a blanket so you won't get cold."

"How thoughtful, C...Hector." She rested her hand on the cisium seat. "The seat is rather small, but it should be large enough for the three of us if we sit close. That should help us all stay warm."

Hector drew a breath. Sitting close to her was certainly going to help him stay warm.

"Let me help you in, and we can start."

Drusilla stepped in front of him, and he lifted her into the seat. She slid over next to the edge and patted the center of the seat. "Sit here, Captain."

Hector turned back to Cornelia.

She stepped close. "I'm ready for you to lift me in as well."

The scent of the unknown flowers grew stronger. His stomach tightened. He'd intended to use a mounting block to help her in. He hadn't planned on placing his hands on her waist and lifting her, but he found that thought strangely satisfying.

That playful smile he loved appeared on her lips. "I'm not so heavy that a man like you can't lift me easily."

"You don't look heavy to me." She was going to twist those words somehow.

Her eyes sparkled, but no tease came. She placed her hands on his shoulders. "Then I'm ready."

Even through his cloak, he felt the warmth of her petite hands. He placed his hands on her waist and lifted her up to the open-fronted seat that sat directly above the single axle.

She was right. She was very easy to lift.

"Perhaps you should sit between us, Captain, like when you taught us to tie knots. That worked very well."

"You're right. That would be best." Sitting so close, breathing her perfume—that was likely to be the best part of the day for him. Did those smiling eyes mean she was thinking the same?

Hector stepped on the hub and swung himself up onto the seat between the two of them. He reached under the seat and pulled out the blanket. After he shook it out, he draped it across all three laps.

Cornelia's elegant hands smoothed the blanket and tucked the end in beside her. Her shoulder brushed his as she settled back in the seat. It was a tight squeeze for three. There was no chance he was going to feel cold during this drive.

He slapped the reins on the mules' backs. The cisium lurched as they began pulling. Drusilla leaned into him, and Cornelia's shoulder brushed against his again. He squeezed his lips to keep the grin from escaping. Sitting between the girl he loved and the woman who attracted him more than he should allow—there truly was no better way to spend a morning.

◆

Cornelia held the reins exactly as Hector had showed her. She glanced at his rugged profile as the mules trotted along the road. He was such a good teacher—able to explain how to handle the reins with a few words, not too quick to take them from her when the mules got stubborn and didn't want to do what she wanted them to.

"Take this turn." Hector crossed his arms and smiled at the ease with which she turned the team. "It leads to a stream near my farm. It's pretty there."

"Near your farm? Will we be driving there as well?"

"No, not today. There's not much there to see."

That was a disappointment. Cornelia was eager to see the farm where she hoped he would take her as his wife.

A man on horseback crested the hill before her, trotting toward them. As he got closer, his noble bearing made her breath catch. His tunic bore the two narrow purple stripes of an equestrian. Her heart pounded, then it relaxed. He was close enough for her to see his face. She didn't recognize him. He wouldn't recognize her.

She expected him to pass them by, but he reined in, blocking their path. Hector rested his palms on her hands and pulled back on the reins. She handed them to him and folded her hands in her lap as he finished bringing the cisium to a full stop.

The Roman nodded once at Hector. Then he fixed his eyes on Cornelia. "Cornelia Scipia. I didn't expect to meet you on a road in Thracia."

"Nor did I expect to encounter someone from home." Her mind raced as she tried to remember who this Roman might be. No luck.

The stranger smiled. "I see you don't quite remember me. Quintus Aemilius Lepidus. I've known your brother-in-law Drusus since he was a tribune serving the governor here. I thought that might be you I glimpsed the other day when I came to look at his colts. You and I spoke about ten years ago in Rome. I haven't forgotten you. No man could." He threw a flattering smile her way.

Cornelia laughed. "Quite so. My beauty has dazzled men for years." Hector tensed beside her. "Do you know Hector as well?"

"Of course." He glanced at Hector, his eyes cooling before he moved them back to her, where they warmed again. "He's a neighbor. I have a large estate in this valley. I share a short length of my border with his farm."

"This part of Thracia is lovely. I can see why you've chosen living here over any of the Lepidus lands near Rome." She glanced at Hector.

His face was stony as Lepidus pointedly ignored him. His hands gripped the reins as his right thumb rubbed back and forth on the leather. The mules fidgeted as if they sensed his tension.

She tipped her head as she donned her social smile. "It's been a pleasure to see you again after so many years, but we must leave you now."

"I'll have to stop by Drusus's house so you can tell me the news from Rome. It's been some years since I last visited there."

"That would be my pleasure, Lepidus. I bid you farewell now."

Cornelia took the reins from Hector's fingers. With a slap against the mules' rumps, she started them down the road, away from the Roman she didn't remember and wished she'd never seen.

◆

The gracious mask that Cornelia had worn facing Lepidus cracked. Hector felt the trembling where Cornelia's shoulder brushed against his and saw the slight tremor in her hands. He lifted the reins from her fingers, and she slumped against him.

When he turned his gaze upon her face, fear had replaced her usual calm. She tried to mask it, and she almost succeeded. He knew her too well now for her to hide it completely from him.

"I don't think you have to worry about what just happened. I've known Lepidus for several years. He's a decent man. His roots are here in Thracia. It's not likely he would know or care about the gossip in Rome. He shouldn't be a threat to Drusilla."

She drew a breath and released it slowly. She straightened, and he was sorry her shoulder broke contact with his own.

"Since you know him, I trust your assurance on that. You're probably right. He has brothers still living in Rome, but they didn't used to be friends of Lucius. I doubt they've become so since we left."

Drusilla pressed closer to Hector. Her wide eyes glistened with unshed tears.

"Don't be afraid, child. Nothing will happen to you. Titus, Philip, and I will keep you and your mother safe."

Drusilla wrapped her arm tightly around his, but her face relaxed. "I always feel safe with you, Captain."

They reached the stream, and he reined the team in. "Did you want to get out here? There's a nice view from the rocks over there."

Cornelia leaned against him again. "Perhaps another day. It feels rather cold. Maybe we should start back."

"As you wish."

Disappointment surged through him. He'd hoped for a longer time with her, but Lepidus had spoiled that.

Her deep blue eyes gazed into his own, and a smile lifted her lips. "I am sorry to ask you to cut our drive short today. I feel quite chilled right now, but I would very much like to come here again. I find this area especially attractive, and I hope you'll show us more of it. Living in this part of Thracia is what I hope to do."

He opened his mouth to suggest going to his farmhouse to warm up so they could continue their drive, but he closed it before speaking. His house was warm and welcoming, but it wouldn't seem like much to someone who was used to a beautiful villa on a large estate. No point in showing her something that would merely remind her he was only a ship's captain, not a landed Roman nobleman. He had nothing to compete with a senator like Atticus or even an equestrian like Lepidus.

He turned the mules and headed back up the hill. "Which of you would like to drive now?"

Drusilla reached for the reins. "Me, Captain. May I make them trot?"

One corner of his mouth twitched up. "I think you're ready for that, but no faster than a trot."

She grinned at him. "Yes, Captain. Will you keep teaching me until I can handle them when they run?"

A laugh rumbled in his throat. "I don't run them myself, but I'll teach you what I can." He glanced at Cornelia and found warm eyes fixed on him. "It's going to take quite a few lessons to teach you all you need to know."

All trace of fear was gone from her face, and she directed an inviting smile at him. "Yes, I think many lessons will be needed for me to learn all I want from you." There were those teasing eyes he loved. "But I hope not more lessons than you're willing to give."

"I'm willing to give whatever you want, Cornelia."

Her laughter was music in his ears. "That's a dangerous promise to make before you know what I want, Hector. An honest man like you can never go back on your word."

He grinned at her. "I'll risk it."

Her grin mirrored his. "And I'll remember it."

Despite the cold shortening their drive, Hector was satisfied. Cornelia wanted more of his company. It had been a very good day.

Chapter 37

CAPTAIN OR HECTOR?

Aunt Claudia had invited everyone to dinner the next day, and Drusilla couldn't have been happier. Captain would be there, and she had something important to tell him.

She swung her mother's hand as they walked up the hill with Aunt Miriam's family. There hadn't been a chance during the drive to tell Captain why Mother hadn't wanted to come to worship at Uncle Philip's house. At least no chance without Mother overhearing. Tonight, she could tell him.

Captain was already there talking with Malleolus when they arrived. She trotted over and slipped her hand into his.

"I have something to tell you, Captain."

He shifted his focus from Malleolus to her. "What?"

She cast a swift glance over her shoulder to make sure Mother was still talking with Aunt Claudia. "Mother was thinking about coming to worship at Uncle Philip's, but she was afraid someone might see us who might say something to someone, and where we are might get back to Father. Aunt Miriam said there were men from Rome there. Mother's afraid they might tell. But I'm sure she'd come if you invite her. You could tell them they shouldn't tell anyone." She glanced again at her mother. "You make Mother feel safe, just like me."

He pushed a strand of hair behind her ear. "That's good to know, child." His eyes warmed as he gazed at her face. "I'll see if I can convince your mother how safe it really is."

199

Drusilla squeezed his hand before slipping away to join Vania and the boy cousins.

◆

Hector strolled over to stand beside Cornelia.

Claudia flashed him a smile. "I want to speak with my chef for a moment. If you'll excuse me, Cornelia, Hector."

Cornelia tipped her head to gaze up into his eyes. "I was just telling Claudia what a lovely time Drusilla and I had yesterday. She was glad to hear that you've started teaching us to drive."

"It's my pleasure to do it."

"It's my pleasure to have you do it."

The serenity of her eyes gave him pause. Sometimes it was hard to believe she was afraid of anything. Was Drusilla right about her only staying away from worship because she feared being betrayed to Lucius? Would his promise of her safety make that much difference to her?

She tilted her head as curiosity lit her eyes. The silence between them began to feel awkward. He should just ask. What was the worst that could happen? She might say no. The best? Next Sunday he might have both her and Drusilla sitting beside him. Maybe she'd sit with Miriam's family during worship, but there would still be a chance to be near her at the meal afterward.

"Drusilla sat with me during last Sunday's worship. I was wondering...would you like to come to worship with me? You seemed interested on the ship. Philip is a much better teacher than I am. I'm sure you'd enjoy hearing him."

"I truly doubt he's much better than you, Captain. I did enjoy listening to you on your ship, but I have concerns about going to Philip's."

"What would those be? Maybe I can help." He watched uncertainty ruffled the serenity of her eyes. "Drusilla would like you there with her."

"I know, but there are some equestrian Romans there. One of them might let Lucius know where we are. I can't risk that."

"I know them all well. They're reliable men, like Titus. If I tell them they should keep you and Drusilla a secret, none of them will tell anyone."

The shadow of worry faded. "Then I would love to go with you. I've wondered for years about the faith of my father-in-law Publius. He was the wisest man I've ever known. Ever since he chose to die rather than sacrifice to Caesar, I've wanted to know what could make him do such a thing. I know Titus and Claudia didn't believe in Jesus before Publius died, but they do now. I would love to learn all about it so I can decide if I should, too."

"Then I'll stop for you next Sunday, and you can begin to learn."

Her lips lifted in a teasing smile. "Being with you has been nothing but a learning experience, Captain, from the moment I boarded your ship. I'll look forward to my next lesson."

Her eyes were dancing, and that smile played on her lips.

But why did she still mostly call him captain instead of Hector? Maybe it was good she did. When she called him Hector and flashed that winsome smile, he sometimes forgot he was only a sea captain and she was a Roman noblewoman. Probably that wasn't good.

But no matter what she called him, she did look forward to the next lesson. And that was enough to trigger his smile.

◆

Claudia made a slight adjustment in her seating arrangements from the first dinner. She switched Malleolus and Hector. That put him directly across from Cornelia, and the two of them provided all the entertainment Claudia needed to enjoy the meal.

Once more, Hector didn't say much, but his gaze kept drifting to Cornelia. Claudia had no doubt of the admiration in his eyes. Any time Cornelia was speaking, his attention focused on her.

As usual, Cornelia conversed easily with everyone, but her best smiles were reserved for Hector.

It was all Claudia could do to suppress a grin when Cornelia turned to Philip after deliberately catching Hector's eye. "Philip, Drusilla told me how much she enjoyed your teaching last Sunday. I was somewhat concerned about attending when I thought word of our being here might get to Lucius, but Hector assures me there's no risk of that." Her eyes focused on Hector, and the gleam was unmistakable before her gaze returned to Philip. "I intend for both of us to be there next time. I want to learn more about your beliefs."

Philip's smile was broad. "I'm glad to hear it. You are most welcome to join us."

Hector beamed when her eyes returned to him.

By the time the final course was served, Claudia found herself contemplating whether the new husband of the woman who'd been her sister-in-law all her life would be considered a new brother-in-law or would he still only be Philip's best friend.

Claudia's maid had finished brushing her hair for the evening. Philip had taken her place behind his seated wife, fingering the thick, reddish-gold tresses that tumbled almost to her waist.

Claudia smiled at his reflection in the dressing table mirror. "It was such fun watching Hector and Cornelia tonight. Every time I see them, it's obvious they like each other more. And when she said she wanted to start coming to our worship to learn...well, I just know God is going to take care of her not being a believer. I'm sure it won't be long before she decides she wants to join us all in following Jesus. That will make her perfect for becoming Hector's second wife."

Philip worked his fingers into her silken hair and pulled them through. "Don't be in a hurry to assume too much. Hector seems to like her, but I'm not seeing anything like the rush to ask for her hand that I remember when he married Damara."

Claudia stood and turned to face him. "That was a long time ago. Young men are always impetuous. Maybe he's forgotten how to court a woman after so many years of marriage. Besides, Hector's so quiet. He might find it hard to ask even when he really wants to. Maybe Cornelia will just have to ask him instead."

A chortle rippled in Philip's chest. "That might work with Roman aristocrats, but it wouldn't be wise to push too hard on a Greek. We make up our own minds."

Claudia stepped close and rested her palms on his bare chest. "That's silly. Greek men aren't that different. I all but begged you to marry me, and look what happened."

He lifted her right hand and kissed her palm. "I'd already decided I wanted you as my wife even before the ship reached Thessalonica. That was more than a week before you tried to persuade me to marry you the night before you moved in with your brother. I was just waiting for you to become a believer so I could ask you."

Claudia traced the rippled scars beside his right eye. "Well, I still don't think Greek men are that different from Roman, and Cornelia's not the kind of woman to miss out on having the perfect husband just because he's shy about asking her. If he's too slow, she'll ask him."

Philip kissed her palm again. "Enough talk about them. Cornelia may or may not be the perfect wife for Hector, but I know perfection in a wife when I see it. It's time for me to enjoy the perfect woman God has blessed me with."

His lips sought hers before he scooped her into his arms.

Anthusa almost laughed aloud as Mistress held out her arms and twirled.

"It was such a lovely dinner tonight, Anthusa." Mistress settled into the chair so her hair could be unbraided and brushed.

"What was so special tonight, mistress?" Anthusa pulled the gold hair pins and the braid tumbled down.

"Hector asked me to go to worship at Philip's with him. I thought that might be dangerous, but he promised me he would talk with the Romans there to make sure it isn't. He's a good judge of people, so I'm sure I can trust them if he does."

Anthusa's fingers unbraided the silken hair. "I'm sure you're right. The captain would never ask you to do something he thought dangerous."

"No, he wouldn't. I saw you enjoy his teaching on the ship. Would you like to go as well?"

Anthusa worked her fingers into the hair and shook it to loosen the last of the braiding. "Yes, mistress. I would."

Mistress Cornelia's reflection smiled at her. "I'm sure he'll be glad."

Anthusa drew the brush through her mistress's hair and watched her glowing eyes in the mirror. She almost looked young again.

"Hector didn't talk much while we were eating, but he seemed to be watching me almost the whole time." The mistress sighed, but it was deeply happy, not sad. Too often those sighs had been sad before coming to Thracia.

"I've never seen a man look happier than he did when I told Philip I was coming to worship with him. Drusilla told me Christian men only want Christian wives. He wouldn't have been so happy if he weren't thinking about marrying me...would he?"

"I don't know, mistress, but it seems that might be so."

"Of course, that's not the only reason I want to go. I want to know more, to understand why Publius loved Jesus enough to die the way he did. But having Hector beside me to explain anything I don't understand...that will be so much better."

"It will."

"I wonder if he'll come tomorrow. I hope so. I don't care what we do when he's here. I just want to be close to him."

"I think he feels the same."

The brushing was over. Mistress strolled to her bed and lay down. "I think so, too." She closed her eyes, but the contented smile remained.

Anthusa blew out the lamp before going to her own bed. The captain almost certainly felt the same. Now he just had to do something about it.

Chapter 38

COUNTING ON THE CAPTAIN

The next day dawned with a cold drizzle. The dull gray clouds dipped low, leaving patches of fog that obscured Cornelia's view down the street toward the sea.

Cornelia's sigh was slow and deep. "I hate it when it rains like this, Anthusa. Everyone just wants to stay indoors where it's warm and dry. Hector's farm is somewhere near the stream where we turned around, so it's a few miles away from here. That's too far for him to ride in this. He'd get soaking wet and chilled to the bone."

"He is a sea captain, mistress. I'm sure he's seen much worse weather and still had to be out working in it. He might still come."

Cornelia brightened. "Do you think so?" Her smile dimmed. "But he shouldn't. I don't want him to come if he has to be out in bad weather. He might get sick."

She turned away from the window and sat at her dressing table so Anthusa could plait and pin her hair "He told Drusilla he would come play Mercenaries. He said he'd come early because he had business to attend to before lunch. When he gives his word, he always keeps it."

"Perhaps he won't today, mistress. He's sensible as well as honest."

Silence fell between them as Anthusa's fingers twisted and pinned. "There. Your hair looks lovely, as always."

Cornelia drifted back to the window. "Such a horrible, gray day." She straightened. A broad-shouldered rider wearing a broad-brimmed hat and draped with a woolen cape that spread across his horse's rump and reached almost to his ankles materialized out of the fog.

"I can't believe it." She turned to face Anthusa. "It's him. He came after all. Quick. I want the attar of roses in my hair." One corner of her mouth rose. "He takes slow, deep breaths when he's close. I'm sure he's enjoying my perfumes, and I can tell that's his favorite." A full grin broke free. "If he's going to ride through the rain, the least I can do is greet him smelling of something that gives him pleasure."

Friday morning was sunny. Hector would have given the second driving lesson to Cornelia and Drusilla, but the side roads that didn't have the benefit of stone surfaces carefully constructed by legionaries were muddy at best and quagmires in the lowest places.

However, that day of sunshine made at least some of the roads passable for the cisium, so Saturday found him driving his mule team through Titus's gate. One more day would be too long to wait before spending some time with the woman whose playful words kept popping into his mind at unexpected moments.

Drusilla came tripping out the kitchen door. "Captain! Are we going driving?"

He looped the reins around the short rod sticking up from the sidewall for that purpose and climbed down. "If your mother wants to. Some of the roads are dry enough, and we'll stay off the ones that aren't."

"I know she'll want to. I'll go get her." Drusilla spun and disappeared through the kitchen doorway.

Nestor emerged from his living quarters adjacent to the stable. "Good to see you, brother." He slapped Hector's arm. "You've been here so often lately that you're almost a member of the household. Someone...ah, something special bring you today?"

Nestor's grin said much more than his words. Hector felt his ears warm. "Drusilla was eager for her next driving lesson. The roads have dried enough. I wanted to take her out before the next rain."

Nestor's grin broadened. "I think Mistress Cornelia is eager for her next lesson as well."

"She said she wanted to learn. It seemed a good idea to teach her while I'm teaching Drusilla." The back of his neck felt warm as well.

Nestor choked back a laugh. "Yes, a very good idea." He glanced toward the kitchen, where Drusilla, wrapped in her cloak, had just scurried out the door. "The first of your pupils is here, but probably not the most eager one." He slapped Hector's arm again. "Enjoy the sunshine."

Hector watched Nestor's back as he walked away. Was it so obvious to everyone that he came to see Cornelia as much as to see her daughter? Was Cornelia as eager for his company as Nestor implied? He wished it were so, but he couldn't tell whether it was just playful friendliness or real interest in him as a man.

He'd watched her with the Romans like the senator in Ephesus and now Lepidus. She responded to them so graciously, even when she was agitated beneath that calm surface. Any man would think she was pleased to talk with him, even when she might not be. She was too good at play-acting, but it didn't feel like she was only acting when she looked into his eyes.

He mentally shook himself. He was letting his desire for her run ahead of what he knew of how the world worked. Liking him as a friend was a far cry from wanting him as a husband.

Drusilla stood in front of him, and he lifted her onto the seat. "Is your mother coming?"

"Yes. She ran back upstairs with Anthusa. She said she'd be right out after she did something."

"Will it take long?"

"I don't think so. I heard her saying something about roses as they went into Mother's bedchamber, but I don't think there are any roses in there."

Hector's eyebrows rose. So, she did wear the perfume that smelled like roses just for him. He fought to keep his mouth more or less straight. He didn't want Drusilla asking him why he suddenly had such a big grin.

A gentle breeze was blowing. Hector had spread the blanket across their laps, but he felt no chill. If anything, he felt a little too warm. The faint scent of roses washed over him as he drove the team along the main road. It raised his heart rate like chopping wood or pitching hay. He had servants to do the farm chores, but it felt good to work his muscles doing some hard labor. It felt even better to be sitting with Cornelia beside him. It was all he could do not to grin.

He reined in and turned the team onto a dirt road.

Cornelia's head tilted. "Isn't this a different road, Captain? I was hoping we might see your farm today."

"It is a different road, but it goes by my farm. After the rain, this one will be drier." He drove a short distance and reined in where the road was already dry. "Who wants to drive first?"

Drusilla was bouncing. "Me, Captain. Can I trot them?"

A chuckle escaped. "For a quarter mile or so. You'll have to walk them when we start climbing the hill."

He turned his eyes on Cornelia in time to catch her suppressing a smile at her daughter's need for speed. Her lips were still twitching when she shifted her gaze from the road to his face.

"So, what new driving skills will you be teaching us today, Captain?" The tease flared in her eyes. "I hope not how to get unstuck from a mudhole. I was afraid it would still be too wet to venture off the stone paving, but I'm sure you can judge that much better than I can." Those blue eyes dragged him in deeper. "You're the only man I know who can steer both ships and mules with unfailing skill."

"You give me too much credit. I've been blown off course more than once by a storm, and I've done my share of pushing and pulling to get a stuck wagon free from the mud."

She laughed. That raised his eyebrows. She laughed again.

"I can't quite picture you covered in mud and pulling like an ox to get a wagon free."

The smile slipped from his lips. He'd done that and much worse before Aristarchus bought him. "A man does what he has to do, Cornelia, even when he may not want to."

Her eyes grew serious as well. "I'm sorry. I hope my laughter didn't offend you. I meant no offense. I know you're right. A woman does what she has to do as well."

Her words took the shine off the moment as it focused him back on the reality of their differences. A noblewoman and a captain—an unlikely combination. A noblewoman and a former slave—an impossibility.

Drusilla pulled him from his thoughts. "We're coming to a fork in the road, Captain. Which way do I go?"

"Uphill." He glanced at Cornelia beside him. He'd come a long way uphill, but he would never reach the mountaintop where queens lived. Cornelia liked him as a friend, but queens married kings and princes, not captains and never slaves.

The scent of roses had faded, but Hector still found himself acutely aware of Cornelia sitting beside him. Her shoulder occasionally brushed his when the cart joggled on the ruts in the road. She was already handling the reins like a woman who'd been driving for years. She didn't really need any more lessons, but he hoped she'd keep coming while he taught Drusilla.

"So, Captain, when will we reach your farm?"

"The olive grove below us is part of it."

"Really?" She pulled back on the reins until the mules stopped. "It's a lovely view from here."

He nodded. He'd always enjoyed riding that road to overlook the farm he'd bought after he married Damara. It had been too painful after the accident, but God had taken that pain during the voyage with Drusilla and Cornelia. It felt good to survey his land again. It reminded him of all the blessings he'd received and how far God had brought him in the last twenty-five years.

"Where's the house?"

Hector pointed downslope to a thick grove of trees. "It's in there."

"I can't really see it. Can we go down?"

"Not today. There's no direct path to this road that isn't still too muddy."

"I'm sure it's lovely. Perhaps we can go there another day."

He nodded without speaking. It was all he'd ever wanted, all he ever would want, but she would be disappointed. It was only a large house, not a villa.

"Lepidus said his estate touched your farm. Where is it?"

Hector tried to mask his disappointment with that question. Lepidus. A Roman equestrian. The master of an estate with a villa. A decent man who'd been a good husband and father. Everything she'd want to marry, if she were to marry again.

"Over there, past my wheat field."

"Your field is very green, much better than Lepidus's. Looks like you'll have an excellent crop of winter wheat. I'm impressed."

She turned her eyes from the field onto him. "I always enjoyed watching my fields green up at home. Lucius had no interest in running the estate, but I found it very satisfying. Malleolus took care of selling my harvests, but guiding the growing of them was my delight."

Her gaze swept his fields once more. "I'll enjoy doing it again after I get some land. The villa was quite beautiful, especially the garden. It held wonderful memories of my boys when they were young, but once they were grown, it was really only a house. It was the land I loved."

The sparkle in her eyes as she talked of her land took him by surprise. The villa only a house? Would she be content not to have another villa? To have something more modest like Titus's house…or his own?

"I know what you mean. When I'm not at sea, I enjoy working my own land."

"One more thing we have in common." Her head tilted as a teasing smile curved her lips. "I wonder what else we'll find that we share. I shall enjoy finding out."

Her eyes held his. Was there an invitation there? He wasn't sure what, if anything, he should say, so he said nothing.

The silence stretched out between them until she broke eye contact.

"Where is the stream where we turned around?"

He pointed to the east. "Over there."

"We should drive there again. It would be a lovely place to eat lunch on a warm, sunny day."

"We can do that."

A sudden gust of wind lifted some olive leaves and swirled them around the feet of the mules. Cornelia shivered.

"You're getting cold. I should take you home now."

"Do we go forward or backward to get there?"

"Back down the hill."

She handed him the reins. "I yield to your superior skill. I have no idea how to turn this cart around on a narrow road."

"Watch carefully, and you'll be able to do it next time."

Pulling back on the first mule with one rein and slapping the second mule with the other, he forced a tight circle turn.

"It will take more than one lesson for me to master that." She flashed the smile that drove up his heart rate. "I trust I can count on you for that."

"You can." *You can count on me for anything. If only you would.*

"I'll remember you said that, Hector. You always keep your word."

Even with those laughing eyes and crooked smile, he knew she'd remember. And she was right. She meant a lot to him, and he would always keep his word.

Chapter 39

Hector rode through Titus's gate on Sunday morning. It was the first time Cornelia was going to Philip's to worship with him. A sense of anticipation filled him, although he didn't know what to expect.

He dismounted and led his mare into an empty stall. After lifting off her saddle, he headed across the courtyard.

Drusilla came from the kitchen door. "Good morning, Captain." She slipped her hand into his. "Mother and Anthusa are almost ready. Come have some breakfast with me."

The warm air of the kitchen wrapped him like a blanket. The scent of rosemary-laced bread filled his nostrils. He stood by the kitchen table and lifted a slice of cheese from the serving tray.

He'd just taken a bite when the music of her voice drifted across his ears. "It's good to see you, Hector. Miriam's family already went ahead. We're ready whenever you are."

He turned to find her standing with Anthusa, dressed in the blue tunic that deepened the blue of her eyes.

"I'm always ready to worship, Cornelia." He motioned toward the door with his palm held upward.

She stepped close as she glided past him. Her head tilted and tipped so she could look directly into his eyes. "I look forward to learning why that is."

He followed the three of them out the door. Then he stepped up to walk next to her. Anthusa and Drusilla fell in behind.

He kept glancing down at her as they climbed the quarter mile to Philip's house. If only she would decide to follow Jesus. His heart couldn't ask for much more. To know she would live forever with Jesus as his sister in Christ—there could only be one thing that would make his joy more complete. No matter how unlikely it might seem for a captain and a queen, he still longed for her to live right now with him… as his wife.

◆

Cornelia walked beside Hector through the orchard and past the side of Philip's house. They turned into the garden at the rear and followed a path to a doorway that led into the courtyard surrounded by the wings of the house. A canvas canopy covered several rows of benches. Several braziers heated the space. Despite the cool weather, it was warm and inviting.

Miriam and Claudia were talking when Hector's party entered, but they broke off their conversation and came to Cornelia.

Claudia wrapped her arm around Cornelia's waist. "I'm so glad you decided to join us. Worship will start in a few minutes." She pressed her lips together to squash a grin as she scanned Hector. "You're welcome to sit with either of our families, but I think someone would rather you sit with him."

Cornelia turned her head to look up at the smiling man beside her. "I believe it's proper manners to stay with the man who brought you."

Claudia and Miriam exchanged quick glances before Claudia replied. "I quite agree."

A young man who looked about seventeen strode toward them. He and Hector embraced before he turned a smile toward Cornelia.

Hector draped his arm across the young man's shoulders. "Cornelia, this is my son, Marcario."

Marcario's eyes bounced from her to his father and back. A broad grin split his face. "It's a pleasure to finally meet you, Cornelia." His gaze shifted to Hector and back again. "I'm glad you and your daughter have kept Father from getting too bored while he's in port for the winter."

The warm eyes of the friendly young man brought a gleam to her own. "Your father made our trip out from Rome a delight. Drusilla and I are very glad he's continued to spend time with us." She fixed her eyes on Hector. "I can think of no better way to spend our time than with Hector."

◆

Hector let the smile her words inspired spread across face. No better way? There was no better way to spend time than with her. To hear her speak it aloud in front of her family and his own son—that was more than he'd expected.

Philip strolled over to join them. "Welcome, Cornelia. I'm glad you've come."

"Hector tells me you're an extraordinary teacher. I'm looking forward to learning much today."

Philip chuckled. "If Hector said that, he gave me more credit than I deserve. God himself gives me the message and guides my words. I'm just the tool the Holy Spirit uses."

Cornelia glanced at Hector before replying. "Perhaps those weren't his exact words, but he said you were better than him. He was such a good teacher himself when we heard him on the ship that I have great expectations. He assured me I would begin to have all my questions answered."

Hector felt the heat in his ears. The suppressed laughter in Philip's eye and the lips pressed to stop a grin as his best friend glanced at him didn't help that at all.

Philip nodded once at Cornelia. "That I am sure God will do. Now if you'll excuse me, it's time for me to ask the Spirit's guidance before we begin."

Philip turned and walked to the stand at the podium where he'd already placed a codex.

Hector touched her elbow, and she fixed eager eyes on him. "I hope you'll sit with me and Marcario." He waved his hand toward a bench.

His heart warmed as she gazed up at him, her eyes glowing. "I'd like to do that. I may need you to answer my questions."

"Whatever you need, I'll try to help." The trust in her eyes was everything he could hope for.

Drusilla slid her hand into his. Hector rested his free hand on her hair. "Come sit."

He settled down on the bench with Drusilla on one side and Cornelia on the other. His heart swelled. Beside him were the little girl he loved, and the woman he hoped might love him. Both were eager to learn about his Lord. Surely Cornelia would hear God's call and choose to follow Jesus, just as he had done so many years ago.

He glanced at her. Among the children of God, there was no Jew and Gentile, no Roman and Greek, no slave and free. If she chose the Lord, maybe all that separated a captain and a queen would no longer matter. He longed to see her saved for her own sake, but it might fulfill the desire of his heart as well.

◆

Anticipation unlike any she'd felt before filled Cornelia. Someone struck a lyre and sang a few words. A glorious blend of male and female voices joined in and wrapped around her. It was even better than the singing on the ship.

After several songs, Philip raised the codex from the podium. The singing stopped, and the silence, like that between rolls of thunder, drove up her heart rate. An unfamiliar tingling coursed across her skin.

Philip closed his eye and tipped his face skyward. "Dear Father, fill me today with your Holy Spirit that my words may bring honor to You and to my Lord Jesus."

He lowered the codex and beamed directly at Cornelia before he opened it to the place he'd marked.

"Today, I'm going to read from Apostle Paul's letter to the believers in Rome. He wrote this in a time not unlike our own, when Emperor Nero was hunting and killing the followers of Jesus."

His gaze locked onto the codex. "And we know that in all things God works for the good of those who love him, who have been called according to his purpose. For those God foreknew, he also predestined to be conformed to the likeness of his Son, that he might be the first-born among many brothers. And those he predestined, he also called; those he called, he also justified; those he justified, he also glorified.

"What, then, shall we say in response to this? If God is for us, who can be against us? He who did not spare his own Son, but gave him up for us all—how will he not also, along with him, graciously give us all things?"

Philip closed the codex and leaned with both hands on the podium.

"In difficult times like these, under opposition and even threat of death, we can sometimes give in to fear and lose sight of God's prom-ises. It's important for us to remember Paul's words and to encourage each other in such times with remembrances of how we ourselves have seen God keep his promises."

His gaze settled on Titus and Miriam. "Any one of us here could tell of a time when God brought good out of something bad. God can use even the things that cause us deep pain to bring us good. And some-times he uses those difficult times to soften our hearts and open our minds so we will hear His call."

Miriam lifted her eyes to Titus's face as his turned down onto hers.

The love that flowed between them, the joy they shared…it was everything Cornelia longed for with Hector. God truly had brought good from bad.

"God knows who will hear that call to follow Jesus and be justified. We all remain sinners, because it's impossible for any man or woman to live a perfect life. Only perfection is fit to be in God's presence. God loves us and wants us to be with Him, but His very nature won't let us be in His presence if we're not perfect."

Cornelia's mouth twitched. Perfect—hard even for the simplest things, impossible for the difficult things that mattered most.

"So what did He do to satisfy both His love and His perfection? He took the form of a man Himself. He came to live among us as Jesus of Nazareth. He lived a perfect life as a man, and He sacrificed Himself on the cross to make payment for all the sins of all people for all time, the payment we as sinners could never make.

"As proof that He could do everything He'd said, He rose from the dead. And when He had done all that, He had justified all who choose to believe in Him and in His sacrifice as clearing them of sin. It's a legal judgment. We are justified, declared to be not guilty even though we really are guilty. We can never be innocent in our own right as long as we make choices to please ourselves, not God. And who doesn't sometimes fail to put God first?"

Cornelia glanced at Drusilla. Put her daughter first—she'd done that. But she'd never considered what God might think when making her choices.

"But God the Father treats us as if we had the perfection of Jesus. He looks at us as if we are fit to be in his presence because He paid for our sins Himself, something we never could do.

"Jesus rose from the dead and appeared to His disciples as proof that He could do everything He'd told them. Then he sent His Holy Spirit to live within us, so we can have a small taste of His presence with us before we enjoy the full banquet of His glory in heaven after we die."

Hector's nod and broad smile declared his agreement with all Philip was saying. There was a truth here that they all seemed to know, a truth Cornelia didn't yet understand.

"As Paul wrote, each of us here has been called to receive His great gift of justification. Most of us have answered yes to that call." He fixed his glowing eye on Cornelia. "And some of us are just now hearing the call. Let us all pray that everyone called will say yes to His offer of justification and become a follower of our Lord Jesus. That will bring peace and joy in this world and even more in the next."

Philip stepped back from the podium and nodded to the man with a lyre. The musician strummed a few notes while he sang the first words of a song, then the entire assembly joined their voices in praise again.

As the music wrapped around Cornelia, her mind focused on how God could use anything for good. Even evil acts by selfish people...like Lucius.

Lucius's first cruel decision put Claudia on Hector's ship, where she and Philip met. Their blissful marriage would never have happened without Lucius. Then came Lucius's horrible decision that would have hurt Drusilla. That was bad, but it led to the good of them being on Hector's ship. Drusilla found a man who loved her like a father, and she found the man she wanted to spend the rest of her life with. God was certainly bringing good out of evil.

But there was still more good in coming to Thracia than finding Hector. If she hadn't left Rome, she would never have come to understand why Publius chose death over denial. If she hadn't been on Hector's ship, she would never have been with Christians worshipping. She felt the pull on her heart more every time she came to their gatherings.

Was that God calling her to Him? She was almost ready to answer yes to that call. It was time to talk with Claudia, ask the questions she had that were too personal to ask Hector or Philip, and make a decision.

That night, Cornelia leaned on her elbows and gazed into the mirror. Anthusa pulled the gold pins and Cornelia's coiled braid tumbled down her back. As Anthusa's fingers began working the strands of the braid apart, Cornelia closed her eyes. A happy smile accompanied a satisfied sigh.

"I so enjoyed the worship at Philip's this morning."

"So did I, mistress."

"As much as I loved sitting with Hector, that wasn't the best part. I'm beginning to understand why Publius made his choice. I understood some when Hector taught. I understand even more after listening to Philip. But it's more than just understanding. I can't explain it, but it's like something is pulling me toward believing Jesus did everything he said."

"I feel that same pull."

"Before next Sunday, I'll ask Claudia why she decided to become a believer. Her faith seems so strong. There must have been more to her decision than becoming a believer just so Philip would marry her."

◆

Anthusa kept brushing. She was almost finished when Mistress Cornelia's eyes in the mirror turned dreamy.

"Of course, I did so enjoy sitting with Hector, almost like we were family. His son was so welcoming. I'm sure he'll be happy for his father if we marry. I know Drusilla would be ecstatic."

Anthusa set the brush down on the table and ran her fingers through the flowing hair. "Maybe that's exactly what will happen, mistress. Time will tell."

Cornelia strolled to her bed and sat down. "Yes, time. There's still more than three months before he starts sailing again." She swung her legs up on the bed, and Anthusa drew the sheets up to her chin.

"Three months is a long time. I'm sure it will be enough."

"I hope so." Cornelia's eyes drifted shut.

Anthusa blew out the lamp and stood for a moment gazing at her beloved mistress. The captain looked at the mistress with eyes filled with both love and longing. Surely three months would be enough.

Chapter 40

A Desirable Woman

Drusilla and Vania were playing in the garden when Quintus Lepidus rode through the gate. Drusilla dashed through the kitchen door and upstairs to the women's room where Cornelia was weaving.

Cornelia startled at her daughter's breathless arrival. "Is something wrong, dear?"

Drusilla took a big breath before answering. "A man in a purple-striped tunic just rode into the garden."

Cornelia's heart skipped a beat. "Did you recognize him?"

Drusilla gripped Cornelia's hand. "It's the man you talked to when we were driving with Captain."

"Quintus Lepidus?" Drusilla nodded. "That shouldn't be a problem for us. Hector said he wasn't likely to let anyone in Rome know about us. Remember?"

"But why did he come here?"

"He said he planned to look at a couple of Titus's colts. Since the animals aren't here, he'll be disappointed."

A servant appeared at the doorway. "Mistress, Quintus Lepidus is asking to speak with you."

Cornelia's brows shot up. "Escort him to the sitting room and tell him I'll be there shortly."

Drusilla's gaze shifted from the departing servant to Cornelia.

"Don't worry, dear. Remember what the captain said about him being a decent man. Lepidus did say he wanted to hear about the happenings in Rome. I'm sure it's just that."

Cornelia parked the shuttle and reached for Drusilla's hand. "You can go back to Vania, and I'll entertain our visitor."

After descending the stairs, Cornelia took a deep breath before entering the sitting room where Lepidus waited. How should she update him on events in Rome without making him curious enough to inquire about her situation from his brothers?

She donned her gracious social face as she glided into the room. As she settled on a chair, she waved her upturned palm to invite him to sit as well. "Aemilius Lepidus. What a pleasant surprise. To what do I owe such pleasure?"

"I was passing by and thought I should stop to see whether Drusus had brought the colts we discussed when he came from his estate yesterday. I'm eager to see them before another buys them. Your brother-in-law is well known for breeding some of the best horses this side of Byzantium."

Cornelia tipped her head, but she masked her skepticism. That was not his purpose in coming. "I've raised some horses myself, and I would agree that Titus's animals are quite exceptional."

Lepidus's brows lifted. "You've raised horses?"

Cornelia released a musical laugh. "Of course. I've run an estate for many years. Lucius has no interest in overseeing the day-to-day affairs."

Lepidus cleared his throat. "I also thought it might be an excellent time for the visit we discussed the other day. I saw my neighbor on a ladder repairing a wall damaged by the recent rains, so I had reason to hope you might be home." A corner of his lip lifted. "It's dirty work, but perhaps he can't afford a slave who knows how to do it."

Cornelia kept the flash from her eyes. "Or perhaps he's just a man who finds satisfaction working with his hands. Pleasure, not lack of money, is equally likely as the reason. There are many things I sometimes enjoy doing myself that my slaves normally do. There is satisfaction in any job well done."

She smiled at the tic her words brought to the corner of his mouth. Such condescension toward the man she intended to marry was not acceptable.

"That's true. I feel that way about working with my horses, especially the most spirited ones. Occasionally rubbing them down after a hot ride strengthens their bond with me."

He cleared his throat again. "Speaking of bonds, Titus mentioned you were no longer married."

She raised one eyebrow. "I find it rather odd that came up during your conversation about his horses."

There was that tic again. "I must admit I asked him directly when I saw you. Titus merely answered my question."

She tipped her head sideways, but masked her irritation perfectly. "I have freed Lucius to pursue whatever pretty young things tempt him." She punctuated her point with a well-practiced unconcerned laugh.

Cornelia was careful to keep her full gracious mask in place. Lepidus didn't seem very skilled in the ways of patrician repartee. Perhaps living in the provinces helped any Roman become less pretentious, less of a play-actor. That was a point in favor of any man.

A slight smile curved her lips. Hector was perfection itself when it came to being a man who never pretended to be anything he wasn't.

Lepidus perked up as he watched her smile. That made her smile bigger. He had no idea she was thinking of the neighbor he looked down on, the man who outshone him in every way.

"I think any man a fool who wants a pretty child when he can have a woman." Once more he cleared his throat. "I, myself, am unmarried now. My wife died three years ago. Metilia was an excellent wife and mother. For all of our married life, she was among my favorite companions for conversation. She knew so much about affairs beyond the confines of our villa. Like you, she found pleasure in activity. She spent many hours tutoring our children in what she knew.

His eyes had turned wistful during that reflection.

He glanced down, then refocused on her. "Our son just left to serve with a legion in Dacia. Our daughter is married and just gave birth to her first child. Like Metilia, I took special pleasure in teaching them instead of leaving it all to the tutors. Your daughter is an age I enjoyed very much with my own Aemilia."

He shifted in the chair. "I miss having young ones around my villa, but what I miss most is the companionship of an intelligent woman. I don't want a silly girl who only thinks of gossip and jewels. If I were to remarry, I would want a woman of experience...like yourself."

It tested Cornelia's self-control not to let him see how funny she thought him at that moment. They had barely met, and he was almost proposing. Still, he seemed a decent, honest man. She would let him down easy.

"I'm flattered by your interest, Quintus, but remarriage is not my objective at the moment. I'm glad you enjoyed so many years with a woman worthy of your affection. I was not so fortunate. For the moment, I'm quite content as I am."

She saw no great disappointment in his eyes. How could there be? He was proposing a companionable partnership, not a love match. Her dowry was her main attraction, even to a decent man like this.

"I understand, Cornelia. No husband is much better than a bad one. I hope you'll remember my interest if you should change your mind. I have no desire to marry an ordinary woman after being married to a special one. From all I ever heard of you in Rome, I know you to be special as well."

Cornelia's respect for him grew as she listened to his last speech. His whole face softened when he spoke of his wife.

"I'll remember." She rose to end their conversation. He followed her lead. "I hope you find Titus's colts to your liking. I expect he'll bring them soon."

She walked him back to the kitchen as she spoke. "The way out is through there. Farewell, Quintus."

"Farewell, Cornelia. I hope we speak again soon." He turned and stepped through the doorway.

Her eyebrow rose after he disappeared from view. So Quintus Aemilius Lepidus wanted her as his wife. A man who was a good husband and father. Hector had called him a decent man. She could see that. Good men did exist among the Roman elite. Lucius certainly wasn't one, but two of them had expressed interest in marrying her in the last month. First Atticus, now Lepidus. Before she left Rome, either would have seemed like a man she could marry.

But it wasn't a Roman she wanted anymore. It wasn't even a wealthy man. It was a Greek sea captain who loved his land as much as his ship. A man who loved his wife so much that her death almost killed him as well. That was the man she wanted to marry, and her heart thrilled at the progress he seemed to be making toward wanting her as well.

Flavian Amphitheater in Rome

Lucius normally went to the Flavian Amphitheater to watch the one-on-one contests after the animals had finished savaging the criminals during the lunchtime break. He enjoyed the skill and courage of combat between two trained men, not mere bloodletting by animal fangs.

But today, the woman who stood in his way as he headed to the senatorial seats to join Marcus looked more like an angry feline than a Roman matron.

He pasted on a friendly smile. "Salve, Didia."

She responded with an icicle smile and a tip of her head. "Lucius. I'd like to say it's a pleasure to see you again, but…"

His toga was draped over his left arm, and she pushed back the edge of it as she placed her hand on his wrist. Then she dug her nails in.

His teeth clenched as he grabbed her wrist. The middle fingernail pierced the skin before he could lift it away, so he pushed back the toga enough to keep the blood off it.

He turned a wry smile on her as he pointedly shifted his gaze from her face to his arm and back. "Perhaps not a pleasure today, but certainly a surprise. Is there some reason for this?"

Didia's lips tightened. "You know there is. I don't like being used by men I consider friends."

"I don't know what you mean."

Her head drew back. "You used me to squash a rumor that was actually true. Cornelia did run off and take Drusilla without your permission. I heard you hired one of the gladiators I like to watch at the Ludus Silani to go to Thracia and take your daughter from her, by force if necessary, and bring her back to you. You tricked me into thinking her leaving was all your idea, and I let everyone who matters know that."

A feral gleam lit her eyes. "They'll all think me a fool when the truth gets out. I won't be used that way, Lucius. I'll make certain everyone knows Cornelia planned all along to steal Drusilla from you and you were too stupid to see what she was up to beforehand." The corner of her mouth lifted. "Lucius Fidelis…outsmarted and outmaneuvered by a woman. That's a rich rumor to spread…because it's true."

She raised her head to look down her nose at him. "I can damage anyone's reputation, and I'll enjoy ruining yours."

Lucius's smile made hers seem warm in comparison. "No, you won't. I don't think you want it known that you were trying to seduce me while your husband was out of town. I enjoyed a long talk with him at Marcus's dinner just before he left. He told several of us that you were chaste and faithful when he's gone. Since you've set your eye on trapping another wealthy husband who suits you better than Flaccus, I don't think you want it known that you're no more faithful than an alley cat before you make that change."

Her eyes widened.

His smile drifted into a smirk. "But I don't think I'll need to say anything. I'm sure you'll agree it's best if neither of us speaks to anyone about our conversation today."

"Well..." She licked her lips. "Perhaps you're right. What happens at the circus should stay at the circus."

He rested his hand on her forearm. "Yes, it should. What faction will you be cheering at the races tomorrow?"

"The greens."

"The same for me." Lucius offered a friendly smile. "It's always a good thing when friends can agree as well as we do."

She opened her mouth as if to speak, but nothing came out.

"I hope you'll excuse me, Didia. Marcus is waiting, and we have something to discuss before the fighting starts. Perhaps I'll have the pleasure of dining with you and Flaccus in the near future."

She tipped her head and pasted on a social smile. "Of course. That would be our pleasure as well."

Lucius turned from her and continued down the steps toward the senatorial seating where Marcus waited. He'd escaped the tigress's wrath with only one claw mark. Soon the men he'd hired would reach Thracia and face the lioness there. His mouth curved into a satisfied smile. Too bad he wouldn't be there to see her face when he won their contest and reclaimed the stolen prize.

Chapter 41

MAYBE A GOOD DAY

The next morning, Hector turned the cisium through Titus's gate. The sky was clear, and the warmth of the sun on his arms promised a beautiful day for their drive.

He reined in by the kitchen door. Drusilla bounced out to join him.

"It's so nice today, Captain. Mother thought it would be a good day for lunch by the stream we saw the first time."

One corner of his mouth tipped up. Lunch. That meant a longer time with her at his side today.

He lifted Drusilla and placed her on the seat. Before he could turn, the aroma of cinnamon and something else drifted into his nostrils. He inhaled deeply. Cornelia was close behind him, but where were the roses?

"Mother smells good today, don't you think, Captain? I put some perfume Aunt Miriam made on her. It's a mix of some of her spices that Uncle Titus likes."

He turned to find Cornelia smiling up at him.

"You don't smell like you usually do."

Her laughter tingled up his spine. "A woman normally doesn't want to hear she smells. I hope my usual smell isn't too offensive."

His ears reddened, but his eyes crinkled as his smile broadened. "I didn't mean you smell bad, Cornelia, and you know it. I like your smell."

Again, her laughter rippled around him. "I have noticed you seem to like roses. Actually, I'm glad you noticed I smell different. In the future, I'll wear whichever you like best."

"Roses are good, but any other way you want to smell is good, too"

"Very well, Captain." That teasing sparkle filled her eyes. "Today Titus's favorite. Tomorrow yours."

She handed a covered basket to Drusilla and turned for him to lift her in.

He climbed in between them and slapped the reins. It would be an excellent day for eating on the sun-warmed rocks by the stream. What could be better than a good meal by a stream, breathing in the fresh smells of the outdoors and the perfume of the playful woman sitting next to him?

Cornelia watched Hector drive the cisium back through Titus's gate. It had been a thoroughly lovely day. The burbling of the small waterfall where the stream cascaded down the rocks had wrapped her in music better than the performances of the finest musicians at her friends' banquets. The sun-heated rocks where she sat on the blanket next to him filled her with a delicious warmth magnified by his closeness. Their simple lunch of bread, cheese, and dates was superior even to Miriam's delectable offerings because his hand had brushed against hers when they reached into the basket at the same time.

She walked into the kitchen. Miriam was there, stirring another of her scrumptious sauces that would delight Titus that evening.

"Cornelia, a letter came for you by horse courier. I put it by your mirror."

The warm glow instantly vanished. No one should know she was here. Cornelia hurried up the stairs to her room.

Her hands trembled as she broke the seal and unrolled the papyrus.

> Tertius Claudius Drusus to Cornelia Scipia, my
> dear mother, greetings. If you are well, then I am glad.
> Father thinks you have run to Uncle Titus, as Aunt
> Claudia did. I am writing this in case he is right. He is
> sending some men to take Drusilla and bring her back
> to Rome. I have sent this by the horse courier service
> that should reach you in nine days. Father told his new
> steward to have his agents leave in two days, so they
> should have left Rome seven days ago. Depending on

how hard they ride, they should reach you eleven to thirty days after you receive this letter.

Father does not suspect me, so I hope to learn if he plans something else. I will let you know if he does. Tell Drusilla I miss her. I hope that you can protect her and that all will be well with you both. May the gods guard your safety.

Her knees buckled, and she sat down hard on the stool. Men coming to get Drusilla. Lucius wouldn't stop until he had her or until she was dead.

Cornelia straightened. Until she was dead...or until he thought she was. But how could she convince him Drusilla had died? She pressed her palms against her cheeks. There had to be a way.

She started pacing.

Anthusa entered the room. "Mistress? Is something wrong?"

Cornelia turned anguished eyes on her. "Lucius thinks we're here. He's sending men to get Drusilla. When they arrive, I need to stop them."

"Master Titus could kill them."

Cornelia shook her head. "No, that wouldn't help. Lucius would just send someone else, and next time Tertius might not know in time to warn us." A sly smile lifted the corners of her mouth. "But if they went back and told him she's dead, that would be the end of it." She snapped her fingers. "And I know what might convince them."

Cornelia hurried down to the kitchen with Anthusa right behind her.

"Miriam, I want to put a gravestone in the garden."

Miriam's eyebrows scrunched. "Why?"

"The letter was from my son Tertius. Lucius is sending men here to get Drusilla, and I need something to show them to convince them she's dead."

Miriam's eyes cleared, and she nodded. "When do you expect them?"

"Tertius thought eleven to thirty days from today."

Miriam handed the spoon to her chef. "Let's find Nestor. He can go right now to the sculptor and get him started on the inscription. I'm sure he can get something ready in less than eleven days."

When Titus came home for dinner, Cornelia met him at the kitchen door. "I received a letter from Tertius. Lucius is sending men to take Drusilla."

Titus drew a deep breath and blew it out. "So, I need to get you away from here. I have an estate a day and a half to the west. Lucius doesn't know about it, so I can send you there. Or we could send you to one of Philip's estates near here or in Moesia."

Cornelia shook her head. "It might only be a matter of time before Lucius tracks us down. He's a vengeful man, and he knows the best way to strike at me is to hurt Drusilla. I thwarted his plans. I outmaneuvered him, and he can't stand that. He won't stop until he gets her. She could never feel completely safe. I have a better idea."

Titus's brows dipped. "What would that be?"

"Drusilla must die, or at least Lucius's men must think she has. Miriam said I can erect a gravestone here. Nestor already went to the sculptor to get it started. Tertius thought the men would arrive eleven to thirty days from now. The gravestone should be ready in five."

Titus's eyes gleamed. "I like it. I have to go to the western estate in a few days, but I'll be back before they come. I can be here ten days from now and stay until after they leave."

Cornelia's smile reflected his. "We won't mention this in front of Drusilla until the gravestone comes. I don't want her to worry before she has to." Her smile grew broader. "Together, we'll put an end to that worm hurting anyone in this family...once and for all."

Anthusa pulled the brush through Mistress Cornelia's hair as she read the letter one more time.

"I'd hoped Lucius wouldn't figure out where we went quite this fast, but I should have known he would. He might be worthless as a father, but he's always been smart." She sighed. "I'm so glad Tertius was there to hear what Lucius was planning. Eleven to thirty days. It's going to be hard to wait. The gravestone should be in place before then, and Titus will be back to help me convince them she's dead."

Cornelia buried her face in her hands, then pulled them sideways to gaze into the mirror again. "Perhaps it's a good thing they're coming. Once they return with the message that Drusilla has died, Lucius should leave us in peace."

Anthusa kept brushing. Gradually the tension drained from the mistress's face.

"I'm sure the plan will turn out well." She worked her fingers into the thick hair and began massaging her scalp.

Time to lift Mistress's spirits. "So, how was the drive today?"

Her mistress's face softened. "It was such a perfect day before I read that letter. We sat by the stream in the sun. I got him talking about his farm. He loves his land just like I do...did. He loves his ship, too. I suppose I'll oversee everything when he's at sea. But maybe Drusilla and I will join him on some of his voyages. She would love that."

"She would, mistress."

Mistress turned to face her. "I want him to take me with him wherever he goes. I never dreamed there could be a man like him. After I convince Lucius that Drusilla is dead, we should be able to start a good life together, the three of us. And you, of course. I would never leave you behind."

Anthusa's heart basked in those words. "I never want to leave you, either."

Mistress Cornelia rose and moved to her bed. "I hope I can sleep tonight. It might be hard."

Anthusa turned down the sheets. "Maybe you'll have a dream about the captain. That's worth sleeping for."

A broad smile brightened the mistress's eyes. "Yes, nothing could be better than dreaming of the captain...except having my dreams come true."

Mistress swung her legs onto the bed, and Anthusa drew the covers over her. "I think they will, mistress. I truly think they will."

Anthusa enjoyed the smile on her dear mistress's lips before she blew out the lamp. If everything went as she hoped, the dreams of both the captain and her mistress would finally come true.

Chapter 42

THE LOGICAL DECISION

The next day, Cornelia, Anthusa, and Miriam were working at their looms, chatting about anything and nothing, when Claudia entered the women's room.

Cornelia parked her shuttle. "I got a letter from Tertius yesterday. Lucius has figured out where we are and is sending men to get Drusilla."

Claudia's hand flew to her mouth. "What are you going to do?"

"I'm going to convince him Drusilla is dead so he'll never bother us again."

Cornelia rested her hand on the loom's frame. "Dead? How are you going to do that?"

"I've ordered a gravestone with her name on it." She pointed out the window. "We're going to put it over there by the garden wall. If that's not enough, Titus will help me convince them. Once they go back and tell Lucius, we should be free of him forever."

Claudia nodded as a smile grew. "That sounds like an excellent plan. Until they come and leave again, I'll be praying for it to free you and Drusilla from the sword hanging over your heads."

She rested her hand on Cornelia's arm. "Can I pray with you right now?"

Cornelia's spine straightened. It would be the first time she asked God directly for something. Then her shoulders relaxed. Several of the people had asked for God's help during the worship at Philip's. If they could do it there, she and Claudia could do it here.

"Please."

Claudia took Cornelia's hand and reached for Miriam's as well. "Father, please protect Drusilla and Cornelia from the men coming from Lucius. Help Cornelia to convince them to return and tell Lucius that he has no daughter left in Thracia. Even more, I ask You to protect Lucius until You give him a changed heart. Lead him to follow Jesus as our father did. We ask this in Jesus's name. Amen."

As Miriam echoed the amen, Cornelia's head snapped back. "How can you say that? For eight years, I've thought about Publius and his dying so willingly when he didn't have to. I've been thinking about what Hector and Philip teach about forgiveness. It sounds good, but it isn't natural to forgive those who hurt the ones you love. How can you not hate Lucius after all he's done? To Publius, to you, to Drusilla and me?"

Claudia released Cornelia's hand. "I can only do it because God himself has helped me. Lucius has done terrible things, but hating him would only make me bitter. That bitterness would eat at me like scavenging dogs until my heart was consumed by it. When I left Rome, I hated Lucius with a raging passion for causing Father's death, and I found no peace as long as I did. I would have gladly murdered him, and what did that make me in my heart? A murderer. It made me as bad a sinner in the eyes of God as Lucius was."

Cornelia crossed her arms. Wanting to kill Lucius and actually doing it, were those really the same thing?

Claudia gazed out the window, then focused once more on Cornelia. "We were both taught the Roman way of vengeance when someone wrongs us. But Jesus taught a better way, the way of forgiveness. Philip tried to tell me that from the beginning, even before I knew he was a Christian. I fell in love with him because he showed me so much kindness. He forgave me when I spoke my hatred for him. He and Aristarchus led Father to believe in Jesus, you know, and I told him I wanted the Christians who did that to die in the arena, too."

Claudia's eyes softened. "I wanted Philip to marry me so much. Even though he loved me as much as I loved him, he wouldn't because I didn't follow Jesus as Lord. I couldn't understand how first Father, then Philip could love Jesus more than they loved me. Then Miriam explained everything to me, like Philip did last Sunday—how much God loves me, how He came to the earth as Jesus to ransom me from my hatred and other sins.

"When I asked God to forgive me, to let Jesus's sacrifice pay for my own sins, He filled me with His Spirit. Then I was able to begin forgiving Lucius, like God forgave me, and that's given me peace."

Her serene eyes were joined by a gentle smile. "I've been so blessed by God. He gave me the desire of my heart in Philip, a new life by forgiving my sins, and peace from forgiving others.

"Father wrote Titus a final letter in his cell under the arena. He explained why he'd chosen to believe Jesus had paid for his sins so he could be at peace with God."

She turned to Miriam. "Titus must still have it."

Miriam nodded. "He does." She turned her gaze on Cornelia. "If you'd like, I can ask him to let you read it."

"I'd like that, if he doesn't mind."

A broad smile lit Claudia's eyes. "He won't. That letter helped Titus decide to follow Jesus himself. Father also told us that he'd forgiven Lucius and that we should forgive him, too. Jesus often said if we didn't forgive others their sins against us, our own sins wouldn't be forgiven, either. When you realize how much you've been forgiven, it becomes easier to forgive someone else."

Cornelia's brows dipped. "I've never even considered forgiving Lucius for everything he's done. He betrayed me with other women for almost as long as we were married. When he got Publius killed and wanted to hurt you, I came to loathe him. When I learned what he planned for Drusilla, it was oil on the fire of my hatred for him."

She twisted the filigree bracelet that had been a present from Lucius after Tertius's birth, then returned her gaze to Claudia's eyes. "You're right that it eats at me, and it does nothing to hurt him. He doesn't care that I've hated him. It's only burned me inside. Maybe I should try to forgive Lucius, like you and Titus have."

Cornelia rubbed her throat. "What Philip said on Sunday, about God bringing good from bad...I never really considered that before. Lucius's callous indifference toward Drusilla pained me every time I saw it. When he decided to give her to his friend's son, even if that killed her, I couldn't think of him without disgust. But that hateful act has turned out to be a blessing for me and Drusilla. We wouldn't be here now without it."

The thought of Hector's eyes crinkling at something she said triggered her smile. "I would never have met Hector, and I am so thankful I did. I understand why you can say you're thankful for Lucius trying to marry you to that horrible Sabinus because that was the only reason you met Philip."

Cornelia bit her lip. "I have a lot to think about. Publius convinced me years ago that the gods of Rome weren't real. When he told me why he believed only in the god of the Jews, I could see his point. If God requires perfection, no one can stand before Him on their own. Publius said He loved people enough to allow the blood of an unblemished animal to cover sins for a while, but only for a while. Only the blood of a perfect sacrifice, of the perfect man, could not just cover but erase the sins for good."

She held one arm across her stomach so she could rest her elbow on it as she rubbed her lips. "I've believed in Publius's God for a long time. Maybe I should believe in Jesus, too. Since I first heard Hector teach, it's like I'm being drawn into a whirlpool I can't escape, but I'm not sure I even want to."

Claudia rested her palm on Cornelia's arm. "Pray about it. Ask God to show you the truth. He'll clear the path for you to come to Him and know peace."

Cornelia drew a deep breath and held it. It was as if a crack had appeared at the end of a long, dark tunnel, and a shaft of light was calling her forward. "I'm going to do that. Hector talked about how Jesus said we should ask and seek. I plan to, beginning today."

Miriam took Cornelia's hand. "We'll both be praying for you to hear Jesus call and come."

Drusilla skipped into the room with Vania right behind. "Cook asked me to tell you lunch is ready."

Cornelia watched her smiling face as Drusilla waved before vanishing through the door. As the women headed to the dining room, Cornelia took the first step toward freedom—she offered thanks to God for at least some of what Lucius had done. Maybe, after she'd convinced his agents Drusilla was dead, she'd be able to give thanks for more.

Chapter 43

Too Soon

Drusus town house, Rome

After breakfast, Tertius strolled through the atrium. That afternoon, he planned to meet Gaius Corvinus at the baths, but to fill the morning hours, he needed something to read.

When he entered the library, his father and Gaius's father, Marcus, sat across the desk from each other. Marcus was leaning over a tabula board and rubbing his chin. Father held a blue disk between his thumb and fingers, slowly turning it end over end.

Father glanced at Tertius, raised a hand in greeting, and focused again on his best friend.

He leaned back in his chair. "You may as well concede this round, Marcus. You're off your game today, and you have to be at your best to beat me."

Marcus flipped his gaze from the board to Father and back. "Not yet. I'm not Cornelia, but I'm still a match for you."

Father's lips tightened, then curved into a sneering smile. "She was good at board games, but she's no match for me. Not when it really matters."

He crossed his arms. "The men I hired to fetch Drusilla are almost there. Paullus arranged for them to leave only a day after I realized she and Cornelia might be with Titus. The *lanista* at the Ludus Silani was willing to risk his men in a sea crossing between Brundisium and Dyrrhachium. That took less than two days. He said they could cover about seventy *milia passuum* each day if they changed horses once. At that rate, they'll take Drusilla from Cornelia within the week."

Tertius's heart dropped into his stomach. But his back was toward Father, so he fought to erase the shock and worry from his face before Marcus or Father saw. He lifted a scroll from the shelf and used it to wave farewell as he returned to the atrium.

He kept walking until he reached the peristyle garden. There, he leaned against one of the columns, breathing heavily. Within the week—that was several days less than the shortest time he'd told Mother it might take for the hunters to arrive. If she and Drusilla were with Uncle Titus, might the gladiators get there before she could find a better place to hide? And if they did, what could he possibly do to protect his little sister after they dragged her back to Rome?

Chapter 44

UNPLEASANT SURPRISE

Hector normally wasn't invited to eat at Titus's house, but this winter had been the exception. As he dismounted and handed his reins to the stable boy, he suppressed a grin. Miriam's cooking was the best in Perinthus, and he owed his frequent opportunities to eat it to Cornelia. He'd be willing to eat stale bread and moldy cheese to dine with her, but he wouldn't complain about the delectable feast that awaited him inside.

He was the last to arrive. When he entered the courtyard, Titus approached and slapped his arm. "Glad you could make it, Hector." His smile broadened into a grin. "Two people are going to find this a much better dinner because you're here."

Hector followed Titus into the dining room. It was set exactly as Claudia arranged her tables, and he settled into place between Philip and Malleolus. Directly across from him sat the reason he came, and her delighted smile when he looked at her pumped up his heart rate.

After asking God's blessing, Titus sampled the purple carrots of the first course. "You're in for a treat, Cornelia. This white wine sauce was one of Miriam's mother's special recipes."

Miriam's eyes softened. "I think of her every time I make it. I've started teaching Vania some of what she taught me when I was her age."

She flipped her gaze from Titus to Cornelia. "Tomorrow, Titus and Philip are going to visit the western estates that are a day and a half from here. I think I'll take my children and go with Titus. They haven't

235

been there for a while. We'll all be back in a week. Would you and Drusilla like to come, too? We're taking our raeda, but it won't hold all of us. We could borrow Philip's raeda or you could drive our cisium if you want."

Miriam fixed teasing eyes on Hector. "Do you think she's ready for that, Hector?"

He cleared his throat. "Cornelia handles mules well enough to be safe on that road."

Cornelia's sparkling eyes captured his. "You give me too much credit, Hector. I still need many more lessons before I'll consider myself skillful enough to be truly safe."

He tightened his lips to stop the grin. Many more lessons. And she'd called him Hector. He liked the sound of both.

Cornelia pulled her eyes from him and directed them toward Miriam. "Thank you for the invitation. We'll miss you, but I think we'll stay in Perinthus." Her gaze returned to him. "For the moment, everything I need to be content is right here."

Hector caught her full meaning, and his ears warmed. He hoped no one noticed, but with the way Nestor teased him, that hope was probably futile. One quick glance at Claudia confirmed his fear. Her eyes lit up and her lips curved into a broad smile. The heat spread to his neck.

Claudia leaned forward. "I'll still be here in Perinthus, so you won't have to get lonely. You and Drusilla can come up to my house if you don't have anyone better to spend your time with."

Even he couldn't miss the knowing smiles exchanged between Claudia, Miriam, and Cornelia. He felt the heat again.

◆

Cornelia watched Hector's ears turn pink. There was something incredibly appealing about a virile man like the captain being embarrassed. It was a sure sign that he felt the attraction she did.

Visiting the western estate would be enjoyable, but now was not the best time. She didn't want to be away from Hector for a week. In only a little over three months, he would sail. She couldn't afford to waste a week away from him. It was time to stoke his fire, not dampen it by being away. There would be plenty of time for visiting estates after he was her husband.

Drusilla's safety was no concern even if they stayed. Nestor and the servants would be there, and Titus would be back a day before the first possible time the agents might show up. It was likely they wouldn't even show up for a few days after that. By then, Nestor would have the gravestone set up in the garden, and she would have flowers and bushes in place to make it look permanent.

She glanced at Drusilla giggling with Vania and the boys at the other table. She'd explain to her daughter that Lucius's agents were coming when she set up the gravestone. There was no reason to worry Drusilla before she had to.

Her eyes returned to Hector. When Drusilla wasn't around to hear, she'd tell him what she had planned. Titus was Drusilla's first line of defense, but Hector should know what was going on so he could be the second.

◆

Dinner was over. The children had gone to bed, and Cornelia was walking along the balcony toward her bedchamber. She could hear the men's laughter coming from the bath below. She'd wondered how extensive Philip's scars were from the moment she met him. Claudia always caressed his scarred cheek whenever it was only family present. He was such a fine man that overlooking how ugly he was made perfect sense, but Claudia actually seemed to enjoy touching his scars. How many more were on his chest? Did she enjoy them as much in the privacy of their bedchamber?

The men would be heading back to the dining room at any moment, and they would be bare-chested. She stepped silently toward the edge of the balcony where she would still be in the shadows but could see them as they crossed the courtyard below.

Philip came out first. Scars covered much of his right shoulder, but they weren't as ugly as she expected. She could have stepped away from the edge then, but she was hoping to see Hector as well. She'd never been one of those silly girls who giggled and gasped over the gladiators, but her heart fluttered at the thought of gazing on his broad chest and large biceps. She'd hoped to see his bare chest every time he escorted her and Drusilla to the baths in the ports where they stayed overnight. How disappointing when he'd actually gone extra distance and out of the way to take them only where the men and women bathed in separate rooms. Finally, she would see what she'd been wishing for.

Her heartbeat accelerated as he stepped into view.

Then her stomach knotted.

She couldn't tear her eyes from him. His muscular build was exactly what she expected, but her eyes were riveted on the crisscrossed pattern of many deep scars from his waist to his shoulders. She'd seen that before…on the naked backs of field slaves at her friends' estates where the lash was freely used.

She froze, transfixed by the implication of what stood before her eyes. It only became worse when he turned back to say something to Titus. She could imagine that the scars came from some horrible accident that didn't require him being a slave, but the brand on his chest removed all doubt.

She stepped back into the deepest shadows by the wall so he couldn't see her. The three men continued across the courtyard and entered the dining room before she risked moving.

Her mind churned. She, Cornelia Scipia, daughter of one of the greatest patrician families of Rome, granddaughter of a senator, great-granddaughter of a Roman consul, was in love with a slave. Well, actually with a freedman, but still. And he'd hidden that fact from her. Well, maybe not exactly hidden it, but he'd certainly never told her.

Why had she ever indulged that girlish desire to look at the handsome man who'd won her heart? Well, more like the handsome man she'd given her heart. He'd never tried to make her fall in love with him, so it wasn't a prize he'd sought to win. It had simply happened because he was the finest man she'd ever known.

But even if she hadn't decided to wait on the balcony to see him, those scars and that brand would still be there. Seeing them this way had only given her a chance to learn his secret without him seeing her shock at the discovery. That would have been even more horrible.

She buried her face in her hands as she shook her head. When they first met in Portus, she'd made him furious by saying most slaves were thieves and liars. Now it made sense that he, once a slave himself, was so offended by what amounted to a personal accusation. He was honest to the bone, and honesty in others was so important to him. She couldn't have picked a worse thing to say to him.

He'd be coming the next day to play Mercenaries with Drusilla. How was she going to face him without him sensing something was wrong? He mustn't suspect her disappointment with his past was also a disappointment with him as a man. Even though he'd been a slave and her head told her his lowly birth meant he wasn't worthy of her, her heart still told her he was superior to every noble Roman she had ever known. She wanted him to be her husband.

◆

Anthusa had seldom seen Mistress Cornelia so quiet as she let the mistress's hair down and began brushing. Silence was not the only source of her concern. There was a moistness at the corners of the mistress's eyes that she hadn't seen since they said farewell to the villa the morning they left for the ship. Mistress had never been one to cry easily, but she was fighting tears now.

Something was terribly wrong. The mistress had been in excellent spirits right after dinner. Right now, she should be repeating what the captain had said and talking about what he planned to do with her and Drusilla tomorrow. What had happened?

Anthusa longed to ask, but it was not her place. Mistress Cornelia confided in her like a dear friend, but despite that, she was only a slave. No matter that she loved the mistress as much as a sister, and her heart ached whenever her mistress's did. She was still only a slave.

Chapter 45

BARRIERS

Cornelia's night was disrupted by dreams of Hector, sometimes free of the lash marks, sometimes covered with them. Just before dawn, she decided a private conversation with Claudia was essential. Normally, she would have talked with Anthusa about any important matter of the heart, but how could she discuss Hector's slave past with someone who was a slave herself? Maybe Miriam would be a good person to talk with, but Titus had actually freed her so he could marry her, so she wasn't unbiased. She would never understand why it was even an issue.

Claudia had married outside the circle of Roman nobility, but at least she'd married a man whose family wealth rivaled even that of the Claudius Drusus family. Claudia did know the expectations for patrician women like them, and she would understand enough to maybe give her good advice.

She rose earlier than normal and dressed without waking Anthusa. When she tiptoed onto the balcony, the first thing she looked at was Titus's bedchamber door. Closed, as she expected. They were leaving that day as soon as Philip came. Of course he wanted this time alone with Miriam before they spent a night on the road with all the children.

But maybe Miriam had crept out to the kitchen to surprise him with something special. Even though she usually confined her own culinary work to the evening meal when Titus could relax and enjoy it, there were times when she talked to what amounted to her underchef before breakfast. Cornelia stood on the balcony and listened for Miriam's voice before descending the stairs to search for Nestor. She found him in the small room on the first floor that was the estate office.

"Mistress Cornelia." He rose from the desk where he had wax tablets and papyrus sheets awaiting his attention. "Do you need something?"

"Yes. I need someone to walk with me to Claudia's house. I need to see her as soon as possible."

"I'll do that myself." He motioned her out the door ahead of him, then turned to lock it. After hanging the key chain around his neck and tucking the key inside his tunic, he led her out through the kitchen and around through the garden to the street.

As they walked the quarter mile to Philip's house, Nestor cast many sideways glances at her. He wasn't a gossip, but Cornelia would prefer none of the household know of her distress. She relaxed her face, erasing the crease between her eyes and flipping her frown into a formal smile.

Philip's gatekeeper swung the gate open as soon as he saw them, and Claudia sent word for Cornelia to come directly to her room as soon as the servant announced her arrival.

Claudia took her hand and led her over to sit on the couch by the window.

"What's wrong?"

"I learned something last night." Cornelia had planned to have a calm discussion about Hector's past and their possible future, but her eyes began to burn. She covered her mouth as the first tears escaped and trickled down her cheeks.

Claudia took her other hand in both of her own and leaned closer. "Is something wrong with Drusilla?"

Cornelia took a deep breath and swept the tears from her cheeks as she shook her head. "She's well. I'm not."

"Is it something I can help with? What did you learn that has you so upset?"

"Hector..." She paused to wipe away the next set of tears that dribbled down her cheeks.

"What about Hector?"

Cornelia looked straight into Claudia's compassionate eyes. "I'm in love with him."

Claudia interrupted. "That's wonderful. He's one of the finest men I know."

"I know he's a wonderful man. That's not the problem." Cornelia wiped away more tears. "Last night, I saw his back. I saw his scars from a flogging...and the brand on his chest. I never suspected he'd been a slave."

Claudia took a deep breath. "And that matters to you?"

Cornelia swept the remaining tears from her cheek, and her chest jumped as she fought against new ones. "Of course it matters to me! The Cornelii Scipiones have helped rule Rome for 500 years. If Father hadn't died before he became a member of the Senate, Roman law wouldn't even let me marry him. He's so far beneath me in social rank I should never even consider him, but he's the most wonderful man I've ever met. He's everything Lucius never was, and Drusilla already loves him like a father." She wiped at tears again. "What should I do?"

"Do you think he's about to ask you to marry him?"

"I don't know! I've been trying to get him to. I think he knows I admire him a great deal. I've given him enough signals that he should know. I don't see how he could fail to see that I want him to marry me. He always seems so glad to see me when he comes to do something with Drusilla. Sometimes it seems he's come more for me than for her. You've seen how he looks at me. A man doesn't look that way if he doesn't care."

Cornelia closed her eyes and shook her head. "He's free now, but he was a slave. I'd be disgracing my family if I marry such a man. But I've never met anyone more wonderful, and nothing could ever be better than being his wife."

Claudia squeezed Cornelia's hand and offered an encouraging smile. "I had almost this same talk with Titus eight years ago when he realized he was in love with Miriam. I'm going to tell you now what I told him then. When God brings a truly good man into your life who loves you deeply, you'd be a fool not to marry him, no matter what his family history might be or what Roman law requires.

"Titus almost didn't marry Miriam because he thought a Claudius Drusus shouldn't marry a slave, but he was smart enough to listen to me and change his mind. Look at how happy he and Miriam are. Philip and I are the only people I know who might be happier together. God brought each of us together with the one who would complete us. I think Hector might be that man for you."

New tears had stopped forming, and Cornelia wiped the last one from the corner of her eye. "Do you think him being a slave is why he hasn't let me know he might want to marry me?" She looked down at the floor before turning her eyes back on Claudia. "The first day I met him, I told him most slaves were thieves and liars, and he got angry at me. Furious, actually. Maybe he thinks I wouldn't want a man who'd been a slave as my husband...or maybe he just doesn't want a woman like me." She looked at the floor again.

Claudia pushed a strand of hair behind Cornelia's ear. "I don't know what he thinks. Men are confusing creatures, and I'm not sure they know why they do what they do themselves. When he left on this last voyage, his heart was still horribly broken by Damara's death. Since his return, I can see how much he loves your daughter. She's filled a large part of the hole in his heart that Charissa's death made. Anyone can see he enjoys your company a great deal. I think he cares for you as much more than a friend. How much, I don't know. He's always been a quiet man who keeps his own counsel. I don't know if his love for Damara has left room in his heart for another woman yet."

Cornelia took a deep breath and let it out before turning her eyes back on Claudia. "So, you think I should forget about him being a slave and marry him if he decides to ask me."

Claudia smiled. "Yes, I do. Maybe you need to find some way to let him know you know and that it doesn't matter to you." She paused. "Or maybe you should let him know you want him somehow and just wait for him to tell you. I don't know which way is the best." She squeezed Cornelia's hand. "I do know that you should pray about what's the right way to proceed. God knows what's best for you both."

Cornelia nodded. She would pray, but she would also think about what to do to get Hector to realize they belonged together.

She wiped her cheeks to remove the last trace of any tears as she stood up. "Thank you for listening." Claudia stood, too, and Cornelia embraced her. "I needed to talk with someone about this so badly, and I knew you'd understand. I don't know what I'd do without you."

"What are sisters for?"

◆

Claudia walked Cornelia downstairs and summoned one of the servants from the stable to walk her back home. As she watched Cornelia head down the hill, she once more prayed that two of the people she cared about most would find God's way to happiness.

Chapter 46

Maybe a Chance

Drusilla had just finished setting up the Mercenaries board when her mother entered the sitting room. She'd come through the kitchen from the stable yard, and she was breathing as if she'd been running. Now she was walking back and forth in the room.

Captain's frame filled the door, blocking the sun that had been streaming in from the courtyard. Mother stopped pacing and turned to face him. She was smiling, but something wasn't right. Something around her eyes as she looked at him.

Drusilla might only be ten, but she knew there were times for private conversations between adults. Mother needed to talk with Captain. Right now and alone.

"I'll be right back, Captain. I need to tell Vania something before she leaves."

◆

Cornelia caught her daughter's wink as she passed. She might have laughed at her not-so-subtle manipulation if there weren't something so important to get clear between them.

She wasn't quite sure how to start the conversation, but the start didn't matter as much as the ending. She knew what she wanted that to be.

She cleared her throat. "Hector, I need to tell you something."

The warmth of his eyes and smile wrapped around her like a blanket. She shivered anyway. What if her next words stripped away that warmth and left her forever in the cold?

She wasn't sure whether it was better to look into his eyes or away from them as she began. She chose to look into them. "I saw you last night."

He tilted his head. His brow furrowed, but his smile remained unchanged. She swallowed and continued.

"When you all came out of the bath." The furrows deepened. "I saw your scars." A flash of understanding smoothed his forehead. "I know you were a slave."

"And that bothers you." He said it as a statement, not a question. She saw the cooling in his eyes as his smile faded. She stood immobile as the shiver coursed inside her.

"No...I just wanted you to know that I know." She mentally kicked herself. Telling him she knew may have been exactly what she shouldn't have done.

"That was twenty years ago—ancient history. If anything, it made me a better man now than I would have been." He stepped closer and looked deeper into her eyes. "It does bother you."

"No. I just wondered why you hadn't mentioned you were a freedman before." Her stomach flip-flopped. She was only digging herself into a deeper hole.

"I didn't tell you because I didn't see any reason why you'd care. I don't see why it would matter to anyone now."

His serious gaze was riveted on her eyes, but the trace of a smile tugged at his lips. "Besides, there's no shame in being a slave or having been one. It's only an accident of birth or because many men don't care if others suffer so they can have an easy life. Sometimes God uses it for his own purposes. Joseph was sold into slavery in Egypt, but by God's will, he became second in command to Pharaoh himself. God used him to save Egypt and many others, including his own family, from a great famine."

"You're absolutely right that it doesn't matter...at least not to me." She couldn't keep her eyes from blinking too fast.

His eyes softened. "You look upset."

"I don't want this to come between us."

The warmth returned to his eyes. "It won't if it doesn't bother you."

She almost told him right then that she loved him and wanted him to love her, too. She began to open her mouth, then stopped. That was too risky. What if he told her that wasn't possible? She bit her lip as she glanced away from him.

His gentle smile broadened to wrap around her heart again. "Do you want me to tell you about it?"

She released the breath she had been half-holding when he made that gracious offer. "I want to know everything you want to tell me."

Her eyes locked on his as he began. "I was born on an estate outside Thessalonica. I was there until I was fourteen. My first master fed us enough and only used the lash on the men who didn't work hard enough to suit him. I always worked hard, so life was good there."

Her eyes widened. She'd never considered how someone might think life good just because he had enough to eat and didn't get whipped. No wonder the slaves had all been so upset when her father-in-law was killed and then so happy when Lucius left Malleolus in charge and nothing changed.

"Then something happened that made him have to sell about a quarter of his slaves. I was big and strong for my age, so he sold me to work on the wharves in Thessalonica. That's when I got the brand. My new owner branded all his men when he first bought them so they'd be less likely to run away."

Through his tunic, he rubbed the brand. "The overseer he put in charge of us liked to use the whip when he was unhappy about anything. I worked hard and showed him proper respect, so I never got more than an occasional tip of the whip just to keep me focused. It wasn't so bad. I was fifteen when my life really changed."

His eyes were so peaceful that Cornelia relaxed. The change must have been a good one.

"I owe what I am today to Philip's father. Aristarchus was at the rail of one of his ships, watching what was happening on the pier as the last of his cargo was being loaded. I was carrying small crates onto the ship tied across from his. There was a small boy running up the pier. He tripped and fell into the captain of the ship I was loading. The captain started kicking and hitting him, and he just curled up in a ball instead of trying to get away.

"I'm not sure why, because I knew it was a foolish thing to do, but I put my crate down and scooped up the boy. I set him on his feet and told him to run. Then I blocked the way so the captain couldn't reach him."

Her hand flew to her mouth as she inhaled sharply. She knew what happened on her friends' estates when a slave challenged the overseer.

"The captain hit me hard as he could on the side of my head, knocked me down, almost knocked me out. Kicked me twice in the gut.

Then he just turned and walked up the gangplank, like he was through with me. I thought it was over, but I should have known better. I picked up the crate and carried it onto his ship. I had to do that even if I'd known what was coming."

She swallowed hard as her mind raced to imagine what happened next.

"The next part might be hard for you to hear, but it's why I have the scars. Should I go on?"

She nodded. No matter what it was, she wanted to hear it. She braced herself to keep tears from forming.

"The captain and two of his crew stopped me. They grabbed my arms and tied me to the rigging. The captain began to flog me. The first few strokes came fast, but then he started taking his time between lashes so the next one would be a surprise. It's harder to brace for the pain when you don't expect it."

A shiver raced up her spine. She'd almost ordered the flogging of a runaway, but she'd sold him instead.

"Aristarchus saw it all. He sent his first mate running to the overseer to offer to buy me for 200 denarii more than I was worth if he could take me immediately. He boarded the ship I was on and started talking to the captain to distract him.

"His first mate came back to tell him the purchase was made and the bill of sale was being drawn up. The captain was about to lash me again when Aristarchus grabbed his arm. I heard him order the captain to stop damaging his property and cut me down."

She clamped her jaw to stop the quiver. It didn't work.

"I remember crumpling to the deck and seeing my blood there. My back felt like it was ripped wide open. Everything started swirling. Then Aristarchus stooped down and slipped his hands under my arms. As he lifted me to my feet, I looked into his eyes. No master had ever looked at me like that before. Like he cared. Like I mattered.

"He half-carried me down the gangplank, across the pier, and into one of the rooms in his cabin. He didn't care that he was getting my blood all over his own clothes. Then he washed the blood from my back, spread something on that helped the pain, and bandaged me himself."

His face blurred as Cornelia took a sharp breath. He was telling her the most appalling thing she'd ever heard, but he was smiling as he told her what Philip's father had done.

The tears started trickling down her cheeks. He reached over and wiped them away with his fingertips. She had longed to have him touch her face, and his fingertips brushing her cheeks made her shiver, but this wasn't how she'd imagined he would caress her for the first time.

◆

Touching Cornelia's face was something Hector had wanted to do for a long time, but she'd never given him an excuse before. He gazed down at her blue eyes. They'd lost that calm self-possession he was accustomed to seeing. They were swimming in tears. He hadn't expected her to be so moved by what he'd suffered.

"As he spread the ointment, he told me he'd just bought me. I would serve on his ship as a seaman as soon as I was healed enough. If I worked hard, I could earn my freedom in five years. I couldn't believe what he was saying. It was too good to be true. I asked him why he was helping me. He told me he'd seen me rescue the boy, and rescuing me was what his own Master wanted him to do."

More tears escaped to follow the damp tracks made by Cornelia's first teardrops. He paused again to wipe them away. He'd been afraid she might not welcome the touch of his fingers on her face. As he swept the glistening drops from her cheeks, her trembling smile assured him she did.

"I was used to cruelty from masters, never kindness like that. Aristarchus took care of me himself the first few days. Being treated like a person by the master instead of just a piece of property...I never thought that was possible.

"All the men on his ship were Christians, and Aristarchus led their worship every Sunday. I listened to him teaching how Jesus, the Son of God himself, cared enough about people like me to give up his own life to save us. I saw Aristarchus try to live what Jesus taught. I decided to follow Jesus myself on that voyage."

Teardrops were still trickling as she gazed up into his eyes, so he placed his palms on her cheeks and swept away the tears with his thumbs. Making her cry was the last thing he wanted, but seeing the true feelings of her heart...that was almost worth it. A sign that she truly cared for him.

She closed her eyes as she struggled to control the tears. Her lips quivered, and the desire to lean over and kiss them surged through him. He hadn't expected the temptation to be so strong. It was time to finish the story while he could still resist.

"Being bought by Aristarchus gave me a new life. I'd always been treated like a work animal. I would have died like one. He treated me like a free man even while I was still his slave. Best of all, he taught me about Jesus, and I follow the same Master who told Aristarchus to rescue me.

"I earned my freedom in five years. Then I became first mate on one of his ships. Philip trained on that ship when he was eighteen. When he got his first ship two years later, he made me captain. My ship brought Claudia to Titus before it brought you and Drusilla here."

He wiped away what he hoped were the final tears. "Now you know my story. It's not a sad one, so you don't have to keep crying. I saved the little boy, and that flogging led to my freedom and put me where I would learn Jesus is my savior. You could call it a gift from God."

Those deep blue eyes were staring into his as the tears began to pool once more "I never thought about how hard it could be...how cruel...how horrible. How stupid of me to think I understood anything about being a slave. You told me so that first day."

She drew a ragged breath, and the river of tears broke free. "Can you forgive me for being such an ignorant, arrogant fool?"

He drew her into his arms. Tears cascaded down her cheeks as she pressed her face against him. He felt the warm wetness against his chest as they soaked through his tunic. She wasn't making any sound, but he felt the jumps in her breathing that told him she was sobbing silently.

He'd dreamed of holding her, just like he used to hold Damara, but he never thought he would. Maybe he shouldn't be right now, but he couldn't stand watching her cry. For the first time, she seemed so vulnerable. An overwhelming urge to protect her forever swept over him.

She'd always seemed so far beyond his reach—a regal woman who didn't need anyone to care for her, a woman who would never let herself fall in love with a man who was only a sea captain with a farm.

But the elegant woman who made the simplest chair seem like a throne had broken down in front of him and asked his forgiveness. If she cared so much about his forgiveness, would she welcome his love?

"There's nothing you could do that I won't forgive."

Chapter 47

Cornelia slipped her arms around him. So many times, she'd imagined how good it would feel to be in his arms. It was even better. His strength cocooned her as he held her. Alone for so many years, she'd grown strong. There was no one else to do what must be done. To have him share life's burdens would be so sweet.

Even through his tunic, she could feel the ridges of the scars from that flogging twenty-five years ago. She slid her fingers back and forth across them. Scars from a costly act of kindness, but God had turned it into an act of mercy toward him as well.

She traced one of the welts with her finger. It stretched from just above his belt almost to his shoulder, and her finger crossed at least a dozen more as it traced the first one. Her head reeled at the thought of his torture.

He'd called that horrible flogging a gift from God that led to his freedom and his faith. Maybe Lucius's hateful ways that made her come to Thracia had been a gift from God as well. If only part of that gift could be Hector's heart.

She relished his arms around her. Tenderness radiated from him as he held her in a gentle embrace. The love of a man like him was price-less. She wanted it more than anything she could imagine, but nothing in her past had taught her how to get a man like him to love her.

The river became a rivulet and finally stopped. One more ragged breath was followed by a deep sigh. She slipped her arms further around him and snuggled into his solid chest. More than ever, she wanted him to marry her and hold her like this for the rest of their lives. How was she ever going to let him know he was the desire of her heart and get him to desire her as well?

◆

Hector looked down at the proud women nestled against his chest. This was exactly what he'd dreamed of even before she left his ship. He'd thought it impossible, but there she was, willing and even happy to be cradled in his arms. Would she consider him for something more than a friend? Would she marry a man who wasn't high-born and wealthy like herself? He would have sworn she wouldn't, but maybe he'd been wrong. Maybe he did have a chance with her. What if she could want him as much as he wanted her? Even considering the possibility sent a wave of anticipation up his spine.

He rested his bearded cheek against the top of her head, relishing the silkiness of her luxuriant hair against his cheekbone where there was no beard. It was good she didn't wear those fancy Roman hairstyles anymore. His short, curly hairs caught in the soft brown strands as he shifted his cheek. His favorite of her perfumes teased his nostrils. Her hair was full of the fragrance of roses. He inhaled deeply.

What if he were to weave his fingers into her thick hair and turn her lips up so he could kiss them? He started to reach, but then he paused. She might not welcome that. At least not yet. It was only the first time she'd allowed him this close. It was enough to just hold her today. He placed his hand on her back once more, but this time he swept his forefinger slowly back and forth.

The tears were over. Their breathing synchronized as he held her close. There was something both peaceful and exciting about that. Did she feel it, too?

◆

Cornelia pressed her ear against his chest. His muscles were so solid and warm against her cheek. The beating of his heart was so steady, so strong. Each th-thud added to her conviction that she never wanted to leave the comfort of his encircling arms. In her entire life, she'd never known the peace and security of listening to the heartbeat of a man who cared about her. Could that caring grow into love? She would give anything to have him love her like she already loved him.

She closed her eyes and soaked up his presence. Had it been in her power, she would have frozen time and remained in his arms forever.

The scuffle of Vania's sandals on the mosaic floor as she skipped into the room broke the spell. He released her, and she stepped back.

"Have you seen Drusilla?"

Cornelia smiled at her niece, masking her disappointment over the end of their interlude. "She left here a few minutes ago."

Drusilla trotted into the room right behind her. Her eyes darted between Cornelia and Hector; then a sly smile crept out.

"Shall I get the dice instead and we can all play together for a while?" She smiled hopefully at Hector.

He dropped on one knee in front of her. "I think that's a very good idea." He smiled up at Cornelia. "Playing games with two of my favorite people suits me just fine."

Miriam stepped into the sitting room to tell Cornelia they were leaving. The sight before her seemed very odd. Cornelia's eyes were puffy, like she'd been crying hard, but the happiest smile lit her face.

"I'll say farewell now. Philip's here, so we're leaving." Cornelia rose from the table as if to follow her to the stable yard. "Don't bother coming out. You three keep playing."

A mischievous smile curved Miriam's lips. "Hector, I hope you'll take good care of Cornelia and Drusilla while we're gone." The smile turned into a grin. "But I'm sure you will without me asking."

Hector's grin mirrored her own. "You can count on me for that."

Cornelia's eyes sparkled at his words.

Miriam raised her hand and left them. Something very interesting had just happened. It was going to be hard to wait a week to find out what.

Anthusa noticed Mistress Cornelia watching her in the mirror as she brushed her mistress's hair before retiring.

"Anthusa, I want to ask you something...something important."

Anthusa's eyebrows rose at that statement. The mistress usually just asked without any prelude. "What, mistress?"

"What would you do if you were free?"

Anthusa blinked several times in quick succession. "I never thought about it."

"Well, think about it now. What would you do?"

This was an unsettling conversation. She wasn't sure what answer the mistress wanted. She didn't want her to think she wasn't happy serving her, because she was. But being free...that was every slave's dream. It was also a frightening thought.

"I don't know. I'm happy here with you. I don't know where else I would ever want to go or what I would do if I left."

"What if you could stay with me as my servant but still be free? Would you like that? Then if something happened to me, no one would be able to sell you or hurt you."

◆

Cornelia watched Anthusa closely in the mirror. First shock at the question, then discomfort with an unclear future, and finally her growing smile as she thought about it.

"I do want to stay with you, mistress, but to be free...I never even dreamed that could be. You say I could stay even if you freed me?"

Cornelia stood and took her faithful friend's hands in her own. "You've been my slave for twenty-five years, but you're also my closest friend. You're the one person I trust most in this world. I would never want you to leave. Of course you could stay."

"Then yes. I guess I would like to be free. It's a frightening thing when a master dies. You never know what the next master will be like. No one else could be as good as you've been."

"Then that decides it. I'll talk with Titus when he gets back about what I need to do to free you. He freed Miriam, so he'll know."

"Thank you, mistress." The happy glow in Anthusa's eyes said more than words could. Cornelia opened her arms, and Anthusa threw her arms around her. As she embraced her dearest friend, Cornelia's smile broadened in anticipation of Hector's reaction to her decision. She would love the look of approval in his eyes.

Chapter 48:

THE NEWEST SISTER

As Hector rode through Titus's gate the next morning to take Cornelia and Drusilla to worship, he expected a very good day. On the road from his farm, the memory of how soft her cheeks had been as he wiped away her tears teased him. He couldn't get his mind off how alive he felt as he savored holding her close while she slowly swept her fingers across the scars on his back.

He'd told himself repeatedly there was no point in thinking about a future with her. She would only marry a high-born man, someone her social equal. Yesterday had shown him the passionate woman underneath the elegant veneer. A woman who seemed to want him like he wanted her. He'd been strongly drawn to the regal Cornelia he'd seen for many weeks. The vulnerable Cornelia of yesterday had finished ensnaring his heart as she cried in his arms.

Surely God had brought her to his ship, to his friend's family, to his own arms so they could be together. It was a little over three months before the sea opened and he took the *Claudia* out again. He wanted to make her his wife before he sailed. Only two things were needed. She must decide to follow his Lord, and he needed the courage to ask her.

Drusilla was already outside, tossing grain to the chickens gathered around her feet. She flung the rest into the air before bouncing over to greet him.

"Mother and Anthusa are almost ready, Captain."

"Good." He swung down and led his mare into the waiting stall.

254

She trotted along beside him. "It's too quiet here with Vania and the boys gone."

A corner of his lip twitched up. "I'm not surprised. It's never quiet with little boys around."

Drusilla grinned up at him. "I'd like to have a little brother to find out. My brothers are all grown up."

She was looking at him like her mother did when she expected him to do something.

"Maybe your mother will remarry, and you will."

Sparkling eyes accompanied another grin. "I hope so, Captain, and I know who she should marry."

Hector fought a grin. He knew who wanted to marry her already. If he were a betting man, he'd wager they were thinking of the same man.

◆

Cornelia and Anthusa emerged from the kitchen to find Drusilla walking back from the stable with Hector.

Butterflies danced in Cornelia's stomach as she watched him stride toward her. Her mind filled with his brawny arms wrapped tenderly around her, his solid chest pressed against her cheek, his trusting words revealing the secrets of his past.

His smile brightened the stable yard better than the sun. "Are you ready to go, Cornelia?"

He stopped three feet from her.

"Yes, Captain." Again, she imagined his arms around her. If she got too near, could she resist touching him after the closeness of yesterday?

Anthusa and Drusilla moved up beside her. Drusilla slid one hand into Cornelia's and reached for Hector's with the other. "Uncle Philip is gone, so who's going to teach? Is it you, Captain?"

Hector shook his head. "I only teach on my ship."

Cornelia tipped her head. "Perhaps you should teach on land as well. I am still thinking about what you read and spoke on the *Claudia*."

"I'm glad, but I only speak as the Spirit leads me. Here I learn instead of teach."

Cornelia would have preferred to walk beside him, but Drusilla still held their hands until they reached Philip's gate.

The gatekeeper swung the gate open to admit them and closed it after they passed through. Excitement coursed through Cornelia. Something special was in the air. God was calling her, and she was prepared to answer. She wasn't sure what would happen today, but she knew it would change everything.

◆

Cornelia settled onto the bench next to Hector. It seemed so natural to be there, feeling his warmth beside her. She glanced at his profile. God had made him such a wonderful man. Claudia was right about God bringing good even out of evil. She could honestly say she was grateful to Lucius for making her flee to Thracia.

An old man with a fringe of silver hair and deep wrinkles moved slowly toward the podium. He looked feeble, until he turned his eyes on her and smiled. Those eyes—piercingly intelligent yet filled with love. His smile—it wrapped her like a cozy blanket. It felt as if he knew something special was about to happen as well.

The lyre man started the singing, and once more it transported her. Finally, the old man raised his hand, and all went quiet.

He raised his hands and closed his eyes. "We praise you, Lord, for this new day to gather and worship you together. Fill us all with your Spirit, that our prayers and praise may give you joy."

He opened the codex. "I had planned to read from the gospel of John today, but God had other plans. So instead, I'll read what He chose a few minutes ago from the gospel of Luke.

"The son of Man must suffer many things and be rejected by the elders, chief priests, and teachers of the law, and he must be killed, and on the third day be raised to life. Then he said to them all: "If anyone would come after me, he must deny himself and take up his cross daily and follow me. For whoever wants to save his life will lose it, but whoever loses his life for me will save it. What good is it for a man to gain the whole world, and yet lose or forfeit his very self? If anyone is ashamed of me and my words, the Son of Man will be ashamed of him when he comes in his glory and in the glory of the Father and of the holy angels. I tell you the truth, some who are standing here will not taste death before they see the kingdom of God.'"

Cornelia's eyes saucered. It was the same reading Hector had chosen the first time she listened to him on the ship. She'd lived the life of someone who seemed to have the whole world, but it hadn't satisfied. She'd lived separated from God by her sins, never fully at peace. Jesus had come and died to change that, and she knew, at the deepest core of her being, that He'd done it for her.

And right then, next to the man who'd started her on the path to hearing God's call, she answered yes. Yes to being a sinner needing a savior. Yes to accepting the gift of Jesus's sacrifice to cover those sins. Yes to the call to follow Jesus as Lord.

The old man's eyes locked on her own. "Someone here today is ready to give her life to our Lord Jesus."

Cornelia rose. "I am, and I will never be ashamed of claiming Jesus as my savior."

He held his hands out to her. "Come."

She walked up to him and knelt.

He placed his gnarled hands on her shoulders. "In the presence of all gathered here, tell our Lord your decision to love and serve Him, and receive the Holy Spirit as He promised."

Cornelia wasn't sure where all her words came from, but as she spoke her heart, she felt surrounded by the indescribable presence of God, and her heart soared as words she never knew poured forth.

When she finished, the whole congregation rose to offer their praise and thanks to God.

The old man held her hand as she rose, and she floated back to stand beside Hector.

He beamed at her. "Welcome to the family, Cornelia. You'll be with me as my sister in Christ forever."

"Forever with Jesus...and you and Publius and Claudia and...I've never felt less alone."

He grinned at her and took her hand as the musician plucked the lyre and the final songs of worship rose heavenward.

◆

After the service, Hector watched Cornelia being greeted as the newest believer by everyone, and his heart filled with joy. She was now his sister in Christ, and he couldn't have been happier about her decision. She was saved from her sins, destined for eternal life in heaven after her death. But he was joyful for one more reason. It was now possible for him to take her as his wife...if she would have him.

That was a very big if. He rubbed the back of his neck. She'd begun thinking about Jesus on his ship. He'd seen it in her eyes. But when did she decide to commit? She'd said nothing during their walk up from Titus's house about being ready to make this step. When a woman loves a man, don't they share their deepest thoughts and dreams? Damara always had.

He shook his head to shake that thought loose. She probably just made the decision during this morning's worship. Surely she knew he would care whether she shared the most important decision of her life with him before she announced it to the whole fellowship.

She knew she could trust him. Hadn't she let him see her true heart yesterday when he told her things about himself that no one else but Philip knew? Surely she knew how much he cared.

But maybe she didn't. He'd never actually told her. She'd been so soft and open when she cried in his arms, but maybe she only felt pity for him when she thought about what he'd suffered. She'd let him embrace her long after the tears were over, but what did that really mean? She'd asked for his forgiveness, not his love. Even a good friend would do that. What if he told her of his love, of his desire to marry her?

Her smiles, her teasing, her eyes...all seemed like invitations. But what if he asked and she turned him down? What if she didn't want him like he wanted her? He'd rather be with her hoping she might someday grow to want him than to find out she never would.

That would be too hard to bear. He'd rather live in pointless hope than certain knowledge that his dreams were impossible.

He would wait and see. Time would tell him whether she could love him. When he knew for sure, he would ask for her hand.

◆

Hector sat next to Cornelia during the fellowship meal. He would rather have had her to himself, but it was such a joyous occasion when someone became a new believer that he didn't expect it. Finally, everyone had expressed their happiness for her, and it was just the two of them, Anthusa, and Malleolus.

Cornelia reached over and touched Malleolus's hand. "Today may be the very best day of my whole life. Only the birth of my children brought such joy. I never dreamed when we boarded the ship that it would lead to this."

She turned to Hector. "It was you who got me started down this path, Captain. You've made such a difference in my life...and Drusilla's. I can't imagine where we'd be today without you. I'm so glad the sea closes during the winter, but you're going to be gone in three months. That's really not much time. We'll miss you terribly. I don't know how we'll ever find a replacement for your company."

Hector's head bounced back. Replacement for his company? Can the company of a person you love be replaced? Not as easily as her words seem to imply.

He didn't know what to say, so he said nothing. She'd spoken those words too lightly, and they sat heavy on his mind.

Had he been fooling himself? Cornelia had noble ancestry and great wealth. He had a farm and made good money from his share of the profits on the cargoes of the *Claudia*, but he wasn't rich or of noble blood. Could an aristocrat like her want a mere captain?

Only a captain—she must still think of him that way, at least sometimes. She kept calling him that most of the time even after he told her to call him Hector. Maybe she only did it because that's what Drusilla always called him, and she was used to calling him that onboard. There did seem to be admiration in the way she said it, but it still meant she hadn't forgotten he wasn't in her class.

Maybe the class difference really was too great. Maybe God only brought them on his ship because he needed Drusilla. Maybe Cornelia becoming his wife wasn't part of God's plan. But when he thought about what she said and how she acted with him, it certainly felt like she might be.

He would pray and watch to see what he should do. In the normal ways of the world, an aristocratic woman would never marry a slave-turned-sea captain. But his slave days were so long ago; they really shouldn't matter. Not to a woman who loved him. Maybe in God's more perfect ways, it might be possible. He should be able to tell within a few days. If she left her heart open to him, like she had yesterday, he would know.

<h1 align="center">Chapter 49</h1>

Too Good to Be True

As Hector escorted Cornelia and the others back to Titus's house, the doubts of the morning slipped to the back of his mind.

Cornelia walked close beside him, so close their hands almost brushed several times. When he glanced down at her, she seemed to feel it every time. Her chin lifted toward him and the happiest smile appeared. They reached the kitchen door much too quickly.

As he gazed into her welcoming blue eyes, a small voice distracted him.

"Can you stay to play a game of Mercenaries, Captain?"

He broke contact with Cornelia's eyes and looked at Drusilla. "I can."

Drusilla and Anthusa disappeared through the kitchen doorway.

He stood in silence, his gaze once more fixed on Cornelia. It might be wiser to wait a few days, but he didn't want to. It felt like it was time. It took all his courage to ask what he was about to, and he took several deep breaths to prepare himself.

That mischievous gleam he liked so well filled her eyes. "Were you going to say something, Captain?"

The jingle of a harness behind him pulled his eyes from hers again. A wagon carrying three men and a gravestone had entered the yard. Nestor came from his quarters and led the driver to a place by the garden wall that had been prepared to receive it. Then the four of them began unloading.

Hector's brow furrowed. "What's that?"

She dropped her voice to a near-whisper. "It's to protect Drusilla from Lucius. Tertius wrote to warn me that he sent two men to get Drusilla and drag her back to him. They could be here in five days. Titus and Philip moved up their trip to the western estates so they would be back by then. The gravestone has her name on it so Titus and I can convince them she's dead."

His stomach knotted. "You should have told me, Cornelia."

"I know. I'm sorry." Her whisper stabbed like a knife.

Drusilla in mortal danger and this was the first she told him of it? How could she say nothing to him if she wanted to be his wife? She should know her welfare and that of Drusilla were his to protect if she thought he should be her husband. Sorry now wasn't enough.

Was this the sign that their marriage wasn't God's plan after all?

His lips tightened. He longed to ask her if this meant everything he feared, but he didn't. The answer might be too painful.

◆

Cornelia saw Hector's lips tighten as his gaze remained locked on the gravestone and the men unloading it.

"Captain."

His jaw clenched as a flash of pain crossed his face, then vanished.

Cornelia's stomach tightened. "After you and Drusilla play Mercenaries, will you stay for dinner?"

His eyes had chilled. Then anger flamed in them. A wall shot up between them.

"No. Since Titus isn't here, I'll eat at the farm with Marcario. Tell Drusilla I'll come tomorrow morning for some Mercenaries. Now, if you'll excuse me."

Without waiting for her answer, he spun and strode toward the stable, leaving her alone by the kitchen door.

She stood transfixed. What had her failure to tell him done?

He tossed the saddle on his mare, cinched it, and jumped up to swing his leg across its rump. He rode past without even looking at her.

Her stomach knotted so hard she thought she might vomit. He was hurt and furious because she hadn't told him about Lucius's men. She'd planned to tell him at dinner the night she saw his scars, but she'd had no chance. She couldn't talk about it when Drusilla or the cousins might overhear. The morning he held her, Lucius and what he was doing were the farthest things from her thoughts. Only Hector filled her mind as he cradled her in his arms, and then Drusilla had come and the chance was gone.

He hadn't been this angry since the first day on the ship when he thought she questioned his honesty. She fought against the tears that were trying to escape.

Drusilla popped out of the kitchen in time to see him ride out the gate. "Where is Captain going? Isn't he going to eat with us?"

She forced her voice to sound calm. "No, dear. He's eating with his son."

"I wish he'd eat with us, but he'll probably be here tomorrow."

"He did say he'd be here tomorrow to play Mercenaries with you."

Drusilla's gaze turned toward the men who were moving the gravestone into place.

"What are they doing, Mother?"

Cornelia took her daughter's hand. "I've ordered a surprise for some men Lucius is sending for you."

Drusilla's eyes saucered. "Father found us?"

"Yes, but you don't have to be afraid. Your uncle and I have put the stone up so we can convince them to go back to Rome and tell your father you died. Then he'll never try to get you again. Go back inside so the men won't see you as they leave."

Drusilla squeezed her hand before turning without a word and walking back into the kitchen.

Cornelia's gaze drifted to the gate where Hector had disappeared. He'd be back tomorrow. She'd explain why she hadn't been able to tell him before the gravestone came. He'd been angry at her before and forgiven her. Once she explained, surely he'd forgive her for not telling him sooner.

She bit her lip. But what if he didn't?

Anthusa had noticed how quiet Mistress Cornelia was all afternoon and through dinner. As she pulled the hairpins in preparation for brushing, she hoped she'd finally find out why.

Mistress drew the deepest breath and slowly released it. "Today started out as the best day of my life. How could it turn bad so quickly?"

"What happened, mistress?"

"I think Hector almost asked me to marry him. He'd seemed so happy after our worship, after I stood in the fellowship and announced Jesus is my Lord. It felt like a barrier between us had dropped away. I was sure he was about to ask at the kitchen door. He stood very close to me for so long without saying anything. Then the wagon with the gravestone arrived just as he was about to speak. He got so terribly upset...hurt and then angry like he was the first day on his ship. It was like all the progress I've made in getting him to want me was swept away. Gone."

Anthusa watched her mistress's eyes moisten in the mirror. "The captain is such an honest man. He probably didn't understand why you didn't tell him about Lucius sending those men."

"I was going to, but I didn't get a chance. Drusilla was around all the time, and I didn't want to frighten her before I had to."

"I know that, but he doesn't."

Mistress Cornelia wiped away the wetness at the corners of her eyes. "I'm afraid he thinks I don't trust him. But there isn't a man alive that I trust more than him. He should know that." She took a deep breath and released a shuddering sigh. "Well, I'll find some way to make him understand when he comes tomorrow. A few minutes alone with him, and I can get this whole misunderstanding cleared up."

"I'm sure you can, if you just tell him everything. I think that's all he wants."

Mistress nodded. Then she wiped at the corners of her eyes again.

Anthusa continued brushing. The mistress had made a grave mistake in making the captain think she didn't trust him. But he was a forgiving man, and it was obvious he loved her. Surely, they would work it out.

The next morning, Hector was up when the first wash of pink lightened the eastern clouds. He hadn't slept all night, and there was no point in lying in bed when he knew he wasn't going to sleep anyway.

In the tool room attached to his stable, he found an ax. He sat at the grinding wheel and began to sharpen it. There was a dead tree at the edge of the grove around the house. He was in the perfect mood to cut it down.

He slid his thumb along the edge of the blade. Almost as sharp as he wanted. As he held it against the wheel again, Marcario walked up behind him.

"Father?"

Hector lifted the blade from the wheel. "Yes?"

"Is there something wrong?"

Before he answered, Hector swept his thumb across the cutting edge. "No...yes, but there's nothing that can be done to fix it. I wanted something that wasn't meant to be. That's all."

"Do you want to talk about it?"

Hector shook his head. Talking would just start the wound bleeding again. "No, but you can do me a favor."

"What, Father?"

"Stop at Titus Drusus's house on your way to work and tell Drusilla I can't come today. She should expect me tomorrow instead."

"I'll do that. Did you want to come in and eat breakfast with me?"

His lips tightened. "No. I'll get something after I chop that dead tree down. I'm not hungry right now."

"Will I see you at dinner?"

"Yes. I'll be here. I have nowhere else to go."

Hector started the grindstone spinning again and held the blade against it. Marcario stood in silence behind him. Finally, his footsteps faded away as he returned to the house.

When the blade was ready, Hector headed into the grove.

Cornelia was eating breakfast when Nestor stuck his head into the dining room.

"Mistress, Marcario was just here. Hector sent word that he wouldn't be coming today. He wanted Drusilla to know he'll come tomorrow instead."

Cornelia's throat tightened. Then she put on her mask. "Thank you for telling me, Nestor. I'll let Drusilla know."

After Nestor left, the mask fell away. Tears welled up. She swept them away and willed them to stop. Drusilla mustn't see her crying. She'd ask why, and if Cornelia spoke the words, she might not be able to stop the tears.

Hector wasn't coming because he didn't want to be near her. That thought tore at her heart. How was she ever going to fix the rift between them if he wouldn't come? She swallowed hard, then took a deep breath.

He wasn't coming today, but he'd said he'd come tomorrow. Hector always kept his word. Maybe it would be better if he had an extra day to cool off.

She popped another date in her mouth. It was sweet and moist, but all she tasted was sawdust.

Claudia Aprensis, west of Perinthus

Maximus and Thrax, gladiators of the Ludus Silani, rode into Claudia Aprenis shortly before dusk. They reined in at an inn on the west edge of town.

Maximus swung his leg over the tired horse's neck and slid off. "The farther we get from Rome, the harder it is to get good mounts."

Thrax joined him afoot, and the two led their weary animals toward the stable slave. "Day after tomorrow, and we'll be there. If Cornelia Scipia won't turn over her daughter, the provincial governor will enforce Drusus's claim. We can take a day or two to rest after we get her, and then we'll start back." He flexed his shoulders and arched his back. "But we won't have to ride twelve hours a day. The girl probably couldn't, and I don't want to. Lanista Lupus said if we get back with her in six or seven weeks, that's soon enough."

The stable slave took the reins and led the horses into adjacent stalls.

Trax slapped his companion's arm. "Time for a good meal and a good night's sleep. If we ride hard tomorrow, we'll be in Perinthus by nightfall. And the day after that..." He grinned. "We'll show Cornelia Scipia that all her money and noble blood are no match against the rights of a father with gladiators to make sure he gets back what's his."

Perinthus

Anthusa had watched Mistress Cornelia wear her mask all day because Drusilla was nearby. But now Drusilla was in bed, and it was only the two of them.

She'd only removed half the pins when the mistress turned worried eyes upon her.

"What am I going to do, Anthusa? He was about to ask me to marry him. I know I've won his heart, just as he's won mine. He's not a man to change his mind about something as important as that. He's so forgiving that he's probably already over being angry at me about the gravestone."

"He is a forgiving man, mistress."

"But I'm afraid this misunderstanding will make him wait longer to ask me. If he waits too long, we won't have any time together before he sails again. What can I do to get him to hurry up and ask?"

"Why don't you just tell him you want him to ask? He's an honest man. If any man would like you to simply tell him you love him and want to marry him, it's the captain."

"Men don't work that way. Especially strong men, and Hector is as strong as men come. They like to think something is their idea. Just telling him would make it seem like it was my idea. That scares men off."

Anthusa pulled the brush through her hair. The captain was a strong man, but he wasn't like any that she'd seen before. The mistress was wrong about that.

"Do you remember Portia Alba? The man she wanted to marry was taking forever to ask her. He was heading out to one of the provinces, and she wanted to marry before he left. She pretended she was interested in a rival. That made him realize he needed to ask quickly or he might lose her."

Anthusa's jaw clenched. That plan was headed in the wrong direction, but it wasn't her place to tell Mistress Cornelia what to do.

"Quintus Lepidus came the other day to tell me he was interested in a marriage with me. Hector said he's a decent man. I can see that myself. He spoke of his interest, but I know his heart isn't engaged. It still belongs to his dead wife. It's impossible for him to be in love with me after two conversations."

A laugh bubbled up. "Three, if you count the one ten years ago in Rome that I don't even remember. He's looking for a companion and an infusion of money with my dowry, not a love match. That would be a suitable choice. He would be disappointed but not hurt when I marry Hector instead."

Anthusa shook her head. "I don't think that's the best idea. The captain might totally misunderstand. He doesn't think like Roman men do. He's already upset that you didn't tell him something important. He just wants to know the truth. Maybe it's best to just tell him."

Mistress Cornelia pursed her lips. "Maybe you're right. I'll wait to see what happens in the next few days. It was only two days ago that he held me in his arms. Surely he could tell I never wanted him to let go. He must know what that means. He should know what to do about it. But if he doesn't do something soon, I might try to make him jealous. I want us married before he goes back to sea in the spring, and that's only a little over three months away."

Anthusa forced herself to say no more. What the mistress was suggesting was a very bad idea, but it wasn't her place to tell her that as forcefully as it would take to convince her. Besides, maybe the captain would ask her before she did something foolish that could drive him away.

Chapter 50

Doomed to Failure

The next morning, Cornelia dressed with special care in the blue tunic that heightened the color of her eyes. Her hair was filled with the fragrance of roses. She'd practiced what she would say to Hector. Everything was ready for his arrival.

She stood at her loom in the women's room, weaving to occupy her mind until Hector came. When she heard conversation outside, she parked her shuttle and walked to the window to see who had come.

Quintus Lepidus was talking with Nestor. Titus had mentioned that he was interested in a young mare after he bought one of the 500-denarii colts. Perhaps that was why he'd come.

But his arrival presented an unexpected opportunity. A satisfied smile curved Cornelia's lips. Hector would be there soon to play Mercenaries with Drusilla. Seeing Lepidus should shake him up a little to get him to propose.

She called from the window. "Quintus. What a pleasant surprise to see you here. Do come in, and we can talk for a while."

The initial look of surprise on Lepidus's face was replaced by satisfaction. He disappeared into the kitchen.

As Cornelia descended the stairs to join him in the courtyard, she bestowed her most gracious smile upon him. A friendly conversation with Lepidus while Hector was there should be all that was needed.

◆

Hector walked through the kitchen into the courtyard. It was hard to make that walk. By the time he finished chopping down the tree and cutting it up for firewood, he had mostly reconciled himself to Cornelia not wanting to marry him. He expected a stab of pain when he saw her, but he'd lived through loss before. Losing Damara had almost destroyed him. Losing Cornelia...well, he couldn't really lose what had never been his anyway. He'd just keep reminding himself of that until the pain passed.

He froze in the kitchen doorway. The last thing he expected to see was Cornelia sitting on a bench talking with Lepidus. He was holding her hand, just like the senator had in Ephesus, and she wasn't doing anything to discourage him. Nothing at all. She was actually smiling at him as if she enjoyed his company.

The cold, hard truth slammed into him again. It was just as he'd thought all along. A ship's captain wasn't the sort of man she'd consider for a husband. It only made sense that she'd prefer Lepidus to him. The aristocrat came from a long-established wealthy family, while he was only a freedman of modest means. His life as a slave bothered her when she first learned of it. She'd told him it didn't matter now, and he'd believed her. But maybe he shouldn't have.

How could he have let himself believe she truly wanted him, in spite of all she'd been born and raised to value? The sight before him made it all too clear he'd been lying to himself. As soon as the first aristocrat showed his interest, she welcomed his addresses.

His stomach clenched. He'd only been a diversion until a more suitable man showed up. She was so good at play-acting. He'd been a fool to believe what he thought he saw because he wanted it so badly.

If she'd ever wanted him as her husband, she would have told him right away about the danger to Drusilla that was almost here. She didn't even trust him with that.

The ache in his chest was almost too much to bear. He should have known better than to let her capture his heart. He knew how the world works. The gulf between their social standing was too wide.

How could he have been so stupid as to expect more than was possible? How could he have exposed his heart to losing another woman he loved? Losing her not to death, but to another man because she didn't think he was good enough.

Drusilla popped out of the sitting room and hurried over to take his hand.

"I'm so glad you've come, Captain. I have everything set up for us." She led him into the courtyard.

Lepidus turned cool eyes on him.

Cornelia smiled at him. It looked genuine, but she was so good at faking he doubted it was. "It's good to see you, Hector. We missed you yesterday."

His throat constricted, and he couldn't answer. He nodded and walked past them. He wished with all his heart he hadn't come.

◆

Sitting at the small table with Drusilla was torture. Hector could hear the low murmur of their voices, punctuated by her laughter. With his mind on the two in the courtyard, he played mechanically, and Drusilla was slaughtering him.

After what seemed an eternity, Lepidus left. Hector had thought it was hard listening to them, but then Cornelia wandered into the room and stood next to him. It was like being chained too close to a fire.

He caged the pain and said nothing.

Drusilla beamed up at her mother. "I can't believe it. I've beaten Captain every game this morning. I've never even come close to that before."

"That is amazing, dear. The captain is usually so good at everything. How is that possible, Hector?"

He kept his eyes on the game board. How could she act as if nothing had just happened in the courtyard? The dagger of her indifference twisted in his heart.

"Captain?"

"Some days are just bad days, Cornelia, and this is one of them."

"What's wrong?" She stepped closer, and the scent of roses accosted him.

He opened his mouth to speak, then closed it. It was better to say nothing.

"You can tell me, Captain. I'm counting on you being an honest man and telling me."

That was more than he could take. He stood so suddenly the chair fell backward. "You want honesty? I'll give you honesty. I couldn't help hearing you with Lepidus. I see your interest in him. He's much more suitable than I am for a woman like you."

The pain and anger consumed him even as he spoke calm words. "I remember the weight of your treasure chests. I know you plan to start over here with a villa on a large estate. I may only be a Greek from the provinces, but even I know an Aemilius Lepidus is a suitable husband for a Cornelius Scipio. Quintus Lepidus is a decent man, and he should be a good husband for you. He'll be good to Drusilla, too."

He dragged in a breath and spoke the words that tore open the wound in his heart. "I wish you happiness together."

He turned away. "Be careful not to tell him about your new faith. He won't allow it."

Her hand gripped his arm, turning him back to face her. When he raised his eyes to hers, he saw naked fear.

"No! You don't understand. I'm not interested in him at all. It's you I want to marry. I was afraid you weren't going to ask me before you leave in the spring, and I thought you might say something sooner if you thought another man wanted me, too. It's only you I love. Only you I want."

Hector's jaw clamped. Red fringed his vision as he clenched his fists at his side before spreading his fingers to relax them.

"That's even worse. Leading another man on just to get me to do something proves you're a liar. If you're willing to fool a good man like Lepidus, how can I be sure anything you tell me is true? Don't you realize what it does to a man to think a woman cares for him when she doesn't? You say you love me, but how can I trust anything you say when I've seen you pretend with men you say mean nothing to you?"

He turned and stormed from the room.

◆

Drusilla ran to the doorway and stared at the captain as he disappeared through the kitchen door. She spun at the choking sound behind her.

Mother had collapsed to her knees, and tears cascaded down her cheeks as she stared at the ceiling.

Drusilla froze and stared at her. Mother was crying. She had never even once seen Mother cry. She spun and ran for the stairs.

"Anthusa! Help!"

◆

Anthusa ran from the bedchamber. "What's wrong?"

Drusilla was crying as she pointed to the sitting room. "Mother!"

Anthusa's feet flew along the balcony and down the stairs. When she saw Mistress Cornelia collapsed on the floor, sobbing, she first went to Drusilla.

"Your mother will be fine. I'll help her. You go find Nestor and ask him for something to do." She pushed Drusilla's hair behind her ears and wiped the tears from her cheeks. Drusilla's lip still quivered. "Go. Your mother will be more upset if she sees you crying. Everything will work out. You'll see."

Anthusa walked into the sitting room and knelt by her mistress. "Mistress, what happened?"

Mistress rose to her knees and threw her arms around Anthusa. "You were right, and I was such a stupid fool." Another sob convulsed her, but she swallowed hard and forced a calm voice. "Lepidus came to see the mare, and I thought it would be good for Hector to see me with him. I was so wrong. First, he told me he understood that I only wanted a nobleman, not a man like him."

Her chest jumped again. "He even wished me happiness. I could see how much I'd hurt him. When I tried to explain I didn't care at all for Lepidus, that it was only him I loved, he got so angry. He told me if I could play with another man's heart, he couldn't trust anything I said. He couldn't believe I really loved him." A sob broke free. "I've lost him. I know I've lost him."

Anthusa wrapped her arms around her mistress and rocked her as fresh sobs racked her body.

"Shhh, all isn't lost. He's angry now, but he'll calm down. Then you can talk it through. I'm sure he loves you. Surely God brought you together, just like He did Philip and Claudia, just like Miriam and Titus. If it's God's will for you, nothing can keep you apart."

◆

Cornelia drew a deep breath. She released a shuddering sigh, and her sobs ceased. Then she rose and offered her hand to Anthusa to help her up.

She wiped the tears from her cheeks and straightened her shoulders. "You're right. Claudia told me I needed to pray about the best way to get Hector to love me. I was a fool to use deceitful Roman ways on an honest Christian man. But God can fix anything, can't He? I know He can, but will He? Maybe it was only me and not God who wanted us together. Oh, Anthusa! What if it isn't God's will at all?"

Teardrops trickled down her cheeks once more.

Anthusa tucked a strand of hair behind her ear. "We can't know yet, but we do know God loves you. Master Philip read to us how God wants only what's best for everyone who loves Him. You and the captain both love Him now, so we need to be patient and pray for whatever's best."

She took Cornelia's hand and led her toward the stairs. "Time for you to rest awhile. Things always look darkest when they first happen. Let's see what tomorrow brings."

Chapter 51

An Honest Woman

Drusilla woke late on Wednesday. She'd watched her mother all Tuesday afternoon and into the evening. Anthusa had been right that she could help, but Mother was still close to tears, even though she tried to hide it.

She always said her prayers after Mother kissed her good night. Usually they were short, but last night she'd prayed and prayed for Mother and Captain. She prayed so long she fell asleep before she finished.

Captain had said during the fellowship meal that he was planning on a driving lesson that morning, but he didn't come. When Mother started crying again, it was time to do something.

Drusilla slipped out the gate and ran up the hill to Aunt Claudia's house. A servant took her upstairs to the women's room.

Aunt Claudia parked the shuttle on her loom when Drusilla was escorted into the room.

"Well, this is a nice surprise. Is your mother with you?"

Drusilla bit her lip. "No. I came for help. Something is horribly wrong between Mother and Captain. They fought yesterday, and he didn't come today like he promised. Please fix it if you can. I want Captain to marry Mother. I was sure they were falling in love, and Captain would be my father soon. And now...I'm afraid he never will."

Tears began trickling down her cheeks. Claudia brushed them away. "What was the fight about?"

"It was over her talking with Captain's Roman neighbor. Captain

273

told Mother he couldn't trust anything she said, and he left so angry. And now Mother is crying all the time. She never cried before. Ever."

Cornelia wrapped her arm around Drusilla's shoulder. "I think I know what might have happened. I'll talk with Hector and see what I can do to fix it. Let's go get one of the servants to walk you back home. Just leave it all to me."

◆

As soon as she sent Drusilla off with the servant, Claudia found Malleolus.

"Cornelia and Hector have a problem, and we need to help them solve it."

Malleolus tilted his head as his eyebrows dipped. "What problem is that? They seemed to be doing fine Sunday."

"They were, until Cornelia did something foolish."

"What did she do?

"She tried to make him jealous with Quintus Lepidus so he'd propose sooner."

Malleolus sucked air through his teeth. "And Hector decided she only wanted a rich, noble Roman instead of him."

Claudia smiled at his perception. "Worse than that. He got angry and told her he couldn't trust anything she said. He hasn't been back since. He just doesn't understand the romantic games people play all the time."

Malleolus's mouth curved down. "No, he doesn't. He would never play them." He slapped his thighs. "Well, it's time for you and me to explain the ways of women to him. Cornelia has been a mystery since he met her." A chuckle rumbled up. "The dear, honest captain will never fully understand women, but we can get him past this so he'll marry the right woman to teach him."

Claudia waved over one of the maids who was cleaning the mosaic floor. "Run to the stable and get Timothy to send a messenger to Hector at his farm. Tell him I need him here as soon as possible."

As the girl scurried away, Claudia smiled at Malleolus. "Now let's pray for the right words to help the two of them get out of their own way and let God give them what He wants for both of them."

Cornelia sat by the window in her bedchamber and wiped away a tear. Hector, the man who always kept his word, had not come for the driving lesson he'd promised them. She swallowed to tame the lump that rose in her throat. Her stupid game-playing had driven him away. If he wouldn't come back, she could never try to explain, never get him to believe how much she loved him, how much she longed to be his wife. If he wouldn't come, she'd made Drusilla lose the only father she'd ever known.

A deep sigh raised and lowered her chest. It was all she could do to keep the tears from breaking through the dam and flooding her face again. She stared down the road, praying for him to come, willing him to come.

Her pulse raced when she glimpsed his brawny form cantering up the hill. She rose and grabbed the attar of roses from the dressing table. She was dabbing it into her hair as she watched him draw closer. Her heart beat in time with his horse's hoofs.

He was at the gate...and then he was past it. He was going to Philip's house, and he hadn't even glanced at Titus's as he rode by. Her heart plummeted.

She placed the perfume back on the dressing table and picked up the sheathed dagger she'd taken from the trunk containing Titus's old armor and weapons. She pulled the blade from the sheath and felt the edge. Razor sharp. Ready to draw blood. Then she slid it back into the sheath and strapped the attached belt to her waist.

The men coming for Drusilla shouldn't be there for another three days, but she'd started wearing the dagger yesterday. She'd dreamed of having a strong man to share life's burdens. That was not to be. Once again, she had only herself to depend on.

No one was going to hurt Drusilla. If anyone tried, she would stop them. If they succeeded, it would only be over her own dead body.

As Hector thundered past Cornelia's house, he kept his eyes locked on the road. It hurt too much to think about what he almost had but lost within those walls. He'd given her his heart. He'd never thought that would happen again after Damara, but it had. Cornelia had brought back his laughter. She'd made him look forward instead of back. She'd made him see possibilities where he'd thought there were none.

But she wasn't what he'd thought, what he'd hoped for, what he'd dreamed of.

He'd been a fool.

The gatekeeper saw him coming and swung the gate open before he even reached it. Whatever had caused Claudia to send the urgent message, he prayed he could help. She was the sister he'd never had, and his stomach clenched as he dismounted and threw the reins to the stable boy. He trotted around to the garden entrance and into the courtyard.

He found Claudia and Malleolus sitting at a table, snacking on fruit and cheese. His pulse slowed. There was no emergency. He strode to the table and seated himself where Claudia waved her hand. It was the same palm-up gesture Cornelia used, and the memory pricked his heart.

Malleolus pushed the fruit tray toward him. "Have some, Captain."

Hector leaned back in the chair. "I thought it was urgent. I'm glad to see it isn't."

Claudia leaned over and patted his hand where it rested on the table. "Urgency is a relative thing, Hector. I thought it was urgent for you to hear a few things. I'm glad you came right away. I think you'll be glad, too, after you hear what I have to tell you."

He cocked his head. "What do you mean?"

A light laugh escaped. "Greek men are the finest in the world, but they aren't very good at understanding Roman women." She leaned forward and rested her hand on his. "Cornelia is deeply in love with you and wants you to marry her more than anything else she's ever wanted."

Hector's head popped back. His brows dropped, his mouth curved down, and he shook his head. "How can that be? I've seen with my own eyes, heard with my own ears how she flirted with Lepidus. He comes from wealth and privilege, just like her. I've suspected all along that she couldn't really be content with a man like me when she could have one of her own kind. She was just settling for me until someone better came along."

"Is that what she told you?"

"No. She said she really wanted me, that she was just using him to make me jealous. But an honest woman wouldn't use a man that way. I'd like to believe her words, but how can I when what she does is just the opposite?"

"Here we go back to Greek men not understanding Roman women. Cornelia was just flirting with Lepidus to get you to realize you want her as much as she wants you. She was afraid you'd take too long to ask her to marry you, so she was trying to make you think you needed to do something before she married someone else. That's just how she learned to do it in Rome. She never thought you'd react the exact opposite of the patrician men she's known all her life. Lepidus won't be hurt by what she did. He understands these romantic games. He probably played them himself before he married."

Hector ran a hand through his hair. "I'd like to believe you, but I've watched her with more than Lepidus. There was a senator in Ephesus. He thought she was happy to see him. He almost proposed in the restaurant. He would have if he'd known she was already divorced."

Claudia patted his hand. "Did you think she was happy to see him?"

"No."

"So, you can tell when she's play-acting. Does it feel like acting when she's with you?"

Hector drew and blew out a deep breath before his answer. "Well, no."

Malleolus leaned in. "I've known Cornelia since she was fourteen, barely more than a girl. That was twenty-five years ago. I know how she thinks, and I know her heart. In all those years, I never saw her in love like she is with you. Yes, she can play-act with the best of the Roman elite. She had years of practice hiding how miserable Lucius made her marriage. He never deserved it, but she was as faithful as any wife could ever be.

"Even before we left the ship, I could see she was in love with you, that she wants to be with you as husband and wife. She might play-act with the Romans, but when she speaks with you, she speaks the truth. She wants and needs you at least as much as I think you want her. Ask her to marry you, and you'll find out how little she cares about noble Roman lineage. She doesn't want a Roman nobleman. She wants a noble man, and she's found exactly what she wants in you. Go talk with her. Clear up this misunderstanding so you can both be happy."

Claudia picked up his hand and held it in both of hers. "Go talk to Cornelia. You'll learn that you really are the man she wants more than anything on earth. God has given you a second chance at happiness, and you'd be a fool not to take the chance He's provided."

Hector rose. He drew a deep breath, held it, and blew it out through pursed lips. "I'll go talk to her."

Claudia rose and linked her arm with his. "Good. Then both of you come back here, and we'll celebrate your betrothal."

As Hector trotted through Titus's gate, his heart catapulted.

Two men stood between him and the woman he loved. Anthusa

stood behind her, a terrified Drusilla wrapped in her arms. Cornelia brandished a dagger, her eyes darting between the two men, backing up slowly as they tried to move apart to flank her and reach Drusilla.

Cornelia's voice reached him. "This girl does not belong to Lucius. He has no daughter anymore. See the gravestone? Her real father is my new husband, a sea captain with a farm not far from here."

He trotted closer. Her face was determined, ferocious. No wonder the men stayed back.

She saw him and yelled. "Husband, tell them! Tell them this is your daughter."

He rode between them, dismounting while his mare was still moving. With legs spread and fists on his hips to flex his arms and display his bulging biceps, he glared at them. They were big men, but so was he, and he had God and love on his side.

"Leave my wife and child alone and get out of here while you still can."

Cornelia moved up beside him, still holding the dagger ready to strike. Drusilla ran from Anthusa to cling to him. He wrapped his left arm around her as she buried her face in his tunic.

The men looked at each other, then back at Hector and the fierce woman still waving the dagger beside him.

The taller one cleared his throat. "It would seem we've made a mistake." His eyes flipped to Cornelia. "Claudius Drusus told us his ex-wife was a tricky woman, not to be trusted about anything. But I can see this is your daughter."

Cornelia took one step toward them, pointing toward the gate with her dagger. "You go tell that worm of a man who used to be my husband that he has no daughter to give to his friend's son to kill. He has no claim on this girl or anything else here in Thracia. Get out of here right now and never return."

Hector stepped up beside her. "You heard my wife. Leave."

The taller man nodded and took two steps back. Then he turned and signaled the other man to follow. Hector stood with his arms crossed until they disappeared through the gate.

From the corner of his eye, he saw her relax. He would have expected a normal woman to tremble, maybe even collapse after the danger had passed. Not Cornelia. Not this courageous woman who would do anything to protect the child she loved. Just as he would.

"I was wrong about you, Cornelia."

"Wrong?"

"Claudia told me what you were doing with Lepidus was just the way women like you play games to get the man you want in Rome. She said Roman women don't think what you did was dishonest. It's what any Roman woman might do to win the heart of the man she loved. I was coming to let you try to convince me that was what was you were doing. I hoped you might be an honest woman after all. But I just found out I was wrong."

She cringed as his words stung her, but that pain would be short-lived. She was a playful, teasing woman. It was part of what he loved about her. It was only right that he should tease her in turn. She'd be smiling at his joke by the time he was through with this conversation. He pressed his lips together so he wouldn't smile himself and give the joke away.

◆

Cornelia swallowed hard. "That's the end, then. I know what honesty means to you."

She looked down at the ground as she struggled not to cry. Then she steeled herself against the crushing disappointment and looked up at his face again. She had gambled and lost everything. She would have to resign herself to the consequences of playing a dishonest game to win his honest heart. Somehow God would give her the strength to bear it if they were not to be together, but her loss shouldn't be Drusilla's as well.

◆

Hector watched Cornelia draw herself up to her full height and square her shoulders. There was that regal woman, ready to try to persuade him to do what she thought should be done. She never gave in to defeat as long as she thought there was any hope of changing it. He had come to love her being that way.

He opened his mouth to speak, but she raised her hand to stop him.

"You don't have to tell me. I know I should never have tried to make you jealous. I know you hate lies and deception. I was only trying to get you to tell me you want me, like I want you."

She still stood erect, but her voice caught as she fought to control the tears that started pooling. "But even if you don't want anything more to do with me, please don't stop doing things with Drusilla. She loves you, too. She shouldn't have to suffer because I was such a fool. Surely you can see she needs you. Besides, what I said about her is absolutely true. You are her father in all the ways her father by blood never has been...never could be. And Lucius really does have no daughter to betroth into certain death. I won't allow that, no matter what Roman law might say."

There was that look in her tear-filled eyes—the look she always had when she assumed he could do whatever she asked, no matter how difficult. This time, what she asked would be easy.

"That wasn't what I was about to say."

Her head tipped as her eyebrows scrunched. She so seldom looked puzzled, and her comical expression forced him to fight the laugh struggling to escape.

"You called me husband. To protect the two of you, I had no choice but to call you wife. You forced me to lie, and I can't abide that. I see only one way to fix it."

He gripped her wrist and took the dagger from her hand. "I don't want you holding this when I tell you." He hurled it point-first into the ground before turning his eyes back on hers. "You're going to marry me and make it true."

Her breath caught as her eyes widened. "What did you say?"

"You heard me. I can't let the lie stand. The best way to fix it is for you to become my wife."

He gripped her arms and pulled her toward him.

◆

Cornelia stepped forward so he could wrap his muscular arms around her. The happiest smile curved her lips before she slipped her arms around him and rested her cheek against his broad chest. A slow, satisfied sigh escaped as she listened to his steady heartbeat. The heartbeat of a man who loved her. As she rubbed his back, she could feel the many ridges—badges of honor for rescuing a child, not scars that branded him once a slave.

"I agree with you completely, Captain. That lie I told about you being my husband can't be allowed to stand, either. You'll have to make an honest woman out of me." She tipped her head back to look up into the depths of his eyes. "I'm going to love being the wife of an honest man."

She caressed his cheek before sliding her hand to the back of his neck. He pulled her closer as his lips sought out hers in their first kiss.

Cornelia melted against him. Pure pleasure wrapped around her in the arms of this man. A real man, worthy of all the love she could give and more. A man more noble than any nobleman in the entire Empire.

When that first kiss was over, both Hector and Cornelia freed an arm to call Drusilla into their embrace. Her arms wrapped them tightly as she buried her face between them.

"Oh, Captain! Nothing could be better than this."

"You'll have to stop calling me Captain. Father is a better name."

She beamed up at him. "I think that's better, too."

◆

As Hector gazed down at the soon-to-be wife and daughter he'd never expected to have, one corner of his mouth curved up. It was funny. His beloved Damara had been a sweet, gentle woman who always needed his care and protection. Cornelia was as strong as any man, independent, ready to face any challenge and fight until she won. Except for their faith in Jesus, they couldn't be more different. How could one man be so in love with both of them? He'd loved Damara with a passion that bound them in life and death, but God had given him a love for Cornelia that would grow just as deep in the years ahead.

But only God understood the workings of the human heart. As Hector once more lowered his lips to hers, he gave thanks that he served the God of second chances.

Chapter 52

THE BEST OF HIS SONS?

Rome, 5 weeks later

It was late afternoon when Lucius returned to his town house from the Baths of Trajan. He wasn't looking forward to the evening. Flaccus was hosting a banquet, and Didia would be there, acting the devoted wife even while on the hunt for a different husband.

She would probably treat him with cool friendliness, as she always did when Flaccus was present, but the razor-tongued cat would be watching his every move, noting his every word to find some juicy gossip to use against him.

The corner of his mouth twitched. Or not. Probably the truce declared between them at the Amphitheater meant more to her than to him. She had much more to lose.

As he crossed the guard-dog mosaic just inside the front door, Paullus scurried into the short hallway that connected the outer entrance to the atrium.

Lucius stopped midstride. His steward glanced over his shoulder like a man out too late with thieves skulking behind him.

"Master, the two gladiators I hired from the Ludus Silani have returned from Thracia. I put them in the smallest sitting room off the atrium."

He glanced over his shoulder again. "They commented on how rich everything looked, and the way they were staring at your silver statues... I had some food delivered to keep them busy in the sitting room and stationed the most muscled of the stable slaves in the atrium with orders to make sure they didn't wander into rooms they shouldn't enter."

A triumphant grin stretched Lucius's face. "Where did you put Drusilla?"

Paullus cleared his throat. "They didn't have her with them. When I asked where she was, they said they'd only tell you."

The grin flipped into a scowl.

Lucius entered the atrium and spread his arms so his manservant could unwrap his toga. When the slave stepped back with the yards of purple-edged white wool in his arms, Lucius ran his fingers through his hair.

"Take me to them."

When Lucius paused in the sitting-room doorway, the muscular pair were lounging in the chairs, eating dried dates from the clay bowl Paullus had provided. They rose when he entered.

He crossed his arms. "Where is my daughter?"

The taller one crossed his arms as well. "Dead and buried in Thracia."

"How do you know this?"

"When we reached your brother's house, there was a gravestone with her name on it in his garden."

The arrogant angle of the gladiator's chin stoked Lucius's irritation. "You were told my wife is a deceitful woman and not to trust anything she said or did. Did you see any girl there who looked my daughter's age?"

"There was a girl there, but your former wife said it was the daughter of her new husband."

Lucius's head bounced back. "New husband?" He sneered. "I don't think so. She didn't have time to find one. She lied to you, and you fell for it."

The gladiator's nostrils flared. "I don't think so." He'd mimicked Lucius's tone. "When we first got there, she and the girl were in the garden with her maid. She drew a dagger on us. Her maid grabbed the girl and stayed behind your wife. She kept waving the dagger and telling us your daughter was dead. Her new husband was some sea captain, and the girl was his daughter. I thought she was lying, like you warned us, and we were flanking her so I could disarm her while Maximus got the girl.

"Then a man rode through the gate and told us to leave his wife and child alone. He looked Greek with darkened skin, like a sea captain. As soon as he got off his horse, the girl ran over and clung to him, just like his own daughter would. The gravestone and the new husband...together they seemed proof enough she wasn't lying. Your daughter is dead."

The gladiator spread his legs, arms still crossed.

Lucius rubbed his chin. "Perhaps so." He relaxed his own stance, and the gladiator did the same. "If you'd brought her safely to me, I'd planned a very generous reward for you. Since you failed...the reward will be less, but I still appreciate your effort. The failure isn't your fault if Drusilla truly is dead."

He turned to Paullus, who stood in the doorway with the stable slave behind him.

"Fetch a denarius a day for each of them and show them out."

Paullus flattened himself against the door frame as Lucius strode past.

In his library, Lucius lowered himself into the desk chair. He rubbed the back of his neck before picking up an engraved brass stylus and rolling it between his thumb and middle finger.

His mouth turned down. It took time to get a gravestone ready. Either Drusilla was dead, or Cornelia put it up as a decoy to fool him. But would she have thought to do that if she hadn't known he was sending men to get Drusilla back? She might have...she was much too smart for a woman. But was it more likely that she'd known they were coming because someone had warned her?

Who could have done that? Maybe Brutus? But he was only an equestrian. His wife wouldn't move in Cornelia's social circles, and he wasn't a ladies' man himself. Besides, he wouldn't know Titus was in Perinthus, so he'd never guess she'd go there.

Lucius had only discussed the matter with Paullus, Brutus, and Marcus Corvinus...but Tertius had been there when he realized where Cornelia had gone. His son had tried to get him to abandon his plan to betroth Drusilla to Gnaeus when he first heard it might happen. And he'd said both he and her mother didn't want Drusilla hurt.

Had the son he trusted and valued most betrayed him by warning Cornelia so she could run with Drusilla? Had he known all along where Cornelia was? Keeping that secret was the same as lying. Had he betrayed him again by warning her that gladiators were coming?

His jaw clenched. Was the one he'd thought the best of his sons actually a traitor?

And if so, what should he do about it?

I'd Love to Hear from You!

If you enjoyed this book, it would be a real gift to me if you would post a review at the retailer you purchased it from. A good review is like a jewel set in gold for an author. Other great places to share reviews are Goodreads and BookBub. If you've read others in the series, it would be great if you post a review of those, too.

I'd also love to hear from you at carol-ashby.com or directly at carolashbyauthor@gmail.com.

Want to hear about upcoming releases in the Light in the Empire series and free gifts only for newsletter subscribers?

For free gifts and other special offers, advance notices of upcoming releases, and info about my latest writing adventures, I hope you'll sign up for my newsletter at carol-ashby.com.

Carol Ashby

Chapter 1

Ready to Help

The woman's scream ripped into Dacius. He dropped his shovel of manure and sprinted into the stable yard.

Flames danced in a pile of straw three feet from the grindstone. The fire was small, but it transformed the skittery young stallion the master's son had just bought into a thousand pounds of lunging, rearing, kicking terror. The horse had ripped its lead rope from the stable boy's hand and run for the open gate in the ten-foot masonry wall—just as the young mistress returned on her litter.

She blocked its escape, and the stallion was determined to get out, even if it had to go through the litter where Mistress Julia sat screaming. The flailing hooves knocked the right rear bearer to the ground. As the stallion's full weight came down on his head, it crushed the man's skull.

Dacius stripped off his tunic as he ran toward the stallion. The horse reared, pummeling the top of the litter with its hooves—right above the mistress's head. The curtain bar splintered, then snapped before the hooves returned to the ground.

Her shrieks fueled the stallion's panic. It started to rear once more. Dacius leaped, caught the lead at the halter, and pulled its head down and sideways before it could strike the litter again.

As the hooves came back to earth, he flipped his tunic across the horse's face and pulled it snug around its eyes. The stallion froze, trembling, when the fire disappeared from view.

He led the horse into its stall and stood with it, stroking its neck. "Calm, boy. Steady, boy."

The fear drained from the trembling stallion as Dacius's voice and hand caressed him. When the last was gone, Dacius released his tunic and lifted it from the horse's eyes.

"Good boy." Two soft slaps to the horse's shoulder, and he left the stall.

The litter escort, a tall, muscular German, carried the limp form of Mistress Julia into the house. Dacius's brows rose. He would have sworn he'd pulled the horse away before he struck her.

A boy of about eleven stood with his back pressed against the wall, his eyes flicking toward the overseer like he was hoping not to be noticed.

Dacius slipped along the wall to stand beside him. "Is the mistress hurt?"

The boy shook his head. "No. She fainted. She can't stand blood."

"Well, I don't really like it myself." Dacius tousled the boy's hair and smiled at his worried face.

The boy tipped his head to look up at Dacius. "You ran up to that horse. Why weren't you afraid?"

Dacius shrugged. "He was only panicked by the fire. I knew he'd calm down as soon as he couldn't see it anymore."

The boy's eyes shifted from Dacius to the overseer, and Dacius's followed. The overseer strode over to the slave who'd been sharpening the hoes and swung the bronze knob on the handle of his three-cord whip into the side of his head, knocking him to the ground.

"Stupid son of a donkey! Didn't you see the sparks going into the straw? Move the grindstone over there." He pointed to the wall farthest from the straw and hay.

The slave stood, rubbing the side of his head. He bowed. "Yes, overseer."

Dacius stared at the whip as the overseer hung it back on his belt. The bronze was polished, the leather supple, as if frequently oiled. The overseer was proud of that whip, and that could only mean one thing. He liked to use it.

The overseer nudged the trampled bearer with his foot to make sure he was dead. "Move this litter out of the gate." He turned to one of the other bearers. "You. Get this body out of here."

The man bowed. "Yes, overseer."

The overseer swung and pointed at Dacius. "You. Clean up that blood so the mistress won't see it again."

Dacius dipped his head. "Yes, overseer."

He drew a bucket of water from the cistern and poured it on the blood that had pooled on the paving stone where the man's head had been. The red diluted and faded in the expanding circle of water, but some had soaked into the stone.

He'd seen war, and he knew too much about cleaning up blood. It would take soap and hot water and scrubbing to remove most of it. And even then, a faint shadow would remain. The water had washed away enough that the mistress shouldn't notice it, but he would always know a man had died there.

Dacius sucked a breath between his teeth and shook his head as he released it. In Roman eyes, not a man. A slave had died there, his body now gone, tossed aside like a piece of broken furniture and just as easy to replace.

The steward had gone to the slave market yesterday to buy Dacius for stable work. He'd be going tomorrow to get another slave for the mistress's litter.

He replaced the bucket by the cistern and returned to the dirty stall. As he scooped up one more shovelful of manure and straw, he sighed. *Slaves, obey your earthly masters with respect and fear and sincerity of heart, just as you would obey Christ.* That was what Apostle Paul had commanded. *Serve with your whole heart, as if you were serving the Lord, not men.*

He hadn't even been in this household a full day, and it was already clear it would be a place to sorely test him as he tried to serve Jesus, his Lord.

Julia awoke in her bed chamber as her lady's maid wiped her cheeks and forehead with a cloth dampened with rose water. Her eyelids drifted open as she threw up her arm to rest the back of her hand on her forehead.

Apicula dropped the cloth in the blown glass bowl. Its blue and green swirls caught the light to make a dancing pattern on the wall as she set it aside on the small table by the bed. She pushed an escaped strand of graying hair behind her ear. "Are you revived now, mistress? What happened?"

Julia started to sit up, then flopped back on the bed. "Not quite. The room is still spinning. That horrible horse my brother just bought—it killed one of my bearers and almost killed me. Someone pulled it away, and then I saw the crushed head. All the blood—you know what that does to me."

She tried to sit up again, and this time she succeeded. "Am I ever going to grow out of this? I feel so stupid when I faint over the smallest amount of blood. A Roman woman shouldn't be so squeamish." She touched Apicula's arm. "I'm glad you weren't walking beside the litter today. You might have been killed, too."

Apicula offered her hand to help Julia back to her feet. "I'm glad, too. Who did the stallion kill, mistress?"

"I don't know. Whoever was standing at the right rear. I didn't notice who was there earlier, and I couldn't bear to look at him all bloody."

"It's a good thing, mistress, that someone reached that horse before it hurt you. Who was it? Perhaps he would like something extra to eat tonight. You could have some of the leftovers sent out to him."

Julia raised her shoulders and arched her back after she stood. Her dizziness was gone. "I like that idea. It was one of the stable slaves, but I don't know which one. I didn't look at him before I saw all the blood and then... Gallio can find the right one. I would think our steward knows all the slaves, even if I don't."

Julia pressed her palms to her cheeks and pulled them off sideways. "I'm planning to go to my sister's house tomorrow morning. It's been almost a week since I went there and played with her little girls."

Five steps took her to the dressing table. Her hair was still tidy, and the reflection in the polished silver mirror showed her color had returned to normal. "I promised Flavia I would do her hair up pretty like mine the next time I came, and I don't want to disappoint her. I need a box to take some of my hair ornaments. I'd better take enough to do Sabina's as well, since she's three now and likes to mimic her older sister."

"Shall I get the box now, mistress? Do you feel well enough for me to leave you?"

"Yes. That's over. Let's pack now so I have everything ready. They're such precious children, and I want to go early."

Apicula smiled her agreement. "You'll make a wonderful mother yourself, mistress. When your betrothed returns from Britannia, perhaps the gods will smile on you and give you a child during your wedding week."

"Wouldn't that be wonderful? I don't remember much about Metilius Nepos, except he's handsome. I was only twelve when we celebrated the betrothal at Metilia's town house, and we didn't talk alone."

Her stomach fluttered. In a few months, she'd marry the man her father had chosen. But that was the Roman way, and Father loved her too much to pick someone unsuitable.

"Metilia says he's such a dear, kind brother. If she thinks he'll be a wonderful husband and father, I'm sure he will. In only a few more months, I'll find out."

As Apicula left the room to find a box, Julia began selecting the ornaments she was sure the little girls would love.

Aulus walked up the marble steps of the cold-water pool at the Baths of Trajan. The bath slave handed him a towel, and he wiped his face. He moved away from the pool edge before toweling his hair. His eyes were closed when something hard rammed into his stomach.

"What the—" He stepped back as he tossed the towel aside. A man muscled like an ox stood before him with a hinged wax tablet clutched in a hand large enough to crush a melon.

"Aulus Julius Secundus?" His voice was a low growl.

A shiver ran up Aulus's spine. "Yes."

The man thrust the wooden frame of the wax tablet into his stomach again. "Take it."

Aulus snatched it from his hand and stepped back again.

With spread legs and crossed arms, the thug glared at him. "Your brother-in-law's cousin, Sextus Sabinus, let you continue to gamble on promise of prompt payment. Four months paying nothing is too long, and his father is calling in the debt." He dipped his head toward the tablet and held out a stylus. "Read and sign."

Aulus flipped the tablet open and scanned the text.

> Marcus Julius Secundus owes Quintus Flavius Sabinus 10,000 denarii for debts incurred by his son, Aulus Julius Secundus. Unless other arrangements are made, M. Julius Secundus will pay in full within thirty days of his return to Roma at the end of his governorship of Sicilia.

A wide finger tapped the wax below the text. "Sign." Two more taps. "Now."

Aulus rolled the stylus between his fingers as his stomach churned. He'd lost money that wasn't his to lose. Everything he treated as his own was legally Father's as *paterfamilias*. And every debt he owed was a claim against his father.

Father's red face on the pier in Portus swirled in his memory. Father's anger at him betting too much on the Red faction to win in the Circus Maximus was seared into Aulus's brain. He'd promised Father he wouldn't do that again while his father was away from Rome. And he hadn't...he'd bet on the Greens, and they almost always won.

He'd been money ahead until that dinner party at his step-sister's house.

He planned to pay the debt, but to sign a legal promise committing Father to pay as soon as he returned...

The thug's mouth turned down. "If you don't sign now, I will come back." His scowl turned into a cruel smile. "But you don't want me to."

His fist hit his open palm, then twisted slowly.

Aulus's clenched his jaw and hoped that was enough to hide his fear. Better another tongue-lashing from Father than a beating from a gladiator.

He pressed the stylus into the wax, concentrating on keeping his letters from wiggling and betraying him.

With a snap, he closed the tablet and handed it back to the brute.

"Wise choice." The thug smirked as his gaze raked Aulus from head to foot and back. Then he spun on his heal and disappeared into the crowd.

"What was that about?"

Aulus jerked at the quiet voice of his best friend, Marcus Drusus.

He ran shaky fingers through his hair. "I'm in big trouble. I was at my step-sister's villa a few months ago, and I gambled with her husband's cousin. I lost 10,000 denarii, and I don't have the money to pay." He rubbed the back of his neck. "Sextus said that wasn't a problem, that he'd give me time to pay him. But now he's told his father, and his father is demanding the money...from Father."

"Your father's rich. He can pay that without even noticing it."

"That's not the problem. Sabinus and Father have been political enemies for years. Sabinus will try to use this to hurt him."

Marcus's brow furrowed. "Your father seems more than a match for anyone."

"But I wasn't supposed to be gambling. Not at that level, anyway. I hadn't planned to, but they had this great Falerian wine. I drank too much of it before we started. "His shoulders drooped. "Father's going to kill me when he comes back to find I've exposed him to his enemy like this. Sextus's father is Quintus Sabinus."

"Quintus Sabinus?" Marcus sucked air through his teeth. "He wanted to marry my aunt Claudia right after Grandfather died. Mother fought with Father for saying yes before Sabinus married someone else."

His brows lowered, then relaxed. "I can ask Father to give me the money. Ten thousand isn't much for him. He'd do anything for his best friend." Marcus nudged Aulus's arm. "He'll let me help mine."

Some tension drained from Aulus's shoulders, but not all. "But what if he won't?"

"Then we'll figure out another way to get it." A twisted smile curved Marcus's lips. "I know. We can fake your kidnapping to get enough ransom money to pay the debt." The smile turned into a chuckle. "But Gallio already took away your key to the strongbox after you bought that stallion that's too jumpy to ride. Maybe he won't want to pay that much for you."

Marcus slapped Aulus's shoulder. "We can fake Julia's kidnapping instead. Gallio would pay any amount to get her back."

Aulus chuckled. "He would." He punched Marcus's arm. "I can always count on you to come up with a good plan." The last of the tension vanished. Marcus's father would help, and his own father would never know.

Chapter 2

A Bad Idea

Dacius had almost finished feeding and watering the horses the next morning when the steward entered the stable yard with the overseer.

The overseer nodded as the steward spoke. "The young master's stallion created a problem, Vilicus. She wants to go as soon as she finishes her breakfast, so I need one the same height. There isn't time to go to the market. Do you have one you can spare?"

Dacius emptied his bucket into Niger's water trough. The steward's request shouldn't affect him. He was the only slave working in the stable. There had been another, but yesterday Vilicus sent him into the garden to help dig a new reflecting pond. No sign of him this morning, so Dacius had to do the feeding, grooming, and cleaning alone. He couldn't be spared from the horses.

He patted the young stallion's neck before fetching another bucket of water from the cistern.

Vilicus didn't like a slave to look directly at him, so Dacius kept his eyes down. Since he tried to serve as unto the Lord, he never avoided work. But it was obvious why the other slaves tried to be invisible when this overseer came near. He'd jerk a man off one task to do another. Later, he'd curse and sometimes strike him for not completing the first task. It was a chaotic place to serve.

As Dacius poured the last bucket into the stallion's trough, he heard the guttural voice. "You."

He turned and bowed his head. "Yes, overseer."

"Go stand by the litter."

He froze his eyebrows to hide his shock. Was Vilicus planning to leave the horses untended? But no matter how foolish the command, he had to obey.

Three bearers already stood by the litter, so he joined them.

Satisfaction lifted the corners of the steward's mouth. "He's the right size. I'll take that one for today. Have him wash to get rid of the stable smell and put him in the litter tunic. She'll be wanting to leave in perhaps half an hour."

Vilicus tipped his head. "Yes, steward." He watched the steward enter the house before spinning on Dacius. "You. Wash that stench off, then dress for litter work."

Dacius lowered his eyes. "Yes, overseer."

The overseer strode through the small archway that connected the stable yard to the garden, and Dacius sighed. It was a good thing he'd risen early. Otherwise, the poor animals would have gone without. He'd barely finished placing the feed and water in the last stall, but Vilicus didn't know that when he ordered him to litter duty.

He scanned the stable yard as he headed to the cistern to draw some water. The horses needed grooming. The stalls needed cleaning. If he were a betting man, he'd bet the work would still be waiting for him when he returned, and Vilicus would yell at him because he hadn't finished.

Slaves, obey your earthly masters with respect and fear and sincerity of heart, just as you would obey Christ. He'd reminded himself at least ten times yesterday. Another sigh escaped. He'd probably hit twenty today.

When Marcus entered his father's library, Lucius Drusus Fidelis had a hinged wax tablet open before him.

"Good morning, Father." Marcus lowered himself into the second chair by the desk.

His father closed the tablet. "A letter from your brother."

Marcus raised his eyebrows to feign interest. "How is he?"

"You know your brother. It's impossible to tell. He never complains, no matter what his situation." Father's lips tightened. "I went to some trouble to get him a good tribune posting near Rome, but he's decided to apply for a posting in a frontier province. He going to ask for Britannia, Dacia, or Judaea. He hasn't decided which."

Marcus pasted on a smile. "That sounds like Lucius. He'll want to go to the most dangerous place where no one else would volunteer to serve, so I'd bet on Judaea."

Father drummed on the tablet with a silver-tipped ivory stylus. "You're probably right. Your brother would put the needs of Rome above his own self-interest. Someone needs to serve there, but I'd rather it wasn't my son."

Marcus picked up a brass stylus and rolled it between his fingers. "There's glory to be found in battle. Lucius probably wants some excitement while he's tribune."

"Judaea isn't like Germania before it was pacified. The Germans fought you like warriors. They didn't stick a knife into you as you were going down the street and then keep walking as if they'd done nothing. Lucius might get himself killed by some zealot and left like the bodies the urban cohorts gather after they were murdered during the night. There's no glory in that." Father rolled his eyes. "But Lucius is too much like his grandfather, so he'll probably volunteer for the most dangerous place."

Father placed the stylus atop the closed tablet and leaned back in his chair. "But you didn't come to discuss your brother." His eyes warmed as they rested on Marcus. "So, why have you sought me out so early?"

Marcus stopped rolling the stylus. "I need 10,000 denarii."

Father rested his elbows on the desk and steepled his fingers. "What for?"

"To help a friend."

"Aulus Secundus? What sort of trouble has he gotten himself into this time?"

"He was gambling when he'd drunk too much, and he lost more than he realized."

His father laughed. "I'm not surprised. Aulus tends to act without thinking, and when the wine flows in, his sense leaks out. I'm glad my own sons are smart enough to keep their drinking and gambling separate."

Father's eyes narrowed. "Why didn't you stop him before he lost too much? He always follows your lead."

"I wasn't there, or I would have. You've taught me what a man should do for his best friend. His father told Aulus not to gamble to excess while he was governor in Sicilia, and except for that night, he hasn't."

Marcus leaned forward. "Will you give me the money so I can help him before his father finds out?"

"Of course. My best friend helped me more than once so your grandfather wouldn't know. Marcus Corvinus and I were closer than brothers at your age. We still are. That's why you carry his name."

"Thank you, Father. Sabinus sent a gladiator to the baths yesterday to make Aulus sign a document committing his father to pay the debt within a month of his return. If Aulus clears the debt now, his father will never know."

Father's head pulled back. "Why would Aulus's brother-in-law use a gladiator?"

"He didn't lose to Antonia's husband. It was her husband's cousin, Sextus."

"Quintus Sabinus's son?"

The edge on Father's voice raised Marcus's heart rate. "Yes."

"Did it say Secundus owed Quintus?"

"Yes. Why?"

His father rubbed his mouth. "That changes things. Secundus and Quintus Sabinus have been political enemies for as long as I can remember. Secundus is an honorable man, but Sabinus...Let's just say he's not a man to cross."

Father rested his elbow on the desk as he rubbed his forehead. "You were only fourteen and living with your mother when he wanted to marry your aunt Claudia. She ran off to Titus in Thracia to avoid that, and Sabinus was ready to kill me over the embarrassment that caused him.

"He spared our family because he found another girl to marry with better political connections. It's been four years, but I still feel the venom in his gaze."

He tightened his lips until they vanished. "If it were anyone else, I'd give you the money, but I'm not going to get between the crocodile and his prey."

"But—"

Father held up his hand. "This discussion is over."

Marcus froze his face to stop the frown. "As you wish, Father." While he could still control his irritation, he turned and left the room.

Aulus was waiting for him in the peristyle garden, sitting on the low wall by the pool.

When Marcus entered, he shot to his feet, smiling. "So, do we go to Sextus or his father to settle the debt?"

"Neither. Father said he'd give me the money; then he backed out when he heard you owed Quintus Sabinus." He spat. "I never took Father for a coward before."

The blood drained from Aulus's face. "What am I going to do?"

Marcus placed his hand on Aulus's bicep and squeezed. "I'll think of something." A slow smile crept across his face. "I guess we need to plan a kidnapping."

"I thought that was a joke." Aulus bit his lip. "We can't actually do it."

Marcus rubbed his chin before the half-shrug. "Why not?"

ROMAN FAMILY LAW: THE POWER OF THE FATHER, THE RIGHTS OF THE MOTHER, THE FATE OF THE CHILDREN

The Roman concept of family was distinctly different from today's nuclear family, defined as an independent unit of father, mother, and children under the age of eighteen. The Roman *familia* consisted of a father, his wife with some limitations, his children whether young or fully grown, and his slaves.

Roman society was intensely patriarchal. The *paterfamilias* was the oldest male and the legal head of the familia. Until he died, he possessed *patria potestas* (the power of the father) over his grown children, both male and female, whether they were married or not.

The paterfamilias had the power to tell any of his children to do something, and they were required to obey him. He had the power of life and death over all except his wife. He had the right to kill his child of any age (*ius vitae necisque*), the right to decide whether a newborn would be allowed to live or would be exposed to the elements to die, and the right to sell his children into slavery. It was not uncommon for an unwanted or defective baby to be exposed. Although it was legal, killing one's children after infancy was generally frowned upon without extreme provocation.

He owned all the family property, with the exception of the wages earned by a grown son from his military service. If a grown son ran a business, the business and the profits all belonged to his father. Grown sons usually had families of their own and lived separately from their father, but they lived off the allowance (*peculium*) he provided. Only at his death did his children finally became independent (*sui iuris*, under one's own authority).

A father could choose to emancipate a grown son before his death. There were two main reasons. The son might have done something that led his father to disown him, but fathers sometimes emancipated their sons so they could inherit from their mother. Since the mother officially remained in the familia of her father, all her property remained subject to the control of her own paterfamilias. Her children wouldn't inherit directly from her if they were still under the control of their father.

Roman marriage took different forms, depending on the time period and the circumstances of the couple getting married. During the early Republic, a woman might marry *in manu*, where she passed from her father's control into her husband's control, or *sine manu*, where she remained under her father or a male guardian. By the time of the Empire, most marriages were sine manu. Marrying sine manu had a major financial effect that contributed to the stability of marriages.

Because a woman didn't officially leave her father's familia, she kept her maiden name when she married. The children took their father's name. When Cornelia Scipia (whose father's clan and family names were Cornelius Scipio) married Lucius Claudius Drusus, their first-born son would also be Lucius Claudius Drusus, and their later sons would be Claudius Drusus but with a different first name. Their first-born daughter would normally be Claudia Drusilla, a feminine form of her father's clan and family name.

A new wife was usually accompanied by a dowry in a sine manu marriage. Because her paterfamilias owned all the family property, the dowry did not automatically become the property of her new husband. The dowry itself remained the property of her paterfamilias or under the control of her guardian, if her paterfamilias had died. The guardian was usually, but not always, the male relative who replaced her father as the new paterfamilias. Her husband could use the dowry and keep any profits it earned, but if the marriage was ended through divorce by either husband or wife, the full dowry had to be returned.

In an attempt to encourage the Roman elite to have more children, Emperor Augustus declared that a freeborn woman would be released from the requirement of a guardian after bearing three children. She could then take control of her own property and do what she wished with it without any man's permission.

A Roman marriage existed by the consent of the couple for as long as they wanted to be considered a family unit. The marriage was recognized as valid when both parties publicly declared their desire to unite in a marriage. But because it was based only on the consent of the couple, it wasn't a legally binding agreement like modern marriages. Either party could decide to divorce the other for any reason. The divorce became "official" when the decision by one to separate from the other was declared in front of witnesses, even if the spouse wasn't present. It was a "no-fault" divorce, and the partner being divorced had no say in whether the divorce happened.

The dowry, on the other hand, was usually established by a legally binding contract. It was the husband's to use as long as the marriage lasted. He owned any profits, but his wife's family still owned the original amount of the dowry. When a couple divorced, the husband had to return the full amount of the dowry. His inability to do so often discouraged a man from divorcing his wife.

Women were often discouraged from divorcing their husbands because any children were the property of the paterfamilias. He had the right to refuse her any further contact with her children after a divorce. Even if her husband died while they were still married, his father could tell the widow that she could no longer see her children.

While reputable women were expected to be faithful to their husbands, it was not considered adultery when a Roman man engaged in sexual activity with an unmarried woman, slave or free, who was not his wife. Promiscuous activity on the part of the man was considered normal, but a respectable Roman matron was expected to abstain from extramarital affairs, at least as far as anyone outside her household knew.

In *Second Chances*, Cornelia tolerated many years of Lucius's infidelity because she didn't want to risk losing her children. But after twenty-five years of marriage, her three boys were grown. When Lucius decides to put their daughter at risk, she has no legal power to stop him. She decides to protect Drusilla by divorcing Lucius without his knowledge, reclaiming her dowry, and disappearing with her daughter before he can stop her.

As the mother of four children, she didn't need a guardian's permission to divorce Lucius or do what she wanted with her dowry. The divorce and immediate return of her dowry were her legal rights, but Roman law gave Lucius all rights to Drusilla.

When Cornelia took Drusilla without her ex-husband's permission, she "acquired and concealed" a Roman citizen who didn't belong to her. Technically, she violated the law against "possessing a citizen in bad faith" (*plagium*). But Roman abduction law was aimed at those who kidnapped a person to make them a slave, not a mother stealing her own daughter from her father to protect her. Given the political prominence of her family, it's not clear how the Roman courts would have dealt with the case if Lucius wanted Cornelia tried for kidnapping.

For more about life in the Roman Empire at its peak, please go to carolashby.com.

Discussion Guide

1) Hector was devastated by the loss of his wife and daughter, even knowing that he would see them again in heaven. Given his background, what do you think made it so hard for him to move past his deep grief? Have you ever tried to encourage a friend mired in grief? What helped?

2) Lucius Fidelis is a self-focused man who arranged his father's death for his own advantage. But he's also a loyal friend, willing to do whatever he can to help his best friend solve a serious problem. Have you ever known someone who easily betrays some but is intensely loyal to others? How do you deal with them?

3) Cornelia is a proud woman and loving mother who tolerated many years of her husband's adulteries and verbal cruelty for the sake of her children. Under Roman law, the children of a marriage belonged to the father. If she divorced him, he had the right to ban her from ever seeing her own children. Have you known a man or woman who's made the same choice she did?

4) When Lucius is willing to risk his daughter Drusilla's life to help out his best friend, Cornelia divorces him, takes Drusilla, and runs halfway across the Empire. Under Roman law, she was a kidnapper. Would you consider doing what she did in the same circumstances?

5) Cornelia is from a family that had helped rule Rome for 500 years. Bloodline, wealth, and her own skill moving in Rome's highest social circles had elevated her to the pinnacle of society. How did that affect her first impression of Hector? How did that change and why?

6) Rescued from slavery by Aristarchus, Hector worked hard to become a landowner and family man, but he knows his social status is far beneath Cornelia's. How did that affect his attitude toward her when they first met? What caused it to change?

7) Drusilla is saddened by leaving her brother and friends, but she's also sorry her mother is sacrificing everything to protect her. Although Hector initially befriends her to cheer her up, he soon discovers that helping her helps him even more. Are there times you've seen the same in your life or the lives of friends?

8) For Lucius, what began as a desire to help out a friend turns into determination to hurt Cornelia for outmaneuvering him by disappearing with Drusilla. Drusilla becomes a pawn in the contest between them. Roman law gave Lucius all the rights to his daughter; today both mother and father have "rights" to their children. When children are turned into weapons in the battle between parents, are there things we can do to help?

9) Cornelia's affection for her dead father-in-law and amazement at his decision to die for his faith make her curious about the Gospel message. Where does that curiosity lead? How does it affect her attitude toward choices of which her upper-class Roman society disapproves?

10) *Second Chances* is a story of loss and longing and the power of love to heal the pain of the past, opening the door to a joyful future. What touched you most? What made you think about what your own choices would be?

What should the future hold for Lucius Fidelis?

Lucius Fidelis got his father executed so he could take control of his own life and the family fortune.in *The Legacy*. When Fidelis betrayed his father, his sons, Lucius, Marcus, and Tertius, were sixteen, fourteen, and ten, and his daughter Drusilla was two. Lucius and Marcus were old enough to understand what their father had done, and the consequences play out eight years later in *Forgiven*. In *Second Chances*, Tertius, now 18, works against his father to protect his sister. When Lucius Fidelis realizes his favorite son may have helped his ex-wife outsmart him, he suspects Tertius poses a danger to himself. I haven't yet decided where that will lead or what Fidelis's ultimate end will be. Will he act on his suspicions? If so, what will he do? I'd love to hear what you think. Please go to my website, carol-ashby.com and share your thoughts in the comment box. Looking forward to hearing from you!

Glossary

aureus	gold coin worth 25 denarii
cisium	two-wheeled cart with forward-facing seat located above the axis
corbita	merchant ship, typical size 90 feet long, 25 feet wide with one large sail midship and a second small angled sail in the bow
cursus honorum	"course of honors," the sequence of military and political offices held by men of the senatorial order
denarius	coin equal to about one day's wage for a worker.
dies solis	Sunday
freedman	a former slave who still owes service to his former master
gladius	short Roman sword used by legionaries
lanista	the head trainer in charge of a gladiator school (ludus)
ludus	a school for training gladiators, who could be rented for tasks needing the threat of force
mille passus (milia passuum)	Roman mile (miles) = 0.92 English miles or 1.48 km
operae	specific duties, such as a certain number of hours of service, owed by a freed slave to the master who freed him and that former master's heir
palla	woman's large rectangular shawl (60 x 120 inches) worn wrapped around the body and sometimes over the head
paterfamilias	legal head of a Roman family with absolute control over all his children, even when grown or married

peregrine	a person who is not a Roman citizen
praetor	a judge in the Roman court system; the second level magistrate in the *cursus honorum*
quadrans	smallest denomination Roman coin worth 1/64 denarius
raeda	a four-wheeled closed-in carriage
second table	the dessert (third) course of a three-course Roman dinner
salve	hello
sestertius	coin worth 1/4 denarius
stola	a long robe worn by married women fastened by clasps at the shoulder and worn over a tunic
tabula	a popular backgammon-like game
vale	goodbye

Scripture References

Scripture quotations marked (NIV) are taken from THE HOLY BIBLE, NEW INTERNATIONAL VERSION®, NIV® Copyright © 1973, 1978, 1984, 2011 by Biblica, Inc.® Used by Permission of Biblica, Inc.® All rights reserved worldwide.

Chapter 13: Luke 8:22-25 (NIV)
Chapter 21: Luke 9:18-27 (NIV)
Chapter 23: Luke 11:9-13 (NIV)
Chapter 25: Luke 8:5-15 (NIV)
Chapter 34: Luke 9:23-27 (NIV)
Chapter 39: Romans 8:28-32 (NIV)
Chapter 48: Luke 9:22-27 (NIV)

/ Acknowledgements

First, I thank God for this opportunity to tell a story of how He can take the sad times of our lives and use them to open doors to happiness we never dreamed possible. I loved writing the story of the healing of Hector's broken heart, the joy he found watching the people he'd grown to love accept Jesus, and the opening of Cornelia's eyes to the love of God and the unimportance of the things she'd been raised to value. There's nothing more satisfying that writing about lives being transformed by forgiveness and love.

Writing the best book I can is only possible with the help of many others. It's with a mixture of joyful remembrances and deep sadness that I thank Regina Fujitani for being my alpha beta reader and dear friend. Despite many health problems, she kept sharing her knowledge of good writing, her spiritual insight, and her warmth until a few days before she died. She's helped me with all of *Blind Ambition*, *The Legacy*, *Faithful*, and *Second Chances* plus a few sections of the next two in the series. I do so wish she would be here to help bring those to completion as well, but she's dancing with Jesus now, and who wouldn't rather be doing that than reading draft manuscripts?

I'm especially thankful for my kindred spirit and treasured friend, Lisa Garcia, who's a great beta reader who understands the human heart and is so good at spotting typos that I'll never need a copy editor. Andrew Budek-Schmeisser shared his invaluable male perspective and impressive writing skill as a fellow author. There were no combat scenes in *Second Chances*, but since I like to work on the future volumes of the series at the same time, he's already helped me with the action scenes in the next two volumes.

My critique partner, Katie Powner, who's an award-winning author herself, helped me spot and fix things only an author would see.

Many thanks to my friends who read shorter sections, looked at draft covers, and gave me helpful feedback: Terry Shoebotham, Brennan McPherson, Patti Stouter.

My line editor, Wendy Chorot, has blessed me with her skill as an editor and with her insights for making the deep spiritual scenes reflect real life. She's a joy to work with as well. If you need a great editor, she's the one to call.

Yet again, Roseanna White has designed a gorgeous cover that captures the time and the theme of the Light in the Empire series. It takes amazing talent to start with a collection of separate images and meld them together to get something that looks like the Romans had color photography. Once more, she came up with a design that's attractive to both men and women. I can't wait to see what she does with the next two in the series. I keep thinking she can't make the next one better, but she always does.

I especially want to thank my wonderful son, Paul, and my beautiful daughter, Lydia, for their love and patience with my obsession with writing. I give special thanks to Lydia, who posed in the Roman woman's costume I made for the American Christian Fiction Writers' genre dinner in 2017. That's her body but not her head as Cornelia on the cover.

But my special thanks go to my long-suffering husband, Jim, who kept me company by watching movies until 2 a.m. when I was on a roll writing and brought me dinner at my desk when I couldn't tear myself away from the keyboard. He's smart, funny, kind, patient...in short, he inspires the best parts of my heroes. I don't need a second chance to find happiness because I got the best man the first time around.

About the Author

Carol Ashby has been a professional writer for most of her life, but her articles and books were about lasers and compound semiconductors (the electronics that make cell phones, laser pointers, and LED displays work). She still writes about light, but her Light in the Empire series tells stories of difficult friendships and life-changing decisions in dangerous times, where forgiveness and love open hearts to discover their own faith in Christ. Her fascination with the Roman Empire was born during her first middle-school Latin class. A research career in New Mexico inspires her to get every historical detail right so she can spin stories that make her readers feel like they're living under the Caesars themselves.

Read her articles about many facets of life in the Roman Empire at carolashby.com, or join her at her blog, The Beauty of Truth, at carol-ashby.com.

LIGHT *in the* EMPIRE SERIES

*Dangerous times, difficult friendships,
lives transformed by forgiveness and love.*

The Light in the Empire Series follows the interconnected lives of four Roman families during the reigns of Trajan and Hadrian. Join them as they travel the Empire, from Germania and Britannia to Thracia, Dacia, and Judaea and, of course, to Rome itself.

NOW AVAILABLE

Forgiven

Are some wounds too deep to forgive?

With a ruthless father who murdered for the family inheritance, Marcus Drusus plans to do the same. In AD 122, Marcus follows his brother Lucius to Judaea and plots to frame a zealot for his older brother's death. But the plan goes awry, and Lucius is rescued by a Messianic Jewish woman. Her oldest brother is a zealot and a Roman soldier killed her twin, but Rachel still persuades her father Joseph to put his love for Jesus above his anger with Rome and hide Lucius until he heals.

Rachel cares for the enemy, and more than broken bones heal as duty turns to love. Lucius embraces Joseph's faith in Jesus, but sharing a faith doesn't heal all wounds. Even before revealed secrets slice open old scars, Joseph wants no Roman son-in-law. With Rachel's zealot brother suspecting he's a Roman officer and his own brother planning to kill him when he returns, can Lucius survive long enough to change Joseph's mind?

Blind Ambition

Sometimes you have to almost die to discover how you want to live.

It's AD 114 in the Roman province of Germania Superior, and being a Christian carries a death sentence. Tribune Decimus Lentulus is on the fast track for a stellar political career back in Rome. When he's robbed, blinded, and left for dead, a young German woman who follows the Way finds him. Valeria knows it's his duty to have her and her family killed, but she chooses to obey Jesus's command to love her enemy and takes him home to care for him.

It's not his miraculous recovery that shakes Decimus to his core. It's the way they love him like family and their unconcealed love for Jesus. In spite of himself, he falls in love with the Christian woman Rome wants him to kill. Can Valeria hide her faith to follow him into the circles of Roman power? Or should he abandon his ambition to help rule the Empire and choose to follow a different way?

The Legacy

When Rome has taken everything, what's left for a man to give?

Betrayed by a ruthless son who'll do anything for power and wealth, Publius Drusus faces death with an unanswered prayer—that his treasured daughter, Claudia, and honorable son, Titus, will someday share his faith. But who will lead them to the truth once he's gone?

Claudia's oldest brother Lucius arranged their father's execution to inherit everything, and now he's forcing her to marry a cruel Roman power broker. If only she could get to Titus—a thousand miles away in Thracia. Then the man who secretly told her father about Jesus arranges for his son Philip to sneak her out of Rome and take her to the brother she can trust.

A childhood accident scarred Philip's face. A woman's rejection scarred his heart. Claudia's gratitude grows into love, but what can Philip do when the first woman who returns his love hates the God he loves even more?

Titus and Claudia hunger for revenge on their brother and the Christians they blame for their father's deadly conversion. When Titus buys Miriam, a secret Christian, to serve his sister, he starts them all down a path of conflicting loyalties and dangerous decisions. His father's final letter commands the forgiveness Titus refuses to give. What will it take to free him from the hatred poisoning his own heart?

Join the people you met in *Second Chances* eight years earlier in this tale of betrayal, hatred, love, and forgiveness, where even bad things can work together for good.

Faithful

Is the price of true friendship ever too high?

In AD 122, Adela, the fiery daughter of a Germanic chieftain, is kidnapped and taken across the Roman frontier to be sold as a slave. When horse-trader Otto wins her while gambling with her kidnappers, he entrusts her to his friend and trading partner, Galen. Then Otto is kidnapped by the same men, and Galen must track them half way across the Empire before his best friend loses a fight to the death in a Roman arena.

Adela joins Galen in the chase, hungry for vengeance. As the perilous journey deepens their friendship, will the kind, faithful man open her eyes to a life she never dreamed she'd want?

A trip to the heart of the Empire poses mortal danger to a man who follows Jesus, especially when he must seek the help of an enemy of the faith for Otto to survive. Tiberius hunted Christians when he governed Germania Superior and banished his own son when he became one.

When Tiberius learns sparing Galen offers a chance at reconciliation, he joins the trio on their journey home. Can his animosity toward the followers of Jesus survive a trip with the Christian man whose courage and faithfulness demand his respect?

Follow the continuing saga of the people you met in *Blind Ambition* from the frontier of Germany to the heart of the Empire.

True Freedom

*The chains we cannot see
can be the hardest ones to break.*

When Aulus runs up a gambling debt to his father's political enemy, he's desperate to pay it off before his father returns to Rome. His best friend Marcus suggests they fake the kidnapping of Aulus's sister Julia and use the ransom money. But when the man they hired kidnaps her for real, Aulus is catapulted into a desperate search to find her.

Torn from his childhood home by Rome's conquering armies and sold as a farm slave to labor until he dies, Dacius's faith gives him strength to bear what he must and serve without complaining. After a deadly accident makes him one of Julia's litter bearers, he overhears Marcus advising her brother to kidnap her. When Dacius almost dies thwarting the kidnapping, a Christian couple pretend Julia and Dacius are their children to keep her brother from finding them before her father returns.

But pretending to be free again makes returning to slavery more than Dacius can bear, while acting like a common woman opens Julia's eyes to dreams and destinies she never knew existed. With her brother closing in and her father almost home, can she find a way around Roman law and custom to free them both for the future they long for?

Find out what happens to Ariana's brother Diegis twelve years later in this tale of hope and a future never imagined until God opens the door.

Hope Unchained

Can the deepest loss bring the greatest gain?

Rome's conquering army took Ariana's family and freedom, but nothing can take her faith in Jesus. When she rescues a tribune's wife from certain death, her reward is freedom and a chance to free her brother and sister. But first she must catch up with the slave caravan before they vanish forever, and tracking them from Dacia to the coast seems impossible for one woman alone.

Discharged from the legion with a hand crippled by a Dacian knife, Donatus faces a future without hope. When the tribune asks him to escort Ariana on her quest, it's the only work he can find. It means four weeks with a Dacian woman and a gladiator bodyguard, but it takes money to eat. A man without options must take what he can get.

But a lot can happen in four weeks. Even battle-hardened men can be touched by love and forgiveness, and it's easier to face an enemy with a sword than to face the truth. When his moment of truth comes, what will Donatus choose, and what will that mean for both of them?

Honor Bound

When the honorable path isn't clear, how do you find your way?

Marcus Brutus owns estates, ships, and gladiator schools that increase his fortune daily, but his greatest treasures are his honor and his wife. When she reveals her faith in Jesus before dying after the birth of their son, he's consumed by hatred for the unnamed Christian woman who led his beloved to abandon the Roman gods, making him lose her in this life and the next.

For fifteen years, Licinia's father hid her Christian faith. But now her father is dead, and a ruthless political enemy is hunting for anything to destroy her brother's career. When she becomes the target, her brother sends her to their estate in Germania. But is that far enough to protect her from an evil man who will stop at nothing?

When a carriage accident leaves Brutus injured and his best friend near death after rescuing Brutus's son, Licinia welcomes and cares for them. But her strange habits and his friend's unexpected recovery make Brutus suspect she's the Christian who corrupted his wife. When her brother's enemies come for her, does honor require him to protect her or turn her over as an enemy of Rome? And when Licinia's heart is drawn toward the pagan man who makes money off death, can she reconcile her growing affection with her love for Christ?

Join some of the people you met in *True Freedom* four years later in this tale of loss and discovery, anger and forgiveness, and the truth that sets people free.

9 781946 139085